THE FLYING DUTCHMAN

BLEAK

FUTURE

Nils Visser

Illustrated by Julie Gorringe

Dear Sofia,

Thanks for the excellent
care!

Nils Visser

COPYRIGHT PAGE

The Flying Dutchman BLEAK FUTURE by Nils Visser
Cover art by Tom Brown and Nimue Brown
Interior Illustrations: Julie Gorringe
Text©Nils Visser, 2022
ISBN 978-1-8382427-1-8

Loosely based on the book *De Vliegende Hollander* by Piet Visser
(1st Edition 1901, 2nd edition 1910, 3rd edition 1918, 4th edition +/- 1930,
Gebroeders Kluitman, Alkmaar, The Netherlands)

The Flying Dutchman BLEAK FUTURE, 2021, Cider Brandy Scribblers,
Brighton, England
(with kind permission from Uitgeverij Kluitman Alkmaar B.V.)
PoD/IngramSpark & Lightning Source Independent Book Publishers

Dedication

This story has been 376 years in the making. It started in 1646, when Willem IJsbrantsz Bontekoe published a journal of his Asian travels.

This work formed a major inspiration for German author Philipp Körber when he wrote *Der Fliegende Holländer* (published in 1849). Alkmaar-based publisher Gebroeders Kluitman had it translated to Dutch in 1870, with a second edition in 1885.

Gebroeders Kluitman asked Piet Visser to do a thorough rewrite around 1900. The first edition of Piet Visser's *De Vliegende Hollander* was published in 1901. It was followed by a second edition in 1910, a third edition in 1918, and a fourth edition in 1927.

I first became aware of this story by my great-grand-uncle in 2018. After reading the story I became inspired to retell Piet Visser's take on the origins of the Flying Dutchman. Kluitman (now Uitgeverij Kluitman), still in business, kindly said that they had no issue with this.

This first book of the planned trilogy is dedicated to my father, Rob Visser.

Nils Visser
Brighton, England, 2022

CONTENTS

Obligatory Opening Curse

PART THREE: ISLE OF WALCHEREN

Obligatory Opening Curse

For him or her that stealeth (or borroweth and

returneth not) this book from its owner:

Let bookworms gnaw their entrails.

Let them languish in pain crying aloud for

mercy & let there be no surcease to their

agony.

Let them be cursed

to sail the seas and oceans...

Forever More.

Part One
Duchy of Brabant

Many stayed forever,
Buried by the waves,
Many boarded by worms
In their watery graves.
But no such mercy
For the Flying Dutchman's crew,
Doomed to sail from Pole to Pole,
O'er the Seven Seas blue.
Like prisoners eternally chained
To waterborne hearse.
Groaning and moaning,
Under an everlasting curse.

(From 'De Vliegende Hollander' by Jan Slauerhoff, 1928. Translated by N. Visser 2018.)

1. An Unexpected Visitor

OYSTERHOUT ~ DUCHY OF BRABANT ~1622

Liselotte Haelen opened the shutters of her bedroom window as quietly as she could. The fields around the house were bathed in the luminosity of the waxing moon. It was a bright contrast to the dark treeline of the forest that surrounded this little corner of the world.

Opening her bedroom windows at night wasn't allowed. These were dangerous times. The truce had ended, and the young Dutch Republic once more faced the wrath of the Spanish empire. General Ambrosio Spinola was massing troops south of the border. Brabant would be the first province to bear the brunt of what the Dutch had come to call the 'Spanish Fury'.

War!

Liselotte shivered. It had been a sunny summer's day, but the night carried a chill.

She had been a toddler at the start of the truce. She was fifteen now, closing in on sixteen, and had grown up during twelve years of uneasy peace. Nonetheless, she didn't need personal recollections of the war to comprehend what horrors might lie in wait. Folk in the nearby village of Oysterhout still talked in fearful tones of beastly Spanish atrocities.

Across the Republic, I suppose.

There was no sign of war on this night though, the only movement a fox prowling along a hedge.

According to Liselotte's father there was another danger in her contemplation of the night. He would have been furious to find her like this, leaning against the windowsill to breathe in the crisp night air. There'd be thunder in his voice.

SIN! SINNER!

Liselotte shrugged. Father was downstairs in his study, working his way through a bottle of brandywine and unlikely to stumble up the stairs to check on his children.

Regardless, she could hear his voice clear enough.

A girl's mind is easily led astray.

Liselotte shrugged again. There had been a time when his words had made her squirm with guilt, but the list of sins to be avoided had grown so much it seemed she was sinning no matter what she did.

Like my very existence is a sin.

She took a deep breath. The dour air that pervaded the house was stifling, the cool night air refreshing.

A barn owl screeched somewhere over the forest. Its shrill shriek was harrowing but commonplace. Other sounds drew Liselotte's attention, a cacophony of startled twitters and squawks at the forest fringe. It was where the dirt road that cut through their little enclave meandered to Oysterhout.

Liselotte frowned. Something had caused a disturbance. Could it be a fox? She didn't think so. Smaller birds – safely perched high up in the trees – mostly ignored the passage of one of the sly red hunters.

She peered at the dark edge of the forest. The broad dirt path that passed by the house wasn't a main thoroughfare. Others rarely used it in daytime and only seldom at night.

Poachers were far too canny to advertise their location in this manner. A drunk perhaps, stumbling away from the nearby Old Cauldron inn.

Or worse...

Not all the scars of the long and vicious war with Spain had been healed by the truce. Bands of unemployed soldiers still roamed the countryside. A gang of them had been waylaying unwary travellers in the vicinity of Oysterhout over recent weeks.

Liselotte took a sharp intake of breath when she saw a figure emerge from the forest edge, marching resolutely along the road. The shape's physique suggested a man. He was wearing a broad-rimmed hat instead of a helmet, but Liselotte saw steel reflected in the moonlight, and what looked like a sword hanging by his waist.

An armed man abroad at night was bad news. Liselotte made to close the shutters, but then stopped.

He'll see the movement if he's looking at the house.

She backed away from the window, edging out of sight, and then rushed out of her room to cross the landing and open her twin brother's bedroom door.

§ § § § § §

Andries Haelen grumbled in protest when his sister shook his shoulders. He resisted, wanting to claw back his dream that had

4

featured Toosje, the miller's daughter. Liselotte, however, was most persistent.

"Andries. Wake up. There's someone outside."

"Whu...wha...who?"

"Shhh. Keep your voice down. I don't know who. A man."

Andries propped himself up on his elbows, reluctantly abandoning his dream of Toosje wading through a forest stream, her skirts hoisted up to reveal shapely ankles and calves.

"He's on the Oysterhout road," Liselotte said. "He might turn our way."

Andries sighed. It had only been three nights ago that his sister had woken him to report a supposed Spanish cavalry patrol in the fields. He was only an hour older than his twin but reckoned himself far wiser. Besides that, even if he'd been the younger one, his gender would have still lent him the greater wisdom. It was well known that female brains were unsuitable for deep thought. Not that this had ever stopped Liselotte from trying, but many of her attempts were nonsensical.

"Liselotte. Have you had your shutters open again? Last time..."

"Ja[1], I know. It was just a herd of deer not Spaniards. But this time...it's for real. There's a man. He's got a sword!"

"A sword?" Andries frowned. Liselotte had a lively imagination but there were armed men out and about in the area.

"To my bedroom," Liselotte urged him. "Quick. Bring your musket."

She slipped out of the room. Andries got to his feet to follow her. He took hold of the doglock musket by the side of his bed. It was new, one of the few things his father was willing to spend money on.

When Andries entered Liselotte's room, he discovered her crouched by the window, her hands deftly working a lady's hunting crossbow. She had inherited it from their mother, who had died shortly after giving birth to Andries and Liselotte – taken by one of the fevers that regularly swept through the city of Rotterdam, where they had lived back then.

Andries joined his sister by the window. "What do you think you're doing?"

"I'll shoot him if he has bad intentions."

---

[1] Dutch for 'yes'.

"Don't be silly. The crossbow is just for hunting. Fighting is men's work." He patted the barrel of his musket.

Liselotte bared her teeth in reply.

Andries quickly changed the subject. "Where's the man now?"

His sister shrugged. They both looked at the window, and then, simultaneously, rose to dare a peek.

Anyone who might have seen them there, clad in threadbare nightshifts by the window, would have seen that they were twins even in the moonlight. Both were slender of build and of equal height. They had red hair and the same oval chin and broad cheekbones. A clear distinction was that Andries's face was one of rounded softness, while Liselotte's had a harder angular edge.

Although both still retained that innocent look of youth, they had been hardened somewhat by their circumstances. Theirs had not been an easy life, the cause of which sat downstairs in his study, getting drunk again.

Unaware we have a visitor!

Liselotte had been right. An armed man was striding along the dirt road. The man turned left onto the broad path that led to the Haelen house.

Andries and Liselotte ducked below the windowsill.

"We have to tell Father," Andries whispered.

"Nay[2]!" Liselotte placed a hand on his arm. "We can't. He'll know I've opened the shutters..." "I think that visitor will be foremost on his mind."

"Andries, you know what he'll do to me."

Andries bit his lip. He knew all too well what Father would do. He asked, "What if the man wants to harm us?"

It was either that, or someone seeking medical help. But those usually arrived in a horse-drawn carriage to take Father to wherever the patient lived. As far afield as Zevenbergen, Tilburg, and Breda because Father had a solid reputation as physician.

Andries continued, "If he wants to attack us..."

"Father has his pistols; we can rush downstairs. You with your musket, me..." Liselotte indicated the crossbow, her eyes shining brightly.

_____

[2] The Dutch for 'no' is 'nee', pronounced as 'nay' which I've opted for to match the Dutch *ja*.

Anyone who might have seen them there, clad in threadbare nightshifts by the window, would have seen that they were twins even in the moonlight.

She's serious about putting up a fight!

Andries shook his head. "He'd admonish me if I came down *without* the musket. But if he's reminded you have Mother's crossbow, he'll confiscate it."

Liselotte nodded reluctantly.

The stranger had moved faster than they thought he would, reaching the doorknocker at the front door.

Tok-tok-tok

Andries and Liselotte stared at each other in silence.

TOK-TOK-TOK

In between the urgent knocking the house seemed deathly silent, as if even the mice huddled in anxious anticipation, their whiskers quivering as they sniffed at the air.

The stranger gave up on the doorknocker, banging on the door with a fist instead.

BAM-BAM-BAM

At least he's not trying to kick it down.

"Doctor Haelen! Doctor Haelen!" Their unexpected visitor's voice sounded loud and clear.

Andries felt some of the tension in him ebb away. Someone had been hurt, probably nearby.

They need a physician, that's all.

Andries reckoned that Liselotte's persistent conviction that thousands of Spaniards – led by Spinola himself – would invade their little enclave in the forest had spooked him a bit. That, and everybody talking about those armed bandits.

BAM-BAM-BAM

"Cease that racket!" It was Father's voice down in the hallway. Andries heard him shuffle to the front door. "I can hear you well enough."

Andries rose to his feet. Liselotte placed her crossbow and quiver of bolts on her lumpy straw mattress, covered them with the blanket, and then followed Andries to the landing. They rushed down the stairs.

Father was just passing the lower end of the stairway, holding a candleholder with a burning candle in one hand, one of his snaphance pistols in the other. He was clad in his night shift, with a soft sleeping cap perched on his head. Listless straggles of his long grey hair fell about his shoulders. His eyes were a bit bloodshot, but he seemed steady on his feet and the expression on his gaunt face was alert.

Simon Haelen looked at his children grimly, nodding his approval when he saw Andries holding the new doglock musket.

"Good lad. Stay well behind me," he growled. "Musket at the ready."

Andries nodded with a dry mouth.

"Doctor Haelen!" their unexpected visitor bellowed.

"*Ja, ja*," Father grumbled, before taking the last few steps to the door. "Hold your horses, I can hear you well enough."

Andries hardly dared to breathe. His heart pounded in his chest, but he took comfort from the weight of the musket in his hands.

2. The Prodigal Cousin

OYSTERHOUT ~ DUCHY OF BRABANT ~ 1622

"Who's there?" Father shouted at the closed door.

Liselotte could sense the tension in Andries. She wished she had brought down her crossbow after all.

The man outside answered, "I'm looking for the physician, Seigneur Simon Haelen. Is he in?"

"That depends," Father answered. "Who are you? What do you want?"

"I'm the physician's nephew. Peter Haelen."

"Peter!" Father exclaimed in surprise.

Cousin Peter!

Liselotte had never met her cousin, but Father had spoken of him often enough. Never positively. According to Father, Peter had been a disobedient child who had run away from home when he was fourteen. All this had happened in Rotterdam a year before Liselotte was born. Peter would be nearing thirty now.

But back then...fourteen. Younger than I am now.

Father always focused on the disobedience and blemish on the family name. He was vague about Peter's fortunes since, other than stating that a disobedient child was likely to grow up destined for the gallows.

Why would Cousin Peter be here, in Brabant?

Father seemed to share that thought. "Family wouldn't come unannounced after nightfall! You could be anyone at all, a tramp...a thief."

"I am Peter Haelen, son of Johan the shipbuilder, one of the physician's younger brothers. I am here on urgent business." The man paused. "One with monetary benefits for my uncle."

"Monetary benefits?" Father asked, curiosity clear in his tone.

Clever!

There were scrapes of protest as Father pulled various iron latches aside. He pushed the front door open with his foot, holding his pistol up with one hand and the candle with the other to cast dim light on the unexpected visitor.

Most of the man remained shrouded by the night's darkness, silhouetted against bright moonlight, but the candlelight illuminated his face. Owlish eyebrows arched over intense blue eyes that were filled with sharp intelligence. A straw-coloured goatee elongated the man's face, but his nose and cheekbones formed tell-tale signs of a Haelen. The man wore his long, fair hair loose, cascading down from his broad-rimmed domed hat.

Father lowered his pistol and grumbled, "You're a spitting image of Johan."

"Uncle Simon," Peter Haelen nodded respectfully. "It's been many years."

"None of which have been kind to me," Father replied. "I suppose you'd better come in, Nephew."

He turned to his children. "Andries. Go light some more candles in my study. Not too many. Lottie. Fetch a flask of ale from the kitchen, be sure to water it down."

"*Ja*, Father," Liselotte and Andries answered in unison. They retreated down the hallway. Andries disappeared into the study. Liselotte went to the kitchen at the end of the hallway. She left the door half open, working as quietly as she could so as not to miss out on anything.

She could hear the tread of boots on the hallway flagstones as Peter entered.

"You'll have to forgive the rude reception," Father muttered, without a hint of apology in his voice. He locked the front door again. "There've been a lot of ill-mannered folks out and about lately. None of them up to any good, I tell you."

"I'm aware of them," Peter answered. "In fact, the reason—"

Father interrupted him, not done grumbling just yet. "You could have arrived during daylight, saved us all a fright. Tis the normal way to do things, Nephew, but I recall you were never one for convention."

The voices neared the end of the hallway, but the men paused outside of the study.

"It was my intention to arrive tomorrow, Uncle, at a Christian time. But something urgent came up."

"Urgent?" Father asked. "If you came begging for investment in one of your hare-brained shipbuilding schemes, you might as well be on your way again. I haven't a *duit*[3] to spare."

---

[3] Coin of low value, idiomatically used in the manner 'penny' is used in English. Plural: *Duiten*.

He pushed the front door open with his foot, holding his pistol up with one hand and the candle with the other to cast dim light on the unexpected visitor.

"You need not be concerned about my finances, Uncle. I've made my fortune in the East Indies."

The East Indies!

Liselotte's eyes widened. She had heard much about the fabled East but had never met an *Oostvaarder*[4].

"But there are others," Peter continued. "Who believe you have plenty of *duiten* to spare. Guilders too, thousands of them."

"Thousands?" Father laughed bitterly. "I wish I had." Then he added a cautious, "Others?"

"I'd settled down for the night at an inn not far from here, Uncle. A place called the Old Cauldron. I overheard talk in the taproom. Four men. A rough looking bunch, former soldiers certainly. They are convinced there are fabulous riches to be had here. They mean to rob you tonight and spoke in crude terms of assaulting your daughter's virtue. I departed as quick as I could to warn you."

A cold shiver ran along Liselotte's spine. These men knew about her? Had they been watching the house?

"But I have nothing to steal!" Father protested in a shaky voice.

"They believe you do, and they'll be here within the hour. They said they intended to leave no witnesses."

"No witnesses!"

They mean to kill us? Liselotte shook her head. She was still trying to get used to her cousin's sudden appearance, and now there was far more to take on board.

The study door opened. Andries said, "Father, the study is ready."

Liselotte took this as her cue to appear from the kitchen with a flagon and two pewter cups.

Father ignored them both, muttering softly, "*Vae Victis...*"

"Woe to the conquered?" Peter cast a curious glance at Andries and Liselotte. "We haven't been vanquished yet, Uncle, I assure you. There was mention of ale?"

"*Ja*, Nephew, this way."

Half-a-dozen candles lit up the study. The room was sparse, with a simple desk, two mismatched chairs, a single cabinet, and a sturdy strongbox in a recessed corner. There were no paintings on the walls, or any decoration other than a small wooden cross over the hearth. There were no curtains, nor a carpet or rug on the oak floorboards.

---

[4] Literally 'East Farer', someone who sailed to Asia.

Andries had already propped his musket in a corner. Father set down his pistol and candleholder on the table.

Liselotte placed the flask of ale and pewter cups next to them. She and Andries lined up by one table edge, hands clutched in front of them and their heads downcast, although they both sneaked curious peeks at their unexpected guest.

Peter wore wide, dark-blue knee-length breeches, a matching doublet, a simple leather jerkin, and a modest flat linen collar. A broad-rimmed brown hat covered his head. His sea boots were worn but in good shape. An orange sash was tied around his waist. A broad, leather baldrick crossed his chest. It held two modern flintlock pistols and carried the scabbard of a short sword. The sword's grip was made of leather bound by spiralling silver wire, but its handguard and pommel were plain, undecorated steel.

Peter's attire was made of superior materials but simple and robust in design. The emphasis was on weathering the elements, rather than preening wealth.

A seafarer from top to toe!

Peter had a large sailor's duffle bag slung over his shoulder, which he slipped off and set on the ground.

"Sit, sit." Father gestured at one of the chairs as he seated himself on the other.

Peter didn't seat himself yet. Instead, he faced his two cousins curiously.

"Andries and Liselotte, I presume? I am your cousin, Peter."

They nodded at him, Andries with a nervous smile, Liselotte with intense curiosity. She made to speak but was cut short by her father.

"*Ja, ja.* How delightful to meet at long last." Father poured ale from the flask into the two cups. "Greetings and pleasantries over and done with. We have more important matters to discuss, do we not, Nephew?"

He handed Peter a cup, only half-full, and then looked at his children disdainfully. "Lowlife bandits intend to rob me of my life on this very night. As I have predicted many times."

"Bandits?" Andries asked, disbelief in his voice.

"I'm afraid the situation is dire," Peter confirmed. "I was planning to stay at the Old Cauldron for the night. I overheard four rogues hatching a plan to rob your house. I asked the innkeeper to bring my supper to my room and told him that I wasn't to be disturbed until morning. Then I tied the bedcurtains together, climbed out of the window, and ran as fast as I could. Hopefully I won't be missed until

14

tomorrow. The rogues wanted to be here at midnight. At worst, we have little more than an hour. At best, they'll drink themselves into a stupor, but they sounded serious and in dire need of funds."

"An hour?" Father asked. "Four of them, you say?"

Peter nodded. "They were getting steadily drunk, an advantage and disadvantage for us."

"Disadvantage?" Liselotte asked. She could understand why being drunk was likely to hinder someone in a fight, not how it might benefit them.

She had spoken out of turn, but fortunately Father didn't seem to notice, and Peter – to her surprise – took Liselotte's question seriously.

He looked at her, his eyes earnest. "Drink is a recipe for false bravado and carelessness, Cousin, they'll be slower to fear us—"

"Fear us!" Father barked a laugh.

Peter ignored him. "The advantage is that any cunning they might possess will be drowned in ale. The disadvantage that they'll have the reckless courage of drunks – with guns, swords, and daggers at hand."

Peter took a sip from his cup. He looked puzzled for a moment. Liselotte knew why, it was more water than ale, but her cousin didn't comment on it.

"In short, Nephew, we are doomed! Four armed men! Soldiers did you say?" Father also took a sip from his cup, pulled a face, and then snapped at Liselotte. "I told you to water it down."

"But Father, I did!"

"Keep your mouth shut." Father turned to Peter. "Children should be seen, not heard, don't you think so, Nephew?"

Peter remained silent. Liselotte could read the disagreement on his face.

Father could too. He chuckled. "I should have known better than to ask. I find some pleasure in the fact that both my brothers' children equal mine in the measure of disappointment they have caused their fathers. Both of Karel's boys perishing in that fever, how very ungrateful of them. And you..."

He looked at Peter shrewdly. "Johan wanted you in his dockyards, to follow in his footsteps as a man's son should."

Andries shifted uncomfortably. Liselotte's brother had shown little interest in Father's profession.

"I chose a different career," Peter said curtly.

"So you did, so you did. The East Indies no less."

It was Andries's turn to widen his eyes at mention of the Indies. Liselotte marvelled again. How long had Peter been there? Which of the emerald isles had he visited?

"Have you any weapons in the house, other than these?" Peter indicated the pistol on the table and the musket propped against the wall.

"There are three more pistols," Andries said. "As well as one more doglock musket, and two old matchlock ones."

Peter raised an eyebrow. "Your household is well armed, Uncle."

"These are ill times we live in," Father said. "And Andries likes to hunt. I'm not averse to the addition of rabbit or pheasant to my larder, for the small expenditure of some powder and shot."

"Do you know how to use the weapons?" Peter asked Andries.

"All of them," Andries replied proudly.

"Good, good," Peter said. "Can you fetch them?"

Andries glanced at Father for approval. He nodded, after which Andries left the study in search of the household arsenal.

"You mean to fight them?" Father sounded dubious.

"Aye, I mean to fight them."

"Four soldiers...against one sailor and a boy?"

"I've faced worse odds at sea, Spaniards and pirates both."

"A regular naval hero. A proper Sea Beggar[5], just like your grandfather. My, my, aren't we lucky?"

Our grandfather? A Sea Beggar!

Peter's face darkened for a short moment. Liselotte shot her father an angry look. Surely Peter's arrival merited more civility.

He answered Father curtly. "I'm proud to be compared to Adrian Haelen. My grandfather fought to free us from Spanish tyranny."

"He was a rogue and a scoundrel," Father countered, gleeful satisfaction in his voice. He only ever seemed happy when denouncing faults in others.

He glanced at Liselotte, and then changed the subject. "I'm grateful of course, for your warning, but curious as to why you should happen to be travelling past Oysterhout precisely at this time." He narrowed his eyes. "It's a strange coincidence after all these years, don't you think so, Nephew?"

---

[5] The semi-piratical 'Watergeuzen', who had contributed a great deal to the Dutch rebellion against Spain.

Liselotte clenched her fists as she struggled to keep her face impassive. Was Father really accusing Peter of being part of some malicious plot to rob his own family?

This time Peter kept his face neutral. "I returned from the East last year, on the East India merchantman *De Blokzeyl*, and am now based in Flushing. I wrote my father, to request his help in some matters, as I am preparing a new voyage to the East on my own ship. I came to recruit."

"Johan always said that you're too clever for your own good. But to leave the seaport of Flushing to recruit sailors in the heath lands and forests of Brabant...how clever is that?"

Liselotte dreaded to think what kind of impression Father must be making on her cousin.

Peter sighed. "The sailors are being recruited elsewhere, Uncle. In ports, as you said. But I also need ship's officers. Reliable and trustworthy officers. My father, in his reply, informed me that you lived here with Andries. I came to enquire if my cousin would be willing to be engaged as midshipman. To learn the ropes as we sail to the East Indies."

It took Liselotte a moment for the meaning of that to sink in. She cried out in horror: "Nay!"

Both men looked at her with surprise.

Liselotte stared back at them in a panic. Andries would be gone for years. What would she do without her brother, stuck in this bleak house with only Father for company? So many of the men who left never came back. What if Andries was captured and eaten by savages? Or drowned in a storm?

"Enough from you, impertinent girl," Father snarled. "I'll take the belt to you here and now. Don't think that I won't, Lottie. Is that what you want?"

Fear was instant. Liselotte shook her head demurely. "Nay, Father. My apologies."

"Good," Father said. He smiled at Peter. "Spare the rod and spoil the child, don't you think so, Nephew?"

Peter didn't answer. Liselotte thought she could read distaste on his face but there was little he could do. It wasn't seemly for a man to interfere with the way the head of a household chose to run his home.

A wave of resignation swept through her. Peter would leave again, taking Liselotte's only companion away, and there was nothing she could do about it.

§ § § § § §

17

Andries returned with the guns, powder horns, and shot. He laid them on the desk. Peter picked a doglock musket up for inspection.

He laid it down and picked up one of the old-fashioned matchlocks. "These are well maintained."

"Bethanks.[6]" Andries glowed with pride.

Father mused, "The lad hasn't shown much aptitude for my trade, much to my disappointment. He's good with the guns, which might stand in his stead regarding your proposal. But tis an expensive affair, an apprenticeship at sea: Fees, outfits, equipment..."

Andries was puzzled by those remarks. He threw a quizzical look at Liselotte, but she was staring at the ground despondently, marooned in a spell of misery.

"I will pay all costs." Peter put down the matchlock and picked up the second one. "Including a modest wage for the voyage to Batavia. A more substantial one if he shows aptitude and is promoted to steersman[7] for the return voyage."

"Many a man has made a fortune in the East." Father flicked his tongue along his upper lip.

Andries looked from his father to his cousin, trying to make sense of it all.

"I've come to Oysterhout to see you, Andries," Peter explained. "I need a midshipman for my new ship. She is due to sail to Batavia soon."

"The East Indies?" Andries asked with disbelief. When Peter nodded, his face was transformed by sudden delight, to be replaced by a guilty glance at his sister.

"I'll be wanting two-thirds of his wages, for the first voyage," Father said. "And one percent of the profit."

"One tenth of one percent of the profits," Peter countered.

Wages! The East Indies!

Andries could barely believe it. Was he really going to the East? He might return fabulously wealthy. A seafaring hero like the men everyone always talked about.

"How much do you expect to make?" Father asked.

"The last cargo I brought back on *De Blokzeyl* for the United Dutch East Indies Company[8] was worth a little over one million guilders."

---

[6] An old-fashioned English version of 'thank you' that survived for some time in the Sussex brogue. Similar to the Dutch *'bedankt'*.

[7] These functioned as Lieutenants to the Schipper/Skipper (Captain).

[8] *De Vereenigde Nederlandsche Oost Indische Compagnie* very commonly referred to by its abbreviation VOC.

"A MILLION guilders?" Father gasped. He furrowed his brow.

"One tenth of one percent of a million," Peter said helpfully. "Is a thousand guilders."

"Done!" Father said quickly, with a happy, hungry grin.

"I'm going to the Indies?" Andries asked, looking away from his sister's desperately unhappy face.

"If those ruffians don't cut your throat first," Father said, his brief enthusiasm ebbing away as he looked at the guns on his desk. "I don't expect any of us will live to see another dawn."

"That should be our primary concern right now, time is running out." Peter looked at Andries. "We'll talk about the Indies later."

Peter's demeanour changed. He asked them a series of questions about the layout of the house and the grounds around it. His tone was that of someone familiar with command, confident and used to having a crew obey his every order. Andries wanted to be like that, more than anything else. More even than he wanted to spend time with the miller's daughter.

Father held his tongue, possibly subdued somewhat by Peter's assumption of leadership. He grew visibly nervous though, as Peter outlined his plan. Father protested only once, when he realised Peter's plan would lead to some damage to the house. "It will cost money to repair the front door!"

"A new front door is a cheap price to pay," Peter said. "In exchange for all our lives."

He summarised his plan, to make sure all had understood.

When he was done, Liselotte asked in a small voice, "And me?"

"You?" Peter was surprised.

"This is men's work," Andries stated with far more bravado than he felt. Taking on armed bandits was not a prospect he relished.

"You, Lottie, will wait upstairs in your room," Father growled. "And bolt your door. Not that it'll do you much good, other than slow them down some. Your cousin told me that the ruffians showed a specific interest in you. Just remember, when they are making the beast-with-two-backs with you, that it's your own wanton behaviour that has brought this misfortune upon our house. It's sins like yours that draw the eye of the Devil."

Liselotte lowered her head. "I shall wait upstairs, Father, as you say."

"They won't come anywhere near you," Andries promised bravely, but shot her a quick query with his eyes.

Liselotte smiled at him, as if comforted, but included a subtle nod.

She'll have her crossbow ready, if all else fails. I hope she's got the sense to stay in her room.

Andries watched his sister give Peter a questioning glance.

"You're not to worry." Their cousin smiled at her warmly and Liselotte gave him a grateful smile back.

After she had left the room, Peter looked at Andries and Father. "Are we all clear on what to do?"

They nodded.

It was time to prepare for bloodshed.

3. Shades of Pain

OYSTERHOUT ~ DUCHY OF BRABANT ~ 1622

They divided the weapons. Peter would take the two doglocks, his own pistols, his own sword, and a Javanese dagger that he retrieved from his duffle bag and stuck in his belt. That left father and son with two pistols and the matchlocks.

Andries accompanied Peter to the kitchen and opened the back door. There was a little courtyard out back, open on one side and otherwise faced by the back of the house and various low outbuildings.

Andries spotted their small wood axe by the chopping block and picked it up. Peter nodded approvingly.

"If all goes to plan you won't have to confront the rogues face-to-face, Cousin. But it's always good to be prepared for the worst."

Andries nodded, afraid to speak in case his voice trembled.

Everything was eerily lit up by the bright moon, or darkly shadowed, which should help Peter find his way through the small apple orchard by the side of the house, and then to the stable that flanked the access road out front.

The building was empty and unused. Father said it was too expensive to keep horses.

Peter and Andries exchanged a last nod, after which Peter made his way around the house. Andries went back into the kitchen, locking the back door behind him. He went to the study to keep Father company. Father grumbled about what he considered the flaws of Peter's plan. Andries was too distracted to pay him much attention, his mood fluctuating between nervous anticipation of the expected fight and elation at the prospect of sailing to the East.

§ § § § § §

Liselotte sat on her bed cradling her crossbow. A hundred thoughts swirled through her mind. Peter's arrival. The planned robbery. The prospect of Andries sailing far away. The danger they were all in.

What if the four bandits killed her relatives? She would be up here, listening to the screams. Then hear the rogues pounding up the stairs. How long would her bedroom door hold?

Not long at all. I'll shoot them when they come in.

The thought wasn't reassuring. She would shoot the first one, but the crossbow took time to reload. The others would be upon her before she managed a second shot. She shivered. She was under no illusion as to what hardened fighters would do to her, drunk and their blood hot from fighting.

She studied one of her crossbow bolts. Maybe she could use her single shot differently. How to aim the crossbow in that manner though? She brought a hand to her throat. Under her chin? She should have brought one of the kitchen knives upstairs. She was unsure if she could do it. It was a sin, to take your own life. But was it so much better to suffer the attentions of the bandits before they killed her? At least it lay in Liselotte's power to deny them their intended pleasure at her expense.

No witnesses...

"This is ridiculous!" she exclaimed. She jumped up to pace her room.

She was being too pessimistic. Peter had been confident that the bandits could be defeated. He had said that he had fought Spaniards...and pirates!

Four against three though, and not even that, really. Father had been drinking.

As for Andries, although Liselotte loved her brother dearly, she feared that Andries lacked the ruthlessness that would be required.

Whenever Father was called away, he was gone for at least a week and sometimes longer. He never bothered to restock the larder when he left. He had also forbidden Liselotte from reviving the old vegetable garden out back, stating that such labour was work for farmers, not physician's children. That had left Liselotte and Andries to subsist on their own.

They had taken to sneaking around farms, vegetable lots, and orchards when the season had something on offer that could be easily snatched. They had also become adept at poaching, taking down hares, pheasants, and the occasional deer.

Whenever they had wounded, rather than killed an animal, Andries always stood by helplessly while Liselotte ended the misery of the hurt animal with a swift knife stroke. Those were always the victims of his musket. Liselotte practiced endlessly with her crossbow when Father was away and never missed any more.

What if she evened the odds? Four against four. They might all have a better chance that way. It was preferable to waiting upstairs until boots pounded up the stairs.

Father would be livid. His fury would know no bounds. Or would it? Maybe Father might even praise her courage. Although Father grumbled about Andries's lack of ambition to learn the physician's trade, he also doted on his son when he was in the right mood, but never expressed such affection for his daughter.

Liselotte shook her head, scolding herself for being so naïve. Father would be furious, no matter what she did. At best he might refrain from thrashing her too hard. He had already suggested it was her fault that the bandits were coming at all. She shivered, wondering again if they had been spying on the house. Anyhow, Father's reaction didn't matter. She had come to her decision. She wasn't going to stand aside and do nothing.

Liselotte tied the belt that held her quiver of bolts around her waist, and then hooked the crossbow onto it. Her window was still open and next to it grew a mass of ivy. She had been up and down it before, so knew it would hold her weight. Once outside, she snuck around the back of the house and then to the stable through the orchard, rather than approaching it directly over the forecourt. Just in case Peter mistook her for a bandit, or either Father and Andries were peeking through a window at the front of the house – even though Peter had warned them not to.

She could see that Peter had opened the broad upper doors to the hayloft and tied a rope to the hoisting beam that thrust out over the loft doors. Concealed in dark shade, Liselotte slipped into the stable and made her way to the back, where a ladder led up to the hayloft. She climbed the ladder nimbly. There was some hay up there still, but it was old and smelled musky. Bright moonlight shone in through the open loft doors. Peter had positioned himself on the floor, one musket in his hands, the other within easy reach beside him.

Liselotte hesitated. Peter had seemed sympathetic in the study but she barely knew him. She was acting on her assumptions of him, rather than anything else. Although Father had spoken of him in the past as a bad example, that had only stoked her curiosity and admiration. Peter had become her secret hero, turning his back on family expectations and running away from home the day after his fourteenth birthday.

Fourteen!

Yet, her first impressions of the real Peter had been mixed. Rather than the proud rebel of her imagination, he had been a contrasting mix between awkwardness, pomposity, and confidence.

Liselotte had no idea how Peter would react to her presence. She was gambling on an ingrained streak of rebelliousness. If she was mistaken her cousin might run off to tell Father. In that case, punishment would follow, regardless of the approaching rogues.

Her heart thumped so loud she was surprised that Peter didn't seem to hear it. Liselotte took a deep breath...

Just don't show doubt, she told herself. *Be confident.*

She cleared her throat.

Peter reacted instantly, rolling onto his back and aiming his musket at the darkness. "Who goes there?"

"It's only me," Liselotte called out. "Your cousin."

She emerged from the darkness at the back of the loft.

"Liselotte?" Peter asked in astonishment when she stepped into the moonlight that fell through the open loft doors.

She stopped, her free hand on her waist, and looked at him defiantly. "What of it?"

Peter looked at her crossbow and the belt replete with a filled quiver of bolts. He shook his head.

"You're no Kenau Simonsdochter," he said.

Liselotte knew that name well enough. Everyone in the Republic did. Kenau Simonsdochter was the shipwright's widow who had helped defend Haarlem during the Spanish siege fifty years ago. Kenau had fought like a lioness on and off the city walls, armed with a pike, musket, and sword, becoming a living legend in the process.

"Nay, of course not," Liselotte answered.

Peter lowered his doglock and gestured at the crossbow. "Do you even know how to use that thing?"

Liselotte had hoped their conversation would reach as far as this. She had already worked the steel string back behind its release latch. She drew a bolt from her quiver and placed it on the crossbow.

"What the..." Peter exclaimed.

Liselotte aimed at one of the loft doorposts and triggered the shot. The bolt sped so fast it was just a blur and brief audible ripple of its leather fletchings, before it thudded into the doorpost, shaking loose a small cloud of dust.

"...Devil!"

"I never miss," Liselotte assured him. She had no idea where she had found the courage to escape the constraints of formality, but she was beginning to enjoy herself. It had been a good shot. Not that she had doubted it. It pleased her to be able to show someone other than Andries her skills.

Peter watched, flabbergasted, as his cousin calmly stepped past him and tugged at the bolt stuck in the doorpost.

"Kenau Simonsdochter was nearly fifty, you see," Liselotte explained. "I prefer Treyn Rembrands. Treyn was sixteen, less than one year older than I am, when the Spaniards besieged Alkmaar. She shot a good many of them with her musket from the city walls."

Peter could have reverted to formality, insisted she speak to him with the reverence due to an elder male member of the family.

Speak only when spoken to.

He didn't. Instead, he engaged. "They were...it was the Spanish Fury. Kenau Simonsdochter and Treyn Rembrands knew what would happen if the Spaniards took their cities. Nobody could forget what the Iron Duke's[9] soldiers did at Mechelen...Zutphen...Naarden."

Liselotte pulled the bolt free. She inspected its blunt steel bodkin tip and ran her fingers along it, before nodding. "It'll still do."

Turning her attention to Peter, she said. "I don't see much difference, Cousin. I don't need my father's wretched reminders to know what would happen if four drunk soldiers got their hands on me."

Liselotte's tone challenged him to deny the truth of it. Peter was uncomfortable with the situation. It was a wholly inappropriate subject for a young lady to be contemplating, but *that* possible outcome of this evening stalked Liselotte's mind like an ominous shadow.

Her cousin remained silent, doubt on his face, so Liselotte added, "At least give me a chance to fight back. Even the odds somewhat. Father's hands will be trembling. Andries hesitates, and you..."

"Me?" Peter asked.

Liselotte took a deep breath. She was about to assume further familiarity they didn't have, but he hadn't admonished her so far. "You, Cousin, aren't as clever as I thought you would be."

"I'm not?" Peter sounded comically foolish. He seemed totally out of his depth, which suited Liselotte because she was too. She only spoke to her brother in this straightforward manner, and Peter was an adult.

"I'll go to my room," Liselotte spoke in the submissive obedient tone she had used in Father's presence. "And wait to be rescued by gallant heroes."

---

[9] Fernando Alvarez de Toledo, 3rd Duke of Alba

Peter's lips trembled, then broke apart in a short laugh.

Liselotte smiled, relieved that Peter had a sense of humour. She looked out of the open loft doors. The house was dark and silent. There was no movement on the patchwork of moonlit fields.

She detached a small iron lever from the side of her crossbow's stock. Hooking it into its slot, she pulled back the string until it was taut and caught behind the trigger mechanism with a click.

Peter wasn't entirely convinced yet. "If Uncle Simon decides to check on you, he'll be alarmed to find you gone from your room."

"Father won't, he'll be far too busy worrying about his own skin," Liselotte said with absolute certainty.

"Your brother..."

"Father won't let him out of his sight. Andries is precious to him." *Unlike me.*

Peter peered out over the fields again, seemingly at a loss. *Things are probably simpler on his ship.*

He began to suggest, "And if I forbade..."

There it is. Obey. Do as you're told.

Instead of scowling, as she wanted to, Liselotte gave him a sweet smile. "You won't."

"I won't?"

"You've been in fights, battles, right?"

Peter nodded. He looked grave as he did so, grim and haunted by memories.

"Then you won't reject someone who can shoot straight." Liselotte used the last argument in her arsenal. "Not when you're outnumbered and uncertain about your other allies."

Peter grinned ruefully, confirming she was right, then looked at her thoughtfully. "But women...girls..."

"Who don't behave like saintly ladies are called names." Liselotte's voice took on a passionate anger. "They accused Kenau Simonsdochter of witchcraft, you know. Because she outsmarted male merchants. They didn't like that. Women who threaten men are called witch...or whore..."

Peter was shocked to hear her use such a crude term. "Women of loose morals, not—"

"Whore. Witch and whore. Those are the words that Father uses when he repeats that particular lesson to the tune of his belt."

"Your father..."

Liselotte hissed. "My father."

Peter tried to provide a justification. "I'm sure that he loves you, in his own..."

Liselotte gave him an icy stare. Then, without speaking – and much to Peter's consternation – she bent down, deposited the crossbow on the floor, took hold of the hem of her shift, and pulled it up faster than Peter could protest, revealing calf, knee, thigh, and then the rounded curve of a buttock.

"For the love of God!" Peter turned his eyes away.

Liselotte was struck by the enormity of her action, but not ready to back down. Andries never wanted to talk about it. She daren't tell her Oysterhout friends. Peter actually listened to her, took her seriously enough to engage in conversation. Real stuff, not idle chat about the weather. It was suddenly of utmost importance to Liselotte that someone knew. Her secret fear was that one day Father might go too far. Not that Peter could do anything about that, but she wanted him to know.

I want someone to at least know.

"Peter. Look," she commanded.

"I will not," he answered resolutely.

Her tone changed, her next words a plea. "Peter. I need you to see this. Please."

He looked. She could tell by his horrified expression that he saw what she wanted him to see. The back of her leg and buttock covered with bruises. Different hues of ghostly pain coldly lit up by the moonlight on her exposed flank. They formed patterns, angry welts left as the impressions of a man's belt, criss-crossed with scabs where her skin had been broken and blood drawn.

"This," Liselotte said in a hard voice. "Is how much my father loves me."

She dropped her shift again, looking at Peter, her mouth set tight and her eyes hard, belying the wave of relief she felt at having shared her secret with someone at long last.

Peter began to ask, "Why did he...?"

Liselotte hesitated. It had been a sin. What if Peter thought...but it didn't really matter, she had crossed just about every boundary already, so confessed, "Because I kissed a boy."

"Kissed?" Peter's eyebrows rose on his forehead. He seemed bemused.

"One short kiss. That was the end of it."

"But Liselotte, if that is...you being here...it might make him angry."

Definitely.

"Perhaps." Liselotte felt a shiver of fear. "But maybe...if I fight well...he might..."

She spoke with intense longing in her voice, after which she felt her confidence ebbing away.

"You want his approval," Peter guessed.

Liselotte nodded miserably, realising her other arguments were possibly weakened by that overriding motivation.

Peter sighed again. When he made to speak Liselotte thought he would put an end to her intended participation, but instead his demeanor changed, from awkward to emphatic.

"Well I know what that's like."

His tone was sincere and the pain in it clear, so Liselotte believed him.

Peter seemed to have come to a decision and assumed the commanding tone of a skipper on his ship. He pointed at the crossbow on the floor.

"Where did you get the crossbow?"

"It was my mother's. She was from a noble family, the van der Krooswycks. She used to hunt in the dunes."

"I remember Aunt Saskia telling me so," Peter concurred.

"You knew my mother?"

"Aye, indeed. You remind me of her. You've taught yourself to shoot?"

"Whenever Father is called away we have seven or eight days of freedom. Sometimes longer. I practise every day he's gone and Andries takes me hunting. I never miss any more."

"I've noticed," Peter said with a wry smile.

He took the sheathed Javanese dagger from his belt and held it out to her.

Liselotte looked at it curiously. "What is it?"

"From the Indies. The natives call it a 'keris'. You may need it, if you're going to join this fight."

Liselotte hardly dared to believe that he was accepting her intended participation. She took the keris reverently, admiring it as she turned it around in her hands. Both the hilt and the sheath were made of carved polished dark wood. The dagger had a curved pistol-grip, rather than a straight hilt. The handguard was asymmetrical, short on one side, whereas the other side was much longer and curved upwards.

Liselotte peered at the carving at the end of the grip. "It's a mermaid!"

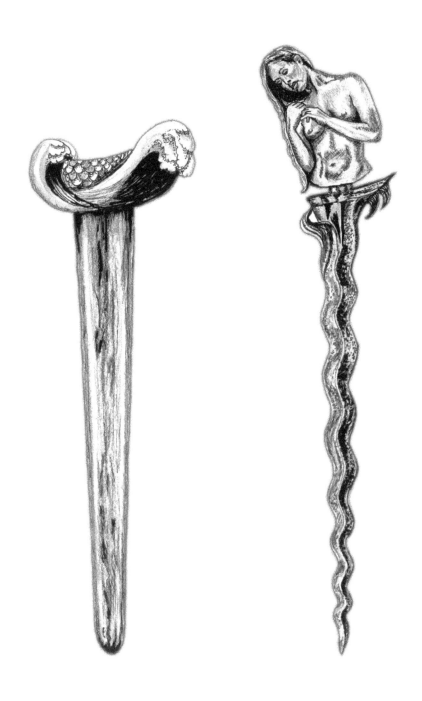

"*From the Indies. The natives call it a 'keris'. You may need it, if you're going to join this fight.*"

"On Java, they have a mermaid they call Eyang, it means grandmother. Also known as 'Nyai Raro Kidul', which translates into Queen of the South Sea."

"Eyang. Keris. Java. Queen of the South Sea," Liselotte said, her face momentarily softened by a dreamy look. "If this is her head..."

"The blade is her tail."

Liselotte looked at the grip, a light frown dancing on her forehead.

"You hold it like a pistol."

She took hold of the grip accordingly. "Why?"

Peter looked out over the fields. Liselotte did likewise, but there was no movement to be seen.

Maybe they got too drunk?

Peter said, "The keris is a stabbing weapon. When you thrust it..." He demonstrated by closing his fist and then driving it forward. "Your palm can deliver extra strength when you pierce."

Liselotte nodded, then pulled the blade out of the sheath. She gasped with surprise.

The blade of the keris had been forged from different metals, causing serpentine silvery patterns to light up against darker curls and swirls. Added to that was the form of the blade, for it wasn't straight but wavy, a total of seven spiralling twirls before the blade levelled out to a straight point.

Liselotte held the blade up, marvel on her face. She had never seen such a beautiful thing. The intricate metal patterns caught the moonlight and the whole seemed to light up, giving the blade a blue-greyish glow. It appeared almost fluid in form, rippling upwards from the hilt like the tail of a mermaid swimming in the sea.

"It's magic," Liselotte whispered, then curled her lips up and bared her teeth at the keris in a wolfish greeting.

"It catches the moonlight. Best put it away." Peter said.

Of course! The reflection.

"*Ja.*" Liselotte slid the blade back into the sheath.

Peter reassumed his position on the floor and scanned the fields. Liselotte stuck the keris in her belt, then picked up her crossbow and lay down on her belly next to him.

The magical sight of the keris blade, however, continued to dance in front of her eyes. After about ten minutes, she whispered: "Peter, did you take the keris from the heathen savages?"

"They are not savages!" Peter answered in a fervent outburst.

"I didn't mean to..."

"I'm sorry. I wasn't angry with you...it's...there was..." Peter waved a hand helplessly.

"Hush. Look! There." Liselotte pointed at the point where the dirt road led out from the woods, the same place her cousin had emerged from not all that long ago.

At first it was difficult to tell. The movements were still concealed in the shadows of the forest edge, but then four dark silhouettes detached themselves from those shadows, clearly visible against the background of the moonlit fields.

The four hastened down the path.

Liselotte took a deep breath, growing tense all over. It was all really happening. Here were the four men Peter had come to warn them about. Intent on robbery, murder, and more.

Peter whispered urgently. "Liselotte. Stay up here when the shooting is done. The keris is only for emergencies, savvy?"

She nodded.

"If you do have to use it, don't hack with it...," Peter mimicked a sideways slashing movement. "It's inaccurate, easy to lose momentum, prone to deflection...also while your arm is out—"

"You're exposed," Liselotte whispered back. "Thrust, not swing. Stab, not slash."

The four dark figures had reached the access road, where they paused to stare at the house. They pointed at it while conducting a hushed discussion. The tallest of them gave the others instructions.

"Aye," Peter continued in an even softer whisper. "Don't stretch out your arm either, keep it coiled, ready to strike. When you've struck, bring it close again. Savvy? If you hold the keris out, it's easily knocked from your hands."

Liselotte nodded again.

Keep it close. Thrust, not swing. Stab, not slash.

Her mouth felt dry.

"Only for self-defence," Peter repeated. "Stay up here when the shooting is done. Those men are experienced fighters, you are not."

Neither is Andries!

"*Ja*, Peter, I understand."

Peter murmured part of a prayer. "Yea, though I walk through the valley of the shadow of death, I will fear no evil."

The four rogues approached the house, walking towards the front door as if making a neighbourly call.

Liselotte briefly closed her eyes.

I will fear no evil.

4. Mercy Was for Them No More

OYSTERHOUT ~ DUCHY OF BRABANT ~ 1622

Father decided to send Andries upstairs on a quick errand.

"We probably haven't the time to get dressed properly. But we'll need our belts for the pistols. Go get them, be quick about it."

Once upstairs, Andries stopped by Liselotte's bedroom door. He wanted to go in and reassure her. Just a few words, but Father had said to be quick, so Andries passed the opportunity. He would go to her straight after the fight to tell her she was safe and receive her admiration for his bravery.

Andries left the study door open after he returned with the belts. They put them on, preparing their small arsenal as they waited in tense anticipation. Nothing happened for a long time. Andries was beginning to believe that an attack might not come when someone started pounding on the door.

"Doctor! Doctor!" A man hollered. "You're needed! An emergency!"

Andries exchanged a glance with Father. The whole situation seemed uncannily like Peter's arrival not long ago, but this time it wasn't a long-lost cousin on the other side of the door. Father and son inserted the barrels of their pistols, two each, into their belts, Andries also slipped the small wood axe into his belt.

"Doctor!" The man slammed his fists against the door. "You're needed man! For the love of God, it's an emergency!"

Following Peter's instructions, Andries and Father waited long enough to give the impression they had been roused from sleep. Andries lit the ends of the matches on the two matchlock muskets. He had to do so carefully. The guns were loaded and primed. It wouldn't do to accidentally snap the serpentine into the flash pan to ignite the priming powder. Andries handed one of the matchlocks to Father. They left the study and walked down the hall slowly, musket barrels levelled at the front door.

"*Ja, ja.* I'm here, stop that racket," Father called out.

Andries and Father stopped about five feet from the front door, Father on the right side of the hallway, Andries on the left. They pressed their backs against the walls, to present smaller targets as Peter had advised. Andries raised his musket to his shoulder, aiming at the middle of the front door.

"Doctor! Doctor!"

Father called out: "I am here, man! What's the matter?"

"It's the vicar!" The man by the door shouted. "In Oysterhout! You're needed! Quick man, hurry!"

Father responded, louder this time. "Go away! Go away at once!"

"The vicar is hurt!"

"I don't believe you. Leave at once...or else!" Father responded. "I shall count to three! One!"

Andries took a deep breath and held it. Father raised his musket.

"Two!"

As planned, Andries and Father didn't wait for the 'three'. They fired. Primers flashed. Stocks slammed into shoulders. There were deafening bangs. Musket balls tore through the front door, followed by shouts of alarm and pain on the other side.

There was another musket shot, more distant this time. Peter upholding his part of the fight. That was followed by two loud reports by the front door, the rogues shooting back, shouting angrily. Their small shot spewed through the middle of the hallway in showers of splinters. Andries tucked the musket under his left arm and drew his first pistol. He pulled the trigger just as Father fired his pistol. More holes were punched through the front door.

There was a chilling scream outside – cut short. Another shot from the stable. Andries transferred his smoking pistol to his left hand – the barrel too hot for his belt – and drew his second pistol.

His ears were ringing. His eyes stung. He could feel his heart pounding in his chest. He couldn't see the front door because the hallway had filled with thick and foul-smelling gun smoke.

Andries fired his second pistol in the general direction of the front door, as did Father, and then the two retreated to the study. Two more shots rang out outside. No balls tore through the splintered door. The rogues were targeting Peter in the stable now. Andries dearly hoped that their shots had missed his cousin.

§ § § § § §

Father responded, louder this time. "Go away! Go away at once!"

Liselotte watched breathlessly as the four men took position by the front door, one of them in front of it, the other three around him, guns levelled. The man at the door pounded on it, shouting for a doctor.

Liselotte had listened carefully to Peter's plan. Andries and Father should now be behind the front door, matchlocks at the ready.

She heard Father's voice, muffled behind the front door. The men shouted again. Father responded, his tone one of inquiry. The bandits pretended that a physician was needed in Oysterhout.

Father raised his voice loud enough for Liselotte to hear his words. "I shall count to three!"

Peter gave Liselotte a quick nod, to which she responded with a nervous grin. All hell was about to break loose.

"One!"

Liselotte tightened her grip on her crossbow stock. Peter aimed the doglock at the group by the front door.

"Two!"

The men by the door began to raise their muskets, but as planned two shots from inside the house marked the count of two. There were shouts of alarm and pain. Peter triggered his first shot. The world vanished in an almighty bang and a cloud of foul-smelling smoke. Two of the rogues fired their muskets through the front door. Their shots were answered by two pistol shots inside the house.

Liselotte waited until the smoke cleared enough to target, and then loosed her bolt with a twang. She watched it streak towards the front door. There was a chilling scream – cut short. Peter grabbed the second doglock and fired. Two more pistol shots sounded from inside the house. There was smoke everywhere, in the loft, by the front door.

Andries and Father will head to the study now.

Liselotte finished reloading her crossbow and once again heard the snap as her steel string sprung forward and another bolt shot out into the night. This time she shot blindly, unable to make out the front door because of the smoke. The men by the door returned two shots at the stable, one ball punching through a plank to the left of the loft doors.

"Wait here!" Peter ordered. "No more shooting."

He dropped the second doglock, rose, and launched himself forward – right out of the loft doors. Grabbing hold of the rope tied to the hoisting beam, he swiftly shimmied down.

Andries and Father barred the study door and then set about reloading their guns. There was plenty of light to see what they were doing because Peter had told them to light as many candles as possible.

"Pistols first," Peter had instructed. "I should be able to deal with the survivors outside, but if they manage to break into the house..."

Andries tried to control his nerves. He reloaded the pistols as quickly as he could. Father was slower, his hands shaking. Father said something, but Andries could barely hear him, his ears still ringing.

What's happening outside? Is Peter still alive?

Much to Andries's relief his hearing slowly returned, but he couldn't place the sounds he heard. There were angry voices at the front of the house, but it didn't sound like men in the heat of close combat. Surely, he should be hearing the ringing of steel blades?

New noises were added. Loud banging and crashing from the front of the house, but it wasn't by the front door.

"The parlour," Father guessed. "They're smashing through the window shutters. So much for our gallant Sea Beggar's cunning plan. I knew it wasn't going to work."

§ § § § § §

Liselotte got to her feet. She was careful to remain out of sight as she approached the open loft doors to peek out.

She saw Peter running towards the front door, his sword drawn and one of his pistols in his other hand. In the thinning smoke she also saw a motionless body on the porch and three men disappear around the far corner of the house.

That wasn't in the plan!

Liselotte made a grab for the rope and climbed down like Peter had, albeit slower.

Once safely on the ground she ran to the front door. She registered that the dead rogue on the porch had a crossbow bolt buried up to its fletchings in his chest, a pool of blood spreading around him.

Peter had halted at the corner of the house. If the rogues were lying in wait around the corner, a hail of fire would await him if he ventured farther.

Liselotte joined her cousin, preparing her crossbow for a next shot. Peter glanced at her, appearing unhappy that she had ignored his instructions, but there was no time to discuss it. Liselotte noted a light trail of dark drops on the ground.

One of them is wounded.

Someone barked orders around the corner. There was a loud crash, followed by another that was immediately succeeded by the splintering of wood.

"Bloody hell!" Peter cursed in a low voice. "They're battering through the shutters."

There was more splintering of wood, this time accompanied by the shattering of glass.

"Teun, stay here." A gruff voice commanded. "Shoot anybody who comes around that bloody corner."

"But Berend!"

"Shut your goddamn mouth and do as I say!"

Liselotte heard men scrambling through the window, followed by the thud of their boots on the floorboards inside.

§ § § § § §

Andries started reloading the first matchlock. The pistols on the table were ready for use.

He could hear the splintering of wood and the breaking of glass from the direction of the parlour. A voice barking orders. Then, the thud of boots on floorboards.

They're in the house now!

A single shot sounded outside; a pistol shot by the sound of it.

Peter! Where is Peter?

There was more than one rogue in the hallway. They were kicking doors open, shouting with triumph when they found the study door locked.

It's all happening so fast!

§ § § § § §

Peter took off his hat and placed it on the tip of his sword. He glanced at Liselotte who quickly nodded her understanding, then thrust his sword forward, hollering as his hat ventured into view of the rogue left to guard the window. A pistol shot rang out. Peter whooped and rushed around the corner, sword at the ready.

Liselotte followed him but nearly collided with her cousin who had come to an abrupt halt. The bandit facing him had a second pistol that he pointed at Peter's chest. The rogue's first one had been cast aside and lay on the ground, smoke curling up from the muzzle.

"Weren't expecting this, were ye?" The bandit gloated. "Ye dumb bastard."

He hadn't registered Liselotte behind Peter's back. She stepped sideways and triggered the crossbow. The bolt slammed through the rogue's right eye, into his brain. The man slumped down, dead.

"Hurry Peter, the others are inside!"

Peter gave her a curious look. "Bethanks."

They made to the window and peeked into the dark room. The door to the hallway stood open. Banging sounds deeper in the house suggested that the two remaining rogues were attempting to force open the study door.

Andries!

§ § § § § §

Something…someone crashed against the study door, which bulged inward for a moment, hinges shrieking in protest.

"God have mercy upon our souls," Father said shakily.

Andries cast a look at the last – unloaded – matchlock.

No time!

He aimed the loaded matchlock at the study door. "Father, take a pistol!"

Another crash, this time the door burst open and slammed onto the ground.

§ § § § § §

Peter scrambled up inside and ran across the room. Liselotte followed. The study's door succumbed with a loud crash. Shouts and shots followed. The hallway was filled with foul-smelling smoke. They reached the study. The door had been torn off its hinges and had fallen inward.

§ § § § § §

Andries triggered the matchlock. His shot once again deafened him. Father picked up one of the pistols on the table but pulled the trigger too soon. The ball ploughed into the floorboards. Two bandits burst into the room. Andries dropped the musket, snatched one of the pistols and managed a last shot that was met by a cry of pain. Then the rogues were upon them, cursing. The largest, advancing on Father, had a long sword in one hand, a pistol in the other. He aimed the gun at Father and pulled the trigger.

The sound of the shot seemed to reverberate in Andries's bones. The room was a nightmare of smoke, bellows, and screams. The second rogue emerged from the smoke, brandishing a sword, his face a hideous landscape of scars and warts. Andries drew the axe from his belt. It seemed puny in comparison to the long and wicked blade held by the bandit, its steel glistening menacingly in the candlelight. The rogue grinned, baring a mouth full of rotten teeth. He advanced on Andries.

§ § § § § §

Liselotte drew back the string of her crossbow even as she tried to make sense of the study – the once familiar room now a confusion of smoke, dim candlelight, struggling bodies, and hoarse shouts. The taller of the rogues stood over Father, who lay prone on the floor in front of the recessed alcove that held his strongbox. The bandit had his sword raised. The second bandit cornered Andries on the other side of the study. One of the man's arms hung limp and bleeding. He hacked at Andries with his sword, but Liselotte's brother parried the blows with the household's small woodcutting axe.

Peter raised his pistol and aimed at the tall rogue. He pulled the trigger. There was a flash, smoke rolled out of the barrel, but it didn't spit out fire and shot. "Damn!"

The tall bandit spun around, sword at the ready. His face was disfigured by a deep diagonal scar that ran across his forehead, through an unkempt eyebrow, a partially missing nostril, the snarl of his mouth, and finally his stubbled chin.

Peter dropped his pistol and raised his sword. The blade met the rogue's with a ringing clash.

The rogue's sword was a Spanish hanger, with a long and narrow blade. Peter's sword was much shorter, with a broader and heavier blade. Peter's shorter sword was far more practical in the small fighting space afforded them by the study. The tall bandit was hampered by the length of his blade and the lack of space to wield it to full effect. He was also bleeding from a wound in his left arm, yet he drove home his attacks with skill. Peter grunted with the effort of countering the thrusts and yielded some ground.

Liselotte's crossbow was reloaded, ready for use, but she couldn't get a clear shot at the tall bandit because Peter was between them. She glanced at her brother and his opponent, but the two dodged around so much that Liselotte worried her bolt might strike Andries instead.

"The Devil piss on you!" The tall rogue thundered at Peter. "You pox-ridden bastard!"

He lunged again. Peter parried, then counterattacked only to find his thrust blocked in turn. He stepped sideways to evade a new powerful lunge. As the tall rogue followed his movement through, Peter slashed into the man's left arm, the razor-sharp edge of his sword cleaving through coat, shirt, and flesh just below the gunshot wound. The man roared with angry pain.

On the other side of the room, Andries managed to knock his opponent's sword out of the man's hand.

"Good lad!" Peter hollered. "Now kill him!"

"Kill him, Andries!" Liselotte shouted at her brother.

"I'll kill you!" The tall bandit shouted at Peter, making a wild lunge that Peter easily countered. Peter failed to retaliate though, his eyes half on the fight across the room.

To Liselotte's dismay Andries hesitated, axe raised but seemingly unable to deliver the killing blow. Her brother and the man circled one another. The bandit drew a crude dagger from his belt, grinning.

"Jaap! KILL THE BRAT!" The tall rogue shouted at his companion, before opening another attack on Peter. "CUT HIS THROAT!"

"NAY!" Liselotte shouted. She boiled with frustration because both Peter and Andries continued to block a clear shot at either bandit.

The tall man launched another series of attacks on Peter, who parried desperately. Their blades crashed together with loud clangs. Sparks flew. Peter grunted. The bandit growled, barked, and snarled. He was forcing Peter to retreat towards the gaping doorway.

Andries uttered a cry of alarm as the rogue he was fighting disarmed him. The axe thudded onto the floorboards. Andries made desperate evasions as the man swung his dagger this way and that, toying with the boy now. Their movement allowed Liselotte a clear shot at the man's back.

A twang. A whir. A sickening wet thud.

"FUCK!" The bandit facing Andries buckled, nearly falling over. He clutched his thigh. The end of a bolt protruded between his fingers.

I missed!

"Well done!" Peter shouted, as he retook the initiative in his own fight. This time it was his turn to drive the tall rogue back in a flurry of attacks.

Screaming curses, the man Liselotte had just shot turned on Andries again, clutching his thigh and slashing with his dagger. Andries only barely managed to dodge the dagger's blade, but he was driven against the wall, trapped.

"I got you now, you little piss-ant!" The bandit barked at Andries.

Liselotte dropped her crossbow and drew the keris. There was no time to think, as the rogue drew his arm back for the fatal dagger thrust that would take her brother's life.

She screamed furiously as she rushed the man, holding the keris close as Peter had told her before stabbing it deep into the man's lower back, and pulling back straight away.

The man arched his back and screamed shrilly. Lumbering around, cumbersome as a wounded bear, he bellowed his pain and anger, slashing wildly with his dagger.

Liselotte felt his foul breath hot on her face. She drove the keris forward again, plunging it into the man's belly. He dropped his dagger, howled, and sank to his knees. Andries picked up the dropped dagger and struck at the man's back.

A shot rang out, loud in the enclosed space. Liselotte faintly registered the thump of a body hitting the floor.

She was desperate to end the rogue, but she and Andries lacked the experience to make a clean kill of it. Andries was hacking at the man haphazardly with the dagger, shouting frantically. Liselotte brought the keris forward again and again, stabbing in frenzy. The man rolled about on the floor, shrilling like a stuck pig. He released his bowels. Liselotte gagged on the foul stench that enveloped them.

"Die, just die!" she screamed at the man. The horror of it all was beginning to overwhelm her, but then Peter was there. He placed his blade across the man's throat and ended the butchery with one swift cut that caused a brief fountain of bright red blood. The rogue lifted his hands, but ere he could begin to claw at the gaping gash across his throat, his life ebbed away.

With a stunning suddenness, the fight was over.

Liselotte sank to her knees, still clutching the bloodied keris in one hand, the other clasped over her mouth, her eyes wide and wild, blood spattered across her face. Andries dropped the dagger, let out a sob, and clutched his sister tightly. Peter took a few deep breaths.

There was a groan from the other side of the room, followed by a grunt of pain.

"Uncle Simon!"

"Father!"

5. The Butcher's Bill

OYSTERHOUT ~ DUCHY OF BRABANT ~ 1622

Liselotte had sometimes been allowed to attend when Father attempted to teach Andries the physician's trade. Unlike her brother, Liselotte had paid close attention. She had expanded her knowledge by talking to the local 'cunning' woman and reading Father's medical books when he was away on business.

Andries had a key to the library because he was encouraged to peruse the books. Whenever Father was away, Liselotte's brother unlocked the library door and 'forgot' to lock it again.

The only book he seemed interested in himself was a Walther Ryff book with coloured anatomical illustrations.

Liselotte had once caught him staring at an image of a blonde woman, privates and breasts bared around a dissected belly that showed her internal workings. One of Andries's hands had been in his breeches, shaking to and fro. Andries had been so absorbed that he hadn't noticed his sister, who had quietly departed.

The best time to read was the first week that Father was gone. It was a good time for study. With the help of dictionaries in her father's considerable library, Liselotte had read as well as she could: Vesalius, Sylvius, Aderne, van Galen, Ryff, Da Carpi, and more. She had also pored over the anatomical drawings in these books, fascinated by the way the human body functioned, albeit in a different manner than Andries.

Most of the time.

After that first week, caution was required even though Father would usually be gone for another two days or so.

If Father's return was to catch them totally unaware, Liselotte had a broom and dustpan at hand. She'd gotten Andries to slam the front door and pace toward the library to storm in. Several times, at different speeds. They had learned that there would be time enough to place a single book back on a shelf *and* be sweeping innocently by the hearth when the library door opened.

Those tense, unknowing days weren't a good time for study, with multiple volumes open at a time. They were perfect for reading a volume of lighter literature. The added aspect of knowing she could get caught enhanced Liselotte's reading experience. If she was swept away by a story, she could get warm or cold, goose bumps, or shudders of revulsion – all magnified by the secret thrill of doing something forbidden.

Father hadn't caught her at it, but she'd never had much opportunity to translate her theoretical medical knowledge into practical application. Not until now that was, kneeling beside her injured father in the study. She quickly saw that there was little she could do for him. Simon Haelen had been wounded twice, one gunshot, and a deep laceration caused by a steel blade. Both wounds were in the abdomen.

Liselotte bit her lip. Her father had spoken of abdominal wounds. He was now doomed to die, slowly in gruesome pain.

She looked up over her shoulder. Peter and Andries looked at her, their faces questioning.

Liselotte shook her head. "All we can do is to make him as comfortable as possible."

"Carry him upstairs?" Andries asked, with doubt in his voice.

Liselotte looked at Peter, who shrugged helplessly.

"Nay," she decided. "We'll take him to the surgery. Lay him on the cot."

Though it was rare, Father sometimes treated patients at home. A front room had been transformed into a makeshift surgery for that purpose. There was a table, a stout cot, bandages, a stocked medicine cabinet, as well as Father's black leather case with his surgical tools.

Although Peter and Andries tried to be as gentle as they could, even the short distance down the hallway was hellish, leaving Father gasping between yelps of pain. Liselotte directed Andries to light candles, whilst she herself retrieved the key to the medicine cabinet from its hiding place, which she had discovered long ago. She opened the cabinet to retrieve a bottle of the opium tincture her father called laudanum, a sedative he swore by for effective pain relief. Anaesthesia had been one of the English physician John of Aderne's recommendations.

"Not too many...candles." Father whispered hoarsely, having drifted into awareness. "Don't waste...the laudanum...costs a fortune."

Both his children ignored his instructions. Andries carried in candles from other rooms as if Father's life depended on the amount of light he could create. Liselotte used generous amounts of laudanum. Father soon drifted away into unconsciousness.

"I'll need hot water," Liselotte told Andries. "The copper cauldrons. Bring the water to a boil first."

He nodded and made his way towards the kitchen.

"Can I do anything?" Peter asked.

Liselotte looked at him blankly for a moment. Her mind replayed various horrendous scenes from the fight. She wasn't much disturbed by the gore; she had plucked pheasants before, skinned and gutted rabbits and deer. However, she had killed something other than animals this night. Ended the life of human beings. The petrified screams of that last rogue echoed in her mind. "*Ja.* The bodies...could you...I don't want them in the house."

Peter nodded his understanding. "I can take them to the stable, but it's best if we leave the broken windows and doors, as well as the blood, until the Sheriff's men have had a look."

"Bethanks."

Peter left the surgery. Soon she could hear him move through the hallway, dragging something heavy out of the house.

Liselotte considered retrieving the ball from Father's gun wound, but decided that he wouldn't live long enough for any rot to set in. She would clean the wounds as best as she could and continue to administer laudanum.

After a while, Andries brought in the cauldrons of hot water she had requested, throwing an anxious look at Father. "Is there nothing...?"

Liselotte shook her head. "Nay, nothing."

"What's going to happen to us now?" Andries groaned. "What are we to do?"

"First things first." Peter came back into the room. "The bandits are all in the stable now. I've gathered all their weapons and put those in the study."

"Will more of them come?" Liselotte asked.

"Nay, I don't think so," Peter answered. "It was just these four at the Old Cauldron. They didn't speak of any others. We should be alright now."

If he hadn't come to warn us...

"Bethanks, Peter," Liselotte said. "For everything."

Her cousin regarded her thoughtfully. "We need to thank you, Liselotte. If you had stayed in your room this fight would have ended differently. I reckon Kenau and Treyn would have been proud of you."

A slow smile spread on Liselotte's face, a warm glow inside, but the moment was cut short by Andries.

"I fought too."

"You did well," Peter confirmed.

Liselotte was struck by her brother's tone; it had sounded almost like a whine.

He's used to getting all the praise when Father is in a good mood. This is new for him.

She hid a grin.

"What do we do now?" Andries asked.

"I think...I think..." Peter began to sway on his feet.

"Have you been hurt?" Liselotte asked.

Peter shook his head. "Just very tired...it's been a long day for me. I've been walking for a few days to get here, as well as the flight from the Old Cauldron and the fight just now."

"Then you need to sleep," Liselotte decided. "There's a spare room upstairs."

Peter threw a concerned look at his uncle, who was groaning with pain again.

"I'll stay with Father," Liselotte offered.

"And me?" Andries asked.

"If Liselotte can stay up with your father, you'd best get some sleep too," Peter answered. "A few hours. As soon as it's daylight you need to go to Oysterhout. Someone in the village will have to send word to the Sheriff of Breda."

He looked at Liselotte. "Are you sure you'll be alright?"

"*Ja.* Andries, can you show Peter the spare bedroom?"

"We'll reload all our own weapons first, Andries, just in case," Peter said. "Keep them close at hand tonight. Liselotte, we'll leave a loaded pistol in here, do you know how to fire one?"

"*Ja.* One of Father's snaphance pistols. Andries taught me how to use them."

"Good. If there is anything to give you cause for alarm, fire the snaphance. That'll wake us up. We'll lock the door to the other front room for now, wait until the morrow to board up the broken windows."

After these matters were seen to the others went upstairs. Liselotte did her best to clean her father's wounds and apply a bandage to his midriff. He wasn't bleeding steadily, but every now and then new blood would well up in copious amounts.

She tried to be as gentle as she could, but nonetheless her ministrations brought Father back to consciousness.

He stared at her without comprehension for a few moments, then his hand shot out with surprising strength. He clutched Liselotte's wrist, staring at her. "Andries?"

"Andries is unhurt, Father," she answered. "He's resting, in the morning he has to—"

"Thanks be to God for saving my only son," Father whispered.

He closed his eyes, relaxing his hold on Liselotte's wrist. When she tried to pull her hand away, he tightened his grip again, with considerable power in his bony fingers. His eyes shot open, full of stern disapproval. "Why are *you* tending me? The healing arts are a man's domain, you know that Lottie. Apart from midwifery, women shouldn't..."

He was seized by a series of cramps, let go of her wrist, clutched at his midriff, and yelped out his agony. Liselotte took a few steps back, out of his reach.

"Au...think...family name...ARGH...they'll call you a witch. A WITCH."

"Father, I..."

The spasms passed. Something resembling relief flooded over her father's face. Then it pulled taut into an expression Liselotte knew all too well, a laden paradoxical mix of longing and loathing. As always, it didn't fail to make her skin crawl.

He was staring at her, but not at her face. Liselotte looked down. The front of her shift was bloodied from hem to neckline. Most of the blood was from the rogue she had struggled with in the study. More was from Father, and she had splashed water on herself when she washed his wounds. Her shift was plastered to her body with watered-down red gore. Liselotte only noticed it now. She shivered with sudden revulsion.

Her father gnashed his teeth. "Have you been dancing again?"

He tried to scramble up. "Jezebel!"

Recoiling with pain, he collapsed back on the bed. Mercifully, he slipped back into unconsciousness.

Liselotte administered some more laudanum, enough to keep him drifting for a while.

If I was merciful, I'd give him enough arsenic to end his pain.

But that Liselotte couldn't do.

She hadn't used the hot water in the smaller cauldron and took it through the kitchen. She spotted the keris on the kitchen table, its blade wiped clean of blood, the carved sheath next to it. Liselotte recalled dropping the weapon when she had rushed to her father's side after the fight. Peter must have picked it up and cleaned it.

Four crossbow bolts lay next to the keris, all cleaned, one with a twisted bodkin. Its thule had imploded, the thin steel layer around the shaft torn, which suggested that the bolt had impacted against something hard like a brick wall. That was probably her second shot when gun smoke had obscured a clear view of the bandits by the front door.

Liselotte picked up the keris and then went out back, hauling the cauldron. One of the small outbuildings opposite the well held a narrow tin tub. She opened the double doors, pleased to notice that enough moonlight flooded in. She wouldn't need to go back inside to fetch a candle.

She poured the water from the cauldron into the tub and then stepped back outside again, taking a deep breath.

Whore.

Liselotte filled two pails with cold water from the well and poured that into the tin bath, her expression grim. She undid her belt and laid the keris aside. She peeled off her blood-soaked shift and stepped into the tub to use a tiny sliver of soap and a rough sponge to clean herself.

Father hadn't always been this way. They had lived in Rotterdam until she was seven. He had barely taken notice of her then, leaving the upbringing of his children in the hands of his household's sole maid. Liselotte had been heartbroken when Father had announced they were moving to the Brabant countryside, and he was ending the maid's employment to save on expenses. Father, son, and daughter had moved into a brick house in Oysterhout. Liselotte suspected that it was only then that it had dawned on Father that raising children required more than just feeding them every now and then.

There were times when he tried to play the fatherly role, although on those occasions most of his attention was reserved for Andries. There were also days when Father was irritable, drunk, or both, and regarded his children as an inconvenient nuisance. The twins rushed through their chores on those days so they could escape the house. Still, apart from the occasional cuff about her ear if she had been slow or sloppy with a chore, there had been no violence. Outbursts of anger but no subsequent physical repercussions.

She had assumed, back then, that his neglect had been her own fault. Deep down she had harboured a tiny hope that if she did her best, he might come to love her yet. She had tried to love him dutifully, but her efforts had remained unanswered.

Liselotte stared down at herself, as she continued to scrub furiously just to feel clean.

Have you been dancing again?

For a long time, she had tried to deny her intuition, the uncomfortable awareness that Father's transformation had set in shortly after her body had begun to change. After that, he was continuously irritable, quick to anger, and forever finding fault in anything Liselotte did or said.

Things had come to a head two years ago, during an exceptionally hot summer. He had been away to treat a patient but returned to Oysterhout much earlier than expected. He had found Liselotte, Andries, and half-a-dozen of their village playmates at play in the large garden behind the house. They had been playing a game of tag. Because of the extreme heat, gowns and doublets had come off and they had been frolicking about in their under shifts or breeches and shirts. The whole of it had been conducted in pure childish innocence.

Father had thundered into the garden.

He had given his children strict instructions that they weren't allowed to interact with the local village children, other than the offspring of the vicar, notary, and schoolmaster. It was irrelevant that the Oysterhout dignitaries didn't have children of their own age. Father had made it clear that the other village children were below their social standing. A physician's child didn't play with common farm children.

Liselotte had first assumed that their violation of this rule had been the cause for Father's fury. He had barked and roared at the other children who had fled as fast as they could. It wasn't until she and Andries had been marched into the house that Liselotte came to understand that most of Father's fury had been roused for a different reason.

He had sent them to their own rooms. Liselotte had waited as she heard him holler at Andries, the sheer anger in his voice unlike anything before. When he had stalked into her room she had been trembling with fear. Without saying a word, he had undone his belt. Then he had seized her, sat down on the bed, thrown her belly-down across his lap, pulled her shift up to bare her buttocks, and lashed her with his belt. It was something he had never done before, only threatened to do with increasing frequency.

The belt had been brought down hard, each lash of the heavy leather causing agonizing pain. She had wriggled around, attempting to get away from the next downward stroke, but Father had held her locked in an iron grip. She had pleaded, then begged for him to stop.

"Father! Nay! Please! I'm sorry!"

"I know you put Andries up to it."

WHACK.

"Au. Nay…nay…I'm sorry…"

"You will *NOT* tempt *my* son with SIN!"

WHACK.

"AUW! I wasn't…"

"Dancing! Dancing NAKED! Like a witch's sabbath!"

"Nay! Please. We weren't…"

WHACK.

"Your legs were bared for all to see. Your shoulders and arms."

"It was hot! Please! Father…"

WHACK.

"Aaah! Stop! Please stop!"

"I could see them jiggling as you ran. Jiggling!"

WHACK.

Liselotte had only been able to scream in pain as reply. She had caught sight of her father's face. It had been awful to behold. His eyes had been bulging, his face red, a string of saliva hanging from his mouth.

"Everybody could see. Exposing yourself shamelessly. JEZEBEL! WHORE!"

WHACK.

Liselotte had screamed again and would do so many more times that night. Her father's fury had seemed inexhaustible. At long last, he had left her bleeding on the bed. It would be days before she could sit down again or walk without pain. Shortly thereafter, Father had announced that they were to move away from Oysterhout and into the forest.

Ever since then, it was as if she had lived multiple lives.

In Father's presence she was timid and submissive, the only state in which he permitted her in his company. She despised herself for the pretence but also grew to hate Father for causing it. She had stopped hoping for better, yearning for his next assignment so that he would just go away.

With Andries, when they were alone, she could almost be herself. There were a couple of subjects related to Father to avoid in conversation. Broaching them would send him away in a sulk. Other than that, isolated out in the forest and often alone for days on end, they mostly only had each other for company.

During Father's absences she would sometimes seek out her friends from the village. Especially on the days they were out working the land, unseen by village gossipers.

Her relationship with the farm girls was a strange entanglement of mutual naivety and knowledge.

Liselotte had considerable knowledge gleaned from Father's library. The farm girls had learned their basic sums and letters but were reluctant readers. Their entire world consisted of Oysterhout and the fields and forests around the village. Desire for travel was restricted to the hope of attending Breda's annual carnival fair, of which they had heard their elders tell wild tales.

On the other hand, they easily surpassed Liselotte in other – more worldly – knowledge. When she had her first monthly bleeding Liselotte hadn't dared to consult her father. She had been unsure if it was ranked amongst any of the many sins he lectured his children about, the family bible in his hand, stern frown upon his brow. The medical books were obscure. She had turned to her friends instead for explanation and advice.

They knew about other things as well. Common country folk were far less concerned about virtue and purity. Their young folk tended to marry whom they wanted. A young bride often had a bulging belly as she said her vows, with nobody batting so much as an eyelid. Liselotte would listen in curious astonishment as her friends related their experimental adventures in vivid detail, envying them their freedom.

Had it not been for that, she might have continued to avoid the severity of that first beating, but it had all gone horribly wrong a month ago. It had been a warm languid summer's eve and Liselotte had been visiting her friends. They had been hard at work in the fields all day and were enjoying a few well-deserved jugs of cider in the shade. Liselotte had been offered a few sips as well. Her friends had cheered and whistled when one of the farm lads had asked to walk her home. His name was Henk. He was tall, handsome, funny, and – she recalled with a sigh –, he had smelled nice even after a day's hard work in the fields. She had willed the walk to go on forever, in the peaceful evening sun, thrilled by the proximity of the charismatic older boy who had seemed to think she was interesting.

When they reached the edge of the fields around her house, Henk had proposed a kiss. Liselotte had been unable to think of any reasons *not* to, other than Father, but he had left for Tilburg a few days before and wouldn't be back for a while yet.

It was a sin, she had supposed, but to judge by her friends' stories about what they got up to, just a minor one. Moreover, in all the books she had read in which such things were mentioned, a kiss was a magical pinnacle of romance. The books remained stubbornly silent on all the other things her friends talked about. So, breathlessly and with a pounding heart, she had answered with a "*ja*".

Liselotte couldn't draw comparisons based on previous experiences, but she had deemed her first kiss a disappointment. Before she had even been able to relish the thrill of Henk's lips pressed against hers, he had abruptly thrust his tongue into her mouth, pawed roughly at her small breasts, and urged a bulging hardness in his trousers against her belly. She had pushed him away and fled home.

That should have been the end of it, but Henk had boasted widely that he'd *had* Physician Haelen's daughter. When Father returned from Tilburg, he had been greeted in Oysterhout with jovial inquiries regarding a wedding date.

The first Liselotte had known of this was when Father returned home: Humiliated and seething. She had been hanging up the washing on the lines out back. He hadn't even bothered to drag her inside, instead tearing at her clothing and thrashing her within an inch of her life right there and then, roaring his fury.

Now he's dying.

Liselotte stepped out of the bath, her skin tingling from her vigorous scrubbing. She looked at her fouled shift.

Should have fetched a clean one first.

She spotted the slow billowing of the linen sheets she had hung out to dry earlier that day, on the grassy clearing at the end of the little orchard.

Picking up the keris, Liselotte crossed the orchard, one arm folded over her breasts. She was halfway when she abandoned the attempt at modesty. Everybody was asleep, dead, or dying. The night was hers. It felt strangely liberating and carefree. It was a sin, of course. Moreover, Liselotte was sure that revelling in her nakedness the way she was would be considered an even graver sin, but she didn't care anymore.

She stopped by the washing lines and raised her arms above her head in a greeting to the moon. It was like having another bath, but this time in moonlight. It felt cleansing. She drew the keris from its sheath, and pointed the blade at the moon, marvelling once again at how the patterns of the steel and curvy blade caught the light.

A shiver fluttered over her arms and legs, followed by goose bumps all over.

A shiver fluttered over her arms and legs, followed by goose bumps all over.

Liselotte pushed the blade back in its sheath, then took down a sheet from the washing line to wrap it around her.

Her eye fell on the stable. That's where Peter had dragged the bodies. Impressions of the fight flashed by and she was overcome by curiosity.

Her approach to the stable was marked by uncertainty. She had never been in a fight before, nor even witnessed one other than village lads throwing a few punches to prove their manhood. Peter had expressed his admiration of her conduct, but Liselotte felt that was misplaced. Using the crossbow had been easy. There had been no need to think about what she had been doing, just hours of practice kicking in. Drawing the keris had been instinctive, driven by the fear that Andries would be taken from her by the bandit's crude dagger. It had seemed as if she'd been a phantom spectator, standing aside as she watched whatever spirit drove her body attempt to kill a man, screeching like one of the *witte wieven*[10] that haunted the heath lands.

Thinking about the fight now, without the urgency of the moment to dictate her actions, all Liselotte could feel was a shudder and the certainty that she should have just run as far away from the danger as possible.

She paused by the stable's double door, which Peter had shut.

There are four dead men in there.

Still, she had to see...what she had done.

Thou shalt not kill.

Liselotte had to know: Were such horrible monsters God's creatures too? Or were they Devil-sent? Would she be overcome by remorse? Guilt? Was she Hell bound now? Perhaps Treyn Rembrands had felt this way, the first time she had blasted her musket at the Spaniards storming Alkmaar's walls.

Liselotte swung the doors open to let the moonlight wash in. Peter had arrayed the men in a row in the aisle between the empty stalls. Their bodies were impossibly still. Visible skin seemed almost white in the moonlight, broken by the darkness of congealing blood.

Their faces puzzled Liselotte, until she realised that Peter had placed copper coins over their eyes.

For Charon! The ferryman who'll carry their souls across the Styx.

---

[10] White hags, evil spirits.

She knew that from books. Father would have been furious had he seen this, denouncing heathen practices as ungodly, but Peter had obviously thought it important. The gesture seemed oddly deferential. Liselotte supposed her cousin sensibly wanted to ensure that Charon wouldn't leave their souls roaming on the wrong side of the Styx.

Apart from fascination, Liselotte could feel nothing but satisfaction as she regarded the corpses. Given half a chance, the four would have killed Andries and Peter. She knew what they had wanted from her. There would have been no mercy, even if she had begged for it.

She spat on the ground by the nearest dead man's feet. "I hope you all rot in Hell."

Liselotte walked out of the stable, closed the doors again, and went back to the kitchen yard to collect her belt and quiver. She didn't want to touch the blood-soaked shift, not this night; she would collect it on the morrow. Going back into the house, she went upstairs to her room to put on a clean shift, over which she donned a threadbare gown. She kept the keris with her, just in case. After that she went back to the surgery, to check on Father.

He had doubled over into a foetal position and was drifting in and out of consciousness. Now and then he uttered a groan of pain, but they were short for he had trouble breathing. His face was sallow and moist with perspiration. The bandage around his midriff was soaked in blood. Liselotte wasn't sure if she should change the bandages, afraid of the pain it would cause him and her memory of his earlier bony grip on her wrist.

Please, let it end soon.

Liselotte pulled up a chair to stay by his side as closely as she dared to. The first time Father came to and opened his eyes to behold Liselotte, he whispered "Saskia? Is that you, Saskia?"

It was heartbreaking to hear the hope and longing in his voice, and a double blow to hear the name of the mother Liselotte had never known. Worst of all, he sounded vulnerable and touchingly human, a state which he had never exposed to his children.

Would that he had.

Liselotte wiped away a tear, as her father drifted into a feverish lapse of consciousness.

The second time he came round, he recognised Liselotte and, between gasping for breath, he hissed his accusations, again and again.

"...Jezebel...whore...witch..."

Gathering all her courage, Liselotte spoke. "Father? Is this not a time for forgiveness? I can find it in my heart to forgive you, can you not..."

"You forgive me?" Father tried to laugh, but it ended in painful gasping. "I have done...you no wrong...ungrateful rat...You would...bite the...hand that...feeds you?"

Liselotte stared at him, taking in the malice he exuded.

I would bite the hand that whips me.

She had tried to be a dutiful daughter, but now she couldn't recall why. The dying man seemed to be an utter stranger, their connection an obscure coincidence.

He was also fading fast now. He no longer had the power for his words to claw at her soul. A tiny nugget within her began to grow, the realisation that she would be released from his dominance over her.

I'll be free.

"...whore...wit...aaargghh..."

Truly free.

There was relief when the dying man blew out his last breath. Relief that the pain and suffering had ended, but also a sense of liberation and subsequent guilt for her soul's elation at that notion.

Liselotte left the surgery and calmly climbed the stairs. She hesitated in front of Andries's bedroom door. Her brother would be devastated, but she couldn't bear the thought of having to comfort him, having to pretend she shared his grief when she felt mostly reprieve. On this bloody night, that lie, more than anything else, seemed a sin to avoid.

She went to the guest room instead. Peter was on his back, fast asleep, but on top of the blanket and fully dressed, he even still had his boots on.

"Peter," she whispered. "Peter."

He woke instantly, sitting upright, reaching for his sword.

"It's nearly dawn," she said. "Father's dead. I need to sleep."

"I'm sorry..."

She shook her head. "Will you tell Andries? Before you send him to Oysterhout?"

He nodded, was about to speak again, then thought better of it. Liselotte turned around and went to her room. The last thing she was aware of was falling onto her bed, after which she fell into a deep sleep.

6. An Uncertain Future

OYSTERHOUT ~ DUCHY OF BRABANT ~ 1622

Liselotte was woken by the sound of the doorknocker. She sat up in bed.

Cousin Peter showed up out of nowhere. Father is dead. There are four dead men in the stable. Is Andries back from Oysterhout?

She could hear footsteps in the hall, moving from the kitchen to the front door. There was also a distinctive metallic click – someone cocking a pistol.

"Belay that knocking!" Peter shouted. "I'm on my way!"

Liselotte wondered if her cousin's considerable volume was intended to alert her. She had fallen asleep in her gown, so was already dressed, other than her cotton cap that she didn't bother with. She grabbed the keris and then rushed out of her room and down the stairs, hair flowing freely.

Father would have given me an earful for that.

Liselotte came to a halt behind Peter as he finished unlocking the battered front door. He swung it open to reveal the Old Cauldron's innkeepers on the doorstep.

The man was an ale-bellied barrel of jollity, the woman tall and wiry, with a shrewish expression that made her seem perpetually sceptical.

Liselotte and Andries had sold them the occasional hare and cuts of venison. The innkeeper was friendly enough, his wife in possession of a sharp tongue but sound judgment. Deciding they weren't a threat, Liselotte concealed the keris in a fold of her gown.

"Seigneur!" The innkeeper wailed. "We met the doctor's lad on the Oysterhout road, so we did. He told us what happened."

"We come to pay our respects, so we have," his wife added.

"'Pon our souls!" cried the innkeeper.

His wife's eyes narrowed. "But then we meets the gentleman, what we took to be honourable..."

"'Tis what I said, Seigneur." The innkeeper wrung his hands. "When you called upon the Old Cauldron last eve, I told my luverly Miep, 'never has such a fine gentleman crossed our threshold', and that be the truth of it."

"But!" The woman raised her index finger and shook it at Peter. "But, what ordered a meal and bed at our fine establishment, and what left without paying his dues."

The innkeeper shook his head and cheek jowls. "Is there none to be trusted these dark and foul days?"

"I did eat, and the food was good." Peter rummaged about for coins in the leather purse that hung from his belt.

"The room is ruined! Me best room!" The innkeeper's wife wiped away an imaginary tear, while not taking her eyes off Peter's purse. "The finest curtain rods in all Brabant. The curtains shred to ribbons, the finest curtains in—"

"All Brabant." Peter finished.

He withdrew more coins from the purse. "I will pay in full for my lodgings then. With my sincere apologies for having run into urgent business to attend elsewhere, and constructing a makeshift ladder to assist my departure."

The finest ladder in Brabant.

Liselotte lowered her face to hide a grin.

Peter offered the coins. The innkeeper took them, then shot a glance at the splintered bullet holes that disfigured the front door. "You're a true gentleman, Seigneur. Tis what I told my Miep when..."

"Bethanks, now if that was all?"

"There are other matters, Seigneur!" The innkeeper hastened to say. "One of lost income which will like as not ruin us...condemning our poor selves to end our days as miserable beggars...We were due some monies, you see..."

"I overheard that conversation. I know who owed you that money." Peter said. "Blood money, to be stolen from my uncle."

"Your uncle, Seigneur?" The innkeeper's wife's eyes grew wide. "I see, I see...such a tragic loss for the family."

She peered curiously at Liselotte.

"Aye, indeed," Peter answered. "Your four other *guests* are in the stable. Neatly lined up. You are welcome to call upon them and ask them for the money they owed you, although you may find them reluctant to speak and just as lean of purse as they were last night. Now if you'll excuse us, there are many urgent matters at hand."

"Of course there be!" The woman agreed. "And I does apologise, Seigneur, but there be one last thing."

"There is?" Her husband looked puzzled at that.

Liselotte, thoroughly amused by the encounter so far, moved a hand in front of her mouth to hide her smile at his comical expression.

"Of a monetary nature, I presume?" Peter asked.

"*Wablief?*[11]" The woman glanced at Liselotte again. "Nay, Seigneur. Tis but a piece of well-meant advice. The children, Seigneur."

"What of them?" There was a warning tone in Peter's intonation.

"Whatever you decide, Seigneur, will be wise. *Ja*, I'm sure of it. But I beg of you, Seigneur, not to leave them in the grubby hands of the Parish Orphan Fund."

Parish Orphan Fund!

I'm an orphan.

"Pray tell me, *Mevrouw*[12], what business this is of yours?" Peter asked. "As I recall neither of you protested when those four rogues were discussing their intentions last night, other than refusing to let them rob me in your own inn."

Peter's tone suggested that a line had been crossed.

The innkeeper looked horrified. "Seigneur! There's not much to be done by the likes of us against the likes of those rotten men."

His wife shrugged apologetically. "Begging your pardon, Seigneur. Tis just that the orphans are rented out for labour. By the vicar and notary both. Tis rare for the Fund to spend even a single *stuiver*[13], but many a coin makes it into their strongbox...if you know what I mean, Seigneur. Tis always been so, the boys are made to work themselves into an early grave...the girls..."

The woman shuddered, and then gave Liselotte a genuine look of pure pity.

Liselotte felt her skin crawl when she realised the implications of the warning. Had she escaped the lurid clutches of the bandits only to land in the hands of others with similar intentions? This new option would be shrouded in hypocritical legitimacy. There would be nowhere to turn for help.

"I understand," Peter said. "Bethanks."

"Seigneur, tis just that I were one meself! A Fund Orphan that is. I know what happens...this little one here shouldn't have to..."

"Your advice is appreciated, *Mevrouw*. Truly." Peter dug another coin from his purse and gave it to her. "Now I bid you a good day."

---

[11] 'What did you say?', a Brabant expression.

[12] Mrs / Missus

[13] 5 cent coins

The woman mumbled "Bethanks", after which the couple departed.

Peter shut the front door and turned to face Liselotte. "I paid them because they were honourable enough to prevent the rogues from assaulting me at their inn last night. It was suggested to them several times."

Liselotte nodded, not sure why it mattered. She stared at Peter in a new light. For a brief time, she had perceived herself to be free, but her cousin, as the only adult relative present, would be the one making decisions about...

The rest of my life.

"I found some rye bread and a basket of eggs in your larder," Peter said. "As well as a lump of cheese I wouldn't feed to bilge rats. Is that all the food in the house?"

"*Ja,*" Liselotte answered.

"This'll last us for today if we don't mind eating the same food twice. Come to the kitchen and we'll break the night's fast. We're about an hour short of noon, so it's none too early!"

Liselotte followed him into the kitchen; dreadfully aware that Father's corpse lay behind the door as they passed the surgery. To her surprise, Peter didn't expect her to make the food. He had already sliced some of the rye bread and started to fry half-a-dozen eggs in a skillet on the wood stove.

"Sit down," he said.

Liselotte took a seat at the kitchen table. The four crossbow bolts still lay on the tabletop. She placed the keris next to the bolts and regarded her cousin curiously. Even though it seemed they had gone through a lot together, she barely knew the man other than the little information she had gleaned when Father took delight in listing Haelen family misfortunes.

Her grandparents, Adrian and his wife Elisabeth had three sons. Liselotte knew little of her grandparents other than they had come to Rotterdam to start a family and were long deceased.

Their eldest son had been Father, who had gone on to university to study medicine. The middle son was Johan, Peter's father. Peter's birth had been complicated. He survived; his mother had died. Peter had one older sister, Jacoba. Liselotte recalled meeting both her uncle Johan and cousin Jacoba, but not very often. Jacoba had been a married woman already and had seemed ill at ease with children.

Liselotte had seen much more of the youngest brother, her uncle Karel. Karel and his wife Mathilda had two boys, Thomas and Maarten.

Thomas had been one year younger than the twins, Maarten one year older. There had been times in Rotterdam when Liselotte and Andries had seen more of their uncle, aunt, and cousins than they had of their father. These were the happiest memories Liselotte had.

Uncle Karel and Aunt Mathilda had always welcomed Liselotte and Andries into their home, a warm, lively place full of affection. Uncle Karel had liked to say that the four cousins were as thick as thieves and more mischievous than a tiding of magpies. But then Father had taken his children away from Rotterdam.

They had been eleven when Father had received a letter with news that Thomas and Maarten had succumbed to an epidemic.

Liselotte now figured that her father had possibly seen those ill tidings as a vindication of his decision to leave Rotterdam. Back then, the triumph in his voice as he told them the news had been a cruel blow. After being dismissed from Father's presence, the twins had fled to the nest of blankets they had made in the loft of the brick house in Oysterhout. They had cried and clung on to one another in grief.

Despite these sad thoughts, Liselotte's belly rumbled as the smell of frying eggs filled the kitchen. She was hungry.

"Your breakfast, Mademoiselle." Peter placed a pewter plate in front of her. It contained three slices of rye bread with a fried egg on each. He added a cup of watered ale, then sat down with his own plate which he attacked with a healthy appetite.

Liselotte did likewise; relishing the food while her memory replayed the alliance she had struck with her cousin in the stable the night before.

She had surprised herself with her own audacity, both the familiar way she had addressed Peter and her impulsive decision to show him the awful bruises. There was nothing Peter could have done about it, since her father had acted within his legal rights. At least Peter's moonlit face had shown revulsion. That meant he was unlikely to treat her as such. It brought her thoughts back to her status. Legally, Liselotte had been Father's possession, until he transferred that ownership to whomever he chose to marry her off to...or died.

And now, I belong to Peter. Unless he chooses to unburden himself of me. What then? The Parish Orphan Fund?

Liselotte finished off her last piece of bread, following that with a sigh.

"Are you feeling alright?" Peter asked, his voice full of concern.

His tone threw her. Liselotte couldn't recall the last time anybody other than Andries and the innkeeper's wife just now had shown heed for her well-being. Was he worried that she wasn't coping with Father's death? She had far more pressing concerns.

"You're going to steal Andries from me," she accused him. "Make him sail on that ship of yours."

"Would you deny your brother a chance to see the world?"

"I wouldn't deny *anybody* a chance to see the world," Liselotte hinted hopefully. It was a silly fantasy of course, but one that briefly sparked into a tiny flicker of hope.

"Things have changed since last night," Peter said. "I'll talk to Andries when he returns from Oysterhout. The offer is still open, but I'd understand if he chose not to."

Liselotte shrugged, that wasn't what she wanted to hear. She felt suddenly shy of asking outright what Peter intended to do with her. This was different than the stable loft. Peter had acted awkwardly then, as if not quite knowing how to deal with his forward cousin. Since the fight, his behaviour had changed, as if they were comrades almost. He had even deferred to her in the treatment of Father's wounds.

Now it was her turn to be awkward. Peter was the new head of the household and wielded total power over her. It made her wary. Could she trust him? She thought so, but her mind doubted her intuition.

Peter is right, things have changed. What's that?

Hoofbeats, multiple hoofbeats, approaching the house at a canter.

Liselotte and Peter rushed to the front door, to hear horses whinny as they were urged to a halt in front of the stable, seven of them in total. Their riders dismounted. One of the men tossed his reins to another and then strode toward the front door. He was in his thirties, with a narrow, pinched face, clean-shaven cheeks, and a rimmed steel helmet on his head.

"Edwin Hartman," he announced. "Assistant to the Sheriff of Breda."

"Peter Haelen," Peter answered. "Retired VOC Commodore. And this is my—"

"*Ja, ja,*" Hartman said, seemingly dismissing Liselotte as unimportant after a quick glance. "What's the matter here then, Commodore?"

"Monseigneur! My brother? Andries?" Liselotte asked. She looked for her brother amidst the other riders, but all were grown men, wearing helmets and leather jerkins, armed with pistols and swords.

Hartman looked at her with irritation. "The boy follows. With the village notables."

61

"Thank you, Monseigneur," Liselotte said.

Peter gave Hartman a quick summary, then offered a tour around the house and grounds to see evidence of the attack.

The two men went to inspect the broken shutters of the parlour. Liselotte stayed behind; she didn't like Hartman all that much. Nor did she feel very comfortable staying where she was. Some of the Sheriff's men were grinning and leering at her.

Do they think that makes them attractive? That I'll come rushing over? "I wouldn't feed you lot to bilge rats," she murmured. She went back inside to the kitchen, to clean the plates and cups, and scrub the skillet.

Liselotte could hear Peter and Hartman progressing through the house, visiting the study and surgery – where Father was still laid out on the cot – before leaving through the front door. Liselotte went out back to fetch water from the well. She spotted her bloodied night shift, decided that it was ruined, bundled it, and stuck it beneath the eaves of one of the outbuildings. It's presence here wouldn't be part of whatever Peter was telling Hartman, and she didn't want to have to explain last night's bath. The thrill of raising the keris to kiss the moonlight was a private memory.

Liselotte went back into the kitchen, poured the water into a cauldron and started heating it, before gathering a mop, a brush, and various cleaning rags. She wanted to scrub the study floor and then the surgery. When the water was hot, she poured it into a pail and mixed in some of the green soap Amsterdam was famed for, one of the rare luxuries Father had always insisted on stocking.

She was somewhat puzzled to hear hoofbeats again, this time moving away from the house, but in lesser number.

Shortly thereafter, Peter came into the kitchen.

"How good are you at scrubbing decks, Sailor?" Liselotte asked him, to match the familiarity with which she had startled them both the night before.

Peter glanced at the bucket and cleaning implements. He chuckled. "Scrubbed a fair few, especially on my first voyage east."

"When you were fourteen and ran away?" Liselotte asked eagerly.

"Aye, indeed. I'll give you a hand. Where did you want to start?"

"The study," Liselotte said. "But, maybe, if you could see to the broken shutters in the front room? Has *Mynheer*[14] Hartman left?"

---

[14] Mr / Mister

"Edwin Hartman," he announced. "Assistant to the Sheriff of Breda."

"He has, along with two of his men. The other four have been posted by the stable doors. There'll be a wagon to pick up the bodies. They'll escort it back to Breda."

"So, he didn't doubt your story?"

"As a retired VOC Commodore I'm a man of some standing. Those four vagabonds are well known to the Sheriff and his men. I suspect there's a reward for their capture."

"Will we...you get any of that reward?"

Her cousin laughed. "Why do you think Hartman was eager to get back to Breda? He'll be claiming it all, I'm sure."

"That's not fair! Can't you do anything about that?"

"Aye. Go to Breda, hire an expensive lawyer, and then wait for months while the lawyers fight it out. I haven't the time for it. I need to get back to Flushing, to my ship."

He burst out with sudden passion, "I want to be on the sea again. The ocean! I want to be with..."

Peter ceased talking. He seemed to be far away for a moment. There was a longing expression on his face.

He's in love with someone!

Peter shook his head, as if to shed whatever daydream he'd been lost in. "A hold filled in the East will be worth a hundred-thousandfold of whatever the reward for these vagabonds may be. Besides that, if lawyers get involved there won't be much left by the time they're done."

Liselotte nodded her understanding.

She picked up the keris from the table. She would have liked to hold on to the magnificent blade a little longer but reckoned it wouldn't do to make Peter ask for its return. She held out the dagger to Peter. "Bethanks for the loan."

He looked at it with a regretful expression on his face. "Would you believe that I never drew her in anger? You were the first to satisfy the purpose for which she was forged. To feed her thirst."

She? Her? He speaks of the keris like a person.

"I was?"

"Aye, you were. A keris is highly personal, Liselotte. I think it would be ill luck to part her from you now."

Liselotte was thrilled. "I can keep it...her?"

Peter shrugged, a bit unhappily. "I believe she has chosen you to do so."

Liselotte beamed. She recalled the goose bumps she had felt the night before, after her bath when she'd saluted the moon with the serpentine blade.

"Thank you so much! So, there is magic in the keris?"

Peter's face fell. He frowned. "It's better not to speak of these things. Folk are burned at the stake from Edinburgh to Lübeck, and Hamburg to Brindisi for lesser offences these days. Things are different in the East."

"I understand," Liselotte said, albeit reluctantly. "I'll put Eyang away and then start scrubbing."

"Eyang?" Peter asked with a smile, then nodded. "A good name. I'll get started as well. I saw some old boards in the stable. I'll clear up the broken shutters, then board up that window."

They had both finished their respective tasks when they heard more hoof beats and the soft rumble of ironbound wheels out front, followed by greetings called out by the Sheriff's men.

Andries!

7. Ill Tidings

OYSTERHOUT ~ DUCHY OF BRABANT ~ 1622

Andries shared an uncomfortable wagon bed with the vicar and notary. Two stout draught horses directed by a local farmhand pulled the wagon along. The second wagon, driven by another farmhand, held a simple coffin; the pale pine boards startlingly bright on the age darkened and stained wood of the wagon's bed.

It had been a long morning. It had seemed to Andries that he hadn't slept at all when Peter had woken him with the news that Father had passed away.

Somewhere deep down, Andries had clung on to the hope that he would come downstairs in the morning to find Father grumbling and complaining, in a foul mood – but alive.

Andries had barely been given time to digest the news of Father's death. Peter had been keen on notifying the authorities as soon as possible and had sent the boy on his way into the day's first summer sunshine, clutching a small hump of rye bread.

The vicar's wife had fed Andries a proper breakfast when he had reached Oysterhout. It had been nice to rest his weary legs while the vicar and notary made arrangements. That included the despatch of a fast rider to Breda. The man had returned much earlier than expected because he had encountered Edwin Hartman. The Sheriff's men had been patrolling the road on the lookout for the bandits who had made travel between Breda and the north a dangerous business.

Two wagons had been prepared, one to carry the vicar and notary, one to carry an empty coffin. It seemed as if all Oysterhout had come to watch the wagons depart. The news had spread like wildfire on parched heath lands. The previous arrival and departure of the Sheriff of Breda's mounted men had already been observed and much speculated upon.

Andries had been pleased to see Toosje amongst the villagers, staring at him with admiration that made him straighten his back and broaden his shoulders. He had been in a deadly fight, he reminded himself. Wielding musket, pistol, axe, and dagger.

I'm a hero.

Andries sagged again when they were out of sight of Oysterhout's spectators. Hero or not, Father's death weighed upon his thoughts.

His travelling companions made an odd couple. The vicar was a corpulent man, tall and fleshy, with prominent jowls and small eyes. The notary was short and thin, with a narrow sour face and shifty eyes magnified by thick spectacle lenses. He was studying a sheaf of papers he had brought along, his brow a continual frown.

The vicar kept up a non-stop sermon, about the will of God and the perfection of Father's new Heavenly home. Andries made the appropriate pious responses when required but wasn't really listening. Instead, he stared dully at the surroundings, not understanding why everything was so utterly normal when his own life had been turned upside down.

Although all the locals called the way home a 'road', it was nothing more than a broad sand path, occasionally marred by hardened outcrops of tree roots. The wagon wheels struggled to plough through the deep sand and caused the wagons to rattle and shake when they crossed the harder ground. At those times, Andries could hear the coffin jolted about in the wagon behind them. Thumping and bumping. It was the most awful sound he had ever heard. He dreaded the thought of Father's body shaken about in such indignity on the way back to Oysterhout.

"This is for you."

Andries glanced in bewilderment at the single sheet of paper the notary offered him.

He took it, managing enough concentration to make out the words and numbers on the paper. It was a bill. For the coffin.

"But… but…" Andries stammered. "I haven't got any money, not even a single *duit*."

The notary looked at him pensively. "I don't think it improper to disclose at this time, unofficially, as it won't be lawful until the required legal protocol is met—"

"I don't understand!" Andries exclaimed in a near panic, his head spinning. *Legal protocol* sounded like trouble, but surely they understood he had no money to pay for Father's coffin!

"…I wasn't finished speaking." The notary said in a sharp tone. "Manners maketh the man."

"Come, come," the vicar spoke. "The boy's been through the Valley of Death and back. Allow him some leeway."

The notary snorted, but clarified nonetheless. "I drew up and witnessed your father's last will and testament, boy."

"His will?"

"Suffice to say," the notary said. "That he has left everything to you."

"Enough to give us a royal tip!" The farmhand turned his head at his passengers, grinning broadly. "Everybody knows your old man was hoarding his wealth, in that run-down house of yours. I've always reckoned it's a clever way to disguise—"

"Shut your mouth, man!" The notary snapped at him. "You're not paid to think, or spread village gossip for that matter. Just to get us there and back."

"*Ja*, Seigneur. Sorry, Seigneur." The farmhand's face betrayed no regrets whatsoever, but he did turn his attention back to his team.

"From what I've heard," the vicar said to Andries. "Your father was a man of means, befitting a renowned physician. We can discuss a more suitable coffin for the funeral after the testament has been read."

Funeral. Will. Testament...Everything!

"Everything, *Mynheer?*" Andries asked the notary. "How about my sister?"

"Her name isn't mentioned in the will," the notary replied.

Andries shut his eyes briefly and took a deep breath. He had never understood why Father had come to loathe Liselotte. Andries had always hoped Father would relent in his plain opposition to his own daughter.

But to omit her name from his will altogether!

It was a denial of her status. It seemed spiteful. It left Liselotte with nothing. Andries resolved to take care of her. She could live in the house as long as she wanted to. He glowed with secret pride, as he envisaged his new role of provider.

Things have changed!

The sound of thudding hoofs in the soft sand announced Erwin Hartman and two Sheriff's men.

Hartman stopped to exchange news. He said that he was riding ahead to Breda to notify the Sheriff that the bandits had been killed. The bodies would be taken to Breda, to be hung and gibbeted as an example.

Andries shivered. He had heard of the practice of encasing criminals in coffin-sized cages and then hung from the gallows, their decomposing bodies on display by the roadside as a stark warning.

Hartman continued speaking, telling them he had spoken with VOC Commodore Haelen...

VOC Commodore?

The notary turned to Andries, "You didn't tell me your cousin was a Commodore of the United Dutch East Indies Company."

Andries shrugged helplessly.

I didn't know!

"*Retired* VOC Commodore," Hartman specified. "But still, hey? The VOC."

He uttered the abbreviation with a respectful sigh. Both the vicar and notary nodded their assent of Hartman's assessment of the Company's legendary reputation.

"I've left some men at the Haelen house," Hartman said "Two for…" He looked at the notary. "The matter we spoke about. Two to escort the bodies of the dead bandits to Breda, for which purpose I am commandeering one of your wagons, in the name of the Sheriff of Breda."

The vicar protested. "How will we get back?"

"Sit on the coffin if you must sit," Hartman replied. "Or walk. I care not. This is Sheriff's business."

With that he and his men departed, speeding their mounts on their way, leaving the vicar and notary to grumble.

"On his way to claim the reward," the notary said sourly.

"VOC Commodore," the vicar murmured. He glanced at Andries. "That might complicate matters?"

The notary shrugged, before turning back to his papers.

Andries barely paid them attention. They would be upon the clearing soon. He would be glad to get out of the uncomfortable wagon. Never mind what Father said about the expense of keeping a horse, Andries would get a team of them, and a proper trap, with a lacquered finish and comfortable seat cushions. With his cousin holding high rank in the VOC, Andries was sure his own star would rise. Liselotte could keep the house for him while he voyaged east, and he'd come home between journeys to travel around in style. Liselotte would sit next to him in the trap, dressed in the finest gown money could buy. 'There goes VOC Officer Haelen', folk would say as he passed. Skipper Haelen before too long. Commodore even, why not!

He would get some new clothes too, to replace his threadbare day outfit, far past its best days. And a new gown for Liselotte! She would be pleased, Andries was sure. He wasn't going to be stingy, like Father had been.

When the house came into view, Andries decided their home would need some attention as well. The gardens were a near wilderness, the paintwork on the shutters, windows and doors faded and peeling.

Peter opened the front door. Liselotte peeked out from behind his back. She hovered there as Peter came to greet the newcomers.

"Well done, Cousin."

"Thank you, Cousin," Andries replied with all the formality he could, then cast a longing glance at Liselotte. There was so much to tell her!

"Go." Peter nodded, and then introduced himself to the vicar and notary.

Feeling overwhelmed by the elation about his new status and deep grief for Father, Andries went to Liselotte. He was sure that she would be as devastated as he felt and in need of comfort. He yearned for a quick hug, a gesture of affection, but scolded himself for his childish needs. He had adult responsibilities now. He had to take care of Liselotte for one.

As Andries approached his sister he slowed down. She didn't look in the least distraught. Her face was pale and thoughtful, but otherwise composed.

She reached her hand out to him, but Andries ignored it, put off by her calm demeanour.

"They are going to take the murdering bastards to Breda and hang them," he announced.

"Hang them? But they're already dead."

"As an example. They'll also be gibbeted!"

Liselotte shrugged. "Not undeserving after what they did. Are you hungry, brother? I could fry you some eggs."

Andries walked into the hallway. "I broke fast in Oysterhout. I was given sausages, bacon, and beans."

Andries quickly looked away from the surgery door, knowing Father was in there. He frowned. "We'll need somewhere to sit and talk."

"I cleaned the study, but maybe the front parlour would be better? Peter boarded up the broken window."

Andries walked into the parlour to look around. Liselotte followed. Peter had done a thorough job; there was no trace of the forced entry other than the boarded window. Peter had already opened the shutters of the remaining windows to let the daylight in. Liselotte quickly went around opening the windows.

"Some fresh air," she explained.

"*Ja, ja.* You mean to eavesdrop."

Liselotte flared up, placing her hands on her waist, eyes blazing. "They might send me out because I'm a girl, but it's *my* life they'll be talking about. *My* future. I should hear it at least."

Andries shrugged. He didn't understand Liselotte's sudden concern about her future. As new head of the household he felt a sudden burst of irritation at her plans to eavesdrop on men's talk. Liselotte should know that he could be trusted to make the right decisions for her.

Also, it might be better if she didn't hear that Father had omitted to mention her in his will. What she didn't know wouldn't hurt her.

He noted that his sister's hair was unbound, her reddish-gold mane cascading freely over her shoulders. "You should go and fetch your cap, Liselotte."

"I'm not a married woman, I can wear my—"

"Father and the vicar equate loose hair with loose morals. Would you provoke the vicar on this day?"

Or disrespect Father?

Liselotte gave him a funny look, then rushed out of the room and up the stairs. Andries went around the room to close the windows again. Outside, the Sheriff's men and farmhands were loading the corpses of the bandits onto the empty wagon. Peter was still talking to the vicar and notary.

Liselotte reappeared far faster than Andries expected. She hadn't bothered to brush her hair and do it up properly, instead bundling it hastily beneath her white cotton cap. She frowned as she caught her brother closing the last window.

"Too much of a draught," he explained sheepishly.

There was no time to discuss it further because Peter led the vicar and notary into the parlour.

"This is men's business." The vicar said, upon seeing that Liselotte seemed intent on staying when the men prepared to be seated.

"We'll discuss her father's funeral," Peter said. "And Liselotte's own future. I would like my cousin to be present."

He spoke with that commanding presence he had displayed the night before. That of a VOC Commodore.

Andries partially resented it now, for Peter seemed to have taken it upon himself to speak on behalf of his cousins. He glanced at Liselotte, to see her raise her hand to her mouth to hide a smile.

"There are also some financial matters to discuss, Commodore Haelen," the notary said.

"Nonetheless, I insist," Peter said.

The notary glanced at the vicar, who shrugged.

"Very well, Commodore," the vicar said. "As you wish."

They sat down, but Peter gestured at Andries to take a place next to Liselotte, standing behind Peter's chair. Andries concurred, hiding his unhappiness at not being counted as one of the adults. He would sit down, he decided, as soon as the will was read.

The will was short and concise. Andries kept an eye on Liselotte. She had assumed a demure position, hands folded modestly in front of her, her head lowered, and her eyes fixed on the floor. Andries could see no emotions on her face during the reading and was relieved that the contents didn't seem to upset her.

Andries took a deep breath when the notary finished reading, feeling he should say something or other on a formal occasion like this. To mark his acceptance of his Father's responsibilities.

A man's responsibilities.

"That being said," the notary raised a hand to ward off Andries's response. "I agree with the Commodore that Simon Haelen's son's youthful inexperience may be a liability."

What?

Andries looked at Peter aghast, then at his sister for support, but she didn't appear to be surprised at all.

"Fortunately," the notary continued. "The presence of an adult male relative resolves matters to the satisfaction of the law. Commodore Haelen has kindly agreed to assume temporary wardship over his uncle's affairs, including the children, until a final arrangement can be made."

Children? I'm nearly sixteen!

Andries struggled to hide his intense disappointment.

The discussion moved to funeral arrangements. Father's body would be transferred to the coffin and taken to Oysterhout, to be stored in the church's cool crypt until the burial three days hence.

"It's an unseemly rush," the vicar apologised. "But it's summer…"

"We don't want things getting more unpleasant than they already are," Peter acknowledged.

The notary scraped his throat, before announcing that he had summoned a lawyer from Breda.

"I expect he'll arrive at Oysterhout around noon on the morrow," the notary said. "I will accompany him here in the afternoon, if that isn't inconvenient."

"A lawyer?" Peter frowned.

"There are some complications," the notary said. "Outstanding rent for one, and…" He glanced at Andries and Liselotte. "Other such matters."

Rent? We don't own the house?

"Very well," Peter acknowledged.

"I'm sorry to raise such a matter on an occasion like this," the notary said. "But a man's debts must be paid."

"As a matter of course," Peter agreed.

"Now as to the children…" the vicar began to say.

Peter turned to Andries. "I made you an offer yesterday. To sail to the East Indies as midshipman aboard my ship. The offer still stands, upon the same conditions. We sail within the month. I will not lie, it's a dangerous journey but the rewards for those who survive are plenty. What say you?"

Andries hesitated. Of course he desired to become a wealthy VOC hero, but he felt a sense of betrayal in Peter's assumption of wardship.

Playing for time, he said, "I appreciate it greatly, Cousin. Truly. But…what is going to happen to my sister?"

Liselotte awarded him a quick smile.

"Well, obviously a ship is no place for a young lady," the vicar said. "Thanks be to God, there is always the Parish Orphan Fund."

"Free of charge." The notary added. "Though a donation would always be appreciated."

"Let me assure you," the vicar said. "That the girl wouldn't be placed beneath her social station."

"In fact," the notary spoke. "I have several nephews of marriageable age in Breda. Their social standing is equivalent to Physician Haelen's daughter. The girl could stay at my house until such a thing is arranged, provided there is a suitable dowry. My wife would be delighted, I'm sure. She's always wanted children, but the Good Lord, in all His wisdom…"

"Amen," the vicar boomed.

Andries remembered the notary's wife from his time in Oysterhout. He doubted that sour and bitter woman had ever been delighted in her entire life.

"Your kindness is appreciated," Peter said. "And it's true that a ship is no place for a girl. But I have no doubt whatsoever that my father – as head of the family now – will be more than happy to receive Liselotte as his kin in Rotterdam."

Rotterdam!

Although Andries had envisaged Liselotte staying in the house in Oysterhout, he was pleased for her. His sister had always missed Rotterdam.

Andries glanced at her again. She kept her face non-expressive, but he could see a bright sparkle in her eyes.

"Thanks be to God," the vicar boomed.

"How will she get there?" the notary asked, not quite managing to hide his disappointment.

"Safely," Peter answered curtly.

There was a knock on the parlour door. It was one of the farmhands.

"Begging your pardon, Seigneurs. But we're ready to place Doctor Haelen in the coffin."

"Thank you," Peter answered. He looked at his cousins. "Andries, Liselotte, you may want to say a farewell?"

"*Ja*, bethanks," Andries said.

"Bethanks," Liselotte said, although Andries was puzzled to note that she seemed reluctant.

Peter dismissed them. Andries and Liselotte walked to the surgery.

Father lay stiff and grey on the cot, his face contorted in an ugly sneer. Liselotte kept her distance, as if she feared Father still, even in death. Andries harboured no such concerns, kneeling next to the cot and laying a hand on one of Father's hands. It felt strangely inanimate and cold. He mumbled a prayer.

When Andries rose, wiping his eyes with a sleeve, Liselotte stepped forward. As quick as she could, she reached for the cord around Father's neck to slip it, and the iron key that was tied to it, over his head.

"What are you doing?" Andries asked.

"It's the key to his strongbox."

"I know that, but you shouldn't have it. You're just a girl. It should be mine. Father said so in his will."

Edging away from their father's cold body, Liselotte clutched the key tightly. "You're just a boy. The key is Peter's now."

Peter, Peter, Peter!

Andries frowned. "Then it's up to me to give it to him. Hand it over."

Shrugging, Liselotte surrendered the key. Andries snatched it, trying to salvage a semblance of his self-respect after having been passed over in the parlour just now. Had Liselotte been involved in that somehow? She hadn't seemed surprised. Had she encouraged Peter?

The farmhands entered the room to transfer Father into the coffin. Andries asked them to wait before they closed the lid and ran upstairs to Father's room to gather some blankets. When he returned, they gave him funny looks as Andries stuffed the blankets around Father's body.

"For the bumping," Andries explained.

"Tis no matter to him, Seigneur," said the farmhand who had spoken out of turn on the journey from Oysterhout. "He's stone cold de—"

"Willem!" The other farmhand scolded his companion. "Enough of that, tis the lad's father." He turned to Andries. "Tis very thoughtful of you, Seigneur."

Andries nodded, at once pleased with the compliment, whilst also worrying it might have been too sensitive. He might not be head of the household as he had imagined he would be, but he was still sailing east. He would be counted a man amongst men before too long. An *Oostvaarder.*

The vicar and notary took their leave. The wagons departed, the first carrying Father's coffin, followed by the village notables on foot. The second wagon held the bodies of the rogues and their weapons, guarded by two of the Sheriff's men. The last two lawmen stayed behind, making themselves comfortable in the stable. "For your protection," the notary had explained.

After the procession was out of sight, Peter shut the front door. He led Andries and Liselotte to the study.

"I'm not sure what to think of the notary's words about debt," Peter told his cousins. "It sounded ominous. If neither of you object, I think it's time to find out what's in your father's strongbox."

Neither Andries nor Liselotte objected. Peter dragged the strongbox from its recessed corner and studied the lock.

Andries produced the key. "I retrieved this from Father."

"Good lad." Peter looked pleased.

Andries shot Liselotte a proud look as their cousin knelt by the box. Peter turned the key and opened the lid. Andries and Liselotte leant closer to see two smaller boxes within the strongbox. Peter lifted one of them out. The box wasn't locked. It was filled with parchments full of spidery writing and columns of figures.

Setting the box with papers aside, Peter turned to the last box. "That'll be the fabled hoard then, I suppose."

"Hoard?" Liselotte asked.

"When the bandits were discussing their plans in the Old Cauldron, much mention was made of your father's reluctance to spend money. The assumption was that Uncle Simon must have been hoarding his earnings."

Andries stared at the small box. He had no idea what was in there. He knew well enough that the villagers had considered Father a miser. It was true that Father turned each *duit* around ten times before spending it, but there were also disturbing rumours from farther afield. From the nearby cities where Father was fetched to for his work.

Peter raised the lid of the last box. Their eyes met the gleam of silver coins...but only a handful scattered around the bottom.

Peter scooped up the coins, shaking his head. "Six guilders. Those rogues died to get their hands on six guilders."

"I don't understand," Andries said.

"I do," Liselotte said. "Father always stayed away a day or two longer, when he was summoned for work."

Andries knew what she would say next. He was hurt by her easy betrayal of Father's reputation. "You would speak ill of Father? On this day?"

"Peter has a right to know. He's our ward now," Liselotte countered.

"It's only rumours," Andries protested. "Gossip by some Breda and Tilburg coachmen. Maybe they were just making fun of us."

"What rumours?" Peter asked. "Your sister is right; I need to know."

Andries stared into the empty box, hard evidence that supported the gossip.

Liselotte explained. "Several coachmen sent to collect him, or return him, told us. From Breda and Tilburg both. Father would stay in taverns. Drinking and gambling. They said he would also lay with—"

"Stop telling lies!" Andries's face grew red with anger. It was true, but Father had only just died...this didn't feel right.

"Peter has a right to know," Liselotte insisted stubbornly.

"Stop the bickering," Peter ordered. "Andries, if you intend to sail to the East with me, you are to become an officer and gentleman. Please behave like one."

Andries threw him an angry look, but Peter didn't notice because he was lifting the box with paperwork. He set it on the table, laid the six shiny guilders on the tabletop, and began skimming the parchments.

Andries quickly took the second chair. Liselotte rolled her eyes at him. He stuck out his tongue, forgetting he was to behave like an officer and gentleman.

"This isn't good," Peter mumbled, frowning. "This isn't good at all."

He worked his way through another stack, before laying the paperwork aside and looking at his cousins thoughtfully.

"Is there a problem?" Liselotte asked.

Peter nodded. "Your father had debts. A lot of debts by the looks of it, well over a thousand guilders."

"A thousand guilders in debt?" Andries cried out in horror.

"More," Peter said, a grim look on his face. "That explains why the notary was so keen to bring in that Breda lawyer. They want to be sure that the debts are paid in full."

"A thousand guilders!" Andries turned to his sister with a helpless look on his face. If he couldn't pay off Father's debts, both of them would be indentured as servants for as long as it took to repay the outstanding sums. That might be a decade or more and ruin any prospects they might have had.

Liselotte's expression betrayed the same realisation.

"We'll be indentured for sure," Andries despaired.

"Not if I can help it," Peter growled. "You, Andries, are on my muster roll, and Liselotte saved my life last night."

"But what can you do?" Andries asked.

"Pay off your father's debts," Peter said. He looked unhappy but determined.

Andries felt relief when he realised that his cousin's wardship meant that Peter, and not Andries, was ultimately responsible for Father's debts. Peter could have shed that responsibility at the drop of a hat, should he choose not to be burdened with another man's debts, but it was clear he meant to see it through.

More than a thousand guilders!

Peter shrugged. "I agreed to pay your father a percentage of Andries's earnings and my profits. Since that deal still stands, I suppose I could advance the sum until we return from the East with a hold full of silk and spices."

"Oh!" Liselotte exclaimed. "Would you?"

Peter picked up one of the guilders. He ran it through his fingers, shaking his head. "Six guilders isn't much of a dowry, Liselotte. Is there any chance your father had money hidden away elsewhere?"

"It doesn't matter, about the dowry," Liselotte said quickly.

Andries knew that she was in no hurry to be married. She had told him that she viewed marriage as worse than a prison sentence because there was no fixed termination date.

"As to the other matter," Liselotte continued. "Nay, I don't think so. We've searched the whole house before, many times when he was gone."

Peter frowned.

"It was Liselotte's idea," Andries supplied hastily.

"He would leave us with no money and an empty larder," Liselotte explained. "We were just looking so we could buy some food. But we never found any."

"That's why you two went hunting?"

Andries and Liselotte both nodded.

Peter tossed the guilder back on the table. "Unfortunately, we're still sailing in troubled waters. I don't carry that kind of money on me. My funds are secured at the VOC Chamber in Middelburg."

"So, we'll have to go to Middelburg?" Andries asked.

"I thought your ship was in Flushing," Liselotte added.

"Middelburg and Flushing are only a few hours apart, but we'll have to negotiate with that Breda lawyer first before we can go there. However, I'm afraid that they'll probably insist that the two of you remain as surety."

"We can stay here for a while," Andries said. Despite the circumstances he felt a thrill of excitement at the prospect of having ample time to say goodbye to Toosje. She would be devastated and would need to be…comforted. Andries blushed as he felt a stirring in his loins. "We've done it before. Stayed by ourselves, I mean."

"They won't let you stay in this house," Peter said. "They'll want to ensure you don't abscond. I suspect you would be temporarily assigned to this Parish Orphan Fund in Oysterhout. It would be with due respect to your social station but…"

Peter looked at Liselotte, a question in his eyes. She shook her head, almost imperceptibly, but Peter responded with a curt nod.

"How long would it be?" Andries asked, not understanding why Liselotte was set against the notion of waiting for a few weeks so they could say goodbye to Father and their friends.

He also resented the fact that it seemed Liselotte and Peter had just made the decision between them. There was a bond between his sister and cousin of the sort Andries imagined a Commodore should have with one of his trusted officers. "Surely Middelburg isn't that far away. We can cope."

He gave Liselotte a pointed look, but she shook her head in disagreement.

Peter picked up one of the guilders. He ran it through his fingers, shaking his head.

Peter divided the coins on the table into two piles of three guilders, pushing each pile toward a twin. "Your inheritance."

Andries wanted to point out that Father had left everything to him but stopped himself. Peter could override that decision. Andries took his three guilders in silence.

"It would still take weeks," Peter said. "For matters to be agreed upon here. For me to travel to Middelburg, make the necessary arrangements, and then return. And therein lays a problem, because I had intended to sail by the end of the month, or at least before the storm season hits the North Atlantic. Moreover, there is another possible complication, one that I'm more worried about."

"What's that?" Andries and Liselotte asked in unison.

"Why do you think two of the Sheriff's men have been left here?"

"They said it was to protect us," Andries said.

"Protect us from what?" Peter asked. "The innkeeper and his wife? Local farmers?"

"They're guarding us?" Andries was incredulous. "Are we their prisoners?"

"No. Not yet anyway." Peter shook his head. "I think they are mostly here to keep an eye on us. The problem is that a lot of folks seem to think there's a strongbox full of silver in this house. Not just those bandits. You heard the notary; he was quick to mention a donation to the Orphan's Fund and a suitable dowry for Liselotte."

"Well," Andries declared. "There is no hoard, so that's too bad for them."

Liselotte looked at her three coins on the table. "But they might not believe that."

"Precisely," Peter confirmed. "If we tell them there is no hoard, apart from those six guilders, they may choose to believe that we aren't telling the truth. That we have hidden the money to keep it for ourselves."

"But why would we do that?" Andries asked.

Peter shrugged. "This is the Republic. It's easier to explain four dead men in a stable than any perceived financial irregularities. Last night you experienced what the lure of money can do to men. If they are convinced your father possessed riches, they might not believe us if we tell them otherwise. We might find our freedom much curtailed at the behest of all your father owed money to."

"*If* we tell them...?" Liselotte asked.

Her cousin grinned. "You're quick on the mark."

Andries pulled a face.

Peter continued. "We could be questioned rigorously."

"Interrogated," Liselotte whispered.

Andries turned pale.

"A sharp interrogation is the normal way of obtaining confessions," Peter said. "Ideally, I'd take off to Zeeland with you two and these papers…" he indicated the box of parchments. "And arrange full payment there, with the resources of the Middelburg VOC Chamber at my disposal."

"I don't understand," Liselotte said. "I thought you retired from the VOC. But they'd help you?"

"The company views my absence as a temporary matter, they continue to make offers. Besides, I have a very good friend at the Middelburg Chamber. The VOC will task one of their lawyers to sort this mess for a friendly fee, as long as I pay the monies owed to your father's creditors. It's the best way to avoid long and cumbersome delays…or worse."

"But Father's funeral," Andries objected.

"I know." Peter nodded. "It's a terrible thing to ask of you. But when the notary brings that lawyer tomorrow, it would be best if we weren't here, or anywhere else within the jurisdiction of Breda. Maybe it wouldn't be as bad as an interrogation, but I can certainly foresee weeks of suspicion and delay."

"We run?" Liselotte asked.

Andries could read excitement on her face. It was not a feeling he shared. He would have preferred to do things properly.

"We have to make a decision," Peter answered. "Either we stay and risk potential trouble. Or we run. Tonight."

8. On the Run

Peter's proposed plan was simple.

"You two pack. Only what you really need, because you're going to have to carry it yourself for many miles. I brought an extra sailor's duffle bag which one of you—"

"That should be mine." Andries was quick to claim it. "I'm going to be a seafarer."

Peter looked at Liselotte. She said, "There's a leather pack in father's bedroom, with back straps. I'll take that."

"Good." Peter proceeded to explain the rest of the plan. He had found two bottles of brandywine in the larder and would gift these to the Sheriff's men in the stable. He would tell them that the family was exhausted and needed an early night, adding a request to keep the noise down. Peter was certain the men would finish the brandywine before too long, dulling their senses – if not sinking them into sleep.

"When that's done and you're finished packing, we should all try to get some sleep. We'll wake at midnight. I'll boil the rest of the eggs before I go to sleep. We can make a meal of them before we leave, without having to relight the stove. I'll also leave a short note for the notary, explaining that a VOC lawyer will be in touch."

"Where will we go?" Liselotte asked.

"The best route to Flushing is through Breda and Rosendael. But we need to avoid Breda, so we'll head west, to Zevenbergen."

"Because that's in Holland," Andries said. "Not Brabant[15]."

"But..." Liselotte said, before stalling, not sure if she could be critical of Peter's plan.

Children should be seen, not heard.

"Go on..." Peter urged her. "You have a say."

"You mentioned Rotterdam to the vicar and notary," she said. "If they remember that, surely they'll suspect we'll head that way? Did you mention Flushing at all, to the Sheriff's men?"

---

[15] In Brabant now, Zevenbergen was part of the County of Holland in 1622.

"Nay, I didn't mention Flushing, just Rotterdam. You're right, Liselotte. That's why I want to leave tonight, to get a head start. We should make it to Terheyden in two or three hours, long before they find out we're gone. From Terheyden onward our route diverges from the northbound road. They'll be expecting us to follow that to the ferries plying the Hollands Deep."

"Where will we go instead?" Andries asked.

"We'll pass to the south of Zevenbergen, head west until we reach the coast. It bends south-west to Bergen-op-Zoom. I doubt they'll expect to find us south-west of Breda if they assume we've gone north."

"But…we'll be going back to Brabant that way." Liselotte pointed out.

"Aye, Brabant again, but out of Breda's jurisdiction," Peter said. "If we follow the coastline south, we'll be in Bergen-op-Zoom's jurisdiction. We should find someone there willing to ferry us across to the Zeeland isles. Once we're in Zeeland, we'll be safe."

"You know this area well," Andries said.

Peter laughed. "This is the first time I've been in Brabant. There's another reason for choosing this route. You two will have to help me navigate the inlands. But once we've reached the coast…I've studied every inch of the Republic's coastline on sea charts. It's all up here." He tapped the side of his forehead.

"You study maps?" Andries asked.

"Sea charts. And so will you, Andries. Stare at them for hours until you've memorised every current, depth, shoal, and sandbank."

Andries didn't look overjoyed at that news, but Liselotte was intrigued. The list of questions she wanted to ask Peter was growing by the minute. It would have to wait though; it was time to prepare. She had fantasised, sometimes, about running away from the joyless house, and now it was actually going to happen.

They left Peter to pack Father's papers in the study and made to go to their own rooms. Andries halted Liselotte on the landing.

"Why didn't you want to stay at the notary's house for a few weeks? It would save us a lot of bother."

"Weeks which Peter said he doesn't have because he wants to sail. Besides—"

"Besides what? Don't you want to attend Father's funeral? It's not right that we don't."

Liselotte evaded the topic of Father's funeral. She had said her goodbyes the night before. It had been horrible. "I'd rather not stay at the notary's house. He makes me feel uncomfortable."

"Uncomfortable! Why?"

"He stares," Liselotte said.

She drew a blank from her brother, so clarified it further, "At my bosom."

"He did? I didn't see that."

Liselotte sighed. She had felt the notary's eyes, seen the tip of his tongue flick out to moisten his thin upper lip each time he stole a glance. She also recalled the warning the innkeeper's wife had given about the Parish Orphan Fund and the men who ran it. Every fibre of her being told her to stay well away from the creepy notary. At least Peter had noticed her discomfort. Liselotte was suddenly glad that Andries hadn't been elevated to head of household, a position in which he'd be the one making decisions for her.

"Peter saw it," she told Andries. "I wouldn't feel safe staying with the notary."

"Ridiculous. Men stare, it's what they do. You and I aren't common folk, they would respect our status."

"What status?" Liselotte was exasperated. "Andries, don't you get it? We're orphans, penniless orphans. The house isn't Father's, it's rented and there's a lot of rent overdue. We're nothing. Nothing at all. All we have is Peter."

"Peter this, Peter that," Andries snorted.

Liselotte stared at him aghast. Peter had just saved them from abject poverty. Moreover, he was offering Andries bright prospects and Liselotte an escape from a dismal future in Oysterhout or Breda. The notary would like as not have auctioned her off to his nephews once he was done with her.

Andries coloured red, seeming to realise the extent of his ingratitude. "Never mind," he mumbled. "I'll go pack. Seems I have no choice."

Liselotte shrugged and went into her room. She was still packing when both Peter and Andries had finished and gone to sleep.

She had started by retrieving the large leather pack from Father's room.

Selecting her clothes was easy enough. She owned three gowns. One was so threadbare it probably wouldn't even survive being packed. Her Sunday best was heavy and cumbersome. She would leave those two behind. She was wearing the remaining gown, so that just left a warm woollen shawl and some undergarments to fold. Her only other possessions were Eyang and her mother's crossbow, quiver, and bolts. But there were things she wanted from the surgery, library, and one of the sheds. That's where the problems began. After having gathered all she wanted, Liselotte realised that it would never fit into the pack. Several selection rounds followed, each more frustrating than the previous, until she at last managed to cram about half of what she had initially wanted into the pack. Only then did she fall onto her bed to be overcome by sleep.

Andries made no mention of the rejected items scattered about Liselotte's room when he came to wake her, a lit candle in his hand. It was dark outside. They ate a hurried breakfast of rye bread and boiled eggs in the kitchen. Peter wrapped the remaining rye bread and foul cheese in waxed paper.

"That cheese will taste wonderful come morning," he promised. "Let's get our bags and go."

Liselotte went to her room to fetch her pack and the haversack in which she would carry the crossbow, quiver, and Eyang.

Sneaking furtively through the house was an odd sensation. It already felt empty, as if she was trespassing in a stranger's home.

Her spirits sank when she tried to hoist the pack onto her back. It seemed to be filled with bricks. She hesitated; maybe it would be better to...

You can do this.

Liselotte felt slightly more confident when she came downstairs and headed for the kitchen. Once on her back, the pack seemed less cumbersome, although she had to lean forward a little to counter the sheer weight that threatened to pull her backward. By comparison, the haversack seemed of inconsequential weight.

Peter and Andries had their duffle bags slung over their shoulders. Each also carried a canvas knapsack with extra powder and shot for the doglock muskets that they had shouldered. Both had a brace of pistols, Peter his own and Andries the snaphances. Peter also carried a provisions sack and Andries had stuck the short wood axe in his belt. Peter had instructed Andries to take the best of the household pistols, and leave the others behind, along with the matchlock muskets.

"You'll be noticing the weight of two pistols and a doglock soon enough," he promised Andries. "Everything you carry will feel like it doubles in weight before long."

That's not a comforting thought.

Liselotte wanted to grimace but smiled instead. She suspected that Peter would object if he found out about the weight of her pack.

Liselotte and Andries knew a narrow poacher's path that snaked through the woods and would allow them to skirt Oysterhout unseen.

It was another cloudless night. The moon's brightness cascaded through the foliage to light their way. Peter insisted they walk in total silence, which made sense because their nocturnal poaching had taught both siblings how far sound could travel at night.

Andries looked back at the house one last time before they disappeared into the woods. He had a longing expression on his face as he did so.

Liselotte didn't look back. Her life here was already a thing of the past, most of it best forgotten. The humble and winding forest path was the beginning of the road to a new life. Any future that didn't involve languishing in Oysterhout seemed promising.

She had no idea what to expect in Flushing, but all sorts of memories of Rotterdam...*Oh, Rotterdam!*

...resurfaced. She recalled the busy streets, bustling with life and energy. All the sights, sounds, and smells that had once been familiar.

Although her own future was still somebody else's to decide, Liselotte felt less apprehensive about that now. So far, Peter had been perfectly willing to involve her in his deliberations, and even paid heed to her dread feelings about the horrible notary. She felt reasonably sure that he wouldn't marry her off just like that.

The only apprehension she felt about Rotterdam was the notion of being housed with Uncle Johan, whom she barely knew.

Maybe, just maybe...I could stay with Aunt Mathilda and Uncle Karel.

Although she was continuously aware of the dragging weight of her pack and the leather straps chafed against her shoulders, she kept up with Peter's brisk pace. They reached the main road to Breda to find it deserted, as was normal during the night. Crossing it, they found more paths through the forest and past the patchwork fields surrounding small, isolated farmsteads.

The landscape changed after several hours. The forested area gradually thinned to make space for more fields, until endless flat land seemed to stretch in every direction. They followed a narrow dirt road, and although they passed a few farms, saw no other people.

Andries looked back at the house one last time before they disappeared into the woods.

It was here that Liselotte started to struggle. The road would often run along the top of a dyke and Peter decided that they were much too visible on such an elevation in the bright moonlight. He led them up and down embankments and over ditches, so they could walk parallel to the dyke roads, over the wet grass and cloying clay of the fields.

Struggling up and down the steep sides of the dykes and through the ditches, Liselotte's pack pulled her this way and that, bucking like a wild animal trying to escape a trap. She clutched desperately at knolls of grass, trying to maintain her balance. It left her gasping for breath at the end of every such scramble, as surreptitiously as she could so as not to alert Peter or Andries to her ordeal.

Earlier elation at having escaped the smothering isolation of Oysterhout was replaced by weary but dogged resignation. Liselotte's arms, back, and shoulders ached. Her legs felt like dead weights as she forced each step. She stopped looking ahead to gauge whatever endless distance remained to be covered before the next dreaded crossing of ditch and dyke, keeping her eyes on her feet instead.

She looked up when Peter pointed at a church steeple and windmill circled by rooftops. "Terheyden already. On to Zevenbergen! We'll find a place to rest there."

Liselotte smiled weakly, inwardly despairing at the notion that they still had much farther to walk. The pain became monotonous, numbing her senses until she lost all track of time or sense of progress. She persisted though, stubbornly dismissing any thought of lightening her load, forcing herself to continue – step after weary step.

After what seemed like an eternity, scrambling across yet another ditch, Liselotte lost her balance. She swayed unsteadily at the top of the ditch, in danger of falling back. Peter grabbed her arm and steadied her. If he noticed the added weight of Liselotte's pack, he made no mention of it, but shortly afterwards he announced that they'd be keeping an eye open for a place to rest. Moreover, he stuck to the roads rather than scrambling up and down the dykes.

They found a potential place at dawn. It was an old barn, set aside from the road, half-concealed by a copse of trees. The roof had partially collapsed at one end, leaving only skeletal beams poking out into the brightening sky. Although the thatch was sagging with age at the other end, it still offered shelter of sorts. Other wanderers had used it as such before. There was a circle of ash with remnants of blackened firewood in a corner stall, but the ashes were cold, and the timbers used to create crude seating places dusty.

"This is perfect," Peter declared as they peered into the stall.

Liselotte sighed with relief. It felt good to slide the heavy pack off her aching back, although she was left dulled by exhaustion. The others seemed equally fatigued.

Peter had thought to bring along three blankets that he pulled out of his duffel bag. Liselotte took the one he proffered her gratefully, wrapped it around her aching body, and then curled up on the ground, quickly succumbing to sleep.

9. In the Old Barn

ZEVENBERGEN ~ COUNTY OF HOLLAND ~ 1622

Liselotte woke to find Andries still fast asleep. Peter was nowhere in sight. Sunlight fell in through the open roof at the other end of the barn.

Liselotte sat up slowly, grimacing at the pain of moving. Her whole body ached. She rubbed her eyes and yawned, wondering how much longer Peter intended to stay here. She already dreaded the instruction to hoist the heavy pack on her back again.

Her question was partially answered when Peter strode into the barn, his arms full of foraged wood.

Good. We'll be here long enough to have a fire.

"I've had a look around," Peter announced, setting down the wood. "It seems we've found a good hideout. We should see or hear any trouble approaching."

"What kind of trouble?" Liselotte asked.

"Horsemen looking for fugitives. Mind you, with any luck they haven't even discovered our absence yet. On top of which, this isn't the direction they'll assume we took. But still, best be cautious."

"Are we still in Breda's jurisdiction?"

"Most definitely not. I went up the dyke road. You can see the rooftops of Zevenbergen from there. We're as close to the city as I had hoped to get."

"We really walked a long way then!"

"Aye, we did. Why is my midshipman still asleep?" Peter nudged Andries with a foot.

Liselotte's brother groaned a protest. "Wazzisit? Waz time?"

"Nearing the end of the Forenoon Watch," Peter answered.

"The what?" Andries struggled up.

"Some seafarer!" Peter jested, before adding, "It's near noon."

They ate the last of the rye bread and rancid cheese. It tasted every bit as good as Peter had promised. That didn't surprise Liselotte. She had gone hungry often enough to know that most food was bearable when a belly was rumbling.

Afterwards, Peter gave Andries a handful of coins and directed him to go to Zevenbergen, to buy bread, cheese, dried sausage, and some flasks of ale.

"Why can't Liselotte go?" Andries complained. "Father always sent her to do the shopping in Oysterhout."

Peter frowned. "You'd send your sister into an unknown city? On her own?"

"I can go," Liselotte said. "I'm not afraid."

"I don't doubt it, but that may be a problem in itself." Peter sighed. "Andries will go, if only because a midshipman doesn't question his skipper's commands."

Andries looked abashed at that.

Peter studied him. "If you leave your weapons here you can pass for an errand boy easily enough, Andries. Sent by his master to purchase some foodstuffs. I'm not sending Liselotte into a strange city on her own."

He raised a hand to stifle Liselotte's protest. "It's simply not safe. As for myself..."

Peter looked down at his seafarer's outfit. "I'd be noticed...and remembered."

Andries left, reluctantly trudging toward Zevenbergen.

Peter climbed up the exposed rafters at the open end of the barn, training a spyglass at the city. Liselotte quickly explored the area around the old barn, partially to find a discreet corner amidst the plentiful undergrowth to relieve herself. When she returned, she scrambled up the beams as well. She was somewhat hampered by her gown but managed to find a perch near Peter.

Liselotte studied Zevenbergen. She could see the tower and roof of a tall church rising above the rooftops, as well as the slowly revolving sail-covered sweeps of a windmill at one edge of the small city. There was a cluster of smaller towers surrounding a larger one, denoting a castle. Zevenbergen didn't have city walls but was protected by low, grassy embankments in the angular patterns that characterised modern fortifications.

Liselotte could make out Andries in the distance, heading for a road on which a few other people were making their way to or from the city, many pulling carts or leading small wagons.

She turned her attention to Peter. He really did look the seafarer now, straddled on a stout beam, peering through his spyglass.

A proper VOC Commodore.

Even in landlocked Oysterhout people spoke in awe of the VOC. The villagers were giddy from the opportunities and riches offered by the spice trade, just like everyone else in the Republic.

Taverns around the Republic were still frequented by the now grey-haired and scarred survivors of the first daring and dangerous expeditions to the north, south, east, and west. Those men rarely had to pay for their ale or brandywine. The drinks kept coming as long as they talked of the faraway places they had visited, the people they had known, and the dangers they had been exposed to on their travels.

Skippers and ships had become household names. Their successes and failures were discussed at length by seafarers and landlubbers alike.

Everybody talked still about the ill-fated northern route expedition led by Willem Barentsz and Jacob van Heemskerck. They had been stranded on Nova Zembla, forcing a winter stay on that most inhospitable island, surrounded by ice and besieged by scurvy and deadly great white bears.

Even the most faint-hearted landlubber, likely to get seasick crossing a canal in a jolly boat, claimed to know better than Skipper Piet Heyn how to transport cloves from the East Indies. The unfortunate Heyn had been forced to dump part of *De Hollandia's* cargo, worth a staggering one hundred thousand guilders, into the ocean when the cloves had started to spoil and became a fire hazard.

Skipper Willem Bontekoe's misfortune was talked of with more sympathy. After an accidental fire had reached the stored gunpowder on board of Bontekoe's *De Nieuw Hoorn,* the ship had exploded with a great loss of life. The survivors, some seventy in number, had found themselves aboard a longboat and a yawl, surrounded by the vastness of the Indian Ocean. Using the stars to navigate by Bontekoe had managed to reach Java, no mean feat in two tiny boats.

Liselotte knew all the stories. She had even heard of *De Blokzeyl,* which Peter had mentioned to Father. It was said to be an unnaturally speedy ship, sailing to and from Java as if chased by the Devil himself.

She recalled that Peter had mentioned the VOC wanted him back in service. Liselotte wasn't sure what the rank of Commodore entailed but knew it had commanded respect from the Sheriff's men and Oysterhout notables.

It must be nice, to have such standing.

"Peter. Will you enter VOC service again?"

He kept peering through his spyglass, but a shadow crossed his face, conveying distaste. "Nay. Never."

The tone of his voice reminded Liselotte of his interaction with the innkeepers, when Peter had clearly thought their inquisitive condolences had crossed a line.

*He really did look the seafarer now, straddled on a stout beam,
peering through his spyglass.*

She hid a grin. She was a Haelen and van der Krooswyck, not an innkeeper. Peter wasn't going to get off that easily. It was the first time they were alone since leaving Oysterhout and there was time at hand. There were a thousand questions that needed answering.

Another opening then.

Peter, when you spoke of wanting to be back at sea, you wanted to be with…someone. What's her name? Is she beautiful? Will she be kind to me?

Too intimate. Maybe when he's in his cups one day.

Peter, do you like to drink? What? When can we get some?

Liselotte giggled softly. Peter didn't react, continuing to peer through his spyglass.

Peter, why were you upset when I asked if you had taken Eyang from the savages?

Peter, how can you be such a different person? Commanding and full of certainty one moment, awkward and fumbling the next?

"Peter…Will you take Andries to the East on *De Blokzeyl?*"

Peter lowered his spyglass to give her a curious glance. "Nay, not *De Blokzeyl*. A new ship."

He paused, and then grinned before speaking with fierce pride. "One I designed myself. There are no others like her."

"Does it have a name?"

"It? '*She*', a ship is a she! And no, she hasn't been christened yet. It's ill luck to name a ship before her launch."

"Ill luck! They say sailors are superstitious."

Peter laughed. "*Mea culpa*[16]. You won't find more superstitious folk anywhere on land."

He frowned. "Apart from some exasperating *Zeeuwen*[17] on the isle of Walcheren."

"So how is this ship of yours different from others?"

Peter sighed so dramatically that Liselotte stifled a laugh.

"I'm sure you won't find shipbuilding very interesting," Peter suggested.

Secretly Liselotte agreed. Shipbuilding wasn't a subject she'd ever given much thought to.

But it's an opening.

---

[16] 'Through my fault' in Latin, i.e., Guilty as charged

[17] People from Zeeland. *Zeeuwen* = plural, *Zeeuw* = singular, *Zeeuws*(e) = Zeelandic

"I'd really like to know," she told Peter. "You worked as an apprentice in Uncle Johan's dockyards, didn't you?"

There was another deep sigh – a clear hint of reluctance.

Liselotte persisted, steering toward the subject she wanted to know about most of all. "Why did you run away from home? Was it to do with the dockyards?"

Peter frowned. "You seem very preoccupied with the notion that I ran away from home."

"Am I?" Liselotte asked innocently. "That's what Father said happened. He said you ran away from home when you were fourteen."

"Fourteen…Liselotte, you mustn't equate…"

"Why not? Haven't you encouraged me to run away from my father's house? A year older than you were back then? We are running away, aren't we?"

She noted with satisfaction that Peter was momentarily nonplussed.

"Rotterdam back then," he spoke slowly. "Oysterhout now…they are very different circumstances."

"Because I'm a girl," Liselotte protested.

"I wasn't even thinking about that. But now you mention it: Aye. The world is a dangerous place for young ladies."

"Because all men can think about…is to bed us."

It was the only thing Henk had really wanted, not her companionship although he had pretended to at first, but…that. It's what those rogues who had killed Father had wanted. It's what the leering Sheriff's men had wanted. It's what the ogling notary had wanted. If she had been placed at some farm as part of the Orphan Fund, or worse, been indentured because of Father's debts, that's what would have been wanted.

"It's how the world works." One of her Oysterhout friends had once said with a shrug, while patting her bulging belly that had been seeded either by the schoolmaster, or else a handsome seasonal worker who had last been seen heading north, blending with the horizon. The friend's shrug suggested nothing could be changed about these things.

Liselotte knew that trying to change the world was an idealistic daydream at best…and dangerous at worst. Yet all the reminders over the last few days had ignited rebellion within her. She looked at Peter defiantly, challenging him to address the truth of the matter.

He complied, harsh in frankness. "Aye. Most men have that on their mind. To be frank, for a girl your age to run away on her own, without family, a protector, employer's references…such a thing would not end well."

"Shame on the family name," Liselotte echoed Father with some bitterness.

Peter frowned. "Family name be damned. I'd be more concerned about the abject misery you'd be subjected to."

Liselotte took a deep breath and stared at Zevenbergen. Peter had sounded most sincere in his expression of concern. She redirected the course of their conversation. "So, Rotterdam, back then, was different?"

Her cousin laughed. "You're as persistent as a blood hound. I fear I won't be able to evade your curiosity."

"Never," Liselotte agreed confidently.

"Alright, I'll tell you. I was fourteen and had completed my apprenticeship, free to go where I pleased as a fully-fledged ship's carpenter's mate."

"But Uncle Johan wanted you to work at his dockyards!"

"And that I couldn't do."

"Why not? Was the apprenticeship horrible? Did they beat you?"

Peter sighed. "No more than any other apprentice. The occasional cuff around the ear. I'm afraid that any comparison between our situations would make my grievances seem petty."

Liselotte shook her head. "You can't always compare these things. You had grievances?"

"My apprenticeship started well. I took to shipbuilding like a fish to water. I'm not sure how to explain…sometimes it was like I understood things before they even finished explaining. It just all made sense instantly."

Liselotte smiled. *Like Father's lessons and medical books for me.*

"But then?" She prompted.

"By the time I had progressed to ship design, there were things that didn't make sense anymore. I think I was about eleven, or twelve when that started happening."

"Things you couldn't learn?"

"Oh, I could learn them all too well. But it seemed foolish to me to design ships the way they were, when they could have worked more efficiently."

"Did other dockyards use better methods?"

Peter shook his head. "They all work with the same methods. From Oostend to Den Helder."

"So how did you find out about them?"

Peter tapped his temple with his index finger. "All in here. The new ideas were mine. But I was foolish enough to talk of them at my father's dockyards."

Liselotte grinned as she envisaged a very young Peter lecturing old and grizzled carpenters on how to do a better job.

Peter managed a wry smile. "It didn't go down too well. I was mocked and ridiculed."

"By your father?"

"My father didn't believe in special treatment because I was his son. He wanted me to make my own way through the dockyards. By the time my shipbuilding heresies reached his ears, the news had spread throughout the shipbuilding community in Rotterdam. I'd become a running joke. They tried to make me see things their way, but I couldn't."

Peter paused, his eyes growing fierce. "Because I knew I was right. About how a hull can be better shaped. How the rigging and sails can be redesigned for maximum efficiency."

Liselotte stared at her cousin in awe. This was a third Peter. Not the awkward one, nor the confident Commodore. This one spoke and shone with a deep passion.

"When my father found out, he was concerned. Worse, he was embarrassed and worried about the reputation of his business. I was summoned to his office. He did, at least, hear me out. Then he forbade me any further thought or talk about newfangled notions concerning ship design."

Peter looked at Liselotte, almost pleadingly. "I did try. I learned to meekly agree with the masters, even though I didn't believe them. I stopped talking about my ideas. But I couldn't keep concepts from flowing through my head. In my own time, I started drawing designs, making the calculations I was able to..."

Peter paused; passion replaced by sadness. When he continued, his voice took on a harsher tone. "I managed to keep that a secret. My father requested a meeting the day after I completed my apprenticeship. To discuss my future in the business. I took all my designs and presented them to him. Quite a collection by then, the efforts of two years. I had rehearsed what I wanted to say to him for months."

"What did your father say?"

"He threw all my designs into the hearth and set fire to them."

"Oh!"

"We had a terrible row. After that, I decided there was no future for me in the family business and left."

Peter trained his spyglass on the horizon again, as if to signal that the exploration of his past was over. Liselotte wasn't having it though – new questions arising as she learned more about Peter's departure from Rotterdam.

"Where did you go...after?"

"To Amsterdam. I wanted practical experience to further my insight. So, I signed up as a carpenter's mate with the VOC and sailed to the East Indies."

"I thought you had to be sixteen, to be mustered."

"In theory. It's remarkable how many obstacles vanish when there's a shortage of seafaring carpenters."

"Ha! So, this was on *De Blokzeyl*?"

"Nay." Peter moved the spyglass away long enough to shake his head. "*De Blokzeyl* came later. This was on *De Assemburg*."

"What are the Indies like?" Liselotte asked eagerly.

"The Indies?" A slow smile spread on Peter's face. "Enchanting. Beguiling."

Liselotte could barely believe she knew someone who had been there. Who had seen those exotic sights, heard the strange native speech and song, and felt the tropical sun on his skin.

"And...?" She encouraged Peter.

"Something is happening," he said curtly.

"In the Indies...?" Liselotte was confused, before realising Peter was more likely to be referring to Zevenbergen.

She peered out at the distant town. Nothing much seemed to have changed other than the traffic on the road, which had increased somewhat – mostly empty carts and wagons heading away from Zevenbergen. Farmers, she guessed, who had sold their wares. She wondered how Andries would be...

There!

...a rider making his way along the road to Zevenbergen. Not at a walk, but in a furious gallop. She could make out other road users hastily moving aside to let the rider pass.

"A messenger," Peter said. "He'll damn well kill his mount if he pushes it any harder."

"A messenger from Oysterhout?" Liselotte asked.

"Could be. But in so much haste?"

Just as the rider was nearing Zevenbergen, Liselotte spotted more urgent movement on the road.

"Peter, look!"

Six riders this time, driving headlong for Zevenbergen at the same frantic speed as the first. Liselotte couldn't make out details, but she could see the glint of steel reflected in the sunlight.

Soldiers, or Sheriff's men.

"We must be more important than we thought," Peter joked, before frowning. "Let's hope Andries uses his brains."

Liselotte bit her lip. It wasn't her brother's strong point, but it would be disloyal to point this out to Peter.

By the time the contingent of new riders approached the city's ramparts there was new cause for concern.

A church bell started tolling in Zevenbergen, soon joined by others. The bells didn't toll at a steady and controlled pace. Instead, they rang in urgent discord.

The town was sounding the general alarm.

Liselotte and Peter exchanged a worried look. Something was amiss in Zevenbergen.

Oh! Andries, be careful!

10. At the Sail & Anchor

ZEVENBERGEN ~ COUNTY OF HOLLAND ~1622

Andries walked towards Zevenbergen in a foul mood.

He didn't like his assigned task one bit. The night's walk had been a long one. He would have preferred a bit more rest.

Liselotte is getting rest!

He would have jumped at the chance of exploring Zevenbergen only a few days ago. Anything to break the dull monotony of Oysterhout. But so much had happened that more new impressions weren't welcome.

A bit of rest would have allowed him to try and get his head around all the sudden changes: Peter's unexpected appearance, the bloody battle in the study, Father's death, Liselotte's strange behaviour, the threat of destitution, village notables, lawyers, and sheriff's men, not to forget his new status as midshipman aboard a ship he had never seen…

Andries had never even set foot aboard a ship! Apart from a few ferries when Father had taken them from Holland to Brabant all those many years ago, but those near-forgotten short crossings didn't count.

There was more, to add to the confusion, but Andries had trouble defining it. Father's loss had hit him hard. Simon Haelen had been a harsh man at times, but his dominant presence had also been an anchor to rely on.

We'll miss his funeral.

Andries still disagreed with that decision. He was sure that the vicar and notary were reasonable men. Peter could have explained the situation, stay for the funeral, and then been allowed to travel to Zeeland to make the necessary arrangements. Peter was a VOC hero. Surely that would have counted a great deal in their favour? But Andries hadn't been able to prevent their swift departure from Oysterhout. Peter was in charge now and Liselotte had sided with him.

Liselotte.

Andries scowled as his thoughts darkened. His sister was cause for a whole new entanglement of confusion. He wondered how much of their hasty departure was because of her strange aversion to staying at the notary's house. Andries had noted the silent communication between his sister and cousin. He resented the intimacy of it. In their relative isolation the twins had always had each other as steadfast companion. Liselotte's strained relationship with Father had made her even more dependent on Andries, but now that seemed to be changing.

Andries kicked at a clump of grass. The readiness with which his sister had transferred part of her loyalty to their cousin was unfair. Especially because Andries needed her more than ever, now that Father was gone.

Does she even grieve for him?

Father hadn't always been kind to her, but as his children they owned him love, respect, and obedience. Andries suspected that reluctant obedience was the most his sister had been willing to offer.

He consoled himself with the prospect of the near future, in which Liselotte would be left in Rotterdam when he and their cousin sailed east. That would end Liselotte's bond with Peter and serve her right for letting Andries down.

There was a spark of restlessness, deep within, but Andries suppressed it. He didn't really want to explore being without Liselotte. Not yet anyway. The twins had never been apart for longer than a few hours before.

Andries reached the end of the fields he was trudging through. A road ran along the top of a dyke and he scrambled up the steep embankment. Not having paid much attention to his surroundings, Andries was surprised how much closer he was to Zevenbergen. He stopped, to catch his breath and inspect his destination.

The road gradually descended to a simple brick gatehouse, about a third of a mile away. It formed part of the low ramparts that curved around the city. A cluster of roofs and chimneys rose around a tall square tower behind the gate, beyond which was a sprawl of red-tiled rooftops, as well as church and chapel towers.

A farmhand, who was pulling a small empty cart away from Zevenbergen, called out a jovial greeting as he passed, following it with a friendly jest. Andries raised a hand in return but didn't smile. He was used to being treated with deference in Oysterhout, where all knew him to be Simon Haelen's son.

"You can pass for an errand boy easily enough," Peter had said. Andries looked down at his threadbare clothes and grimaced. If folk judged him by his outfit, they would assume Andries was a lowly servant to an impoverished or miserly master.

Embarrassment burned within.

I'll have to get some new clothes.

Andries dismissed the thought. Right now, his outfit was perfect for his task, to slip in and out of a city without drawing too much attention to himself. He took a deep breath. Perhaps Peter had sent Andries, and not Liselotte, because he trusted Andries to get the job done.

Andries resolved to return the next greeting to passing folk more cheerfully, to better fit into his assigned role. He immediately failed miserably in this intention. The next two passers-by were two dairymaids, their blonde hair braided and healthy apple glows on their cheeks. He had already raised his hand and started smiling, but when he registered them properly, he stood tongue-tied, unable to utter a word. The two girls dissolved in giggles. Andries's face flushed bright red. When they had passed, Andries continued his journey in a temporary state of deflation.

Just wait!

They would take him seriously when he returned from the East Indies, broad-shouldered and dressed in the best velvet and silk finery that could be purchased with the ample profits of the spice trade.

"A VOC officer," the likes of the dairymaids would tell each other in hushed tones, before competing for his favours. He would know how to sweet-talk them, being a man of experience by then.

Talk them right into bed. I'll have both at the same time.

He pictured himself falling on a soft goose feather bed, the dairymaids joining him even as they undid their bodices. His thoughts then turned to the exotic beauties that awaited him in the East Indies. He had heard they walked about stark naked.

Lost in his daydreams, walking awkwardly because his arousal strained against his breeches, Andries was barely aware that he had reached the city gate.

"Hey, you!" A gruff voice barked. "You there."

Andries came to a halt, surprise on his face as he looked at two guards. They wore breastplates and helmets, carried swords at their sides, and held short pikes in their hands. One was frowning at Andries. The other laughed.

"I reckon there's a village out there short of one idiot," the cheerful one commented, grinning at his own wit.

The frowner didn't smile, scowling at Andries instead. "Where do you think you're going?"

Andries stared at him in terror. Maybe word from Oysterhout had already reached Zevenbergen and Andries would be apprehended as a fugitive. He had a sudden vision of himself constrained in a gibbet, crows picking at his rotting corpse through the bars.

The other guard stopped grinning, narrowing his eyes. "Well, boy?"

"I...ahem...uh-uh...shopping," Andries stumbled, before blurting out: "Food for my master! My master sent me to buy food."

He prepared himself for the interrogation he was sure was bound to follow, but to his surprise, the guards lost all interest.

"Be on your way then," the gruff one said.

"Try not to get lost," the other added.

Andries nodded his thanks and hurried on, through the open gates into Zevenbergen.

His spirits lifted as he strode through the meadows behind the overgrown ramparts, a castle rising over a cluster of treetops to his left. So far, the mission was going well. Although more by accident than intention, Andries's impression of a dull-witted servant boy had got him past the guards at the city gate. There was a sense of adventure now, like he was a master spy infiltrating enemy territory.

Andries straightened his back and whistled a martial tune as he passed the castle. The great keep's height was imposing, the battle platform atop cornered by four round guard turrets. All in all though, the building spoke of decay. Some parts had intact roofs, but many of these were thatched with straw, rather than clad with red roof tiles. Smoke curled up from the flues rising over the intact roofs. Open shutters revealed glass windows, some bathed in warm light that suggested hearth-fires in the rooms beyond. Other parts of the castle had gaping holes instead of windows, and no roofs other than the blackened stubs of roof beams clawing at the sky.

Andries was somewhat confused by the city proper. It was massive compared to Oysterhout, but Andries's definition of a city was dominated by his memories of Rotterdam. Zevenbergen was much smaller. The city seemed to consist mostly of two lengthy streets on either side of a long inner harbour that bristled with masts and rigging. There wasn't much behind the far street at all other than a scattering of workshops and outbuildings, and the meadows that separated the buildings from the outer ramparts. A few narrow streets and alleyways backed up the closer street, but that was the extent of Zevenbergen.

Walking into the city, Andries noticed the lack of prosperity already advertised by the decaying castle. Many buildings needed repairs, a fair few were boarded up, and one or two had even collapsed.

At first glance, there appeared to be a great many ships berthed in the inner harbour, but upon a closer look they occupied less than a quarter of the ample berths along the quays. All the ships were small single-mast inland freighters, sloops, and barges.

Peter had been right about him being noticed. None of the crews looked like seafarers, more like regular labourers dressed to spend a lot of time in cold, wet, and miserable weather.

Andries set to his tasks. There was no trace of the dull-witted servant boy when he haggled with shopkeepers over quantities and prices. This was familiar territory for him, a skill he had picked up when trading game for other foodstuffs back in Oysterhout.

He collected his purchases in a jute sack and swaggered a little as he made his way to one of the city's taverns to buy the flasks of ale. He had saved them for last because of their weight.

Andries was pleased with the bargains he had driven. He smiled as he imagined Peter's compliments when Andries returned with all the required purchases and a handful of copper change to boot.

Andries drew a few curious glances as he passed, but nobody paid him any particular attention. Just another errand boy. How different it would be when he returned from the East. Andries wouldn't wear that simple stuff Peter wore. He'd have a silk shirt. Black boots so polished you could see your reflection in them. Velvet breeches and doublet, intricately embroidered of course. An elaborate ruffled lace collar. His hat would be near invisible beneath the fine plumes of exotic birds that swayed with regal elegance.

He neared a tavern. The faded sign swaying in the wind proclaimed it to be the *Sail & Anchor*. Andries took this to be a positive omen. He was a seafarer now, after all, and on a proper ship, not these small inland tubs that frequented Zevenbergen harbour. Bravely, he swung open the door and strutted inside, the jute sack swinging over his back as if it were a sailor's duffle bag.

The small taproom was hazy with smoke from a reluctant fire in the hearth, as well as the tobacco smoke that rose from the long and curved white clay pipes that many of the clientele were smoking. Much of Andries's bravado had melted away by the time he reached the barrels and casks stacked up on the far end of the taproom.

There was tension in the air. The tavern's customers seemed divided into two distinct groups. The smaller group consisted of eight soldiers spread out around the large centre table, wearing orange sashes across their breastplates and swords at their sides. They had placed their rimmed helmets on the tabletop. They raised their tankards in frequent toasts, puffed on their pipes, and produced a great deal of noise as they shouted, jested, and laughed.

The larger group, consisting of riverboat men and labourers, were spread out at the edges of the taproom and far more subdued. They spoke in low voices, occasionally throwing the soldiers sour looks.

Andries resolved to depart as soon as he could.

He relayed his order for three flasks of ale to the tavern-keeper, a large bulking man with receding grey hair.

"Ale?" The man thundered, as if Andries had broken some sort of rule.

"*Ja*, please," Andries replied nervously. "Three flasks."

The man shook his head. "*Ja, ja*. But what kind? We got fancy stuff all the way from Haarlem, and from three Rotterdam breweries, damn their enterprising souls! Tilburg, Rosendael, Den Bosch — though that last will cost you plenty—, and cat's piss from Breda which I'm practically having to give away."

Andries was at a complete loss, before he recalled a Rotterdam ale Father had complimented once or twice — inadvertently hinting at his habits when treating patients in nearby cities.

Andries asked, "Have you got White Lion, from Rotterdam?"

"Have I got White Lion he asks!" The tavern-keeper boomed loudly at nearby local customers. "Have I got White Lion!"

The locals laughed or chuckled, although Andries didn't know why.

The tavern-keeper leaned closer to Andries, squinting suspiciously at the boy's garments. "The real question is, can you pay?"

Andries took the little leather purse from his belt and teased it open to show Peter's coins, nestled on three shiny guilders.

The tavern-keeper nodded. "Very well. Wait here. I'll go tap your flasks."

He disappeared through a narrow door half concealed behind a stack of barrels.

Andries looked around him. The soldiers were ignoring everyone and everything, except their own rowdy presence. Most of the others avoided looking at them, or at Andries for that matter. Behind the small door, he could hear the tavern-keeper talking "...more money than common sense, I reckon..."

Andries resolved again to make a hasty departure. He'd had enough of Zevenbergen. He wanted to leave. Go back to Liselotte to tell her about his adventures.

"Three flasks of White Lion," a melodious voice said behind him.

Andries turned around to drown in two bright blue eyes sparkling merriment at him. They belonged to a tavern wench, only a year or two older than Andries. Golden hair cascaded around her rosy face; full lips formed a teasing smile. She was a bit taller than Andries and slender in a willowy way. Her simple skirt and low-cut blouse accentuated rounded curves.

"Like what you see?" she asked with a sweet smile.

Andries mumbled incoherently, quickly looking away and hoping the flush on his face wasn't visible in the taproom's murk.

"Your ale," she reminded him, holding the flasks up.

Andries was pleasantly surprised when the girl named the price. It was less than he expected to pay and increased the small hoard of saved coppers.

He handed over the money, took the flasks, and placed them in his jute sack.

When Andries looked up again, she asked, "Anything else? Will you stay to keep us company for a while?"

There was nothing in the world Andries wanted more than keep the girl company. "*Ja*. A tankard of White Lion."

It was the first time he had ever placed such an order in a tavern, like a man come to soothe his thirst after a hard day's work. Andries broadened his shoulders and assumed an expression of nonchalant disinterest when the girl handed him a full tankard in exchange for some of his remaining coppers.

Andries felt a brief pang of disappointment when he noted that his hoard of saved coppers had halved. Still, he would have some change to hand back as evidence of his ability to perform a simple task. Peter needn't know it had been more. As far as Andries was concerned, he deserved a little reward for his efforts.

The tavern wench was called away by another customer. Andries retired into a recessed corner with his sack of purchases and tankard. He raised the tankard and took a large swig.

The rich full taste made him gasp in wonder. He had only ever drunk ale at home, where it had been so watered down on Father's instructions that it was hard to discern any taste at all. The White Lion was heavenly. Andries eagerly drank more of it. A tingle spread through his body. His mind became pleasantly clouded.

He leaned back on the short bench, feeling more relaxed than he had been for a while. Andries beamed at his tankard, savouring its contents, in between letting his eyes roam through the taproom to follow the blonde wench around. She took orders, refilled tankards, and brought two grizzled fishermen bowls of steaming stew, all the time joking and laughing, as well as deftly evading most of the hands reaching for her bottom. The soldiers would cheer when one of them managed a pat or squeeze. The girl would retreat, laughing and calling friendly insults while Andries seethed with envy.

Andries picked up snatches of conversations. Most of it was in complaint. The soldiers were unhappy by the depletion of their garrison and the neglected ramparts.

"...won't stand a chance if the Dons show up..."

"...Spinola won't head this way. There's nothing to be had in this dump for him..."

"...well, if push comes to shove, I say the Cap'n would do best to march us to Willemstad. If we add our strength to their garrison, we can hold out forever. The fortifications there are superb..."

Andries liked that last comment, it was fighting talk. Nonetheless, it didn't go down well with the locals.

"...this lot here won't even put up a fight..."

"...what's the use of us having to pay for a garrison..."

"...bad enough that we had to put up with the Dons in the castle all those years..."

"...they ain't going to be in a merciful mood if they retake Zevenbergen, mark my words..."

Not all the local conversation centred on the soldiers. The price of wheat, peat, and cattle concerned many, as did the summer, which some considered far too hot and dry, and others disappointingly cold and wet. The coming and going of riverboats and their skippers was discussed.

Andries heard other nearby cities in Holland, like Rotterdam and Dordrecht, talked of with bitter scorn. He gathered that Zevenbergen had been on the front line before the truce and had suffered accordingly. The local view was that their neighbours were awash in prosperity enabled by those who had made the actual sacrifices, and precious little had been offered in return for the loss of life and income.

The conversation that interested Andries most focused on Skipper Jan Willemsz Dik, who had recently returned to Zeeland from the East Indies on the VOC merchantman *De Middelburg*. The ship's large hold had been filled to the brim with riches. The man telling the news of *De Middelburg's* return claimed that every man, woman, and child on the isle of Walcheren went about draped in silks and pearls. When disbelief was expressed, he admitted it was only in the cities of Middelburg and Flushing that the inhabitants were so dressed.

Andries's head was spinning from the many conversations. It became more difficult to keep all the strands of narrative apart, and the resultant fusions didn't make sense. He emptied his tankard in the hope it would steady him.

The wench was at his table before he had a chance to set the empty tankard down.

Andries looked at her like she was a heavenly sent angel. He wanted to say something, but instead blinked in surprise when he realised he was swaying...or was it the taproom?

Something was swaying at any rate.

The girl shook her head and laughed. "I suppose that'll be your last then?"

Andries bristled at the suggestion. He growled: "I'll have another one."

"Are you sure?"

Andries answered by giving her the last coppers from his purse.

She shrugged, laughed, and then went to the barrels with his empty tankard.

Andries stared at her bottom, definitely swaying, along with the rest of the taproom. He was stung by a brief pang of guilt about spending all his savings but reasoned that returning with the shopping was accomplishment enough. He had earned those coppers himself.

The girl returned with a full tankard. Andries hoped she would stay by his table a little longer.

"I'm a seafarer, bound for the East Indies," he blurted out, as she set the tankard in front of him.

She laughed and placed her hands on her waist, inspecting Andries from top to toe. "Seafarer?"

Andries wilted a little, knowing he didn't look the part. "It'll be my first time...to sail to the East Indies I mean. I'm to be a midshipman."

"Going to the other side of the world, leaving me here in the *Sail & Anchor*." The girl pouted. "All by my lonesome self."

Andries was overcome by a fierce longing not to leave the poor girl all alone amidst this crude company. He wanted to wrap her in his arms and promise her protection. Not knowing what to say, he took a large gulp from the tankard, then another.

"I'll come back a rich man," he promised.

"Or not at all," the girl replied, pulling a sad face. "So many die on the way, such a waste of handsome sailors..."

Andries drank some more ale and shrugged. "Not everyone is cut out to be a seafarer. I'll make it. I'll come back and buy you a drink."

"One measly drink? Is that all I'm worth to you?" She tutted. "I want to be draped in silks and pearls, like the good folk of Middelburg!"

"That too," Andries said hastily. "Of course."

The girl leaned down over the table, bringing her face close to his. Her blouse hung so low that Andries had an unobstructed view of her breasts. His face flushed and he didn't know where to look, unable at any rate of tearing his eyes away. Arousal was quick to cause stiffening in his breeches.

"But why wait?" The girl murmured, her breath sweet and warm. "It'll be years before you return, Sailor. Life is short, why not enjoy it now?"

Andries stammered something unintelligible, and then shut himself up by taking a long swig from the tankard.

"Cat got your tongue?" The girl asked. She rose again. "Well, do you want to?"

Andries hurriedly got up, then blushed again as he feared all and sundry would notice his arousal. Nobody paid him the least bit of attention though. Andries picked up his jute sack and the tankard and took a first step. The room spun around and for a moment Andries was afraid that he would stumble and fall because his legs were so wobbly.

He followed the girl out of the taproom and down a murky corridor, sure that he was dreaming. She opened the door at the end of the corridor, letting bright daylight spill in. Andries blinked as he stepped into a courtyard, his eyes adjusting to the change of light. He wasn't given much of a chance to look around because the girl took his hand and pulled him across the courtyard and into a stable. The stalls were empty and smelled of fresh hay. The girl selected one of the stalls and fell onto the hay, pulling Andries down with her.

He fumbled at her breasts. Toosje had shown Andries hers once, when they had been alone by the stream in the forest where they sometimes secretly met. After much persistent urging, Toosje had lifted her undershirt shyly to reveal her small, pointed breasts, but she hadn't let Andries touch them. The tavern girl didn't seem to mind. Beneath the fabric of her top, they were soft and firm to the touch of his eager hands.

When he discerned a hardening nipple, Andries was overwhelmed by a primal instinct. He grew so hard it hurt. He growled and made to pull down the girl's top...or up, he frowned, desperate to work out what would bare her bosom quickest.

"Whoa, Sailor!" She brushed off his hands and scrambled into a sitting position. "First things first."

"First things?" Andries was puzzled. Ought they have kissed first? He wanted to and leaned in to bring his face closer to hers.

"Don't you play the fool with me," the girl said curtly. "I want money."

"Money?" Andries asked.

She held out a hand, using the other to slide her skirts over her knees, revealing her bare lower legs. Then she spread her legs a little, in unmistakable invitation.

The embarrassment at having misunderstood the situation almost defeated Andries, but he was overridden by something far stronger, a near uncontrollable urge.

SIN! Father's voice thundered through his mind, but Andries dismissed it. Wasn't this precisely what Father had done in taverns all over western Brabant?

My coppers are all gone!

Andries peered into his purse. He took out one of his guilders. "How much..."

The girl snatched the coin out of his hand. "Precisely that," she said, as she deftly made the guilder disappear in the folds of her clothing. The glint in her eyes told Andries that he had paid far too much but it was...

She lay down on the hay, grabbed the hem of her skirt, and pulled it up over her belly without further ado. Spreading her legs wide, she said: "Well, do your business then."

Andries stared, aghast. This wasn't how he had imagined it would be like. In his imagination there was a build-up...affection of sorts. But that was his mind talking. That other urge driving him made Andries unbutton his doublet, and then wrestle with his belt and breeches.

She'll see my...

He paused, but decided it didn't matter, not with the girl's legs spread wide. He couldn't take his eyes off, trying to equate what he saw with the vague expectations his mind's eye had formulated when he had thought of such matters. Quite a lot over the last year or so – anxiously aware that to even think of it was a sin, but unable to stop his mind exploring the subject and his body demanding guilty pleasure.

"Well? I haven't got all day," the girl said.

Andries glanced up at her face. She looked bored. He looked back at her open thighs. So much more complex than he had thought, like the intricate overlapping folds and curls formed by a rose's petals. What was he supposed to do next?

Then she spread her legs a little, in unmistakable invitation.

He swallowed nervously, horrified when a small squeak escaped from his throat.

"Hell's bells," the girl sat up again, her bundled skirt falling over her thighs. "You haven't a clue, do you?"

Andries shrugged unhappily, humiliation burning on his cheeks.

The girl took pity on him and softened her voice. "Not to worry, you'll figure it out as we go along."

She tugged at his breeches, until they slid down over his buttocks, freeing his erection to stand at attention.

The girl giggled. "Ginger above, ginger below." She ran her hands over his flanks. "Stop shaking, I don't bite. It's not scary."

"I'm not…" Andries began to deny the obvious, then sucked in his breath as she folded her hands around him. He stared, mesmerised by the sight of her slender fingers curling around that, which had only ever been held by his own hand.

She smiled encouragingly. "It all seems in working order. Now, let's give you something to think about during long months at sea."

She tightened her grip and tugged.

Andries shuddered. He felt a familiar rush.

Nay! Not now!

His hips began to spasm. He cried out in sheer delight as he ejaculated.

She laughed, let go of him, and wiped her hands on the hay. "Well, that was easy. Get your breeches back on, Sailor."

"Nay! Wait." Andries protested. "We weren't finished yet."

The girl raised her eyebrows. "I'm pretty sure you finished. You got what you paid for."

"That's not fair!" The languid intoxication of his release was replaced by rising anger.

The girl narrowed her eyes in response to his shifting mood. She rose to her feet, straightening her skirt over her legs. "You want another go, it'll cost you another guilder, Sailor. But your bowsprit is sagging." She pointed at the obvious.

Andries scrambled to his feet, hoisting up his breeches. "I already paid you a guilder! A whole guilder. I want…" He reached out with one hand to grab her by the arm.

Anger flashed through her eyes. She shook her arm loose. "SEM! SEM!"

Sem turned out to be a lumbering, six-foot tall stable hand, whose bare arms were bulging with muscles and covered in tattoos. He must have been skulking about close by because he strode into the stable almost immediately, blocking the open door of the stall. "Truusje?"

The girl pointed at Andries. "Got a customer with a complaint."

Sem turned his head slowly, to take in the sight of Andries who hastily fastened his belt.

"No, I wasn't..." Andries shook his head. "I was just on my way out."

"Good. See him out please, Sem."

"My pleasure," Sem growled, and moved his bulk towards Andries, spreading his bear like arms.

Andries had been awhirl with a wide range of emotions, but the sight of Sem advancing on him brought about a single overriding focus. The ale befuddled him, but he still had more wit and speed than the bulking stable-hand.

Snatching the jute sack, Andries made to go to his right. When Sem threw his weight and attention that way, Andries swerved to his left. He crouched low, evading Sem's arm, and bolted out of the stall.

"Uh?" Sem looked around him, bewildered.

"*Klootzak!*[18]" Truusje screamed at Andries.

"Ha!" Andries fled out of the stable and across the courtyard. Tearing open the door, he made through the corridor and burst into the taproom.

Andries found himself the focus of everybody's attention after barrelling into their midst: Out of breath, clothes dishevelled and covered with bits of hay.

Two of the soldiers jumped up. It only took them a few strides to block the front door. "Where do you think you're going?"

Andries gulped, then turned, in a crouch, ready to propel himself in whatever direction offered escape. There was none. Most of the clientele had risen from their seats, surrounding him in a broad circle. Truusje and Sem came in through the corridor door, to join the tavern keeper who stepped forward to confront Andries.

"What's going on here then?" One of the soldiers asked, seeming to direct his question at both the tavern keeper and Andries. He assumed a sudden, officious air.

"He...! She...! We...!" Andries pointed wildly.

"He was stealing!" Truusje shouted. She snatched the jute sack from Andries.

---

[18] Literally: Testicular sack. Figuratively: Asshole! Plural, *Klootzakken*

He made to grab it back, but the two soldiers behind him took hold of his arms and restrained him.

"He stole ale," Truusje said. She investigated the bag. "And food! He's raided the kitchen!"

"NAY!" Andries protested. "I bought those things! They are mine. I paid for them!"

There were hostile murmurs around him.

"…stranger, never seen 'im afore…"

"…vagabond…"

"…not from round here…"

The tavern keeper took the jute sack from Truusje, glancing at the contents. He demanded in a loud voice: "Did anyone see this scoundrel pay for his ale? Well?"

The taproom fell silent. Andries looked around at the clientele. Some looked away, some looked bemused, and a few were grinning. None spoke up.

Andries's belly sank like a lead weight. His voice quavered. "Please, you saw me pay, for three flasks. White Lion. I paid!"

The tavern-keeper and Sem looked around grimly. None spoke up. Truusje flashed Andries a triumphant look.

"He took money too!" She shrilled. "Two silver guilders. They're in his pouch."

"You!" Andries tried to shake himself loose from the soldiers' grip, but to no avail. They tightened their hold on him so much it hurt.

The tall soldier stepped forward and expertly emptied Andries's purse.

"Those are mine!" Andries shouted. "Please, those are mine…they were my…"

He fell silent, remembering he wasn't supposed to reveal who he was. He wanted to cry and struggled not to. "I'm a VOC midshipman!"

A roar of laughter met his claim.

The tall soldier let the coins glide through his fingers, showing them to the crowd, before he tossed one to the tavern keeper who caught it mid-air with surprising speed.

"The other one," the soldier declared, looking the tavern-keeper in the eye. "Is evidence. We'll hand it over to the Sheriff along with this miserable little thief."

The tavern keeper's mouth tightened as he stared at the soldier. Then he gave a curt nod to indicate his acceptance of the proposal, much to Andries's horror.

"Right, you lot," the soldier ordered his remaining companions at the table. "Drink up, it's time we left."

There were low murmurs of agreement from the townsfolk. The soldiers ignored them, emptied their tankards, and grabbed their helmets. The tall soldier nodded at the two holding Andries. "Take him outside."

Andries struggled as he was dragged out the Sail & Anchor. He threw one last look at the jute sack, engulfed by the totality of his failure. How could he ever face Peter again? If at all, his deepening despair told him. Theft was dealt with severely. He'd be branded, possibly hanged.

Adjusting to the bright daylight again, Andries became aware of a singular focus from all passers-by — and it wasn't the sight of a dishevelled boy led out of the Sail & Anchor, the hands of strong soldiers clamped down on his shoulders. Instead, their attention was focused on a dusty horseman, a soldier, thundering over the street's cobbles. The man was shouting wildly.

"You there!" An officer, wearing a richly embroidered coat and a finely engraved breastplate and helmet, strode forward and held a hand up in command. "Stop your horse. What's the matter?"

The rider brought his mount to a halt, wrestling with the reigns. "The Dons! They've crossed the border! Tens of thousands of them. It's war!"

War.

The word was repeated by the growing crowd around the officer and the horseman.

The Sail & Anchor emptied, its occupants emerging to see what all the fuss was about. Folk streamed from other buildings too. Solemn church bells tolled haphazardly, soon after joined by other church and chapel bells, all adding to the frantic mood.

More horsemen came thundering down the street that led to the castle. They too were shouting.

"It's war! It's war!"

More details emerged in overheard snatches of conversation between the horseman and the officer, as well as the new riders answering dozens of questions.

Fragmented information passed through the crowd.

"...The Catholics in Bergen-op-Zoom opened the city gates for the Dons..."

"...they were shut in the nick of time by patriots..."

"...bloody Papists tried to betray us..."

"...war!"

The two soldiers in charge of Andries muttered curses under their breath. Their grip on Andries's shoulders had lessened to a great degree, and their attention for him ebbed to a low.

Although staggered by the news that the invasion of the Republic had begun, Andries had more urgent things on his mind, like avoiding a red-hot iron sizzling on his skin to brand him a thief.

Shaking his shoulders loose, he ducked down and scrambled away. Crouched low, he worked himself into the crowd.

"Hey!" One of the soldiers exclaimed.

His fellow shouted: "Halt that thief! STOP HIM!"

The two of them gave chase but were slowed down by the press of people they clumsily ploughed through; allowing Andries to increase his head start. Folk in the crowd were looking around, slowly realizing something other than war was amiss, but none of them connected that with the frantic boy weaving his way through their ranks.

The other soldiers who had been in the Sail & Anchor belatedly joined the chase, hindered by the crowd's confusion.

Their shouts amplified the message:

"Halt the thief! HALT THE THIEF!"

Andries was given renewed courage by the first glimpse of emptiness beyond the crowd. He had nearly made it through when one of the soldiers shouted something that was echoed around, closer and closer to the crowd's perimeter.

"He's a Papist spy!"

"PAPIST SPY!"

Andries burst free from the crowd's edge. The soldiers were still hopelessly entangled with the many bystanders, but he was no longer hidden. Heads turned as eyes were drawn to the sight of the boy rushing toward the castle street.

"There he is!"

"The Papist spy!"

"Get him!"

Boots thudded on the cobbles behind Andries, as a mob parted from the main crowd in pursuit of the presumed spy.

"Get him! Hang the Papist scum!"

Andries dared a quick glance over his shoulders. There were at least a score of angry burghers hot on his heels, joined by the first of the soldiers. The hateful anger on their faces was emphasised by predatory braying as they howled for his blood. A brick flew through the air.

If Andries was caught now, they would tear him apart. That chilling realisation lent him desperate speed as he ran for his life.

11. On the Road to Prinsenland

COUNTY OF HOLLAND -1622

The evening sun mellowed the sky. Its sinking rays cast pastel colours on the stately towering clouds that were drifting in from the south, throwing long shadows on the flat green countryside.

It was long after Zevenbergen's bells had stopped tolling. Liselotte had been greatly worried about her brother. She was immensely relieved when he returned at long last – bursting into the old barn in a frenzied rush.

He was panting for breath, wet and muddy. His clothes were filthy and torn. Liselotte rose to welcome him in a tight embrace, not minding the mess Andries was in as long as he was safe.

Andries uttered confusing snatches of explanation between deep gasps for air and stifled sobs.

War.

It was war. The Spanish had invaded and struck at Bergen-op-Zoom. Andries didn't know if the city had been taken, he had heard something about Catholic inhabitants opening a city gate.

As for the rest of it...Andries said that he had finished buying all the provisions. He had been about to leave when army riders had galloped into the city with their ill tidings from the south. Folk had been suspicious of the stranger in their midst, accusing him of being a Papist spy.

"And then, and then..." Andries's voice trembled. "People took up the cry. Spy! Papist! They grabbed hold of me. They took my bag of shopping. They took the coppers I'd saved. They took Father's silver guilders! They wanted to hang me. Papist spy, they called me. Get him. Hang him." He shivered. "I pulled free and just ran. Half-swam and half-waded through the moat."

"Wisely so," Peter said. "Once a mob gets a thirst for blood there is little reasoning to be done."

"Like animals!" Andries confirmed. "Like wild animals."

Liselotte reckoned there were things Andries wasn't telling them. Now and then she sensed he was shying away from the full story, with something of a furtive look in his eyes. However, she put this down to the terrifying experience he'd been through. It was unfair to expect him to provide a comprehensive report after he had been robbed and come so close to being torn apart by a ferocious mob. She hugged him again, relieved that her twin had come back to tell his tale.

"It's war then," she said, with wonder in her voice. "The Spaniards have come."

"It was bound to happen," Peter said. "Ambrosio Spinola isn't the type to twiddle his thumbs with an army of fifty thousand at his disposal. That, and all of Spain howling for Dutch blood."

"Bergen-op-Zoom!" Liselotte exclaimed. "It might have fallen."

"That's where the Dons are!" Andries cried out. "We have to change our plan. Why not go north to Rotterdam?"

Liselotte was inclined to agree. She knew Peter wanted to get to his ship, but now a whole Spanish army lay between them and Flushing.

She asked Peter. "The Hollands Deep is much closer than Bergen-op-Zoom, isn't it?"

"It's closer," Peter acknowledged. "But there are only so many ferries and there'll be a flood of refugees headed north. We'd risk being caught up in a mass of people. We'd be helpless if anything happened, trapped by the chaos. Or fighting our way onto a ferry, which would like as not capsize or sink if swarmed by a desperate crowd."

That made sense to Liselotte, but Andries wasn't as convinced.

He said, "But surely you can't still mean to go to Bergen-op-Zoom? If the Dons didn't take it, they'll be laying siege to it."

"We'll avoid Bergen-op-Zoom," Peter agreed. "Instead, we'll head west for Prinsenland. We should be able to find a crossing to the isle of Tholen. Zeeland is safe, there's a large fleet at Flushing. But we'll have to move fast, and we'll have to go as soon as possible. This very moment, in fact."

His cousins' faces fell.

"We don't have many choices," Peter told them. "Zevenbergen might send men to look for Andries if they think he's a spy. They'll surely know about this barn. If they find us, with suspicions set aflame by war, all three of us will be suspected of spying. My VOC standing will be of no help to us."

He used the tip of his boot to shift the burning logs of their fire apart. "We'll have to risk stopping at a farm to buy some food. But not until morning, when we're as far away from here as possible. We'll march on an empty belly until then."

"Wait!" Liselotte exclaimed.

She had set some snares before she had joined Peter on the barn's roof earlier and ran to check them. She was grinning when she returned, holding up several lengths of twisted brass wire with running loops, and two plump pheasants. Andries and Peter were scooping dirt on the expiring fire. Both looked at the birds in astonishment, before happy grins spread on their faces.

"You're a good poacher," Peter said. "Well done. We'll stop for a break in a few hours, long enough to roast your catch. But first, we march."

Liselotte attached the pheasants to her pack. Her shoulders groaned when she hoisted the pack up, but she managed to keep her balance and conceal the weight of her burden.

It was still light, but the evening was dying when they left the barn. The clouds had consolidated in a compact mass, so Peter decided that they could stay on the hard surface of the road this night, instead of ploughing through soft soil and grass. "Our silhouettes won't be as noticeable, and speed is of the essence now."

As on the first leg of their journey from Oysterhout, Liselotte's pack seemed to grow heavier by the minute. However, not having to scramble up and down dykes and through ditches made the steady pace set by Peter a lot more bearable.

"What if we run into the Dons?" Andries asked.

Peter swept both arms outward, open hands indicating the endless sameness of everything. Outstretched fields and winding dykes. An occasional copse of trees around a farm. A few church spires denoting the presence of small towns and hamlets. Canals and small rivers spanned by narrow bridges.

"If the Spaniards actually managed to take Bergen-op-Zoom, they will have to advance on Rosendael before they go anywhere else."

"Maybe they've already taken Rosendael," Andries suggested.

Peter chuckled. "Big armies don't move fast. Notoriously slow, in fact. Besides, we're close to the fortified and garrisoned towns of Willemstad and Clundert. Oudenbosch and Steynbergen are fortified as well. They will shield us from the worst."

Liselotte recollected Oysterhout elders speaking fearfully of the mayhem caused by the Count of Mansfeld's cavalry when the commander had tried to break Prince Maurits's siege of nearby Geertruidenberg in 1593. Nobody had been safe in the entire region.

She doubted that the three of them would have much chance against a mounted squadron. She asked, "but they could send outriders, couldn't they?"

"At great risk," Peter answered. "There are a lot of garrisoned towns within a bell's toll of each other. Spinola knows the dangers. He'll want to keep a tight leash on his troops, lest he loses them to Dutch ambushes or to the lure of easy plunder. When a regiment becomes undone, it's nigh impossible to force them back into the fold. For now, I'm more worried about Dutch patrols. They'll be on edge and ordered to keep their eyes open for anything odd and unusual."

"Liselotte is odd and unusual," Andries jested.

Liselotte considered poking him for that but decided not to break her stride.

"We'd best avoid all soldiers," Peter said. "Fortunately, they tend to be noisy creatures. If we hear them coming, we run for shelter. The ditches at the bottom of a dyke if necessary."

The road divided into two, both offshoots meandering over broad dykes. Peter chose the road to follow without hesitation.

Andries said, "I can't wait for Prince Maurits to march south. He'll teach the Spaniards a lesson like he did at the Battle of Nieuwpoort!"

Peter was doubtful. "He beat Parma and Mendoza. He didn't do so well against Spinola before the truce. The Prince of Orange is fifty-five years old, and, from what I heard, not in great health. I wish it were otherwise, but I doubt Maurits will be able to deliver another Nieuwpoort."

Andries shook his head in disbelief.

Liselotte shared her brother's misgivings. They were both proud of the Republic. Proud that a small number of stubborn rebels – arrogantly dismissed as beggars or 'men of butter' by Spanish aristocrats – had taken on the world's mightiest empire and fought it to a standstill. They had grown up believing Captain-General Maurits van Nassau, son of Prince William of Orange, to be a rock-solid guarantor of their liberty.

"It's good to be optimistic," Peter said. "But wise to temper patriotism with realism. At least this time the Republic is prepared for war. But Imperial military might is still a force to be reckoned with."

"Well, if we run into Spaniards," Liselotte declared, patting her haversack. "They'll find that Treyn Rembrands isn't the only girl ready to fight them."

"Girls shouldn't fight the Dons," Andries stated. "War is men's work."

Liselotte drew a deep breath, but Peter intervened before she was able to retort.

"The garrison of Alkmaar reported that they only withstood repeated Spanish assaults because the whole city mobilised. Men, women, boys, girls. Even the youngest children, prying loose the street cobbles and carrying them to the walls. Treyn Rembrands wasn't the only girl wielding a musket or sword on Alkmaar's walls. Credit where credit is due, Andries. The women of Alkmaar made war their business. Can you blame them? The cities that had fallen to the Iron Duke were subjected to savage barbarism. The whole of Alkmaar knew wat terrors awaited them if Spanish soldiers gained a foothold in the city."

"See!" Liselotte gave Andries a triumphant look. "Women can fight! Like Treyn Rembrands and Kenau Simonsdochter!"

"When needs be," Peter said. "And at risk of life and limb. Remember, Kenau Simonsdochter was murdered by Norwegian pirates in northern waters."

"Which wouldn't have happened if she'd stayed home," Andries was quick to point out.

Liselotte countered, "Women die at home too. Childbirth. Pox or plague. Drunken husbands who beat them bloody."

"But that is normal," Andries said. "Women dying in war ain't."

"Drunk husbands with loose hands are normal?" Liselotte asked. "They shouldn't be. What do you think would have happened to Alkmaar's women if they hadn't fought back? If the Spaniards won and went on a rampage?"

"The Spanish Fury," Andries admitted.

"That's what Alkmaar's women and girls reckoned," Peter said. "But mark this, Liselotte. They paid a price. When the dead were buried after assaults, there were women and girls laid to rest along with the menfolk. Slain by Spanish blades, musket balls, and cannon shot. Did Uncle Simon never talk to you about Alkmaar?"

"Father? Alkmaar?" Andries asked. "Why would he?"

"I suppose he wouldn't have," Peter continued. "Mine never did either. But the fact of the matter is that their father, our *Opa*[19] Adrian, fought at Alkmaar as well."

"He did?" Andries asked incredulously.

"Aye, indeed," Peter confirmed.

Liselotte proudly stated, "*Opa* Haelen was a Sea Beggar."

"I never knew," Andries said.

Twilight had set in, casting its peculiar half-light on the flatlands they were traversing, but it didn't impede their steady progress.

---

[19] Grandfather

"*Opa* was in the thick of it," Peter confirmed. "Den Briel, Haarlem, Alkmaar, Leyden, Nieuwpoort. If there was fighting to be done, Adrian Haelen was there."

"The Sea Beggars are heroes!" Andries exclaimed. "Why wouldn't Father have spoken of him?"

"I suspect there is shame of his humble origins. He was a common sailor. Perhaps there is also shame for his part in the war."

"Why?" Liselotte asked. "Without the Sea Beggars…"

"I agree," Peter said. "William of Orange's uprising wouldn't have succeeded without the Sea Beggars. But they were still rogues. Ill-educated and rough mannered. There a fine line between operating as privateers in the Prince of Orange's service and blatant piracy. That line was crossed regularly, much to the prince's frustration."

"So, I'm descended from a pirate?" Liselotte asked.

"In a manner of speaking, aye." Peter confirmed.

Liselotte smiled her approval. "Do you think *Opa* knew Treyn Rembrands?"

"It's conceivable that their paths crossed. But I doubt they would have known each other well. Treyn was a patrician's daughter from a well-to-do merchant family. *Opa* was a common patriot and at least half-a-pirate."

Andries frowned. Liselotte reckoned he found it difficult to conceive of commoners – *pirates!* – as heroes. Father had always said common folk were an unfortunate necessity, best avoided by their social betters.

"Did you know *Opa*?" Liselotte asked Peter.

"I met him once that I can recall. I was very young. It was a brief visit." Peter paused. "I remember him telling me that building ships was a fine occupation but sailing them a much finer affair. My father scowled at him for that, but I was mightily impressed by his words. *Opa* died in '07, in the service of Jacob van Heemskerck at the Battle of Gibraltar. The year you two were born. But he had done well for himself. He was skipper by then, and wealthy enough to ensure his sons were able to climb the social ladder."

"To become ashamed of their own father's origins," Liselotte pointed out, disapproval in her tone.

"And perhaps their mother's." Peter smiled. "He married an Englishwoman. The Sea Beggars were stationed on the Kent and Sussex coasts for a while."

"Euw, the English!" Andries pulled a long face.

"*Oma*[20] Elisabeth was English?" Liselotte asked, fascinated by this new information.

"Aye, she hailed from a notorious family of smugglers in Rye," Peter said. "*Opa's* sons are part English, part smuggler, part pirate...and don't like to speak of it."

"So how do you know so much about *Opa* and *Oma*?" Andries asked. "If your father didn't like talking about them?"

"One of the old tars on *De Assemburg* told me a lot about Adrian Haelen. Niklas had been shipmates with our grandfather and held him in high esteem. He said *Opa* was an excellent sailor and canny fighter."

"*De Assemburg*?" Andries asked.

"The first VOC ship Peter sailed on," Liselotte explained. "When he was our age! All the way to the Indies."

"Our age? Really?"

"Fourteen when we sailed from the Tessel roadstead," Peter confirmed. "Sixteen when I returned."

"A two-year voyage!" Liselotte gasped, dreading that long without her brother.

"Two-and-a-half years, actually," Peter said.

"It takes that long?" Andries asked fearfully.

"It doesn't need to. You and I will do it in less than half that time!"

Andries muttered, "more than a year."

Liselotte contemplated the inevitable parting their journey led to. She would be safe in Rotterdam, but Peter and Andries were to go on to face much greater dangers, maybe never come back at all.

Even if they did return, they would be gone for years. She'd be alone with the man who had set young Peter's shipbuilding plans on fire. Father's brother. Were they alike?

Twilight waned into night and darkness enveloped them. The moon remained shrouded, reducing the world to each other's shadowy presences and a few meters of dirt road around their feet.

The roads and tracks they followed atop dykes meandered ever forward in broad curves, sometimes broken by a bridged canal.

Occasionally they came to an intersection and a subsequent short halt. Peter would use the few lights that denoted the presence of hamlets and towns as navigational marks, before coming to a decision about the way to follow.

---

[20] Grandmother

The breeze that had brought in the clouds strengthened into a persistent wind.

When Peter once again indicated their direction after pausing at a fork in the road, Liselotte asked, "I thought you didn't know the inlands that well?"

He sighed, sounding content. "Can't you smell it?"

Liselotte sniffed at the air, then took a deep intake of it through her nose. There was a trace of brine to it, something that she hadn't smelled for a long time. "The sea!"

"Aye, we're on a parallel course to it."

They only ran into potential trouble the once. They had just reached a crossroads. All four roads were dyke top roads. A copse of trees nestled below in the embrace of two of the crossroad arms.

When they stopped at the centre of the crossroads, all heard it at the same time: A slow and steady rhythm of hoof beats and a distant murmur of conversation. Far away but coming closer.

The clouds parted to reveal the moon. The increased illumination allowed them to see a little as they hurriedly scrambled down the embankment.

Liselotte struggled to retain her balance as the heavy pack bucked, the straps burning into her aching shoulders, but she made it down in one piece. They sought shelter amidst the undergrowth in the copse.

They couldn't hear the voices and hoof beats from their new position. The tense waiting that followed seemed to go on forever.

When the sounds drifted into their hearing once again, they were louder, headed straight for the crossroads.

The moon vanished behind the clouds once more. Its last beams gleamed on the breastplates and helmets of eight mounted soldiers as they rode past, speaking Dutch.

Despite Peter's warning that any soldiers they might run into could be on edge, this patrol seemed remarkably relaxed. The mounts plodded along without urgency, the men bantering at ease. The main topic of conversation concerned floral descriptions of the bosom of one of the barmaids at a tavern they frequented. This interspersed with lewd comments regarding all the things they intended to do with, or on, said bosom.

Liselotte rolled her eyes. None of it sounded remotely romantic, or very comfortable for that matter. She suddenly felt far less confident in the Republic's ability to fend off the Spanish Empire.

They didn't even glance into the copse of trees, which was large enough to hide half a regiment.

Don't they know about the war?

When the voices and hoof beats died down, Peter led them back up to the crossroads, chose a new direction, and reset the pace of their march.

§ § § § § §

Andries had no idea for how long they walked after their brief break at the crossroads. He was tired after a long day and night and becoming a bit annoyed by Peter's relentless pace.

His legs felt leaden, but Liselotte appeared to be keeping up effortlessly. Andries didn't want to be the first to request a much-needed break. Admitting weakness was a girl's job. He was somewhat irate with Liselotte for not doing so. She must have been as tired as he was. If she wasn't, that was purely because she'd been given rest when Andries had risked his life in Zevenbergen. Surely, he deserved some consideration?

At long last they stopped, by an empty cattle shed amidst a huddle of trees. The walls only reached halfway to the straw roof, but it offered a semblance of shelter. Andries dropped to the ground, counting his aches. Peter gathered wood to build a small fire while Liselotte plucked the pheasants before gutting them.

Feeling nauseous at the sight, Andries looked away. He had never understood Liselotte's ability to prepare game without retching.

Before long the pheasants were roasting over the fire, spitted on Peter's sword. The sizzling of the meat and warmth of the fire did much to make Andries feel better. His belly rumbled in anticipation of something warm to eat.

"So, Peter, what did you learn?" Liselotte asked.

"Learn?" Peter sounded as confused as Andries was by that question.

"You told me you mustered on *De Assemburg* to learn about practical matters," Liselotte clarified. "Did you?"

"Aye, very much so." Peter nodded. "A painful set of lessons."

"Painful?" Andries didn't like the sound of that.

126

At long last they stopped, by an empty cattle shed amidst a huddle of trees

"First of all," Peter mused. "I learned that I had been right about the inherent flaws in the design of East India merchantmen. That they could be constructed to be far more practical and efficient. But…"

His face hardened. "Until then I had always considered the matter in terms of hull shape, sails, and rigging. *De Assemburg* taught me about the human cost extracted by poor design. A price paid in suffering and death."

Peter fell into a short silence, his expression altering from hardness to pain, and then determination. "East Indies merchantmen are far too small for the full complement of over two hundred crew and passengers. The ships have been designed with cargo in mind, not comfort."

"Why do they overcrowd the ships then?" Liselotte asked.

"There's sheer irony in it," Peter said. "A third, even half the crew, can perish on a return voyage to the East Indies. They overcrew in expectation of those fatalities. Yet, I reckon a significant percentage of those deaths are caused by that very overcrowding."

"That doesn't sound very clever," Liselotte said.

Andries was inclined to agree, somewhat concerned by the low survival odds.

"It isn't," Peter said. "Improved ship design would be the right thing to do, but…"

He waved his hands in helpless frustration. "Another important lesson I learned on *De Assemburg* was that the practical knowledge from my father's dockyards and hands-on experience gained on a tour of the East, weren't by themselves sufficient to successfully design a new ship. I needed more knowledge. Schooling in Mathematics. The sciences."

"Bah." Andries pulled a long face.

"Not so, Cousin, not so." Peter shook his head. "Having lost so many shipmates on *De Assemburg* gave me more motivation than ever to pursue my goals."

"So, what did you do?" Liselotte asked.

"We returned to Tessel with a severely depleted crew. The ship's carpenter had died of scurvy. I had taken his place, but I was also taking watches as temporary third steersman. The skipper wanted to keep me on *De Assemburg's* muster roll, he offered me a position as second steersman even, but I took my pay and share of profits. Then I went to Leyden."

"Leyden?" Andries was puzzled.

"The university?" Liselotte made the connection.

"Aye, indeed." Peter acknowledged. "I enrolled at the University of Leyden and was to spend the next five years of my life with my nose in books."

"Ugh!" Andries said. "It's a wonder you didn't die of boredom."

"Boredom?" Peter sounded surprised. "Not at all. I found what I was looking for. I learned from the sharpest minds in their respective fields. I merged my practical experience with their theoretical knowledge. All the while, I continued working on my own designs until I had perfected them."

"I don't understand," Liselotte said. "If your ship design was completed, why did you sail on *De Blokzeyl* next, and not your own ship?"

Peter scowled. "Building a ship requires financial backing. I took my plans and calculations to dockyards, shipbuilding masters, merchants, and the VOC. Once again, I was mocked and derided. The best offer I received was to become second steersman on *De Blokzeyl,* provided I dropped all notions of redesigning what were considered perfectly fine ships."

He snorted. "I figured that if I wanted to build my ship, I'd have to finance it myself. I'd never earn enough working at a dockyard, but another voyage to the East Indies held the promise of possible riches, so I mustered on *De Blokzeyl*."

"Did that work?" Andries asked.

"In a roundabout way," Peter answered. "It took two voyages to the East Indies on *De Blokzeyl,* not just the one. Six years of my life, but I am now master of my own dockyard and the fastest ship on the Seven Seas. But..."

He looked pained.

"So, you made lots of profit?" Andries asked.

To him that was the main point of sailing to the East. Peter seemed to be making everything needlessly complicated. His cousin was also far wealthier than Andries had imagined because he'd not heard talk of Peter's own dockyard before.

Andries would have to wait for an answer though because the pheasants were ready. Eating them was far more important than talking. Or table manners for that matter, they all tore into the meat with ravenous hunger.

It began to rain as they gnawed at the last scraps of meat on the bones. It was only a light drizzle but that was deceptive. They'd be soaked before too long if exposed on dykes without shelter.

Peter studied the dubious cover offered by the ramshackle straw roof. Then he let his eyes rove over his cousins' outfits, ill-suited to withstand prolonged foul weather.

"There might be better shelter ahead somewhere," he said pensively. "Or nothing for miles. We'd probably best catch our rest here, keep the fire burning, and take turns staying awake in case there's another patrol. I'll take the first watch, Andries the second, Liselotte the third."

Andries saw his own relief mirrored on Liselotte's face. Warmed by the fire, with a full belly, he cared little for what the next day might bring as long as he could rest now. With a contented sigh, he rolled himself into his blanket and was soon fast asleep.

12. The Fall of Steynbergen

STEYNBERGEN ~ DUCHY OF BRABANT ~ 1622

Andries woke to the distant sound of deep rumbling, somewhat like rolls of thunder, but with a regimented regularity he couldn't place. Rubbing his eyes as he sat up, he established that it was daytime and that it had stopped raining, although the wind still chased lead-coloured clouds low over the flatlands.

Yawning, he joined Liselotte and Peter who had walked to the road and were looking at the southern horizon with sombre faces.

"Cannon fire," Peter explained to Andries. "From the direction of Bergen-op-Zoom."

"Then the city hasn't fallen," Liselotte said. "They're resisting."

"It might be thunder?" Andries suggested. "Maybe there's a storm drifting in down there."

Peter shook his head. "I know cannon fire when I hear it. My guess is that Spinola is laying siege to Bergen-op-Zoom."

"So, we're in the middle of a war," Andries said despondently.

"Not quite," Peter corrected him. "We're on the edge of one. Best be on our way. The faster we reach Zeeland the better."

The distant rumbles continued, though more sporadically than the fast-paced opening salvos of the siege.

The three Haelens met the first refugees before too long. Common folk pushing or pulling carts laden with belongings, frail elders, and weeping toddlers. All were headed in the opposite direction, northeast toward Zevenbergen and Hollands Deep. Some were submerged in misery, others looked warily at Andries and Peter's array of guns.

"There'll be more of them," Peter predicted.

"No horses to pull their carts." Liselotte observed. "Nor any livestock."

"They'll have met soldiers then," Peter said. "Armies have to eat and are always short of horses to ride. Dutch soldiers I suspect. The Spaniards would have been more forceful in confiscating mounts and livestock, more like as not to slaughter the owners and help themselves to the..."

He stalled, glancing at Liselotte.

"Girls and women," she completed his sentence.

There was bitterness in her tone that Andries couldn't understand. Perhaps this was one reason why women weren't suitable for warfare. They were fussy about things that happened naturally during wartime. Besides, he would protect his sister from any harm, as he had told her often enough.

The clouds still formed a single mass but moved slower.

Far to the south, they could make out a dozen rising columns of dark smoke.

"Farmsteads," Peter said. "War is ugly business."

"Those poor people," Liselotte spoke softly.

Andries refrained from comment. As far as he had been able to tell, the refugees were all farmers and labourers. He hadn't seen any of the fashions that would have denoted important people, proper burghers from the merchant classes. He knew Liselotte was of a different mind regarding commoners, but she'd always had a soft spot.

"We'd best try and buy some food before there's none to be had," Peter decided.

They stopped off at the first farm they saw, a small one some way from the road. House and main barn shared a sloping thatched roof that had the shape of an upturned boat hull.

There was some commotion on the farmyard when they were spotted. A welcome committee was hurriedly assembled: A weather-beaten mountain of a man holding an antiquated blunderbuss, flanked by two stout youths clutching pitchforks. A woman and a young girl observed from an open door.

"*Donder op[21]!*" The farmer thundered. "Be gone or I'll shoot."

Andries eyed the ancient gun in his hands. The farmer's eyes suggested nervousness as he took in the muskets and pistols Andries and Peter were armed with.

Andries tentatively brought a hand to one of his pistols, but his cousin reached out to stop him.

"We mean you no harm," Peter told the farmer. "We come in peace."

The farmer grunted his disbelief. The two young men at his side increased their grip on the pitchforks, their faces conveying resigned determination.

Liselotte broke the tension, stepping away from Andries and Peter to move closer to the womenfolk at the farmhouse door.

---

[21] Literally 'Thunder off', used as 'Fuck off'.

A welcome committee was hurriedly assembled

"A good morning to you," she said brightly. "I'm Liselotte."

The girl's eyes widened with uncertainty, but the woman mumbled her own name in reply, seemingly embarrassed to be reminded of normal behaviour.

"And your name?" Liselotte asked, giving the girl an encouraging warm smile.

"Bettie," the girl said shyly, daring a small smile back.

"A pleasure to meet you." Liselotte said. "We've been travelling for a while and have nothing left to eat. We came to ask if you could perchance spare—"

"That might be, *Lieffie*[22]. But it's you and everybody else." The woman pointed at the refugees on the nearby road. "It's been busier than a carnival fair this morning."

The farmer added his voice. "Half the world seems to be making their way to our door claiming hunger and hardship. We're good Christian folk, but we'd have nothing left for ourselves if we started feeding all that's come by so far."

"And likely to come yet." Peter nodded his understanding. "As they run from the Spaniard, aye, indeed."

He patted his purse so that the coins inside chinked promisingly. "We can pay. We're after some bread, cheese, perhaps some dried sausages or ham. Just to keep us going for another day or so."

The farmer lowered his gun, and the youths relaxed their grips on the pitchforks. The farmer eyed Peter's orange sash. "Do you serve in the prince's army?"

"Nay, I'm an *Oranjevaarder*," Peter said proudly.

Oranjevaarders[23] had replaced the Sea Beggars. They were more organised and disciplined and had taken the war against Spain to the Americas and Asia. They ensured naval dominance in home waters and occasionally lent England a helping hand against the common foe.

The term covered every Dutch sailor with a deck below his feet and a sail over his head. Even the steersmen of a cattle barge were expected to flock to the orange banner when it was raised. This meant Peter's claim was vague. It could mean a warship, but just as easily any of the many smaller auxiliary craft pressed into temporary national service.

---

[22] Term of endearment, used like the English 'my dear', or modern usage of 'sweetheart' / 'luv'.

[23] Literally: Orange Seafarers. Figuratively: In the service of the Prince of Orange at sea.

Nonetheless, the farmer and the youths were clearly awed. Andries's chest swelled up when he realised that he and Peter were following in *Opa* Adrian's footsteps. They were heroes of the Republic, to be sure.

"*Ja*," Andries said. "We're *Oranjevaarders*."

The farmer's wife wasn't as easily impressed. "If you're an *Oranjevaarder*, where's your ship?"

Peter pointed west. "Flushing. We're on our way to Zeeland."

The farmer studied Peter's outfit. He nodded his acceptance of this explanation. "We can sell you some food."

Liselotte was invited into the farmhouse by the farmer's wife, to select and pack the foodstuffs.

Andries broadened his shoulders to feel less puny in the presence of the strong farm lads, who easily exceeded him in height and broadness of chest. Then he mimicked Peter and scanned the southern horizon.

"You'd best hurry, Seigneur," the farmer pointed at the distant columns of ominous smoke. "Damned Dons are swarming out over the countryside now."

It seemed to Andries that the columns of smoke had increased in number, but he wasn't entirely sure. Getting away from the Spanish army as far as possible, however, sounded like wise advice.

"They're far more active than I anticipated," Peter admitted. "How about your family?"

The farmer spat on the ground. "We've been told to rely on the garrisons in Oudenbosch and Steynbergen. Fine theory for fancy regents in faraway offices, but in real life Steynbergen is toothless."

"Oh," Peter said. "How so? There's a garrison, isn't there?"

"They got soldiers," the farmer confirmed. "But no cannon. Bloody women."

"Women?" Peter asked.

"Steynbergen was offered cannon and cannoneers," the farmer explained. "But the town's women refused to have them. Them was worried it would be viewed in bad light by the Dons and invite the Spanish Fury. Steynbergen is like as not to surrender at the first sight of a Spaniard. The garrison know it, so I suspect they'll leg it if they have any sense. Everyone remembers what happened to Haarlem's garrison."

Andries nodded. After Haarlem had been starved into surrender, every single soldier had been hanged, beheaded, or bound with rope and thrown into the Spaerne River. Two thousand men had been executed in a single day.

Peter looked concerned.

Andries surged with righteous anger at the cowardly inhabitants of Steynbergen. They sounded bereft of patriotism, not willing to die in glorious defence of the Republic.

"Bah," Andries said, and spat on the ground like the farmer had. "Women. I'd show them Dons a thing or two."

The farmer ignored him, but Peter cast a sideways glance at his cousin, raising an eyebrow. The two youths were amused, one of them grinned and the other sniggered. Andries felt his cheeks flush.

He was saved by Liselotte's return. She said cheerful goodbyes to the woman and girl, and then beamed at Peter, as she held open a sack filled with bread, cheese, onions, and a smoked ham.

Peter and the farmer reached an agreement over the price.

"We're truly grateful." Peter told the farmer. He counted the coins into the man's large and gnarled hand. "All considered, it might be wiser for you to evacuate?"

"And go where?" The farmer asked. "Become a beggar by the roadside, like them other poor sods? My family have farmed this land for generations. We'll stay."

Peter nodded. "I wish you good fortune, God willing."

"God willing," the farmer agreed.

"Peter," Liselotte suggested. "We could leave them a pistol?"

Andries shook his head, his hands protectively reaching for his snaphance pistols. Liselotte had gone mad. They were finely crafted and expensive.

And had belonged to Father.

Peter considered the farmer's ancient gun. Nodding, he removed one of the pistols from his baldric and held it out to the farmer. "Andries, leave one of your pistols behind. Along with some powder and shot."

"What? Nay! I need them."

"You'll still have a pistol and musket left. As will I. We've got to get you a sea officer's sword in Flushing anyway, so we'll get you another pistol then."

"But…but…" Andries stammered, surging with outrage at the unfairness of it. He shot Liselotte an angry look.

"They mean to show the Spaniards a thing or two," Peter said. "Isn't that what you wanted, Midshipman? The least we can do is give them a fighting chance."

"For the Republic," Liselotte added.

Andries reluctantly surrendered one of his pistols.

The farmer's demeanour changed entirely as he showered Peter and Andries with clumsy but earnest praises, also insisting on returning the coins. The two youths eyed the guns appreciatively and the farmer's wife brought her hands to her heart, uttering a heartfelt. "God bless you!"

The Haelens left the farm, walking back to the main road that had grown busier with evacuees in their short absence.

Andries couldn't keep his unhappiness from surfacing in his demeanour and kicked at pebbles on the road.

"A sea officer's sword, Andries," Liselotte said cheerfully. "You'll look dashing, I'm sure."

Andries gave her a vexed look. He knew she was trying to cheer him up, but he'd still have both Father's pistols if she'd just kept her mouth shut.

Like a respectable girl ought to.

"Should have given them your crossbow," he grumbled, although he did cheer up somewhat at the thought of a fine sword and scabbard at his hip.

Liselotte is right, I'll look very dashing.

"Come now, Cousin," Peter said, also trying to make light of the situation. "Your sister has proven herself to be a proper Frisian shieldmaiden of old. Would you deny such a Valkyrie her weapons of choice?"

Andries cast a glance at Liselotte to see her beam with pride at the pagan references from the days of yore. For a brief instant, he too felt proud of her, but the dark cloud that had enveloped his sense of well-being with some frequency over the last few days quickly displaced that.

Heresy! The Frisians worshipped false idols.

"She shouldn't be fighting," he muttered.

"What kind of *Oranjevaarder* are you?" Liselotte asked. "Everybody should be fighting."

They negotiated their way around a lopsided cart that had one wheel stuck in the soft grassy verge. It rocked to and fro as a group of men heaved at it.

"Liselotte is right," Peter said. "When we sail east, we'll be flying the Republic's colours. Duty bound to oppose Spanish or Portuguese ships when and where encountered."

"We're on land now." Andries protested, inwardly groaning at yet another understanding between his sister and cousin.

"Still obliged to oppose the Spaniards," Peter said. "You heard that farmer, they intend to stay and fight. Better they have more firepower to do so. We did our duty."

"As if they have a chance." Andries retorted; his words somewhat harsher than he intended.

"They don't," Peter said curtly, following that with a softer, "not a chance in Hell."

Liselotte turned to peer at the distant farmhouse shrinking in the fields, alarm on her face. "We should—"

"I advised them to leave," Peter said. "But you heard the man. It's their decision. If they're lucky, they'll stay out of Spinola's reach."

"I agree with Peter," Andries said quickly, pleased with the opportunity to outvote Liselotte.

They stopped. There was commotion ahead. Another heavily laden cart blocked half the dyke road. It had a broken axle and couldn't easily be shifted, causing a considerable congestion of anxious refugees behind it.

Peter indicated a smaller roadway leading north, not much more than a dirt track. "We need to get off this road. It'll become increasingly difficult to make any speed. Those people are on the verge of panic. Also, this track leads away from Steynbergen."

"We wanted to be west of Steynbergen, didn't we?" Liselotte asked.

"In a roundabout manner now." Peter grimaced. "It turns out that Steynbergen isn't as secure as I thought."

"They don't have cannons," Andries told Liselotte. "To defend themselves with."

They followed the track across the fields until they reached another dyke road, this one nearly empty of evacuees, and there turned left to resume their south-westerly course.

The dyke ran parallel to the sea, or rather an expanse of mud lands exposed by the low tide, with more distant deeper channels marked by small choppy waves. Gulls swooped by overhead, screeching plaintively. Inland, small clusters of trees and rooftops formed islands in the green spread of fields. Peter identified the largest of the clusters as Steynbergen.

Some of the more distant columns of smoke were thinning, but new ones replaced them – closer by. The bombardment at Bergen-op-

Zoom continued unabated, but Andries barely registered the low rumbling anymore.

The sea dyke road followed a broad curve, curling around the countryside surrounding Steynbergen. The spread of brown mudflats to one side and the flat green expanse to the other offered minimal variation that made it hard to mark progress. Passage of time was marked by the incoming tide as the sea crept over the edges of the mud banks.

They stopped long enough to cut some slices of bread and cheese for a hurried meal, casting worried glances at the multiplying columns of smoke on the southern horizon. So far, they had managed to stay on the edge of war, but it was advancing steadily.

War caught up with them not long after their meal break.

It started with fresh columns of dark smoke. This time the columns were behind them, to the northeast, the direction from which they had come. They stopped, turned, and stared.

Those farmers.

Andries glanced at Liselotte who had turned pale.

He searched for words to console his sister, but then, without warning, the rumbling from Bergen-op-Zoom was completely drowned out by new bursts of artillery fire. Much closer by, the mighty thunderclaps assaulting Andries's eardrums.

"Tarnation!" Peter cursed. He drew out his spyglass as he looked in the direction that spewed flame, shot, smoke, and uproar.

Steynbergen.

Even bereft of a spyglass, Andries could make out low banks of murky smoke drifting away behind the cluster of trees and rooftops. The implication hit him. "Steynbergen has no cannon."

"That means Spaniards at their gates," Peter said, training his spyglass on the town.

"Shooting guns at folk that can't shoot back!" Liselotte frowned. "Why would they do that?"

"I'd guess it's to intimidate the defenders into a quick surrender," Peter answered. "Those are light field pieces firing, not heavy siege guns. I can't see troops on this side of Steynbergen, so they're concentrated on the other side. More likely an advance column. A large army intending a serious siege would be digging in all around the town. There are many folk leaving by a gate on this side."

The guns roared again.

Peter added darkly. "At least half of them soldiers. That farmer was right, the garrison is running."

139

He folded his spyglass and tucked it away. For a moment, he looked at an absolute loss.

Facing the twins with an earnest expression, Peter said, "I owe you my apologies. I had not foreseen this. We shouldn't have come this way. I'm truly sorry."

"You were right about the flood of refugees," Liselotte said. "All heading to Hollands Deep it seems. A great mass of people."

She shuddered.

Andries recalled the panicked congestion behind the cart with the broken axle. He tried to imagine what it would be like if Spanish soldiers showed up and attacked such a nervous crowd. He concluded with the satisfying image of himself storming out of the terrified mob with axe and pistol in hand to drive the Dons off. It was too bad he didn't have that officer's sword yet.

Peter nodded at Liselotte's words but didn't seem convinced. He scanned the horizon behind them, darkened by the smoke pouring from burning farmhouses. "We can't head back. Our best option is to push on as fast as we can. I know you're both tired, I certainly am, but we need to stay ahead of the folk fleeing Steynbergen...and any Spaniards that may be hot on their heels."

Andries nodded. They were short on options. They resumed their journey, at a quicker pace and in silence as they marched into the war.

13. To Hell and Back

STEYNBERGEN ~ DUCHY OF BRABANT ~1622

The clouds had darkened with foul promise. They shed localised rain that traversed sea and fields in dark and hazy funnels, occasionally crossing one of the columns of smoke. In contrast, the sky was tearing gaps in the darkness to let brilliant displays of sunshine cascade down in golden celebration.

Liselotte stared at a bright rainbow that appeared over the rising sea. There were more rainbows forming broad curves over the ravaged land.

Life had become as surreal as the contradictory horizon that managed to be both ominous and joyous at the same time.

War.

She'd thought of it plenty since the ceasefire had ended.

The Republic was awash with patriotic pamphlets. Plenty had circulated in and around Oysterhout. They were designed to provoke moral outrage. Graphic illustrations accompanied by lurid descriptions of the Spanish Fury.

The images had burned themselves into Liselotte's memory.

Inhabitants of Zutphen, stripped naked and hung upside down from tree branches to freeze to death in icy winter weather.

The burghers of Naarden, herded unarmed into their large church, followed by bloodthirsty Spanish soldiers with drawn swords and loaded guns.

The citizens of Antwerp, who had discovered that allegiance to the King of Spain hadn't spared them from being burned alive in their homes or raped on the streets by the King's men.

The young women of Oudewater led out of their burning city like trophies, with ropes and halters around their necks, weeping for the slain that were left behind, lifeless on the streets.

Everywhere, good protestant folk condemned to a fiery death for reading the wrong bible or humming the wrong hymn. Tied to rows of stakes, hands clasped in prayer and eyes piously raised to the heavens as flames consumed them.

Bodies outstretched on racks and wheels, sawn in half, or swinging from gallows. Hacked off heads and limbs. Dutch folk toyed with, rent asunder, buried alive, violated, and destroyed.

The creators of the pamphlets hadn't spared their readers a single gory and sensational detail.

It was one of the things Andries didn't like talking about. He always ended attempts to broach the subject with a confident assurance that, unlike Liselotte, he wasn't scared and would protect her from any harm.

Liselotte's friends talked of little else on the occasions she managed to sneak away to the fields. Earnest discussions about preferable ways to die when the Spaniards came had sown seeds of anticipated horrors. Raped, buried alive, burned at the stake, drowned, strangled by hemp, pierced by steel...the terrible possibilities had seemed endless.

Yet...

...far away, distant somehow, surreal. It was something that happened elsewhere to other people and couldn't possibly shatter the peace in Oysterhout.

Now, here, exposed on the broad curve of the sea dyke that marked the edge of Brabant, it was rapidly becoming all too real.

Liselotte couldn't help but think of Bettie. Earlier that day, with her gown so dishevelled that Liselotte had looked more like a beggar than a young lady, the farmer's wife had assumed her visitor was a servant and shared her low social status. They had chatted amiably in the kitchen, unimpeded by social conventions. Liselotte had fast become friends with the young girl as well.

Her memory supplied images of their faces – Bettie's shy smile – and the broken bodies displayed by the pamphlets. Liselotte didn't doubt that one of the newer columns of smoke to their north hailed from Bettie's farm.

Where was the girl now? What had happened to the family when the soldiers came?

Please, let it have been quick and painless for Bettie.

Liselotte's hand patted her haversack, feeling for the familiar shape of her crossbow and the less familiar yet assuring presence of Eyang. She wondered if she would have the courage to turn Eyang on herself if they were captured by Spaniards, once again weighing up the sin of such an end against surrendering herself to the rough hands of merciless soldiers.

The new pace set by Peter was relentless, making the initial walk from Oysterhout to Zevenbergen seem like an easy amble. However, the bombardment of Steynbergen formed a continuous reminder of what was at stake. The urgency of the moment overcame Liselotte's fatigue, as well as the agony of her shoulders.

There are worse things.

For a while, she became acutely aware of their surroundings, alert to the slightest sensory input.

Birds. There were birds everywhere. Wading over the mudflats. Soaring over the dykes. Feeding and nesting in the reeds that grew in the ditches that separated fields. Floating by on canals in stately splendour or jester-like squabbling. Gliding high above, sharp eyes scanning the fields below. Circling over Steynbergen in an ever-growing, dark...

Ravens! Crows!

War.

Bettie and her family.

The Spanish Fury.

The thoughts swirled round and round. A dire sense of foreboding made itself at home within the entirety of Liselotte's being. Intrusive. Unwanted. Tenacious.

The road and sea dyke parted ways, both curving out in opposite directions. Peter examined the narrow track that ran along the departing sea dyke. It was half overgrown with grass and rich in puddles. "No point in twisting our ankles. We'll follow the road for speed."

That brought them down to the level of the fields. It was something of a relief that the view was more limited here, the smaller world somehow less threatening. The sunlight that fell through gaps in the ceiling of clouds mellowed, taking on warmer tones as the Haelens walked into a long summer's evening that was marked by the rumbling of artillery near and far.

Liselotte's earlier hyper awareness of her surroundings dulled. Fatigue set in. It hadn't yet lessened her stride; she was still able to keep up with Andries and Peter. Her leg muscles and back hurt, but that pain had become a vague presence rather than a pressing concern, as if she'd pushed through a barrier where such things mattered less.

Her mind though, was sapped of energy, as if all was required to feed that forced automatic motion of her legs.

After some time, they reached a forest. There was a crossroads at its centre and...things that Liselotte couldn't immediately comprehend.

It took Peter's loud "By God's gonads!" to shake Liselotte out of her stupor.

Her cousin had come to an abrupt halt. She nearly stumbled into him. Swerving around him, Liselotte came to a halt as her eyes struggled to make sense of the bloody scene.

Three carts, one large, two small. Overturned. Their contents scattered on the road, boxes broken open, torn sacks spilling bedding and clothing.

There were lifeless bodies everywhere. Scattered around the cart, mostly clothed men, hacked or shot down. They had been armed with clubs and pitchforks but that hadn't done them any good. Liselotte only saw two dead soldiers, and they wore the Republic's orange sashes. No swarthy, plumed, and moustachioed Spaniards.

Hanging in clusters from the branches of two large oaks...

...Liselotte gasped...

...women and children. Dangled upside down from rope bound around their feet. Bereft of clothing. Their faces frozen in anguished terror. Their bodies sticky with drying blood and gore. Criss-crossed by untold blade cuts...

...Andries collapsed onto his knees, bent over, and retched...

...and on a broad bed of moss on the other side of the crossroads, four young women lay spread-eagled, their open thighs a sticky mess of blood and semen. Their throats cut...

...Peter stared with horror and seemed frozen to the spot.

Liselotte thought she could discern recognition in his eyes.

He's seen these...he's seen it before.

Flies buzzed around the bodies.

Liselotte faintly registered that the artillery fire at Steynbergen had stopped but was more immediately concerned with voices around the forest-lined corner of the southbound road. Then more such voices from the road ahead.

Loud, boisterous, confident. Competing in volume of jest, insult, and raucous laughter. Voices that swaggered like soldiers. Approaching the bloodied crossroads.

"Andries," Liselotte hissed at her brother. "Get up! On your feet!"

Andries groaned a protest but slowly scrambled up.

"Peter." Liselotte tugged her cousin's sleeve.

Peter had a faraway look in his eyes, like he was elsewhere altogether.

"Peter!" Liselotte shook his arm.

His eyes refocused. "It's Lontor all over again," he mumbled. Noticing that Liselotte didn't understand, he added "Wandan", which clarified nothing.

Liselotte noted a fifth extension of the crossroads, a narrow dirt path half concealed by the foliage through which it tunnelled, angling westward from the larger northbound road.

"Andries, that way!" Taking hold of Peter's arm, Liselotte pulled him toward the path. "Peter, we have to go. There are soldiers coming."

"Soldiers!" Peter snapped out of his daze and followed Andries and Liselotte down the path.

They stopped when they were hidden from sight, to assess the situation by ear.

The two groups of loud men met and mixed at the crossroads, but their banter didn't suggest any alarm at the scenes of slaughter. Nor was there an attempt to depart, explained by the loud mocking of absent comrades who were still expected to arrive.

In Dutch.

Peter motioned the twins to follow him farther down the path, at a steady run.

Those soldiers spoke Dutch! But they weren't surprised by the bloodshed. Did they...?

After endless minutes, just as they were all starting to gasp for breath, Peter stopped them again.

He whispered, "they were expecting more, perhaps from other directions." He nodded at the path ahead. "Load your weapons, quick as you can."

Liselotte and Andries nodded and set to work, as did Peter. Liselotte belted her quiver around her waist and attached Eyang to her belt. She drew the crossbow string back. She didn't dare place a bolt yet. It was too easy to accidentally trigger the crossbow, but she held the bolt ready in her other hand.

They resumed their way down the path, no longer running, but striding fast.

The initial fright of the near escape was countered by the reassuring weight of Liselotte's crossbow in her hands. At least she wasn't helpless. The sheer terror of the massacre lingered, her mind replaying the tableaus arranged by hellish design. Gruesome details surfaced that made Liselotte swallow sobs.

How could anyone be so monstrous?

They came to a small clearing that harboured a simple thatched cottage and some rickety outbuildings. The homestead appeared deserted, other than the motionless bodies of a man and woman by the front door. They were silver-haired, wrinkled by life's troubles, and bloodied by death.

Peter motioned the twins to slow down, and approached the cottage cautiously, musket levelled.

A scream sounded behind the cottage, then another, followed by angry shouts.

A blonde farm girl – a year or two younger than Liselotte – appeared from behind the cottage. She ran frantically, fear on her face. A breast-plated and helmeted man, swearing loudly, dashed after the girl and grabbed one of her braids. He dragged the girl out of sight to the sound of her screams. Neither of the two had spotted the Haelens.

"Liselotte! Nay!" Peter hissed, but he was already too late.

She raced towards the back of the cottage. Peter's boots pounded after her. Andries came in motion as well.

They stormed around the corner of the cottage to come to an abrupt halt, taking in the scene. There were two soldiers wearing orange sashes, a dozen steps from each other. One held a struggling boy with dark curly hair, about twelve or thirteen years old. The lad was desperate to reach the other soldier, who clutched the girl they had seen. The man ripped at her clothing.

Liselotte placed her bolt and aimed. She hesitated for a fraction of a second. This wasn't a hare or a deer she was aiming at, but a living, breathing man.

The brute succeeded in ripping the girl's top open, laughing at her terror. "The little bitch got itty-bitty titties!"

No, a monster.

"Hey!" the other man spotted the newcomers. "What the—"

Liselotte released her bolt. It sped toward the monstrous man groping the girl's budding chest. The bolt pierced his throat, throwing him backwards, croaking and clutching at the missile embedded in his throat. The girl scrambled away from him, clutching at her torn clothing.

The other man pulled out a pistol, aiming at the Haelens. He had an arm folded around the curly-haired boy's head to restrain him. The lad bit down on the man's hand hard. The soldier roared with anger, and delayed firing his gun until he had shoved the boy away.

That was all the time Peter needed. He surged forward, sword in hand, and skewered the soldier with the blade, holding his hand against the man's mouth to stop his screams as he sank down.

The lad had hit the ground with a loud thud.

"Jasper!" the girl exclaimed. She rushed to his side, throwing her arms around him.

The two looked fearfully at the newcomers. Liselotte clawed back her crossbow string, Peter wiped his bloody sword on the grass, and Andries stared at the children intently with levelled musket in his hands.

"Good folk," Liselotte said. "We're on the same side."

What side though? These dead bastards wear orange sashes.

Having established that there was no immediate further danger, Peter turned to Andries. "Help me drag the bodies into the undergrowth."

Liselotte kept her focus on the children. "Are you hurt? Can you get up?"

The two shook their heads and scrambled to their feet.

"Jasper, right?" Liselotte asked the boy, before looking at the girl. "I'm Liselotte."

The lass was older than Bettie but Liselotte connected the two nonetheless. She was grimly satisfied that at least she'd been able to save this farm girl from brutish soldiers.

"Katja, Miss," the girl said softly. "I live here with my grandpar..."

Her voice trailed off as she looked at the cottage. She let out a sob.

She knows.

Peter emerged from the undergrowth, followed by Andries. "Well, they won't be found instantly, in case their friends come looking for them."

He had retrieved the crossbow bolt, wiped it clean on the grass, and handed it to Liselotte.

"Peter," Liselotte said. "Were they Dutch soldiers? Who did all this?"

"*Ja*, they were Dutch," Jasper said bitterly. He spoke with a distinct Flemish accent.

"If they ran from Steynbergen, they mutinied." Peter said. "Deserters on a rampage have no allegiance other than to their own evil urges. We must assume they're operating in the same gang as the men at the crossroads. We can't stay here."

He looked at Jasper and Katja. "We have to move on, we can't stay to protect you. Do you have a safe place to hide?"

Katja shook her head, her lower lip trembling. Jasper paled. They clutched each other tightly.

"We're not leaving them behind," Liselotte decided.

"Liselotte!" Andries protested.

The two looked fearfully at the newcomers.

"We're not leaving children in the hands of these monsters." Liselotte said stubbornly. "You saw what they did at the crossroads."

Andries looked at Peter, who sighed.

"It appears, Cousin," Peter said. "That we're not leaving the children behind."

"I'm not a child," Jasper told them. "I'm a soldier."

Peter looked around him. "The next question is: Where to go? None of the roads will be safe. And the forest isn't endless, there won't be any cover out in the fields."

"Seigneur." Katja looked at Peter hesitantly. "My *opa* has...had...a fishing boat."

"A boat?" Peter brightened.

"A yawl, Seigneur. Just an old one."

"Does it float?"

"*Ja.*"

"Excellent!"

"Peter," Liselotte urged. "I can hear voices coming our way."

Her cousin nodded at Katja. "Lead the way."

Katja dashed down a narrow path beyond one of the outbuildings. The others followed her.

14. Tholen Ho!

ON THE EENDRAGT RIVER ~ BETWEEN BRABANT AND ZEELAND ~ 1622

The old yawl was dilapidated, its bottom boards covered by a layer of water. Andries didn't reckon it looked safe, but Peter was satisfied.

"It'll do," he said.

The yawl was moored to a rickety jetty that was nearly wholly hidden by clusters of reeds. There were no trees here, but the reeds grew high enough to restrict the view entirely. They rustled in the wind in a chorus of whispers.

In the distance, Andries could hear the bawdy presence of deserters at the small cottage, still the tune of belligerent audacity to suggest they were in good cheer.

Andries recalled the morbid sights at the crossroads. He shuddered. They had taken their time with the women and children, as if finding enjoyment in their grisly handiwork.

"Andries," Peter ordered. "To the bow, have your axe at the ready to chop the mooring line. Liselotte, same at the stern. Eyang should suffice. On my command, savvy?"

"*Ja.*"

They climbed aboard. Andries wrinkled his nose at the strong smell of fish. Liselotte deposited her pack on the dry hatch amidships with an audible sigh of relief.

"How about us?" Katja asked fearfully.

"Either of you ever sailed a boat before?" Peter asked.

"*Ja*, I have." Jasper answered. "This one as well."

"Good lad," Peter said. "Can you manage the tiller?"

"Aye-aye, Skipper," Jasper straightened his back.

Peter turned to Katja, pointing at a pail by the bow. "Can you start bailing?"

"*Ja*, Seigneur."

Jasper helped Katja scramble onto the boat. Peter retrieved a long pole that was secured to the mast. He took position amidships, both hands on one end of the pole, shoving the other end into the water.

There were shouts of alarm from the cottage.

They found the bodies!

"Now! Cut the mooring lines!" Peter commanded in a low voice.

The lines came loose, their severed ends splashing into the water. Peter heaved at the pole and pushed the yawl away from the jetty.

"Andries, Liselotte. Stay low down by the gunwales. Keep your weapons trained on the jetty. Fire at will if anyone shows. Shoot to kill. Jasper, to larboard."

It sounded as if the deserters at the cottage were spreading out in various directions, looking for whomever had killed their comrades.

Peter began to heave at the pole. His face was tense with the effort as he pushed the boat towards a gap between the reeds, gathering modest speed.

The girl who Liselotte had insisted on bringing was bailing water. Her torn shift hung down low when she bent down to scoop up another pail. Having already stared when they had been back at the cottage, Andries knew there wasn't a great deal to look at, but he eyed the small fleshy nubs on her chest with fascination.

When she rose again, she caught his eye and frowned.

Andries quickly looked away, at the jetty that was rapidly receding from sight.

Fire at will.

He patted the stock of his musket. He was an *Oranjevaarder* now, ordered by his skipper to fire at will. He was a sailing soldier. Proper heroes deserved better than the disapproval Liselotte's stray had just shown.

Who does she think she is? Living in that ramshackle hut. We should have left them behind.

The jetty was lost from view, the distant voices fading. All around them was nothing but a forest of reeds that parted reluctantly for the yawl, or briefly receded somewhat to form narrow waterways.

They couldn't see anything else, other than the broken sky above. The clear patches of sky glowed a deep red, the edges of the dark clouds lit up in amber. The clouds, though their dark underbellies were still menacing, were breaking up and drifting apart.

Liselotte's stray still bailed, but she was tiring and her pace was slowing.

Andries wondered if he ought to instruct her to work at it harder. It was the sort of thing he imagined an officer-in-training should be telling the crew. It would also remind the girl as to the difference in their stations. That would be as satisfying as the stolen glimpses offered by her ravaged top.

Peter spoke in a low voice, "open water ahead."

The reeds were thinning, the channels of water broadening until they formed a whole. Away from the shelter of the reeds, white-capped edges of choppy waves were bright in the gathering dusk.

"We'll hit a sea channel," Peter told Jasper. "Set course to larboard. I'll hoist the main. We'll be running before the wind."

"Aye-aye, Skipper," Jasper answered.

Peter stopped poling the yawl, lifting the dripping pole aboard.

"Andries, help me." He started to undo the bindings that wrapped the yawl's mainsail to the boom.

Andries relinquished his position – and view – at the bow with reluctance. Aiming his musket at imaginary enemies and sneaking glances that stirred his loins was more to his liking.

He stepped past the mast to the boom and looked at the incomprehensible knot with which the nearest binding had been fastened. It seemed complex and the dying twilight was of no help.

"Like this," Liselotte joined him, and helpfully reached out to the knot.

"I can do it." Andries shooed her hands away.

Liselotte shrugged and took to the next binding. Andries was still fumbling with his first knot when she started on her third, much to his chagrin.

Peter did a quick round, tugging at rigging, peering up the mast, and judging their distance from the choppy waters – before deciding they were ready to hoist the main sail.

"Help me heave, Andries."

Andries took hold of the rope behind Peter and was surprised by the weight of the sail as the yard slowly slid up the mast, pulling up the canvas spread.

"Too slow," Peter muttered.

Liselotte and the girl took hold of the rope behind Andries and added to the effort.

"When the sail catches the wind," Peter warned. "The halyard is going to want to jump out of our hands. Brace yourselves."

He took the brunt of it when the sail, three-quarters of the way up, came alive, booming as it filled with wind.

The yawl responded immediately, jerking forwards, deck tilting at an angle. Andries struggled to keep his balance as the halyard tore at his hands.

"Ease her up a bit," Peter told Jasper.

"Aye-aye," Jasper adjusted the tiller so that the deck angled back and the increase of their speed declined some.

"Good work, keep her steady," Peter called out. "We're nearly there crew. Heave! Heave!"

They pulled the yard into its topmost position.

Peter deftly secured the halyard to one of the cleats at the bottom of the mast.

He rose and turned to find all four children staring at him expectantly.

Peter noted that Jasper had taken hold of the mainsheet to control the boom and gave the boy an approving nod. "Pleased to have you aboard, Sailor."

Jasper beamed.

Peter turned to Katja, earning himself a smile when he said, "This yawl of yours is quite splendid indeed. Bethanks from the bottom of my heart."

Facing his cousins, Peter said, with evident relief in his voice, "through the eye of a needle, cousins. That was a close call."

"They were Dutchmen!" Liselotte fumed. "At the crossroads and the cottage."

"Like the Dutchmen who ravaged the Flanders coast all those years." Jasper said.

"Why, you!" Andries glared at the Flemish boy angrily.

"Now, now, Andries," Peter raised an open hand. "The north contributed to a fair share of atrocities."

"They were just doing to the Dons what the Dons did to us," Andries protested.

"That's what Admiral Lumey said," Peter responded. "But personally, I doubt murdering monks and nuns contributed to a cause that claimed to be righteous and just."

Andries shrugged.

"Or killing innocent folk in fishing villages," Jasper added. "Who were Flemings, not Spanish."

Andries gave him a hard stare.

Liselotte changed the subject, addressing Peter, "There's still cannon fire from Bergen-op-Zoom. A lot less, but still now, at night?"

She looked around at the rapidly darkening sky.

"Keep the defenders on their toes," Peter explained. "Deprive them of a night's sleep."

Andries reckoned that worked both ways, wouldn't besiegers hear the same thunderclaps? He couldn't imagine anyone sleeping through such a racket.

Liselotte wasn't done sharing her observations yet. "We're sailing towards the cannon fire, aren't we?"

"Alas, but there's nothing else for it." Peter acknowledged. He pointed at the open water behind the stern.

"If I recall my Zeeland charts correctly, we're at the mouth of the Eendragt, the Skelde river arm that separates Brabant from the isle of Tholen. Going north to the Slaeck would entail sailing head to wind. If I had half-a-dozen *Oranjevaarders* on board, I'd have no hesitation repeatedly tacking – even in the dark. But as it is, we're a bit short on sailors."

"We can learn," Liselotte promised.

"*I* can learn," Andries corrected her quickly, to remind her that he was a midshipman now. Liselotte was better off learning how to instruct servants and should start practising on her two strays.

Peter nodded. "I have no doubt the two of you can. But these aren't the circumstances for learning. It's heavy work that requires quick reflexes. I don't know about you two, but I'm utterly exhausted. Twould make a dangerous chore and the Slaeck is open sea to boot. It can get rough out there and this is an old boat, the hull is flimsy."

Three cannons barked in the distance, one after the other.

Peter pointed at the shores to either side of them. One was formed by a sea dyke that hid all land behind it, the other marked by the forest of reeds. "We're between Brabant and Zeeland now. The wind and tide are opportune for sailing down the Eendragt." He nodded at the water beyond the bow. "Yonder lies the city of Tholen. It's heavily fortified and has a large garrison. We'll be safe there. A few hours away at most. Pray the wind blows steady."

"Seigneur," Katja said. "There's a jib."

"Ah," Peter replied. "But who'll—"

"We worked the jib sail before, Skipper," Jasper said. "When Katja's *opa* took us out on the water."

"Have you now?" Peter asked. "It's dark though."

"We can do it," Jasper said confidently.

"Very well, I'll take the tiller. You two hoist and man the jib."

Peter seated himself next to Jasper, taking over the tiller and mainsheet. Jasper and Katja walked to the mast to retrieve the jib sail from a compartment. Liselotte went to help, leaving the afterdeck – as was appropriate – to the ship's officers.

Andries took place on the nearest thwart, his musket back in his hands.

"That Jasper is quite a find," Peter said thoughtfully, keeping his voice low.

Andries disagreed. "I think he's a Papist."

"If he's from Flanders he's likely to be a Catholic," Peter acknowledged. "But I subscribe to William of Orange's vision of a Republic that is free for all without such distinctions. I'd muster that boy in an instant were he willing. Like a fish takes to water, I wonder where he learned his ropes."

Andries recalled his useless fumbling at the binding. "I'm sorry I don't—"

"You'll learn. Your knots for one…"

Andries looked down in silence.

"There'll be a lot to take in, Andries. Things to pay attention to. And on board, I'll be the skipper, not your cousin. You'll need to fend for yourself if you want to fare well. If we weren't trying to outrun Spinola and Dutch mutineers, I'd start teaching you to sail right here and now on this yawl."

Andries took in the small ramshackle boat.

"Isn't your ship much bigger?"

Peter chuckled. "Aye, a little bit. But you start learning in these smaller boats before you can handle a proper ship."

The moon appeared, revealed by a departing cloud. It cast a pale shimmer over the Eendragt.

The three at the bow succeeded in hoisting the jib. The triangular sail added to their speed. Jasper and Katja settled down at the larboard gunwale, clutching on to the jib sheet to control the jib. Liselotte found the pail and started scooping out what was left of the water sloshing over the bottom boards.

Andries stared at his cousin in awe. Seated on the tiller bench, lit by the moon, tiller in one hand, mainsheet in the other, Peter looked supremely confident and in his element, every inch the *Oranjevaarder*.

Andries was cheered by Peter's palpable elation at being back on the water, deck below his boots, wind in his sails, and a lively tiller at hand.

The speed with which the yawl pushed through the water provided a sense of freedom and relief that they were leaving the day's earlier horrors behind.

We made it!

"So, what's the plan now?" Andries asked.

"Find an inn in Tholen. It's late, but we should be able to find one in the sea quarter." Peter yawned. "Get a good night's rest. With a lie-in tomorrow, I should think. Then on to Flushing. We'll book passage on a billander, howker, or flyboat. There's lively traffic between the islands. I daren't risk the open sea with the state this yawl is in. Besides, it belongs to Katja and we don't yet know what she means to do."

"Well, if they're safe in Tholen…" Andries suggested hopefully. He wasn't happy with the praises the curly-headed Flemish boy was getting, and still resented the accusation in the girl's eyes earlier.

"I'll offer Jasper a chance to sail east with us," Peter said. "He's made of the right stuff. You two will have to make your peace, do you understand, Andries? It helps to have allies on board, it really does. This is a good opportunity to start making friends."

Andries nodded reluctantly.

Ally, maybe. If I must. But friends with a Papist? Never.

"As for Katja…I suspect Liselotte will have a thing or two to say about the girl."

Andries shrugged. Peter was in charge. There was no need to consult Liselotte about everything.

Recalling comments he had heard Father make, Andries paraphrased these to Peter. "She'll befriend anyone, without reservation. There were no young ladies her age in Oysterhout, other than farm children. Rotterdam should be a good reminder for her as to appropriate behaviour and acceptable companions."

Peter answered after some thought, "She's like your mother in that, Andries. It stood Aunt Saskia in good stead. Do remember that she married the son of a Dutch pirate and English smuggler. Don't look down on common people. I've learned to trust them with my life. And their lives in my hands. It is a strength of unity that will carry a crew through the heart of the worst storm."

Liselotte made her way to the stern, clearly curious. She set down her pail. "That's about as much water as I can bail out."

"Bethanks," Peter acknowledged. "We were talking about the rest of our journey."

"To be honest, Skipper," Liselotte said. "I could use some sleep."

"Sleeping is top of the list," Peter promised. "On feather mattresses in Tholen with fluffy pillows and warm blankets."

Andries thought he could hear his tired bones growl with appreciation.

"Then on to Flushing. My ship is nearly ready. I've given it some thought, and I suspect it'll be cheaper to buy most of the required supplies for our journey East in Rotterdam. More so because my father will refer me to honest traders. So, we'll take you there ourselves,

Liselotte. I'd like to see my father and sister again before Andries and I depart."

As per usual, Liselotte had her questions ready. "Have you seen him often? Your father I mean, since you left Rotterdam?"

"Not since that meeting in his office many years ago," Peter said. "But a friend of mine persuaded me to make amends, so I started corresponding with him four years ago."

He paused. "My friend was right. My father is pleased we're in touch again. Every letter ends with an invitation to visit. You'll be welcome there, Liselotte."

"He burnt your papers," she answered, confounding Andries who didn't understand what she meant.

"That was between him and me," Peter assured her. "He'll view you in your own right. As daughter of Simon Haelen and Saskia van der Krooswyck. His family. Not the stubborn comrade-in-arms of his prodigal son."

Liselotte laughed. Andries offered an unconvincing smile, unhappy with the camaraderie between the two.

I fought just as well.

"But don't tell him about the poaching," Peter advised. "I don't care much for social conventions myself but I think I'm an exception in the family."

"I won't," Liselotte said glumly. "How about Katja and Jasper?"

"That is something to decide in Tholen. I'll pay for their lodgings at whatever inn will take us in this late and treat them to a hearty breakfast tomorrow. That will be a good time to discuss their future."

"Excellent," Liselotte agreed. "But we're not leaving anyone behind."

Peter sighed. "I'm an *Oranjevaarder*, not the Pied Piper of Hamelin."

Liselotte laughed.

"And now," Peter said. "Time for some food. I'm starving and there's plenty left in our provision sack for all of us."

They all bit down hungrily on portions of bread, cheese, and ham, invigorated by the food and the sense that the worst was behind them.

Andries nodded off after the meal, unable to keep his eyes open, soothed by the yawl's steady progress as it cut through the water.

He woke when Liselotte prodded him and called his name.

"We're here," Peter said.

A solitary boom sounded from the south, much closer by than the last one Andries recalled hearing.

He sat up straight on the thwart, looking around him. Peter was still at the tiller and Liselotte was taking a few steps back from Andries after poking him. Jasper clutched the jib sheet, but the girl had fallen asleep, head resting on the boy's shoulder.

They were sailing much slower than they had been before, the dying wind too lacklustre to fill their sails with any conviction. The sky was clear of clouds other than a few wispy stragglers.

The Eendragt took a broad turn, slowly revealing the outline of a small city. Its spires and rooftops, as well as a tall windmill, were resplendent in the moonlight. Closer by, imposing bastions connected by stout ramparts loomed on both sides of the river.

"They have fortifications on the Brabant side?" Andries asked.

Peter confirmed this. "The Slickenburgh, with bastions of its own and plenty cannons. This time the *Zeeuwen* want to prevent the Spaniard from marching where he pleases. The whole of the Eendragt is fortified. If Bergen-op-Zoom falls, Tholen might be next, but Spinola will find it a hard nut to crack."

"They have so many soldiers," Liselotte said.

"True," Peter agreed. "But theirs are out in open fields that can be flooded, ours are well dug in behind ramparts. Our fleets have yet to enter the fray. The Republic can bring a great deal of firepower in support of besieged coastal strongholds. The Spanish will find that the Iron Duke's 'men of butter' have become men of steel."

"Dug in like they were at Steynbergen?" Andries asked.

"I think Steynbergen's morale was an exception to the rule," Peter said. "Most places should have determined garrisons."

Andries wasn't sure. He recalled the soldiers at the Sail & Anchor complaining about Zevenbergen's poor defences, but didn't want to argue the point. It would be better to say as little as possible about his experiences in that town.

"See those masts on the city's riverfront?" Peter pointed. "That's where we'll moor. Jasper, take in the jib if you please. I'll need you at the tiller."

Liselotte went forward to support the sleeping Katja. Jasper deftly lowered the jib, gathered it in his arms and looped it around the forestay. Then he came aft to take the tiller.

"Steer for the quay," Peter instructed. "I'll drop the main. Sharp to larboard on my command."

"Aye-aye, Skipper. And come to by the quay."

Peter made to the mast, hollering: "Ahoy! Tholen Ho!"

Next to Liselotte, Katja stirred awake, yawning.

A dark helmeted shape approached the edge of the quay, his musket outlined against the moonlight.

"Who goes there?" The figure shouted.

"Good folk!" Peter called back. "Friends."

The man stepped back without answer.

"Ahoy," Peter hollered again.

"Now!" Someone on the quay shouted.

A small bell tolled in alarm. A ragged line of helmeted men appeared, muskets at the ready.

"*Klaar*[24]," the commanding voice called out. "*Richt*[25]."

"No!" Peter shouted. "Good folk! We're frien—."

"*VUUR!*[26]"

All hell burst loose as the muskets discharged in rapid succession. Flames flashed out of muzzles into the night, briefly blinding those on the yawl.

Most of the shot landed in the water, spewing up small fountains. One impacted on the edge of the gunwale at the bow, sending splinters flying. A single musket ball was right on target.

Peter cried out in pain, then crumpled onto the boards, clutching the left part of his chest.

"No!" Liselotte called out and scrambled to her feet.

A loud "Reload!" sounded on the quay.

"Tack! Ware boom!" Jasper called out as he gave the tiller a mighty wrench.

The yawl changed direction, turning sharply back to the centre of the Eendragt. Liselotte reached Peter and crouched next to him. Jasper hauled in the boom.

The main sail was bereft of wind for a moment. It flapped indecisively until the yawl turned far enough for it to find the wind again. The boom swung ponderously over the deck.

Andries ducked as it passed by before it came to an abrupt halt at Jasper's command, filling with enough of the meagre wind to lend them some speed at least.

The dark figures on the quay were reloading their muskets, preparing to unleash another volley.

Jasper coaxed what speed he could from the yawl. Katja was sobbing. Liselotte called out Peter's name without getting a response.

---

[24] Ready

[25] Aim

[26] Fire

All hell burst loose as the muskets discharged in rapid succession.

Andries despaired.
Peter was dead or dying.
All was lost.

Peter's Story
Despair & Hope

TWO WEEKS EARLIER

FLUSHING - COUNTY OF ZEELAND - 1622

Peter Haelen peered into his pewter tankard, surprised to find it empty. He looked around him, trying to make sense of the busy tavern. He saw everything through a drunken haze. Catching the eye of a pretty serving wench, Peter lifted his empty tankard. The girl nodded, evaded a laughing sailor's groping hand, and then made her way to Peter's table in a murky corner of the noisy taproom.

"Skipper?"

"...shome mow of djis..." He lifted the tankard and tossed a coin on the table.

"Haven't had enough yet?" The wench laughed. "Anything else?"

"...Cjistene...I want... Cjistjene..."

"Christine? Turn you down, did she? Broke your heart? Oh dear, that weren't very nice of Christine now, were it?" The wench shook her head, picked up the coin and empty tankard, and made to the stacked barrels in a corner.

Not being a drinking man, Peter was unused to the daze of intoxication that clouded his brain. He had been driven to the tavern by desperation, and downed tankard after tankard of ale in the hope of forgetting...just about everything.

Christine.

By all rights Peter should have been here in triumphant celebration. He was nearing the culmination of a project he had been working on since he was twelve years old. He had been mocked, scorned, and derided as a madman every step of the way. He had nearly achieved what everybody had said was impossible...he was so close now. Steel-willed determination had seen him through, but still they refused to believe, even with the evidence right in front of them. His resilience had begun to falter.

"Peter! You scoundrel! They said I'd find you here."

161

Peter looked up to see a richly dressed man of his own age standing by the table. The man had twinkling hazel eyes and a clean-shaven thin face framed by long dark curls. He was wearing salmon-coloured, brocaded knee-length breeches, a matching doublet with slashed sleeves, and a wide and elaborate lace collar. His broad-rimmed, high-domed, black hat was adorned with ostrich feathers. His footwear consisted of polished black boots. His sword was sheathed in a fine scabbard, its grip, handguard, and pommel intricately decorated. He was every inch the dandy gentleman.

Peter's mind struggled to understand the unexpected presence of an old friend in his current location...and predicament.

"Marnix?"

"I didn't believe them," Marnix said, shaking his head in disappointment. "I told them: 'Not Commodore Haelen, Peter barely touches a drop. I'll vouch for him'. That's what I said. I suppose that means you've made a fool of me."

"Fool? Marnix! Why? What!"

"The end of our friendship should be a foregone conclusion, really. But since you've made me rich, I suppose I'll have to make an exception and forgive you. Come on!"

Marnix cheerfully took hold of Peter's arm and pulled him up. Peter rose groggily, still unable to make any sense of his old friend's presence.

The wench returned with the tankard. "The skipper wanted another."

"He's had quite enough, I should think," Marnix beamed his charm at her and she giggled. "Have it yourself, or else sell it to the next drunken sailor."

He tossed her a coin that she caught deftly. "Thank you, Seigneur."

"My drink..." Peter muttered, as he watched the wench depart.

"Is waiting outside," Marnix answered.

He escorted Peter out of the tavern and marched him onto the narrow street. It was lined by a haphazard selection of low buildings in the shipbuilding quarter, just outside of Flushing's ramparts. A few passers-by glanced at the pair, but most didn't. The sight of a drunk stumbling out of a seaman's tavern was commonplace in a seaport.

Marnix directed Peter to a long and broad wooden trough filled with water for horses and oxen.

"No, wait..." Peter protested, when he perceived what destination his friend had in mind. "Marnix! I outrank you..."

"Only on the quarterdeck, Commodore. Out at sea. Not on land," Marnix said happily, and then pushed Peter forward with sufficient force to launch him into the trough.

Peter's hat went flying. The water closed around him with a cold shock. He reached for the rims of the trough and pulled himself up, gasping.

"Feeling better?" Marnix asked.

"A pox on you! I ought to have you keelhauled."

Peter drew himself out of the trough, got to his feet, retrieved his hat from the ground, and faced Marnix.

Apart from the one being soaking wet and the other bone dry, the men were different in many other ways.

Both were from Rotterdam, but Peter had been trained as an apprentice in his father's dockyards at the Geldersche Kaay, and Marnix came from an established patrician family from the Hoogstraat. He had been schooled in mathematics and handled numbers and sums with astonishing dexterity.

Marnix was a just a year older than Peter. In appearance he appeared frail and slight, but this was deceptive because Peter knew his friend to be surprisingly strong. Whereas Peter's usual mood was one of solemn and stoic introspection, Marnix's face was usually animated and he had an easy, outgoing charm.

Despite their differences, the two men were firm friends. As young boys social status had kept them apart in Rotterdam. On land, the Geldersche Kaay and Hoogstraat were worlds apart. They had met in service of the VOC. The two Rotterdammers had served together during two East Indies voyages aboard *De Blokzeyl*.

Noting with relief that the alcohol-induced fog in his brain seemed to have cleared up somewhat, Peter stopped glowering, no longer able to keep up the pretence of anger.

He grinned. "Marnix! What the Devil are you doing in Flushing?"

"Business."

"Still working for the VOC?"

"Only for a few more months. Closing down my last assignment. I've accepted a position in the West India Company."

"The West Indies!" Peter's face fell. "The fever islands."

"I shall be alright," Marnix assured him. "I'm far too interesting and important to die of a mere fever. And you, my friend, I heard you've gone and built that ship of yours."

Peter's face fell.

His friend frowned. "I would have expected something of a smile, Peter. You've talked of little else but building that bloody ship since I met you."

"They call it *The Coffin*," Peter said softly.

"*The Coffin*? Who?"

"The locals, here in Flushing. In Middelburg as well. And most of the rest of bloody Walcheren."

"Why?"

"Same reason as ever." Peter pulled a sour face. "It's different. It isn't what they know. It deviates from their precious norm."

"May the damn bastards bloody well choke on dead maggots."

Peter grinned wryly. "Spend too much time in the company of sailors, Marnix, and you start talking like them."

Marnix shrugged. "Seriously, Peter. Who cares what they think? You do your thing, that's what you've always done."

"I care only because I'm ready to launch from the dockyard, after which I can complete the masts and rigging. Ready to sail, Marnix! I don't need much of a crew for the launch, but I haven't been able to recruit a single sailor. Not even one. Plenty of unemployed seafarers in Flushing, and I've even offered double wages. But they've convinced each other my ship is ill-fated...none will set a foot on board."

"But you got local men to build it?"

"Ship's carpenters, from a firm in Domburg. I pay them well and they're not half as superstitious as sailors. But I'll need them on the land for the launch."

"Well, that won't do at all. Your ship has to sail, and it will! I might be able to help. Wait here a moment, don't go anywhere."

"Go where?" Peter asked. "I'm as good as marooned on this godforsaken island."

Marnix looked pained. "Have I ever let you down?"

"No, you haven't," Peter said softly, as he watched his friend walk towards the crossing past the tavern and then disappear down one of the side streets. "But this would take a miracle."

He felt a bit better, having had a chance to spew his bitterness. He was also pleased with Marnix's company. His friend had a quick mind, quicker wit, and an unshakable optimism, all of which had done much to sustain Peter during six long years aboard *De Blokzeyl*.

He got odd looks from passers-by, standing as he was by the trough, still dripping wet. He heard the murmurs.

"...these Hollanders bain't normal..."

"...the Indies sun baked his brains..."

"...*The Coffin's* crazy captain..."

Peter glared at them. He had hoped that upon seeing the project near completion, people would understand what a seaworthy craft she was.

Wagging tongues however, had put a stop to that. Local shipbuilders had made no secret of their resentment of the young, upstart shipbuilder from Holland who had landed in their midst. They did all they could to blacken the reputation of what they perceived to be unwelcome competition.

Flushing had been flooded with talk of ill fate, the ungodly ways of Hollanders, the crazy captain, divine retribution, and '*The Coffin*'. The only folk who defended Peter were his own ship's carpenters, but the opinions of Domburgers carried little weight in Flushing. People had retreated even further into their stubborn traditionalism and *Zeeuwen* were notorious for their headstrong character as it was.

Peter took a deep breath, not wanting to honour the secret looks and barely audible comments by rewarding them with his anger. They were not worthy of his attention. Instead, he did what he had long learned to do, swallow his fury and store all that anger somewhere deep within.

I shall not yield.

Marnix returned in the company of three large rough-looking men; weathered, bearded, and covered in tattoos depicting mermaids, anchors and other nautical images.

One of them shouted out, "Well 'pon me life, if it bain't our old skipper!"

Peter beheld them with disbelief. He shook every man by the hand, his delight clear on his face and in his voice. "Jan-Pier! Tjores! Korneel!"

They were all first-rate seamen who had sailed with him and Marnix on both *Blokzeyl* voyages.

"Lads!" Peter beamed his pleasure. "How fares it with you?"

"As well as could be, Skipper," Korneel answered.

"This fancy peacock..." Tjores indicated Marnix. "Found us in Amsterdam and hired us to escort him safely to Zeeland."

"Only to be mocked with crude insolence." Marnix complained. "You'd be flogged out at sea for mistaking me for a bird, Tjores. Seeing as to how I don't lay eggs." Marnix looked at Peter and said plaintively, "They've measured out the boundaries of landbound behaviour in specific detail."

"Must have been an interesting journey," Peter acknowledged.

"We've often talked about you, Skipper, haven't we, lads?" Jan-Pier said enthusiastically. "But we reckoned you'd be living in one of them posh houses on the Hoogstraat in Rotterdam by now, far too good for us simple seafaring folk."

"On the contrary," Peter said. "It's the seafaring folk who appear to be avoiding me. I'm trying to muster a crew, lads, but none will sail with me! I'm between the Devil and the deep blue sea."

"A skipper like you?" Korneel laughed. "I don't believe it."

"No, it's the plain truth. I've been in and out of every tavern in Flushing to recruit a crew, offering double wages even."

"Not even for double wages?" Jan-Pier asked, with disbelief in his voice.

"A new ship?" Tjores asked. "Anchored at Flushing? Which one?"

"On the dry, at the Jayakarta Dockyard. Black hull."

"*The Coffin*!" they all cried out at once.

Peter pulled a long face.

"Begging your pardon, Skipper," Tjores said. "But that's what they all call that ship. We've only been here a few hours and it's the talk of the town."

"I know, lads. No offense taken. But you all know me, won't you at least let me give you a tour around the ship?"

"Only because it's you, Skipper," Korneel conceded. "No one else could get me to set a foot on that deck. They say she's cursed."

The others expressed similar sentiments.

"Grown men wilted by old wives' gossip," Marnix commented. "How very impressive my would-be protectors are."

"She's only a few minutes away," Peter said. He led them to his dockyard with a quick step, infused by new optimism.

When they arrived and approached Peter's brainchild, Marnix said, "Well, she's delightfully morbid."

The ship was upright on rollers, her hull propped up by sturdy beams. The main parts of the three masts, as well as the lower rigging, were in place. The hull was sleek, slightly shorter than the average East Indies merchantman and not as broad, although the upper deck was wider because the hull didn't follow the traditional inward slope as it rose. It had been painted pitch black, with a broad white stripe running from stern to bow along the length of the lower deck gun ports, seven on each side. Both the forecastle and aft superstructure were much less pronounced than traditional ones and lower in height. The figurehead, an elegant, brown-skinned mermaid, her arms outspread as if in an oriental dancing pose. Above her seaweed-crowned head protruded a bowsprit that was double the normal length.

Jan-Pier whistled. "Now there's a shallow draft if I ever seen one on a ship this size."

"The bowsprit is good for poking Dons in the eye!" Korneel laughed.

"Real mermaids have got bigger boobs, begging your pardon, Skipper," Tjores commented, though he admired the figurehead nonetheless.

They went aboard. Peter grew more and more enthusiastic as he pointed out this and that. He had supervised every detail of the construction process with meticulous devotion. Not a single piece of wood, not even a single nail, had been used without his approval. All this dedication shone through in his explanations as he led them around the ship.

"Just fifty men?" Marnix asked in amazement, after his old friend cited his crewing needs.

"Just the fifty," Peter confirmed. "And she can be sailed with less if necessary. Far more space, lads, for the crew, for cargo, for fresh food. That and double wages."

"What if we're boarded?" Korneel asked.

Peter noted the 'we' with pleasure.

"They'd have to catch us first," he answered confidently. "Trust me, she's fast. She'll outsail the old *Blokzeyl* without even trying. She'll make Batavia in half the normal time."

"Quicker voyage, less men to feed, more fresh food to last them…" Jan-Pier was quick to understand the implications.

"Someone will have to scrub that mermaid every now and then." Tjores said. "I wouldn't want her getting lonely now."

"Double wages, I like the sound of that," Korneel said thoughtfully. "And for a good skipper, best I've ever sailed with." He glanced at Marnix. "We're still in your service, Seigneur."

Marnix beamed. "More useless than landlubbers, all three of you. You promised to bring me to Zeeland safely, but I distinctly recall getting a few specks of mud on my boots at Rosendael. I'm going to fire all three of you for that breach of contract. I'll pay your wages until midnight tonight."

The sailors grinned.

"I'll sign, Skipper," Korneel said.

"Add me to the muster roll." Jan-Pier nodded.

"Me too!" Tjores added.

Relief washed through Peter. Three men were a start. These three first-raters in particular, were worth their weight in gold.

"I'll sign you on as second officers," he told the men. "Korneel as boatswain. Jan-Pier as coxswain. Tjores as constable."

They seemed delighted with the promotions and implied trust.

"Another forty-seven men to go," Marnix remarked dryly.

"I need half of that to get her launched," Peter said.

Korneel took to his new role instantly. "Well, that can be done. Some of the De Zierikzee folk arrived in Middelburg yesterday. I could go there and talk some sense into them."

"Thank you, Bosun." Peter nodded. On his last voyage, he had commanded a small flotilla consisting of De Blokzeyl, Zierikzee, and Feniks. The men aboard all ships had come to know Peter's worth, and he theirs.

Encouraged, Korneel turned to Tjores and Jan-Pier. "The two of you, a round of the Flushing taverns tonight methinks, bash some heads together if need be."

Peter provided them with funds.

Korneel returned from Middelburg two days later, in the company of seven first-raters who had served on De Zierikzee, as well as Hidde Tjippema, a tall Frisian who had been the third steersman on De Feniks.

Tjores and Jan-Pier had less luck. For two nights they treated all in Flushing taverns to free ale and talked endlessly of their adventures on De Blokzeyl, as well as the qualities of their skipper. Once it became clear what ship they were recruiting for, however, their audience melted away. They only managed to rustle up three sailors, all down on their luck and in dire need of the muster bonus and a dry place to sleep off a hangover.

That made a full complement of fifteen, including officers. Not enough to launch and the three desperate recruits would need to be watched in case they tried to abscond.

Marnix visited Peter's office at the Jayakarta Dockyard to discuss the continued predicament. Peter poured them both a gin.

"To your health." Marnix raised his glass.

"Death to the Spanish."

"Sulphurous farts of the Devil that they are. So, what are you going to do about mustering a full crew?"

"I've been thinking about that. What seems to work is appealing to men who have sailed with me."

Marnix nodded his agreement.

"So, I'll ask Tjores and Jan-Pier, along with some of *De Zierikzee* lads, to tour the Republic. Rotterdam, Dordrecht, Amsterdam, Hoorn, Enkhuizen…the major ports. I'll give them money for travel and lodgings, and they can divide the ports between them. I'll ask them to look for men who sailed on *De Blokzeyl, Feniks, Zierikzee*, even *De Assemburg.*"

"That's what I would have proposed. Shouldn't take more than a few weeks. How about more first officers?"

Peter frowned. Though ship's officers tended to think of themselves as more enlightened than common seafolk, they could be just as superstitious. News travelled fast between ports; the name *'Coffin'* was likely to have spread already.

"I know you don't have any brothers," Marnix said. "But cousins or nephews, perhaps? Doesn't your sister have a son?"

"My sister's boy is just five or six years old. I haven't been back in Rotterdam since I left to muster on *De Assemburg*, but I have been corresponding with my father for a few years now, as you recommended. I had two male cousins in Rotterdam, but a plague took them. That leaves my uncle Simon's lad, Andries. He's fifteen, lives in Oysterhout, Brabant."

"We passed by Oysterhout on our journey. I should think any young lad would jump at the chance to escape that godforsaken place. It's a few days away, you could be back in a week."

Peter considered this. "I think I can trust chief carpenter Jan-Leyns Visscher to supervise work on the ship for a few days."

"Plus, he'll have Korneel and Tjippema looking over his shoulders now. Hidde was always appreciative of your improvements."

Peter nodded his agreement. "Hidde understands. And Korneel is a good man."

"I'm heading back to Middelburg tomorrow; my presence is required at Biggekercke House[27]. But I'll keep my ears and eyes open regarding any unemployed officers who might be amenable to your shipbuilding heresies. I'll write a few letters to people I know as well. You go on to Oysterhout. A short respite will do you good. View it as a well-deserved holiday, and hopefully return with an eager midshipman. Visit me in Middelburg when you return, and we'll talk some more."

Although reluctant to leave his ship, Peter recognised that his resilience was frayed. He knew from experience that a change of

---

[27] Main offices of the Zeeland VOC Chamber.

purpose and scenery was fortifying. Besides, after all the dangers he had faced on the oceans, as well as the African and Asian coasts, a short jaunt to Brabant shouldn't pose too many problems. What could possibly go wrong?

Part Two
County of Zeeland

'Twas o'er. A lurid lightning flash,
Lit up the sea and sky
Around and o'er the fated ship;
Then rose a wailing cry
From every heart within her,
Of keen anguish and despair;
But mercy was for them no more,
—it died away in the air.

(From the poem 'The Flying Dutchman' by John Boyle O'Reilly, 1867)

15. What Could Go Wrong?

ON THE EENDRAGT RIVER ~ BETWEEN BRABANT & ZEELAND ~ 1622

The expected musket volley didn't roar over the Eendragt. The yawl gained distance from the quay, but the defensive wall that separated the river from the moat around Tholen's bastions ran on for considerable distance. The sentries were pounding along the top of the wall, clearly hoping to get another shot from a better position.

Shouts of alarm sounded from the Slickenburgh redoubt on the Eendragt's Brabant shore.

Jasper, at the tiller, murmured calm reassurances at Katja who had fled to his side.

Liselotte was on her knees by Peter's prone body. Andries approached her cautiously. "Is he dead?"

Liselotte shook her head. "Still breathing. I don't know how bad the wound is."

"There's blood everywhere." Andries trembled. "What's to become of us?"

"We need to clear Tholen," Liselotte suggested.

"What's the point?" Andries's shoulders slumped.

"*Mejuffrouw*," Jasper spoke urgently. "Miss Liselotte."

Liselotte turned to face him.

"If we could hoist the jib…"

More speed.

Liselotte scrambled up. "Katja, with me. Andries, stay with Peter. Find a blanket and arrange it under his head."

"Blanket?" Andries asked, looking at his sister without comprehension.

She was already scrambling to the bow. Katja joined her there to unwrap the jib from the forestay. They stepped back to the mast and hoisted the triangular sail.

"Miss," Katja tugged at Liselotte's sleeve.

Liselotte was on her knees by Peter's prone body. Andries approached her cautiously. "Is he dead?"

Liselotte had already seen the danger. The sentries running along the defensive wall were drawing level with the yawl.

"Hold the jib sheet," Liselotte told Katja. "But stay low, keep your head below the gunwale."

Katja nodded.

Liselotte made her way to the stern.

"We're making more speed," Jasper told her. "But I wish the wind would pick up a bit."

"Can you sail away from them a bit more?" Liselotte indicated the soldiers, now pulling ahead of the yawl.

"We're as far as it's safe, *Mejuffrouw*. In case them soldiers in the Slickenburgh have muskets pointed at us as well. But we'll clear the redoubt soon."

Not soon enough.

The order to make ready sounded from the wall. *"Klaar!"*

"Everybody down!" Liselotte hunkered down. "Stay below the gunwales."

"RICHT."

Katja had already tucked herself away. Jasper understood and slid down without letting go of the tiller. Andries made himself small next to Peter.

"Stay down," Liselotte commanded.

"VUUR!"

The muskets banged.

The soldiers had aimed too high. A few holes appeared in the mainsail as the shot hurled by overhead.

"Ha!" Jasper exclaimed. "Useless *platbroecken*.[28]"

He quickly reassumed his position on the tiller bench, ascertained that they had passed the redoubt on the other side of the Eendragt, and steered the yawl closer to the Brabant shore.

They were clear of Tholen before the soldiers had a chance to reload.

Liselotte took stock. Both shores were defined by tall dykes that hid the respective hinterlands from view. There was no movement to be seen. No lights other than the bright moon, a magnificent emerging starscape above, and the city of Tholen's lights receding to their stern.

---

[28] Literally, 'flat trousers', used to indicate impotence and incompetence. 17th century Dutch.

The yawl seemed safe in Jasper's hands and Katja had control of the jib.

Andries – Liselotte swallowed her disappointment – was not dependable right now.

She looked at Peter's immobile form. She had to examine his wound as soon as possible. She looked up at the sky dubiously.

By light of the moon?

Katja guessed what Liselotte was thinking. "Miss, there's a lantern, candle, and tinderbox in the rear locker."

"Andries, could you please take the jib sheet?"

He responded constructively this time, to Liselotte's relief.

"Thank you. Katja, can you fetch the light?"

Liselotte knelt next to Peter. She reached over to drag her pack closer and undid the leather fastenings.

"We should find a physician," Andries suggested. "Jasper, where is the nearest city? Other than Tholen."

"Bergen-op-Zoom."

"Oh."

Katja joined Liselotte and started fussing about with the tinderbox. Liselotte used the time to pull a spare shift from her pack and employed Eyang to cut it into broad strips.

When the lantern was aglow, Katja held it up to provide Liselotte with some light.

Liselotte turned her attention to Peter. He had begun to twitch and utter the occasional moan, but his eyes remained shut. His left shoulder was soaked in blood.

I must stop the bleeding.

She contemplated his finely crafted doublet for a moment, but couldn't see any way to take it off normally without knowing the exact nature of the wound. She used Eyang to cut the garments open at the front and around the shoulder, and then peeled them away from Peter's injured left side.

Using some of the strips from her cut shift, Liselotte carefully dabbed at the blood on Peter's bared chest and shoulder. She was relieved to discover that the bleeding had slowed significantly.

She tried to recall all that Father had said about gunshot wounds. He hadn't encountered them often, but he had been fascinated by their treatment and was well informed on the subject.

And well equipped for the eventuality.

Liselotte's mind wandered back to that last evening in Oysterhout, when the time had come to pack. Her shoulders ached at the reminder of lugging the heavy load.

She found the entry wound. "The musket ball went in just below his collar bone."

"What does that mean?" Katja asked.

"Not any vitals then?" Andries asked, demonstrating that he had at least paid a little attention during Father's lessons.

Liselotte took a deep breath. Peter had been lucky. A fraction of an inch higher and his collarbone would have been shattered. Two thumb-lengths lower and his lung would have been pierced. "Could have been far worse, but there's still nerves and arteries to consider," she said, although the lack of fresh blood flows suggested that arterial damage was limited. Father had mentioned that shot often had a cauterising effect.

Slowly, and as carefully as she could, Liselotte turned Peter over to examine the back of his left shoulder.

"Cat's piss!" Liselotte hissed. "There's no exit wound."

"Is that bad?" Jasper asked.

Liselotte nodded. "*Ja*, that's bad."

She was surprised to hear Katja share an explanation. "That means the musket ball is still in him. The wound might rot."

Liselotte shut her eyes for a moment, taking another deep breath. It would have been better if the shot had gone clear through. Father had emphasised that it was imperative to remove shot from gun wounds as soon as possible. If wound rot set in this close to head and heart, Peter was done for.

A matter of days.

"The ball has to be extracted," she decided.

"Can we wait until daylight?" Jasper asked.

"Nay, that's hours away yet." Liselotte said. "The flesh will become inflamed and swell up, making it much harder to find the shot. We have to act fast."

"Take it out?" Jasper stared at Peter's wound. "But...how?"

"Liselotte," Andries said. "With what? That savage dagger of yours? It's complicated, you ought to know that. We haven't got the equipment. Peter was right, he failed us."

Liselotte said firmly. "Not if I can help it."

She turned to Jasper. "First things first. We need to moor the yawl and get Peter on land somewhere. The boat is too unstable and I'll need a fire."

"Not on the Brabant shore," Jasper said. "We're too close to Bergen-op-Zoom and the Spanish army. I'll get us closer to Tholen's shore."

"Please do."

"*Ja, Mejuffrouw* Liselotte. We'll have to tack again."

Katja was still staring at the gory red hole with blackened edges that disfigured Peter's shoulder.

When she glanced up uncertainly, Liselotte offered the girl a smile that she hoped was reassuring. "Our father was a physician."

Katja's mouth dropped open. "Really?"

"One of the best," Andries confirmed. "But Liselotte, I can't…"

Liselotte examined the wound again. As it was, she knew what needed to be done.

In theory, she reminded herself. She fought off a wave of fear.

What if I fail?

Shaking the angst off, she decided it was better to at least try, rather than wait for Peter to die a gruesome death.

"I can."

"You can?" Katja asked, in awe.

"Surgery is men's work." Andries snorted. "Father always said girls shouldn't—"

"Oh, just shut up, Andries." Liselotte shot him a withering look. She was as surprised as he was by her irate reaction, but Peter's life was at stake and Andries wasn't being helpful.

Her twin gave the jib sheet a few short angry jerks and settled into a sulk.

They found the location Liselotte required a short sail later. Positioned near the foot of the Tholen sea dyke was an islet, not much more than a sand bank, partially covered by grass and host to a few clumps of trees.

Jasper guided the yawl in. They lowered the sails at his instructions. Liselotte and Andries were at the bow when it scraped over the shore, jumping knee-deep into the water to haul the yawl securely onto the islet.

They got back on board. Jasper and Andries worked the anchor – a flat round stone with a rope looped through a hole in its centre – over the side. The anchor landed with a squelching thud. Jasper shortened the rope. "The tide has turned, but better to be certain the old girl isn't going nowhere on her own."

Peter was still unconscious. He was carefully lowered over a gunwale and carried to a flat patch of grass, over which Katja spread a blanket on which they laid the *Oranjevaarder's* prone body.

Liselotte then brought her heavy pack and the lantern ashore, setting them down by Peter.

She asked the others to search the small island's measly copses for firewood, and then started unpacking her backpack.

Andries was the first to return, lugging a fallen log. He cast a glance at the packages, wrappings, and bundles strewn around Liselotte.

He opened his mouth. Liselotte warmed to note his expression, the one of curious glee that had always accompanied them on the brink of an Oysterhout adventure.

It clouded over.

Andries shut his mouth, and set to the rotting log with his axe, investing anger into his blows.

Still upset.

Liselotte took a deep breath and glanced at Peter. She forced Andries's angry axe chops out of her awareness and focused on the primary task at hand. She began her preparations; grouping small bottles, lidded pots, and a crucible; laying a bar of green Amsterdam soap next to one of their smaller household's copper cauldrons; and unrolling wraps to reveal pocketed displays of the gleaming instruments that had been Father's tools of trade.

Andries stopped chopping and stared. "Those were Father's."

"And would have been the Sheriff of Breda's, or some lawyer's, if I hadn't carried them all the way from Oysterhout."

"Father left everything to me."

Now? You want to argue about this now?

Liselotte scrambled to her feet and placed one hand on her waist as she stared at her twin fiercely. With the other hand she held out one of the surgical tools that Andries was belatedly claiming ownership of.

It was a terebellum, the bullet extractor screw with its distinctive rectangular hilt, elegantly curved turning handle, and long rod with sharp screw at the end. If a ball was too tightly embedded to be otherwise removed, the terebellum's wicked point could be screwed into the projectile. Father had said that it caused agonising pain if the ball was lodged against a bone and that it was a last-resort remedy.

Liselotte dearly hoped that she wouldn't have to use the instrument, but if she had to, she would. She doubted Andries could confidently claim the same.

"You do it then," she said, thrusting the instrument at him. "With *your* terebellum."

Not unexpectedly, Andries recoiled from the surgical tool.

He looked sheepish, as if realising he'd been foolish. "Liselotte..."

She erupted in a fury. She pointed at the unrolled mats of instruments and pots and bottles. "Whatever else, this I respected Father for. You've always had much more. Can't you at least let me have the one thing that I treasure about him?"

A tear of righteous anger ran down her cheek.

She continued, "If you cared about it before, *you* would have brought it all this way. But you left it for the lawyers to auction off, didn't you? But *now* it suddenly matters to you?"

Her anger triggered renewed vexation in Andries. "You shouldn't be in charge. I should be in charge. I'm the man."

"Man?" Liselotte laughed derisively but stopped when she saw how much her laughter wounded his silly pride. She took a deep breath. "Listen, Andries, in all seriousness, if you had led when it needed to be done, I would have followed you. Into the fires of Hell. But you didn't. Not at the crossroads, or the cottage, or at Tholen. We had to act!"

"You took it away from me!" Andries exclaimed angrily.

"Andries! That's not fair."

"I'm going to find more wood." He walked away, ignoring Jasper and Katja who had returned with arms full of dead branches and kindling.

Clamping her jaws together, Liselotte inspected their growing collection of firewood. There was more than she had dared hope for.

"Jasper," she said. "I need a small fire that'll keep burning for a while, for the cauldron and crucible."

She pointed the vessels out. The boy nodded his understanding and set to work arranging the kindling.

Liselotte turned to the girl. "Katja, that cask by the tiller bench, it has drinking water in it, doesn't it?"

"*Ja,* Miss."

"Can you bring it ashore? I'll need to boil some water. We'll also need the pail."

Katja went to the yawl to fetch the cask and pail.

A roar sounded behind Liselotte.

"DAMN YOUR EYES!"

Liselotte shot around to see Peter try to prop himself up on his arms, only to bellow with pain as he put strain on his left shoulder.

179

Liselotte was by him before he fell back to the ground. She cradled his head on her lap.

"Nghhh," Peter stared at her without comprehension in his eyes.

"Calm now, Cousin," Liselotte murmured, as if to a small child. "Everything will be alright, but don't move. Hush now."

"Christine?"

"No, I'm Liselotte. Your cousin. Keep still."

There was no recognition in his eyes. He tried to struggle up again, though subsided willingly when Liselotte gently pressed him down.

His eyes widened. "Dewi!" His face expressed infinite agony. "Dewi!"

"Hush, Peter. I'm Liselotte. Keep still. You've been shot."

"Shot?" Peter squeezed his eyes shut. When he opened them again understanding dawned in them. "Liselotte?"

"And Andries," Liselotte's twin announced as he returned to the small beach.

"As well as Katja and Jasper, the Pied Piper of Hamelin's catch," Liselotte added.

That brought a faint smile to Peter's lips, ere he frowned. "Shot? Tholen!"

Andries deposited the few sticks and branches he was carrying by the rest of the firewood.

"Like you said," Liselotte explained the conclusion she had come to. "Folk are on edge, what with Spinola's army across the Eendragt."

"Trigger-happy sentries, Skipper," Jasper added his agreement.

Peter discovered that he could turn his head a little without causing renewed surges of pain. He took in Liselotte's preparations with curiosity.

"So that's what you've been lugging around."

"Ja."

"My shoulder, it hurts."

"You were shot just below the collarbone. The musket ball is still in there."

Peter understood the implication. "That's not good."

He glanced at the display of surgical equipment once again. "You're going to…"

"Extract the shot, Cousin." Knowing how impossible that sounded, Liselotte decided to exaggerate her limited theoretical experience a little. "Father taught me how to."

"That's good," Peter said. He rested his head on her lap again and closed his eyes, clearly tiring fast. He murmured, "good to know that I'm in safe hands."

Liselotte smiled at that. It was the final encouragement she needed to try her hand at surgery.

16. A Surgeon's Skills

The water in the small cauldron reached boiling point. Liselotte asked Jasper to set it aside to cool some. She then brought the crucible and various bottles and pots over to the fire. When she finished making her tincture, she set the crucible on the edge of the fire so that its contents would remain warm.

Liselotte poured the contents of the cauldron into the pail, added some cold water from the cask, and slipped in some Amsterdam soap.

Rising to her feet, she assessed Peter. He was far-gone, his mind transported far away by the laudanum she'd applied.

Liselotte contemplated her gown, which had already suffered during the journey. Still, it was her only one and she didn't want to get too much blood on it. She took her last clean shift from her pack, a sleeveless one. Liselotte pulled it over her head to use as makeshift apron, after which she rolled up the sleeves of her gown.

"I'm going to need everyone's help," she told the others.

"*Ja, Mejuffrouw.*"

"*Ja,* Miss."

Liselotte looked at Andries, hoping that he wouldn't refuse his co-operation. This wasn't about the unresolved spat they'd had earlier. This was about Peter. She could see by his expression that he reached a similar conclusion. He gave her a brief nod.

"All of you have to roll up your sleeves." Liselotte indicated the steaming pail. "And give your hands and arms a good scrub."

"Wash our hands?" Katja asked, blinking at the notion.

"Why?" Jasper asked.

Andries sighed loudly. "Isn't that obvious? How uneducated are you?"

Liselotte ignored Andries, responding to Jasper instead. "I don't rightly know why. But Father always said it was of great importance. Something he'd read in a book by John of Arderne."

Father had delighted in gleefully reporting the doubt and ridicule expressed by other physicians in response to his outlandish notions regarding hygiene. It hadn't mattered to him that they had considered him a madman of sorts. Father had been certain about his views. He also had a much lower butcher's bill than all the others, so Liselotte reasoned that Father had been getting something right that others weren't.

She revelled for a moment, in her chance to be loyal to him in this at least. Of course, he'd be horrified if he knew Liselotte intended to treat a gunshot wound.

"Witch," Liselotte whispered.

Jasper and Katja crouched by the pail to wash their hands and arms.

"This is really nice soap," Katja exclaimed. "I didn't know soap could be so soft."

"Ours," Jasper added, "back home in Flanders, was like being scraped by a blunt sawblade."

Andries sniffed haughtily. "Fancy never having heard of Amsterdam soap before."

Normally Liselotte would have poked him for a remark like that, but the lingering anger between them stopped her. They were going to have to resolve that, but this wasn't the time to light temporarily shortened fuses.

After she and Andries scrubbed their hands and arms, they all approached Peter.

The *Oranjevaarder's* face was lit up from two sides. His left by the steady glow from the lantern, his right by the irregular light from the small fire. He formed an odd sight being so helpless. A far cry from the determined and worldly cousin who had confidently led them through a landscape marked by war.

Liselotte asked. "Katja, are you squeamish?"

"I don't think so, Miss."

Liselotte had assumed Katja wasn't. Liselotte's friends in Oysterhout lived close to their livestock: At hand when the animals were mated, gave birth, and were butchered. Liselotte had seen that Katja's grandparents had kept pigs, goats, chickens, and geese. Katja wasn't all that different from Liselotte's Oysterhout friends, likely to be familiar with the sight of blood.

Nonetheless, it was better to ask. It wouldn't do to have anyone faint right on top of Peter.

"Do you think you could help me? Hold some things for me?"

"*Ja,* Miss. I'll do that for you."

Liselotte eyed her brother and Jasper. Andries was larger and stronger, but best placed where he could look away from the operation.

"Peter might struggle," she said. "I need you to hold him down. Andries, his right shoulder and arm. Jasper, his left arm."

The boys acknowledged her instructions solemnly, awed by the moment.

Liselotte crouched down by Peter's left side. She indicated that Katja should take place between Liselotte and Jasper, the girl's knee by Peter's head.

Liselotte inspected the laid-out items to make sure everything she needed was in reach. She ran through a mental checklist, hoping she hadn't forgotten anything.

"Hold him down firmly," she told the boys. She handed Katja a small pewter tray. "Please hold this up for me. And with your other hand, hold the lantern close by."

Liselotte used a small pincer and a tiny, blunted spoon-like scraper to clear the wound's opening of scraps of fabric that had been torn loose upon the musket ball's impact. She was pleased to note that Peter's shirt was made of silk. It was a wealthy man's preferred garment for fighting, because it was known that the torn strands of other materials were quicker to cause inflammation.

Liselotte deposited the scraps of silk she removed from Peter's torn flesh on the pewter tray.

She selected a scissors-like dilator, which she inserted gently into the wound to press it open to allow deeper access for her pincer. Peter groaned a few times but gave no other reaction as Liselotte removed the remaining strands of silk that she could see, far fewer inside. There was no tell-tale gleam of metal that she could spot.

The shot is lodged deeper in the wound.

That could spell more trouble. If Peter had been lucky, the ball would have followed a straight trajectory, but it wasn't unknown for shot to take a meandering course through struck bodies, randomly twisting and turning.

After setting dilator, pincers, and scraper aside, Liselotte laid a pile of her makeshift bandages next to Katja. Next, she selected a seven-inch long steel needle, with a sturdy looped string threaded through its head and a small bulbous end instead of a sharp point. She held the probe up to inspect it in the available light. It gleamed. Father had been forever cleaning and polishing his instruments.

Liselotte told Katja, "I need to know how deep the bullet went. If I damage an artery the wound will bleed. If it's a heavy flow, staunch it with the fabric. Press it down tight."

Katja nodded. "I can do that."

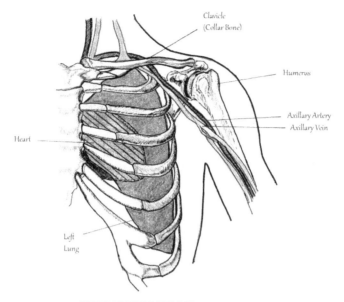

FRONT OF LEFT SHOULDER

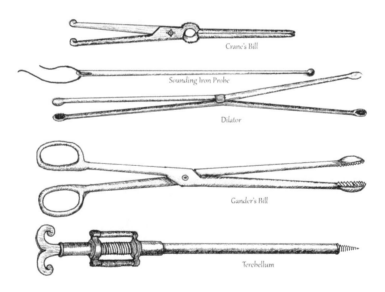

Crane's Bill

Sounding Iron Probe

Dilator

Gander's Bill

Terebellum

Liselotte inspected the laid-out items to make sure everything she needed was in reach

185

"Good," Liselotte said, dearly hoping that it wouldn't be necessary.

She brought the probe down toward the wound but stopped when she noticed her hand was trembling.

Liselotte took a deep breath.

You know how to do this.

Her mind's eye summoned images of illustrations and diagrams in the books she had devoured. Father's voice elaborated on the subject, this intrusion of his presence in her thoughts one she welcomed.

She briefly touched the keris in her belt with her free hand.

Eyang. Queen of the South Sea.

Her hand steadied. "Hold him down tight."

She inserted the probe into the wound and then ever so carefully drove it forward, eliciting a few moans from Peter, but nothing more. The laudanum was at work.

Anaesthesia was frowned upon by old-fashioned physicians. Father had condemned some of his colleagues for being barbarian fools because of their churchly notions that pain cleansed sin and was therefore a positive development in preparing a patient for the afterlife; the more pain here, the less time spent in Hell.

"Fairy tales! Patients can go to Hell in their own time," Father had been fond of saying. "But not during the hours of my attendance."

His piety hadn't been without limit. There had been a solid border where medicine was concerned.

And at the thresholds of taverns.

Liselotte bent down low, to bring her ear closer to the probe as she continued to slide it into the wound.

She sighed a breath of relief when she could hear a soft metallic chink and felt pressure countering the probe's forward motion.

"It hasn't gone in that deep," she reported, and gently pulled the probe out. "Straight trajectory. Just a little beyond sight."

Katja and Jasper stared in fascination; Andries's face was turned away to the fire.

Liselotte selected the dilator and a long thin rod with a round spatula at the end, in the shape of a goose bill.

"The bullet scoop is the least intrusive," Liselotte said, finding that it calmed her to explain what she was doing.

The tool worked best on simple gunshot wounds though. The projectile that had buried itself in Peter's shoulder proved elusive to the bullet scoop's limited grip.

Liselotte withdrew the scoop from the wound reluctantly, having hoped the least complex choice would work.

Pondering her next options – the terebellum shimmering in the light as if to remind Liselotte of its dreaded existence – her eyes wandered over the alternatives.

Crowe's bill. Swan's beak. Drake's bill. Crane's bill. Parrot's bill.

She selected the crane's bill, which was slender with curved, serrated ends. Its circumference exceeded that of the probe and scoop she had used before.

Liselotte looked at Katja, to confirm that the girl was ready to staunch any sudden flows of blood, then at the boys to ensure their recognition of the situation. Andries had stopped looking away. His eyes were firmly fixed on his twin. There was no animosity in them, just wonder. Jasper's eyes contained puppy-like trust.

They understood why she sought eye contact and nodded their understanding, strengthening their grip on Peter.

Using the dilator to press the wound open again, Liselotte inserted the crane's bill. This time Peter began to struggle weakly.

"Hold him tight, good, just like that," Liselotte said, without taking her eyes off her handiwork with the crane's bill. "Katja, fold an arm around his head, so he doesn't bash it on the ground."

Peter continued to fret, despite the strong sedative qualities of the laudanum.

Liselotte gritted her teeth, ignoring the pain she was creating for her cousin. He faced far worse if the bullet didn't come out and wound rot set in. He would watch himself mummify, dying inch by inch. He would smell himself decomposing. He would likely go fully insane before death.

She took in a sharp breath when she heard the tiny chink of metal. She managed to work the serrated ends around the musket ball, but their grip slipped when she tried to withdraw. "Cat's piss."

Liselotte tried again. This time she got a firm hold. Resisting the urge to extract the ball as quickly as she could, she gradually drew it out of the wound, pausing whenever Peter jerked in pain at the passage. Andries, Jasper, and Katja – mercifully – kept him pinned down.

When it was done, Liselotte held the crane's bill up to regard the extracted ball with relief and triumph. "Got it!"

She scanned Peter's wound, some blood had welled up, but there was no tell-tale flow indicating newly ruptured arteries.

She examined the ball more closely, wiping it clear of blood. It was intact; no slivers of it remained in Peter.

She put the instrument and offending article aside. The starlit night had a chill to it, but to her surprise Liselotte noted that her forehead was sheathed in perspiration. She used one of the shift strips to mop it off and turned her attention back to her patient.

A few more strands of silk had been dragged up the wound with the crane's bill's upward movement. Liselotte repeated her earlier action of carefully removing all visible offending items.

"Katja, can you pass me the crucible, that small pot? Wind a strip around it, it might still be hot"

"What's in it, Miss?" Katja asked, as she passed the wrapped crucible to Liselotte.

Having just worked with all the ingredients, listing them was easy. "Oil of roses, turpentine, myrrh, powdered frankincense, gum resin, and saffron."

Katja nodded, as if she was familiar with the materials.

"Do you think you can handle the dilator?" Liselotte held up the instrument.

"*Ja*, I watched you do it, Miss."

"Hold him down tight again," Liselotte told the boys.

Katja demonstrated that she had paid close attention to the earlier use of the dilator, when she used it to press open the wound.

Peter twitched, then struggled feebly when Liselotte poured the hot tincture into the wound.

"Keep it open," she instructed Katja.

Liselotte had left a little tincture in the crucible. She inserted a small strip of fabric into it and ran it around the crucible until it had absorbed most of the remaining content. She rolled it up until it was shaped like one of the lozenge arrowheads of her crossbow bolts.

"We'll insert a 'tent'," she explained to Katja. "To keep the wound open. Father always said it was best to keep a gunshot wound open to allow further treatment. Right, it's in. You can close the dilator now, slowly. Well done."

Liselotte got the boys to position Peter into a sitting position and hold him there so that she could bandage the operated shoulder. They eased him back on the blanket when she was done.

"Katja, could you put some new water in the cauldron and heat it up on the fire?"

After Katja proceeded to do that, Liselotte mopped her brow again and sighed a breath of relief. She had done it. Without making things worse. Here, in one of the oddest surgeries she could imagine, on a forlorn strip of Zeeland by lantern and moonlight. A great deal of tension ebbed away.

She looked at her brother. He, more than the others, had enough knowledge to comprehend what Liselotte had just done.

If it had been him, Father would have been proud as a peacock.

She could barely believe it when she saw the understanding in his eyes.

He nodded. "It was well done. But what do we do next? Where do we go?"

Liselotte had no idea. Her entire focus had been on the urgent treatment required by Peter. She was drained of energy and bereft of ideas. All she wanted to do was sleep, but that probably wouldn't be wise at this location. They'd be in full view of folk on both sides of the Eendragt come daylight.

She returned the question, "What do *you* think we should do, Andries?"

He wants to lead. Let him lead. I just want to sleep.

A cannon at Bergen-op-Zoom added its low boom to the discussion.

Andries shrugged uncertainly. "We can't stay here. But we need to keep clear of Spinola's army."

"If we follow Tholen's coast," Jasper suggested. "We'd be heading away from Brabant. We could cross the Oosterskelde to South Beveland. Head for Yerseke, or Goes?"

Liselotte recalled their reception at Tholen. A repetition of that was less likely if they sailed into a harbour at daytime, but still...

"Peter has a ship and dockyard at Flushing," she said. "We could try to make our way there? He'll know people, surely. He mentioned a friend he has there."

"What's the name of this friend?" Andries asked.

"I don't know, but we can find out once we're in Flushing. Someone there should be able to tell us which dockyard is owned by Peter Haelen."

Jasper said. "Walcheren is the next island over after South Beveland."

He looked at the yawl. The tide was receding and had left the boat sitting much higher on the dry, with just the stern still in touch with the Eendragt. "We'll have to drag the yawl into the water." He looked at Andries. "Could you..."

"I'll help you," Andries said.

Liselotte asked Katja to bring the cauldron over so that she could clean the instruments she had used, another one of Father's stipulations.

The boys lengthened the anchor rope.

When Liselotte was done, she started carefully packing things away.

"Miss," Katja asked nervously, throwing a glance at the boys who were heaving at the yawl.

"*Ja*, Katja?"

"There's a proper needle in there..." Katja indicated one of the instrument rolls. "Isn't there?"

"I've got some special needles and thread for stitching broken skin together, but with gun wounds it's better to leave them open."

"It's not the Seigneur's wound, it's just that..." Katja looked nervous, fidgeting with her torn top.

Liselotte recalled that the damaged had been quite revealing at times. "Would you like me to mend your top?"

Katja nodded. "Your brother...he stares."

Liselotte's face clouded, her mouth set tight and grim. Katja was just a child and under Liselotte's protection. What was Andries thinking?

Men stare, it's what they do.

"I'm sorry," Katja said. "I shouldn't have—"

"It's not you who needs to apologise," Liselotte said quickly. "Come here, we'll fix it."

She retrieved what she needed and made quick repairs.

"Not my best needle-work," Liselotte told Katja. "But it'll keep you covered."

She was touched by Katja's grateful smile.

"Huzzah!" The boys shouted simultaneously, in celebration of getting the yawl afloat.

"I have to pack," Liselotte said, clutching on to the very last remnants of her depleted energy.

"I'll help," Katja said, and proved adept at it.

The boys climbed aboard and busied themselves on the yawl, before making their way back to the fire as Liselotte and Katja finished fastening the straps on the backpack.

"We spread a blanket out on the hatch," Jasper said. "And rolled the other one up into a pillow. Is that one..." He nodded at the blanket occupied by Peter. "Much bloodied? There are a few blankets in one of the lockers, but they'll smell funny."

"Some blood, at one corner," Liselotte answered. "We can reverse it. At worst it'll stain his boot. Keep the other blankets for us?"

"I'll bring the lantern over to the yawl, so we have light there," Jasper said. "Are you done with the pail, *Mejuffrouw*?"

Liselotte nodded. Jasper picked up pail and lantern.

"I'll take your pack," Andries offered.

It was his way to make amends, blithely unaware that he had just raised her ire again by Katja's hesitant revelation.

Not now. He'll flare up and we haven't time for this.

"Thank you, brother," she said, at the very least pleased that she wouldn't be reminded of the backpack's weight at this moment when fatigue numbed her entire being.

Andries made to pick the backpack up, but, misjudging its weight, almost fumbled. Lifting the pack onto his back with a grunt, he looked at Liselotte with wide eyes.

She gave an apologetic shrug. "I should have warned you it was a bit heavy."

"A bit heavy?" Andries asked. He shook his head and walked to the yawl, grumbling, "Atlas shrugged."

Liselotte was pleased that he was experiencing the weight of the pack for himself. She was also relieved that the vexation of the earlier flare-up seemed to be fading. Still, part of the smouldering anger within her would not be doused just because he had remembered how to behave normally.

Jasper returned with the pail, filled with water from the Eendragt, and set it by the fire.

"I'll come back for the blanket and then douse the fire," he said. "When we've got the skipper aboard."

That had to be done with care. It took all four of them to transfer Peter to the yawl and onto the hatch. Jasper dashed back to put out the fire and returned with the blanket and empty pail.

Liselotte and Katja helped the boys retrieve the heavy stone anchor, after which Andries and Jasper pushed the yawl away from the shore, clambering on board with wet boots.

After helping Andries and Jasper hoist the mainsail, she sank down next to the hatch.

She checked on Peter who was still lost in opiate dreams, and then laid her arm along the hatch's edge and rested her head on her arm.

Her eyelids sagged, then dropped. Sailing into the unknown as they were, towards the occasional thunder of cannons that marked an active battlefield, was likely to bring new dangers. She would have to trust that Andries and Jasper would cope. Liselotte had given this day all that she could possibly offer, and succumbed to sleep.

17. Remorse & Amends

ON THE EENDRAGT RIVER ~ COUNTY OF ZEELAND ~ 1622

The wind was enough to prevent the yawl's mainsail from slackening altogether. The outgoing tide, however, lent them extra speed as it bore the boat down the Eendragt to the Oosterskelde.

Andries was perched on the rear thwart, musket in hands as he scanned the dark shorelines to either side of them. Liselotte had fallen fast asleep by the hatch on which Peter lay. Andries's cousin was breathing, but otherwise still. Katja had cuddled up to Jasper on the tiller bench. She was dozing off, but the Flemish boy seemed wide awake and alert to his task.

Andries looked at Liselotte's sleeping form with new respect, guilt, and some residue of his earlier anger.

He'd had no idea just how heavy the pack was that she had somehow carried all the way from Oysterhout. In a moment of self-honesty, he admitted to himself that he would have likely abandoned such a burden, had he even thought of bringing it in the first place.

The earlier disagreement with his twin had stunned him. They liked to bicker about opposing points of views but those were well-trodden paths. They rarely had a real argument. Liselotte had never before displayed the fierce scorn that had overwhelmed Andries back on the islet.

Some of her words stung deep. Especially the ones about not taking charge – which were, he conceded, on the mark. He'd been swept up in events, feeling helpless to control them where, somehow, his sister had taken the lead.

Watching the operation had triggered his self-reflective contrition. He had tried not to watch, because it made him feel queasy, but his eyes had been drawn back to the procedures again and again.

He had recalled enough of his lessons to recognise the enormity of what Liselotte had been doing. Other than once stitching his knee when Andries had taken a fall in the forest, his sister had no practical experience. Just whatever knowledge she had gleaned from attending some of Father's lessons, the Oysterhout cunning woman she had sometimes met in the woods on her own, and those books she was always nosing in.

Father would have been livid. Women couldn't practice medicine other than midwifery – and a physician's daughter should never stoop so low as to become a midwife. Her God-decreed place was supervising servants in a respectable household and honouring a husband of sufficient social quality. Not to harbour unnatural thoughts.

Andries had heard it all often enough. He had assumed it to be the truth, but that assumption had become meaningless weighed up against the sight of Liselotte carrying out a series of complex procedures as if she had been doing it her whole life.

That is where she really belongs.

Father wanted me to learn that.

But it was Liselotte.

She saved Peter.

Guilt had swept through him, guilt at failing Father's expectations and guilt at causing disappointment.

He had resolved to do better and had been trying since.

Andries focused on the dark landscape. The moon was still riding high, but its light had lost intensity, growing dimmer.

Andries repeated the conclusions he had drawn. Other than physician, Father had also wanted Andries to become a good midshipman and officer. So did Peter and, he was sure, Liselotte. If Peter survived, that was something Andries could do. There was a lot to learn, Peter had told him, but this time Andries would apply himself to the lessons. He would make them all proud, especially his sister.

As far as the medical instruments and supplies were concerned, Andries acknowledged that Liselotte had earned them. It was too bad that Liselotte hadn't asked him for permission to take Father's things. He would have granted it gladly, and then they could have avoided the whole row.

He started to doze off, so he stood up to stretch his legs a little to keep himself awake. He yawned.

Andries took in the tiller bench as he sat down again. Katja was asleep, snuggled against Jasper. The boy held the boom sheet in a loose grip and leant on the tiller. He had propped Peter's musket at the other end of the bench, within easy reach.

Andries gave it a glance, disapproving of its appropriation without permission, but acknowledging that if they ran into trouble two muskets would serve better than one.

Jasper had a sound mind. Andries recalled Peter's advice to connect with the boy – easier now that they had shared elation at their exertions in getting the yawl afloat again, but still...

Andries remembered some snide comments he himself had made. Where to begin mending fences?

Pointing at the musket, Andries asked, more brusquely than he intended, "Do you even know how to use a doglock?"

"Of course," Jasper said. "I told you I was a soldier."

Andries chuckled. "Well, you're a good sailor, I'll give you that."

"Not as good as the skipper is," Jasper indicated Peter. "What keeps him floating? His own ship, I mean."

"My cousin is an *Oostvaarder*."

Jasper's mouth dropped open. "An *Oostvaarder*?"

Andries nodded. "Three return journeys. I'm to go along on his fourth as midshipman, on his very own ship this time."

"You are?" Jasper followed his disbelief with excited chatter. "Then you're a lucky devil, er, *Mynheer*. Congratulations. I've tried to muster as ship's boy twice now, but they said I was too young. Come back when you're sixteen. Bah."

"You want to go to the East Indies?" Andries asked with some surprise. He had always thought that the call-to-adventure was a characteristic of Hollanders, *Zeeuwen*, and Frisians. The Flemish, as far as Andries was aware, liked to eat, drink, sleep, and receive absolution for their sins.

"More than anything," Jasper confirmed. "See the world, have adventures, come back with riches. I had it all planned out."

Recalling what Peter had said about mustering Jasper, Andries told the boy, "I'll have a word on your behalf with my cousin, when he's up and about again."

"You would do that for me?" Jasper looked at Andries with wide eyes. "But *Mynheer*, I thought you…didn't like me."

Andries shrugged awkwardly. Jasper's quick wit, resourcefulness, and undoubted skills were eroding his conviction that Catholics were by definition an evil foe. This one was mildly amusing and had proven useful. Peter had ordered him to make peace at any rate. "People can change their minds about things. You've been very helpful."

Jasper nodded, as if that settled things for him. He muttered dreamily, "to sail east, to become an *Oostvaarder*."

"Where did you learn to sail?" Andries asked.

"I grew up in a small fishing village called Heys."

"And the Sea Beggars came there?"

"Before I was born. They burned the church and put an end to our fishing fleet. We were poor after that."

Katja was asleep, snuggled against Jasper.

"So, what were you doing in Brabant?"

"Spinola's men came to the Bruges area last winter, to press fishermen into service for his ships. I was taken too but made a drummer boy in the army. I told you I was a soldier."

"You're in Spinola's army?" Andries asked warily, clutching his musket a little tighter.

"Was," Jasper corrected him. "I didn't like it, so I left."

"They just let you go?"

"Oh, nay. If they catch me…" Jasper pointed in the direction of Bergen-op-Zoom. "I'll be dancing the gallows' jig in the blink of an eye."

"So how did you manage to get away?"

"I rose from the dead."

"*Wablief*?"

Jasper grinned. "It was very dramatic. There was a skirmish. I hid beneath some of the dead. Covered in blood I was, none of it mine. I waited until everyone left, and then rose, scaring the devil out of a couple of foxes and a murder of crows."

Andries laughed. "And then came north to the Republic?"

"I couldn't go back to Heys, folk would have guessed I deserted. It wasn't safe for me in Flanders. Soldiers everywhere. So, I headed north. I roamed about Zeeland and Brabant, doing odd jobs for farmers and fishermen. Ouwe Gerrit, Katja's *opa*, took a liking to me. I stayed, slept in the barn, and helped out."

He glanced at Katja's head resting on his shoulder. "And Katja is a *lieffie*. She thinks I am too."

Andries cast his eyes back on the Eendragt. He noted that the air had filled with a faint haze, shimmering eerily in the moonlight.

He yawned.

"When's the last time you slept, *Mynheer*?"

"Too long ago," Andries admitted. "We haven't been getting much in the way of sleep."

"Why not get some sleep," Jasper suggested. "I'll wake you up if we run into trouble."

Andries regarded him. Peter trusted the boy and Jasper's sailing skills seemed sound.

"How about you, Jasper?"

"I'll be all right for a few hours yet, *Mynheer*," Jasper assured him.

"Bethanks then," Andries said gratefully. "But wake me if anything happens. I may not know much about sailing yet, but I'm a good shot." He lowered himself to the bottom boards, lay down, and closed his eyes. It was uncomfortable but he drifted away almost immediately.

18. A City of Ghosts

THE DROWNED LANDS SEA ~ COUNTY OF ZEELAND ~ 1622

Andries awoke, reluctantly, to the urgency in the voices of Liselotte and Jasper as they talked.

Sitting up, rubbing his painful back, he found that the world had changed – drastically so.

A new day had begun but all Andries could discern was a thick fog all around the yawl, limiting their visibility to a few yards no matter which way he looked. The yawl's mainsail hung limp and useless, though the boat was still in motion, presumably drawn by the tide.

A cannon boomed nearby, its thunder somewhat muted by the fog.

Still too close to Bergen-op-Zoom then.

Peter was still out, Katja by his side mopping sweat off his brow.

A fever?

"I think we're on the Oosterskelde," Jasper told Andries. "But I lost sight of Tholen in the mist. It rose devilishly quick."

"And no wind." Liselotte indicated the limp mainsail.

"That's not all," Jasper said. "The tide will be turning soon and push us to the Brabant shore."

Several cannons at Bergen-op-Zoom roared in quick succession, as if to remind them what reception awaited them there.

"Our best course of action would be to make landfall before the tide turns," Jasper said. "Use the oars."

"But where?" Andries asked.

Jasper pointed at the direction the cannons had sounded from. "Well, that is to our east. If we course west on the outgoing tide while we can, we should find South Beveland. Make landfall. Wait for the tide to go out again later and catch a ride on it to sweep round South Beveland, and then see how to best cross to Walcheren. It's a big mess of sandbanks yonder way."

"Tell us what to do," Liselotte said.

Jasper asked Katja to take the tiller. He and the twins lowered the mainsail. "If the wind picks up," he explained. "It might catch us unaware. The yawl is old and a bit brittle, she won't stand much abuse."

He then asked Andries and Liselotte to take a seat on the midthwart and man the oars. He himself took place on the bow, holding the long pole ready to push against any obstacles that might loom through the thick mist.

Andries struggled with the oar at first.

"You're splashing, *Mynheer*," Jasper said. "Dig in deep."

Rowing was far harder than Andries had anticipated, and it took him a while to get used to it so he could row in sync with Liselotte.

The next cannon blasts were followed by another sound. A church bell tolled forlornly, seemingly not far to larboard. It was joined by another, farther away, and then yet more, a few closer even, until it seemed more than a dozen bells were sounding their sombre calls.

"Land!" Liselotte called out.

"We should head that way," Andries added.

"Nay," Katja shouted.

Jasper was puzzled. "We must have drifted much farther south than I thought, if those are the bells of Hulsterlant."

"They aren't in Hulsterlant," Katja called out, agitated. "We shouldn't go there."

"We need to make landfall, before the tide comes in," Andries reminded her.

"Not there, not there." Katja rose. She addressed Liselotte frantically. "Miss, it's the Drowned Lands. It's dangerous. We mustn't go to the bells. We mustn't!"

"The Drowned Lands?" Jasper turned to ask Katja. "Are you sure?"

"*Ja!*"

Jasper shivered. "Then we should avoid it."

There was a sudden thud, followed by splintering wood and an almighty jolt as the yawl shuddered to a halt. Jasper was nearly thrown off his feet. Katja staggered and fell back on the tiller bench.

Andries stared in horror at the jagged end of a tree trunk that had embedded itself in the stricken yawl, protruding between smashed strakes and two shattered ribs at the starboard bow.

Tugged by the tidal flow, the yawl's stern began to drift to starboard. The pressure of the movement caused more strakes to crack and splinter around the embedded trunk.

Jasper, having recovered his balance, took charge.

"Row backwards," he called out to Andries and Liselotte. "Give it all you got."

He placed the pole end against the partially submerged log and pushed with all his might. "We've got to get loose, or else it'll rip the whole yawl to bits."

Andries and Liselotte worked their oars. Jasper heaved and strained at the pole. Another piece of strake broke with a loud crack. Cannons thundered, and the bells tolled.

The yawl broke loose from the log, leaving a gaping hole at the waterline. Water poured in at the lower edge.

"We're sinking!" Andries cried out.

"Not yet," Jasper replied, working the jib sail loose from its stays. "Keep rowing, we want to be clear of that damned tree."

Andries and Liselotte hauled at the oars for all they were worth.

Jasper attached new lines to the jib. He called Andries and Liselotte over to help him draw the jib underneath the boat like an oversized bandage, its broader foot on the side of the devastation. They secured it as tightly as they could.

"The jib won't stop the water," Jasper said, as they surveyed their handiwork. "But it'll slow it down. I'm sorry, I didn't look for just a few seconds, and then wham!"

"It was real low in the water," Liselotte told him.

"Not your fault," Andries added.

Jasper nodded, not entirely convinced. He urged Andries and Liselotte back to the oars, and they turned the yawl to face west. Jasper alternated between keeping a lookout at the bow and bailing. Enough water had poured in to fill the bilge and then surface above the bottom boards, especially at the bow that was dragged down by the yawl's wound.

The sound of the bells died down and the guns at Bergen-op-Zoom ceased thundering for a spell. All Andries could hear was the sound of oars, his own and Liselotte's laboured breathing, and Jasper bailing. The mist appeared to be thinning a little, their circle of view expanded.

Andries hoped that straying away from the bells, indicative of an inhabited polder with villages, wouldn't cost them dearly.

We could be rowing right next to land and never see it in this fog.

What if they didn't find South Beveland, and the currents carried them out to the open sea?

If we even make it that far.

The water in the boat was rising, creeping ever closer to the stern despite Jasper's best efforts. If the yawl sank, they'd have to surrender their baggage and weapons to the sea. Even then, how could they keep an unconscious Peter from drowning? Andries and Liselotte had learned to swim, but in a small and calm forest lake. Could Jasper and Katja swim? Most people in the Republic couldn't. Many sailors refused to learn, claiming it was better to go down quick.

"Why, hello there!" Jasper announced cheerfully. "Mind your oar, *Mejuffrouw* Liselotte, as we pass."

Andries looked up to see a dilapidated rooftop – with gaps between the tiles exposing the wood framework beneath – emerging from the mist.

He did a double take, but sure enough they were rowing past a roof rising from the waters in the middle of – Andries looked around – somewhere.

Which is better than nowhere.

"There's another one." Katja pointed at a ruined roof to larboard.

"Very pleasant news." Jasper set the pail down and took hold of the pole.

"Jasper, my feet are going to get wet," Katja announced.

"Not much longer now, *meissie*[29]," Jasper promised. "I know where we are, Ouwe Gerrit took me here once."

"Where are we then?" Andries asked.

"A city of ghosts," Jasper said happily. "But all considered, I prefer phantoms to becoming fish food."

"Reymerswal!" Katja exclaimed.

"The water is about halfway to the hatch," Liselotte noted, casting a concerned look at Peter.

"I hear you," Jasper said. He placed the pole in the water, found the bottom, and pushed, increasing the yawl's forward motion.

He alternated his poling between starboard and larboard, urging Andries and Liselotte to keep rowing hard.

A tentative breeze started to break apart the mist.

"The tide is beginning to shift," Jasper said. "We're just in time."

The guns at Bergen-op-Zoom rumbled back into life – a little farther away than previously.

Ahead of them the mist was torn into separate patches that started to drift away. Some retreated past stout brick walls and watchtowers with crenelated parapets.

Andries watched, astounded, as the mist revealed the outline of a considerable city.

---

[29] Lass (*meissie* = singular *meissies* = plural)

"Ladies and gentleman," Jasper announced. "I give you Reymerswal."

"The city of ghosts," Katja added somewhat miserably.

The city was eerily still. Not a sound could be heard behind those grim walls, nor could Andries see a single living soul, not even watchmen on the battlements or watchtowers.

"Who lives here?" Andries asked.

"None that are alive," Jasper answered. "Reymerswal was deserted many years ago."

Andries noted that many of the walls and towers had started to crumble, and some of the brickwork showed long, ominous cracks.

They coursed to a breach in the walls that allowed a peek at ordered streets of brick houses with stepped or bell-shaped gables. It would have been an ordinary sight in the Lowlands, except that the sea ran straight through the breach to cover the streets and conceal the ground floors of houses from view.

It was most surreal to row a boat along a flooded main thoroughfare, countless gaping empty windows all around them, and tendrils of mist weaving sinuous patterns over submerged streets.

Jasper sang a mournful song.

One who has lost himself
Has been gifted to the mist
The bells that drowned alongside
Toll, unheard, day and night
But nobody knows the place
Where beneath the waves
They vanished without a trace.[30]

Andries felt a shiver run down his spine. "Hell's bells. Couldn't you think of something more cheerful?"

"It's about Reymerswal," Jasper said.

Closer by, it was clear that the buildings had suffered much damage from the tide surging in and out, eating away at brickwork and wood. Green slimy fronds hung limp from the walls, marking the extent of high tide. Andries saw a school of fish – startled by the yawl – turn tail and flash into a gaping doorway.

---

[30] Author's loose translation of Gerrit Achterberg's poem 'Reimerswaal', which appeared in the bundle *Limiet* (1945).

It would have been an ordinary sight in the Lowlands, except that the sea ran straight through the breach to cover the streets and conceal the ground floors of houses from view.

Here and there a building had collapsed, and they had to slow down to let Jasper use the pole to determine the extent of submerged rubble.

Rowing was increasingly hard. Room to swing the oars was much limited and the yawl had begun to list to starboard, sluggish to respond to pole and oars.

Andries's oar scraped against a building, and then again.

"Pull the oars in," Jasper said. "Then try to use them as poles, it's shallow enough now. We're nearly at the market square."

The water was getting lower, revealing ground floor windows and upper halves of doorways, menacing darkness behind them.

Andries found solid ground below when he thrust the oar down. Using the oar blade's grip on the uneven cobblestone surface of the flooded street, Andries pushed with all his might. Liselotte did likewise. With three of them poling now, the yawl managed one last stretch of water while it resembled something that had the properties of a boat.

The water on board lapped up to the edge of the hatch.

The houses that flanked them fell away, to reveal a broad city square that was faced by imposing buildings with ornate gables. Church towers reached high up; outreached fingers formed by the jagged beams that had once supported spires.

Lifeless dark windows all around eyed the incoming yawl with a mix of suspicion and accusation.

"I feel like we're being watched," Liselotte said, shivering.

"*Ja*," Andries agreed. "It's unsettling."

Half the square itself was submerged, but the other end rose from the water, the large paving stones forming a forbidding beach. The slope was dark and moist at the bottom, with seaweed spread about, but grey and drier at the top. It suggested that the submerged part of the city, besieged by tides, was slowly sinking.

Jasper announced, "*Mynheer* Midshipman, *Mejuffrouw* Liselotte, time to lay down your oars, you are mighty rowers both."

He gave one final shove with the pole, before he lifted it on board as the yawl limped toward the pavestone beach.

"*Mynheer*," Jasper said to Andries. "You and I to pull her in?"

"*Ja*, I mean aye-aye. Erm, carry on, Sailor." Andries joined Jasper at the bow.

They jumped overboard as the yawl scraped over the bottom, their boots splashing in the shallow water. The boys seized the gunwales to propel the sinking boat forward.

The yawl scraped over the stone slabs, urged on by the boys, and then came to a dead stop, refusing to budge.

Jasper and Andries strode onto the dry, to turn and look at the damage. The jibsail rig already looked worn and torn by the splintered hull's jagged edges. Water from the boat seeped out steadily.

Liselotte and Katja came to the bow.

"How bad is it?" Liselotte asked.

Jasper looked at Katja. "I'm afraid she's done for."

Katja nodded slowly.

It occurred to Andries that the yawl had been her sole possession, a link with the world she had been ripped from so abruptly.

Remembering his promise to apply himself better, Andries said, "I'm sure your *opa* would've been proud that the yawl brought us this far."

Katja looked surprised, then said, "Thank you, *Mynheer.*"

"Ouwe Gerrit would have been cackling with glee," Jasper confirmed. "And proud of you as well, Katja. Damn proud."

"I haven't done anything," Katja said softly.

"Come now," Liselotte shook her head. "Surgeon's Assistant and first-rate ship's girl."

Katja perked up a little.

Jasper addressed Liselotte. "She's lodged tight now, but will float loose when the tide comes in. She won't float for long though. The damage is beyond my ken to fix."

"Abandon ship?" Liselotte asked.

"I'm afraid so, *Mejuffrouw.* We'll never haul her up the beach high enough."

It stung Andries a little that Jasper turned to Liselotte. He should have been consulting Andries as Peter's most senior officer present.

He pushed the vexation aside. Jasper just had to get used to the reality of the situation.

They first carried all their gear off the yawl, depositing the baggage and weapons higher up. Peter was the last to be carried off board, to be placed carefully by their belongings. He showed signs of response, groans and moans, little jerks of the legs and arms.

Liselotte knelt next to him, smiled at Katja who was lugging the heavy backpack closer in case it was needed, and then inspected Peter's bandages.

Jasper ran off to explore, leaving Andries to take in the unsettling sight of all the deserted buildings peering over the artificial lagoon. Maybe the buildings weren't empty. For all he knew there could be hundreds of people huddled in the murky gloom behind the windows, all staring at the intruders.

Andries shivered.

"All right?" Liselotte came to stand next to him.

"*Ja*. But this place is spooky. How is Peter?"

"Coming out of his laudanum dreams soon. We have to find shelter."

"Can't you give him some more?"

"It'll be easier to find out how well he's healing if he comes out of it. If the pain is really bad, I'll give him some more. But Andries, I'm worried for all of us. You and I have only had short snatches of sleep, Jasper's been up all night, Katja is tired as well. We won't be any use to Peter if we drop down from exhaustion."

Andries agreed with her. "We need a place with a roof then, and a fireplace to get nice and warm."

"Away from all these lifeless spies." Liselotte indicated a row of particularly foreboding windows.

They frowned simultaneously when they perceived an odd rumbling sound from a narrow street.

"Huzzah! Huzzah!" Jasper's voice accompanied the rumbles. When he emerged onto the square, they could see he was pushing a broad rickety old wheelbarrow – with squeaking wheel – over the pavestones.

Using a spare coil of rope, the yawl's oars and the pole – chopped in half by Andries – they fashioned a crude stretcher for Peter. Jasper also rescued the lantern, pail, and other items from the yawl's lockers, including some blankets that smelled both musty and briny. After depositing their baggage in the wheelbarrow, they placed the stretcher and Peter on top of it.

Andries and Jasper lifted the wheelbarrow's handles and started pushing the considerable load. Liselotte and Katja were to either side, hands on the stretcher to steady the wheelbarrow and prevent it from toppling over.

Andries was reminded of the refugees streaming to Prinsenland.

What a sight we must make.

Abandoning the yawl to the mercy of the tide, they left the square behind and disappeared into the city of ghosts, eager to be away from the sea's surreal intrusion into Reymerswal.

19. Handmaid in the Guardhouse

REYMERSWAL ~ COUNTY OF ZEELAND ~1622

They followed the streets with a slight upward incline. This brought them to the westernmost edge of the city, to a stout gate that was flanked by two round watchtowers – crowned by the remnants of steepled roofs. Most of the wood gate had rotted away, and heaps of sand filled part of the passage that led to the grassy dunes they could see outside the city.

There was a small guardhouse next to the gate, with ramshackle but intact door, shutters, and roof, as well as a hearth in its single room. They found a pile of old rags in a chest and they used these to sweep the room out as best they could.

When Liselotte was satisfied that the worst of the sand and dust was cleared up, they laid out a blanket on the floor near the hearth and brought Peter inside.

After that they wheeled the old wheelbarrow into the guardhouse, parking it in the far corner.

Liselotte asked Andries and Jasper to scour the neighbourhood for wood that could be used to light a fire in the hearth.

"I'll need you here," Liselotte told Katja, as she began to retrieve items from the wheelbarrow.

The girls placed Liselotte's pack close to Peter and inspected the provisions bag.

"Not much food left," Liselotte said. "If we're careful it might last us until tomorrow. I could set a few snares in the dunes."

"You poach, Miss?"

Liselotte chuckled. "It's what respectable ladies do. How much water is left in the cask?"

"A little over half."

"I'll need some to clean Peter's wound, but we'll have to use it sparingly. We have to drink, and I doubt there are working wells left in the city. We'll need to make a broth as well, see if we can get some nourishment into my cousin."

Peter began to moan, and then feebly writhe about until Liselotte gently held him down.

When her cousin opened his eyes, they were unfocused. "Nay, nay."

"Hush Peter, it's alright, we're safe."

He shook his head. "We must stop them! We have to stop them."

"Stop who?" Katja asked.

"He's delirious," Liselotte said. She laid her hand on Peter's forehead to feel it glow hot beneath her touch.

"Dewi!" Peter exclaimed, before groaning, "*Tebing Yang Menjerit*."[31]

"What's he saying?" Katja asked.

"I don't know. It didn't sound Dutch. Maybe something to do with the East Indies? Peter is an *Oostvaarder*. Could you get the cauldron and crucible out of my pack? And fill the cauldron with some water already?"

"*Ja*, Miss."

Liselotte carefully unwrapped Peter's bandages. She took in a deep breath when she beheld the wound, the blackened edges almost innocuous compared to the angry red swelling at the musket ball's entry point.

Katja asked. "Is it bad?"

"I don't know," Liselotte admitted. "The fever might be a symptom of wound rot, but it might not be. Same with the red swelling."

The books had mostly agreed on the overlap between early symptoms of various possible complications. They hadn't mentioned the healer's frustration at not being able to read a patient properly.

"We need to stay put a while, to let Peter rest. And check on his wound, if we see or smell decomposition then—

"It's wound rot," Katja said. "I'm not sure...don't laugh at me, please, Miss...but country folk around Steynbergen always came to *Oma* if they couldn't afford a doctor."

Liselotte was intrigued. The books were scathing about what they called heathen quacksalvers, but she knew that countryside folk – so-called flatlanders – stubbornly relied on the services of cunning women. Father had hated the Oysterhout cunning woman, mostly because he was affronted by the notion that he faced considerable local competition from a woman. It was an assault on his dignity. He had frequently lectured the twins about the ungodliness of women stepping beyond their divinely destined role in life.

---

[31] In the context of this story: 'Cliff of Screams' in Indonesian.

Obedience. Obedience. Obedience. Amen.

Liselotte hadn't dared to visit Oysterhout's cunning woman in her cottage in the woods, although she had been tempted to. They had met though, in the forest by accident. Liselotte had been on her way back home with snared wild fowl as dawn banished the night's darkness. The cunning woman had been out because – as she explained – she liked to gather certain herbs at dawn.

"Picked midday, most be as useful as a gin-sodden drunk in bed. Some are as potent as a prince when the sun rides high, but a great many fare best at dawn."

Despite the woman's friendly smile, Liselotte had been somewhat intimidated by her piercing eyes, which seem to suggest her soul was an open book to the cunning woman. She had raised the audacity to ask a daring question. "And by moonlight?"

The kind patience had changed into instant wariness.

Herbal medicine was not, in itself, a heresy. It was dubious because it was mostly practiced by women.

And what do we know about healing? Isn't that right, Father?

Moonlight, however, potentially added magic to the mix. Sorcery was frowned upon and punished severely.

The cunning woman had stepped closer, staring at Liselotte with blazing eyes. "You be the doctor's girl? Bain't it so?"

Liselotte had nodded timidly.

"That brandy-sodden bible-thumper, what would just as lief see me tied to the stake?"

Liselotte had nodded again, unwilling to deny this highly accurate reading of Father and his opinions.

"And yet, you dare ask this question of me?"

"I'm not him," was the best Liselotte had been able to offer.

The cunning woman had laughed heartily, then beheld Liselotte again, inspecting her from top to toe. "You're a curious one, aren't you? And..." she frowned. "A healer."

Liselotte had shrugged unhappily. "I haven't healed anyone."

"Not yet. Very well. *Ja*, with some plants the strongest essence is begot when gathered in the light of a particular phase of the moon. Some like to be sung to softly, each their own tune, others like to be caressed first ere the deed is done."

The woman had run her hand along Liselotte's cheek slowly, causing goose bumps all over. Liselotte had shivered with thrilled trepidation. "Can you teach me?"

Despite the woman's friendly smile, Liselotte had been somewhat intimidated by her piercing eyes, which seem to suggest her soul was an open book to the cunning woman.

The woman had stepped back, breaking the intimate connection. "Corrupt an innocent Christian child? Win her soul for the devil? That's how 'twould be seen."

"I'm not innocent," Liselotte had insisted, having already been thrashed within an inch of her life for the mortal sin of playing tag in the garden.

The forest had rung with peals of laughter. "Oh *Lieffie*," the woman had said. "Oh *Lieffie*, if only you knew."

With that she had departed so fast it seemed she had vanished in the light morning mist. But the next time they had met, by carefully co-ordinated 'coincidence' on Liselotte's part, she had taken Liselotte on a stroll through the woods to point out plants and their characteristics. They had repeated those walks when Father had been away. A few nights before Father had returned to be met by amiable enquiries about imminent nuptials between Liselotte and Henk, his daughter had been out at night. To help dig up roots deep in the woods in exchange for knowledge about their qualities.

If Father had found out about that, Liselotte doubted she'd have regained her ability to walk at all by the time Peter had arrived.

Witch.

"Miss?"

WITCH.

"Miss?"

Liselotte shook her head, to release it from captivity by the past. "I'm sorry Katja, my mind was elsewhere."

"Never mind I said that, Miss," Katja said. "About *Oma*. Tis just a countryside thing for simple flatlanders."

Liselotte shook her head fervently, seeing Katja in a new light. If Katja's Oma had been anything like Oysterhout's cunning woman...

Recalling how adept an assistant Katja had been so far, something dawned.

"You helped your *oma*, didn't you, Katja?"

"Sometimes, Miss. We weren't doing no wrong."

"Can you teach me?"

"Teach you?"

"*Ja*, please."

"I don't ken much."

"Teach me what you know. How would your *oma* have treated wound rot?"

"Maggots."

211

"Maggots?" Liselotte had heard of the practice, but only in thunderous terms of condemnation.

"You insert them into the wound. *Oma* always said they eat the dead flesh."

Of course. When mortification occurs, to prevent it from spreading.

"We'll have to find maggots then," Liselotte decided.

"You would try that, Miss?"

"*Ja*, I would. But keep that between us."

The boys came in with a load of wood, remnants of doors and shutters, as well as bits and pieces of broken furniture.

They deposited their loads next to the hearth, before departing immediately again to return shortly, triumphantly bearing a rickety table and four mismatched chairs.

"Fit for kings," Andries pronounced, seating himself on one of the chairs. "What's for breakfast?"

"Food," Jasper said hopefully. "I've always been told food makes a pleasant ingredient for a good breakfast."

Their faces fell when Liselotte told them about her intent to ration the little that was left, but lit up again when she suggested they place snares in the dunes.

The boys left after lighting a fire – looped snares from Liselotte's pack in their hands – boasting about the enormous catch they'd haul in.

"We'll have a cornucopia to consume, if the boys are to be believed," Liselotte said, as Katja placed the cauldron on the fire.

"*Wablief*, Miss?"

"Horn of plenty."

Katja's face lit up and she rubbed her tummy. "I'd like that."

When the water had boiled and cooled sufficiently, Liselotte cleaned Peter's wound, extracting the tent in the process.

Peter was restless.

"*Lautan Tulang*[32]," he murmured, repeating it louder. "*Lautan Tulang*."

"*Lauwtan tulan*?" Katja asked.

Liselotte shrugged, found some bottles in her pack, and took them, a stirring spoon, and the crucible to the fire.

---

[32] In the context of this story, 'Ocean of Bones' in Indonesian.

"Miss?" Katja said. "When I woke for a bit, last night on the tiller bench, I heard the boys talking. Jasper wants to go to the East Indies on your cousin's ship."

"He's a bit young, I think?" Liselotte carefully added a few drops from one of her bottles to the crucible and stirred.

"Your brother said he'd put in a good word for Jasper."

"Andries did?" Liselotte was surprised; until she recalled that the two seemed to have reconciled their differences somewhere between their initial skirmishing about who-did-what-to-whom and landfall at Reymerswal.

"He did, he said he was one of your cousin's officers."

Liselotte chuckled. "Andries sometimes likes to exaggerate his own importance. Jasper knows far more about sailing a boat than my brother does. Andries still has a lot to learn."

"I wish Jasper wasn't so good at sailing though." Katja sighed wistfully.

She wiped away a tear that welled up in her eye.

"Katja?" Liselotte asked, full of concern.

"I don't want him to sail away east, Miss." Katja's lip trembled. "I'd be left all by myself. I'll be all alone."

Liselotte knew that feeling all too well. She laid a hand on Katja's shoulder. "Same for me when my brother and cousin sail off. I understand."

"You do?"

"Very much so. But I'll tell you what, Katja. You and I can stay together. That way we won't be totally alone, we'll have each other." Liselotte warmed to the idea as she spoke the words.

"We can do that?"

"Of course," Liselotte stated confidently. "If I'm to go to Rotterdam and act like a proper young lady, I'll need a handmaid and companion, won't I?"

"You'd have *me* as handmaid?" Katja asked, incredulity in her expression. "In Rotterdam!"

"More importantly, as companion. Nobody else. Unless you don't want to?"

"I do, I do!"

"Good, that's settled then."

"Miss? I'm sorry but...but..."

"What is it, Katja?"

"If I'm a handmaid, will I be able to...when Jasper returns from the East Indies...can we..." Katja turned bright red.

"Can we what?"

"We were to get married," Katja said.

"Married! Did he ask for your hand? So young?"

"Oh, nay. Of course not."

"But you've spoken about it?"

"Well, nay."

"So, you haven't actually talked about it with him? Nor he with you?"

"Nay, but I just know. And Jasper knows. And he knows I know. And he knows I know that he knows. And *Opa* and *Oma* always joked that we would."

Katja said that with such confidence and certainty that Liselotte felt a little envious.

To be so sure of something so important must be wonderful.

"Well, I'm sure that wouldn't be a problem."

"It wouldn't?" Katja's eyes lit up, then her expression changed into an inquisitive one. "Miss, what does a handmaid do, exactly?"

Liselotte considered this for a moment. "You know, I haven't got the faintest idea."

They stared at each other, and then burst out laughing.

"We'll work it out as we go along," Liselotte promised.

Having mixed and warmed the ingredients in the crucible, Liselotte and Katja lifted Peter up so that they could spoon-feed him the concoction.

"It'll help him fight the fever," Liselotte told Katja. "Next we'll heat some lye to pour into the wound."

Lowering Peter back onto his blanket, Liselotte decided she would apply some laudanum as well. She didn't want to wait until the boys returned to hold Peter down for the lye treatment. It was clear Peter's shoulder would be too painful for him to bear just yet. If he trashed around too much it would likely put a lot of strain on the wound – and spill some of her modest supply of lye.

They had completed the procedure, with Peter bandaged up again, when the boys returned.

Liselotte estimated it was noontime.

They ate a little, too tired to speak much, and then settled down for some much-needed sleep.

20. The Drowned Land of Reymerswal

REYMERSWAL ~ COUNTY OF ZEELAND ~1622

Liselotte was the first to wake. She was wholly disorientated at first, until she recalled she was in the guardhouse next to a Reymerswal city gate.

Dim daylight peeked through the cracks between the boards of the shutters and door. She hadn't slept that long then, just enough to defeat the worst of her fatigue.

Her back hurt and she was keenly aware that she hadn't had a bath since that fateful night back in Oysterhout. She was even still wearing the bloodied under shift she'd pulled over her gown as surgeon's apron. Yawning, and scratching at an itch on her head, she took in the sleeping forms of the others, smiling when she looked at Katja and recalled their pledge to stay together.

At least I won't be completely alone.

She checked on Peter. His forehead was still hot to the touch, but he was breathing calmly and seemed to be at peace.

The others woke one by one, yawning, grumbling, and stretching.

"How's Peter doing?" Andries asked sleepily.

"He'll be under for a few more hours," Liselotte said. "Which is good, because I need some fresh air. You and Jasper can keep an eye on him for me."

She looked at Katja. "Will you come along?"

Katja nodded.

"Where are you going?" Andries wanted to know. "It's not safe. One of us should come with you, with pistols and a musket."

"I'll come," Jasper offered.

Liselotte lifted the haversack that contained her crossbow, quiver, and Eyang. "This is protection enough. Besides, I intend to have a wash."

"I don't mind, *Mejuffrouw*," Jasper said cheekily. "I'll pretend you're a mermaid."

"Jasper!" Katja admonished him.

Andries shrugged. "On your own head be it."

"A clean head." Liselotte said. "Come on Katja, let's go."

They walked out of the guardhouse. Liselotte led them out through the city gate. She was pleased they didn't have to roam through abandoned streets to be assaulted by forlorn echoes from the past.

It was still a bit misty, but their range of vision was greatly expanded compared to the morning.

There wasn't much land beyond the gate, though it was the largest part of the small island on which the city's ruins rested. A series of sandy dunes stretched into the distance, hooking southward at the end. The dunes were dotted with patches of grass and low shrubs. The air seemed less oppressive away from the brooding remnants of the city. A briny breeze tugged at Liselotte's hair and frolicked with the hem of her bloodied shift.

They walked into the dunes. A wide sea-arm ran along one side of the narrow strip of land.

The Oosterskelde?

A sea inlet stretched south on the other side. Its waves lapped gently on a wide sandy beach, the high tide having spent itself and beginning to recede.

Liselotte made out the dark outlines of flat land through the haze to either side of the inlet. She guessed that the land to her right was South Beveland. To her left was the Brabant mainland with its occasional rumble of cannons at besieged Bergen-op-Zoom. The inlet itself was still shrouded in a blanket of mist.

She walked through the dunes to the sea. Strands of ginger hair spilled generously from her cotton cap. Katja's simple clothes were as dishevelled as Liselotte's. The girl had lost her cap altogether and the thick braids of her long sunny hair had long lost tightness, the original design hard to discern.

Liselotte was pleased to be out Reymerswal's decay. Away from the surreal and fearful sight of the sea flowing in and out of half-submerged streets – inhabited only by fish. It was good to breathe fresh sea air.

Stopping where dunes and broad sand beach met, Liselotte kicked off her shoes and worked off her tattered stockings. She laid her belt and haversack on the ground and then removed the makeshift apron and her gown, leaving her clad in her under shift.

"Coming?" she asked Katja.

The girl shook her head and lowered herself onto the soft flank of the dune instead. "I'll keep a look-out."

Liselotte walked to the surf, the loose sand beneath her bare feet gaining firmness. She stopped just short of where the low rolling waves tumbled onto the beach. The sand was cold and wet. She wriggled her toes, and her feet sank a little, water and sand creeping over the sides.

The water felt far colder than Liselotte would have liked. She shivered at the thought of exposing more than her feet to the sea's chill. However, her desire to wash was stronger. Taking a deep breath for courage, Liselotte broke into a run, splashing through the low choppy waves until the water rose to her thighs. There she dove headlong into the sea, completely submerging herself.

She gasped when she resurfaced – sure she would freeze to death. She washed as quickly as possible, and then ran back up the beach. Her teeth were chattering when she reached the embrace of the dry blanket Katja had thought to bring. Liselotte wrapped herself in the wool folds, which countered the chill on her wet skin.

It was good to be cleanish, even though the salty water would leave her hair stiff and unmanageable. Liselotte picked up her bloodied shift and shook it out for examination. She sighed, doubting she'd ever get the stains out.

No spare shifts left. But there are worse things. Like soldiers, Spanish or Dutch.

She shivered as she recollected the near escapes of late. It was safe for the moment, on this desolate miniature isle between the Duchy of Brabant and the many islands that made up Zeeland, but what to do next? Liselotte had no idea how to proceed, although she was keenly aware the burden of that decision now rested on her shoulders.

Andries can't and doesn't. But who am I? To make decisions for all of us? I'm just me.

A rumble of distant thunder rolled across the sea, an ominous reminder of war's proximity.

We can't stay here. The Spanish army is too close.

A sound blended in with the rumbling of the artillery and the steady low rush of the sea. The same sound they had heard that morning. It was the chime of a chapel bell, joined in by more, as well as the deeper tolls of larger church bells. Oddly enough, the tolling seemed to be coming from the sea inlet, not the land to either side of it.

If they had continued sailing towards the bells in the morning, they would have headed away from land, out onto a mist-shrouded sea in the aging yawl.

Recalling Katja's reaction in the morning mist, Liselotte looked at her young travel companion. It was a relief to note her new friend showed no sign of the panic she had displayed earlier at the sound of the bells. Instead, Katja gazed warily into the haze over the sea.

Liselotte turned her head that way to see the mist over the sea recede. It remained hazy along the Zeeland and Brabant shores to either side of the sea inlet, but looking straight over the water, Liselotte could see for miles.

It was a strange seascape. A great mass of small choppy waves as could be expected, but here and there tall rectangular silhouettes rose from the water like giant monolithic gravestones.

The sight caused a tingle to run up and down Liselotte's spine. "Church towers!"

"The Drowned Land of Reymerswal," her younger companion spoke solemnly. She pointed at one of the towers. "That was the church of the village of Duvenay. Over there, Kouwerve."

She continued her inventory, pointing at the towers. "Kreke. That big one, Nieuwkerke. There was Tolsende."

"What happened here?" Liselotte asked. "I can't see any houses. Who is ringing the bells?"

"No one is, Miss."

"No one? Is it just me? Can *you* hear them ringing?"

"I've heard 'em afore, Miss. Now as well."

"But...someone has to be ringing them..."

"Miss..." Katja hesitated. "There are no bells."

"No bells? How..."

"They took them away, to make cannon to defend Bergen-op-Zoom."

On cue, cannons rumbled menacingly from the direction of the besieged city.

Liselotte stared intently at the nearest tower. All that remained was the eroded shell of the bare brickwork. Yet a bell tolled insistently from the tower, loud and clear.

A bell that isn't there.

She folded her arms around herself and shivered.

Rung by no one.

"Katja, what happened here? To Reymerswal? The Drowned Land?"

"You *don't* know?" Katja was astonished.

"I'm not from here."

218

Oysterhout was far away, Rotterdam so far it seemed wholly out of reach. Worlds apart from Zeeland at any rate. "Please tell me."

"It's a long story, Miss."

The chiming and tolling of the bells slowed and then ceased altogether. The surf's crash and sea birds' cries seemed to mourn their passing. A long story suited Liselotte, a human voice to distract her from the loneliness of an island saddened by melancholy and whispering of long-gone glory days. Days when there had been life here, instead of desolation.

"Tell me."

Katja began to tell, hesitant at first, but soon gaining a confidence that suggested she had heard the story often enough to be able to recite it from memory, using far more complex language than Liselotte had heard her use before.

"A hundred years ago Reymerswal was the third city of Zeeland. A rich city surrounded by rich land, ruled by Adrian of Lodieke. Lord Lodiek and his wife Johanna had a son called Bartoen. They lived in Lodiek Castle, not far from the city. Over there..."

Katja pointed west, where the last of the dunes fell away to mark the end of the small island. Liselotte could see a similar but smaller ridge of dunes across a stretch of water, forming another miniature island.

Katja continued. "Bartoen was handsome to look at, with hazel eyes and brown curls. His skin was browned by the sun because he spent much of his time outdoors; hunting, swimming, wrestling, and learning his swordplay. He wore the finest clothing because his parents spoiled him. When Bartoen rode the land, folk would point as he passed and say: 'There goes our Prince'.

"One summer, when Bartoen was sixteen, he went out riding near the castle. He heard a strange and unexpected sound. It was a girl's voice and she was singing. Her voice was so beautiful that Bartoen thought an angel must have come down from Heaven. He rode his horse to the banks of the Oosterskelde to see who owned the enchanting voice.

"What he saw bewitched him. A girl his own age, up to her waist in the river, singing while she washed her hair. Her skin was white as a lily, her breasts perfectly rounded, her hair golden as if spun from sunrays, and her eyes the colour of the sea. When she saw Bartoen staring at her, she smiled and waved, inviting him to join her. Bartoen didn't hesitate. He dismounted, took off his finery, and ran into the water.

"The girl told him her name was Hille and she seemed to like Bartoen as much as he liked her. They teased, laughed, and frolicked in the water like two otter cubs at play. They went deeper into the water, but never did Hille go nearer to the shallows of the riverbank. Bartoen gave it no thought; he was smitten, drunk on her presence. When Hille told Bartoen it was time for her to go home, he begged her for a kiss."

Katja stopped telling, giggling instead.

"Go on," Liselotte urged. "What happened?"

"They did the kissing thing. Euw. Bah." Katja scrunched up her nose.

"They kissed." Liselotte sighed dreamily. Her mind's eye pictured the unlikely pair, Bartoen dark as the earth and Hille light as the sky, shyly pressing their lips together.

"Tsss..." Katja rolled her eyes, before she continued. "Bartoen was so bewitched by Hille that he couldn't bear to be parted from her. He asked her to come back to Lodiek Castle with him. Hille laughed and told Bartoen that he was sweet, but this was impossible. She didn't say why. Bartoen assumed that she didn't want to, because he couldn't imagine anything being impossible. He always got what he wanted. None but his father dared to say 'nay' to the future Lord of Reymerswal. He repeated that he wanted to take Hille home and again was met by gentle refusal. This time Bartoen became angry. He took hold of her arm and demanded that Hille go with him."

"What a rotten bilge rat!" Liselotte exclaimed.

"I think he was," Katja agreed. "And Hille now found out he was. She became angry and struggled to break free from Bartoen's grip. They wrestled, but this time it wasn't in fun play. This time it was serious. Bartoen was surprised at Hille's strength. Even as they fought, there were times she managed to pull him deeper into the water. He realised why when he finally succeeded in forcing her out of the water, onto the riverbank. He nearly let go of her in surprise, because..."

"Well?"

"Where her legs ought to have been, he saw a great fish tail, the scales shimmering in all hues of blues, greens, and silver."

"I knew it! Hille was a mermaid!"

"*Ja*, she was. When he had recovered from his surprise, Bartoen tied Hille up and laid her across the saddle of his horse. He brought her back to Lodiek Castle in triumph, boasting that he had captured one of the merfolk and everyone was much amazed. Lord Lodiek ordered a large wooden cage built. They put Hille in the cage and lowered the cage into the castle moat so that she could be in water. At first, she hissed and spat at her captors. Then she swam into the farthest corner of the cage and turned her face away from all of those who came to gaze upon her.

"That night Hille started singing again. This time it wasn't a beautiful, enchanting song. This time it was a dirge she sang, in plaintive notes. Bartoen complained that he couldn't sleep. His father ordered some of his retainers to tie a gag around Hille's mouth to silence her. They bound her hands as well, so that she couldn't undo the gag."

"Poor Hille," Liselotte commiserated.

To be caged...Hille hadn't deserved to be locked up and scorned.

Katja nodded. "But what Lord Lodiek didn't know was that Hille wasn't *just* any mermaid. She was the daughter of Nollekin and Drimmeline, the King and Queen of the merfolk."

Liselotte liked the sound of that. She hoped that Bartoen and his father would be punished.

"King Nollekin and Queen Drimmeline despaired when Hille didn't come home. They swam around all of Zeeland, but none of the merfolk or sea creatures they asked could tell them where their daughter was. There was no other choice for the king and queen. They had to engage with the landfolk, whom they usually avoided.

"King Nollekin went to Steynbergen, presented himself off the quay, and humbly begged for information. Now as it happened, the folk of Steynbergen had already heard of Hille's capture. But they were devout Christians and took the merfolk to be demons in league with the Devil himself, so they gave no answer to poor King Nollekin, other than laugh at his desperation.

"Bastards," Liselotte commented.

"Erm, *ja*, Miss. They were. But not all landfolk were. Queen Drimmeline went to Bergen-op-Zoom and hailed the city folk from the harbour. She found a kinder reception. She was offered refreshments because they could see she was tired from her efforts to find Hille. Then they told the queen that her daughter was held captive in the moat of Lodiek Castle. She thanked them and summoned her husband and all their subjects to the Oosterskelde riverbank near the castle. They arrived late in the evening and were told by a dolphin there that Hille's dirge had been heard the previous night but that all had been silent since. Fearing the worst, King Nollekin and Queen Drimmeline struck up the same keening dirge, joined by all the other merfolk who had emerged from the depths.

"But what Lord Lodiek didn't know was that Hille wasn't just any mermaid. She was the daughter of Nollekin and Drimmeline, the King and Queen of the merfolk."

"Once again, Bartoen complained that he couldn't sleep. This time he was scared as well, because it sounded like there were hundreds of Hilles lamenting their grief all at once. They soon discovered that it wasn't Hille who was singing, for she was still secure in her cage, hands bound, mouth gagged, eyes wide. The noise was coming from the river. Alarmed, Lord Lodiek urged his retainers to arm themselves. He arrived at the Oosterskelde riverbank astride his war-horse, wearing his best armour and followed by a small army of helmeted and breast-plated men armed with swords, spears, and crossbows. Lady Johanna and Bartoen came along as well."

"There was a battle," Liselotte whispered.

"Not at first, Miss. Only a battle of words. King Nollekin asked Lord Lodiek for the release of Hille, 'as a courtesy from one Lord to another Lord.'

"Lord Lodiek laughed loudly and then told King Nollekin that a domain made of muddy sand banks couldn't hope to compare itself to the rich land of Reymerswal.

"Then Queen Drimmeline appealed to Lady Johanna to release Hille, as a 'Mother's Mercy'. Lady Johanna scorned the merfolk queen. She said that Bartoen was a devout Christian, who couldn't be compared to a grotesque monstrosity like Hille.

"'She's mine now!' Bartoen cried out. 'You can't have her back.'"

"Those people were horrible!"

"*Ja*, Miss. They were cruel. They laughed cruelly when the king and queen begged for their daughter's release. They laughed when the queen offered them the wealth of the sea for Hille's safe return. 'There is no wealth which I don't already possess,' boasted Lord Lodiek. 'There is nothing you can give me.'

"At that, Nollekin and Drimmeline became very quiet. Then the king hissed: 'There are things that we can *take* away.' Lord Lodiek laughed at him and said: 'Then I'll invite you to come ashore and try.' At that, Queen Drimmeline rose higher out of the water, spread out her arms, and spoke a curse:

Bergen-op-Zoom will prosper and grow,
For Steynbergen nothing but woe,
And o'er Reymerswal streets,
Fish'll dart through seaweeds."

Liselotte shivered, her mind's eye conjuring up the half-submerged streets of the drowned city. A merfolk curse was not something to be taken lightly.

"Lord Lodiek, his family, and all their men laughed again. Then King Nollekin and Queen Drimmeline, as well as all the other merfolk, disappeared into the Oosterskelde. Far to the west the sky rumbled, and lightning shot through dark clouds.

"The Lodiek family went back to the castle, but Lord Lodiek took the precaution of posting guards on the sea dyke by the Oosterskelde, and by Hille's cage in the moat. All seemed calm again, but deep in the night that distant storm reached the land of Reymerswal. The wind howled around the castle towers. A vicious rain whipped the land and the guards outside. The storm clouds hurled down bolts of lightning. These shook the castle foundations when they impacted nearby and deafened those within the castle and village of Lodiek, and then the rest of Reymerswal."

Katja indicated the sea inlet in front of them.

"Lord Lodiek was urged to raise the general alarm, upon which all able-bodied men would be mobilised to guard the outer sea dykes. But the Lord of Reymerswal was a proud man and concerned people would say he feared the merfolk. 'The dykes will hold', he said. 'No alarm.' He did order the guards to be withdrawn, because he deemed any hostile action by the merfolk to be pure insanity in the horrible weather."

"That probably wasn't smart of him," Liselotte suggested.

"Nay, it wasn't. But there wasn't much they could have done. Merfolk fight their wars differently from us landfolk. The tide was being driven in from the sea by the storm. The waters around the Land of Reymerswal rose fast, waves assaulting the dykes, sheets of spray whipped up and over the dyke tops...and the merfolk were hard at work below."

"Work?" Liselotte asked, although she could guess.

"Digging. Clawing away the earth. At Lodiek dyke but in other places as well, all around the Land of Reymerswal."

"To dig through a whole dyke..."

"They didn't need to, Miss. They just needed to cause a small breach. After that they let the sea do the work. The water broke through with such force that the breach grew wider quickly, until there was a long gap, which is called Lodiek Gap to this day. It's right behind that last big dune over there.

"The merfolk came in with the water that rushed through. The inner polder dykes were weaker than the outer sea dykes. The merfolk dug breach after breach until the whole of Reymerswal was swallowed up by the raging sea. Even in the city, where the water reached the market square, as you have seen for yourself."

Liselotte stared at the monolithic towers rising from the sea. She envisaged the horrors of that night, as the ravenous flood cascaded down upon unsuspecting villages and farms. "Those poor people…"

"Eighteen villages drowned that night," Katja said. "As well as Lodiek Castle and part of the city."

"The castle! Did the merfolk find Hille?"

"Hille was freed. Lord Lodiek and Lady Johanna managed to escape to Bergen-op-Zoom. All the riches the Lord of Reymerswal had boasted of were lost to the sea. His people were drowned or dispersed. He never returned and died in poverty."

"And Bartoen?"

"Bartoen was dragged to the Oosterskelde by merfolk. Screaming his head off. They pulled him under the water and that was the last that was seen of him."

Liselotte was glad of that, but that satisfaction was much diminished by the knowledge that the entire population of Reymerswal had paid a high price for their Lord's pride and cruelty. There must have been untold hundreds of people in those eighteen villages. The alarm hadn't been raised. They would have thought themselves safe up to the moment the angry sea had roared through doors and windows, blocking any means of escaping the ferocious water.

Liselotte shivered again.

While Katja had told the story, the girl had run a hand through the sand, letting it spill between her fingers. As the story progressed, she had uncovered part of a larger item and had been slowly sweeping it clear of sand.

Liselotte hadn't paid attention to the details of Katja's absentminded handiwork, her mind occupied by images conjured up by Katja's words. She glanced at it when Katja lifted it from the sand.

It was a long, carved whalebone, like a spearhead, but with a great many barbs of different lengths and thicknesses, all of which suggested a vicious ability to maim and kill. Though the whole was smoothed by sea and sand, the spiky barbs still looked sharp. Despite that deadly aspect, it was curiously elegant and ornamental.

"What in the name of Orange is that?" Liselotte asked.

"A merfolk weapon," Katja said without doubt. "We find them now and then, back at home too. Here, have it."

"Thank you." Liselotte took the merfolk weapon with reverence. She could barely believe she was holding part of a deadly weapon once wielded by a merman or mermaid, maybe even in the battle to free Hille from Lodiek Castle. The carefully crafted whalebone leant Katja's story a sense of reality that was breath-taking.

21. The Blood Oath

REYMERSWAL ~ COUNTY OF ZEELAND ~1622

A battery near Bergen op Zoom fired in quick succession. The echo of the booms drifted over the sea, as did renewed and encroaching mist, already concealing the farthest church towers. The bells started tolling again, mournfully so.

Liselotte tore her eyes away from the merfolk spear blade, and looked at her young companion, who looked tired from telling the long tale.

"Thank you for telling me that story, Katja."

"Of course, Miss."

"You must call me Liselotte, none of this 'Miss' business."

Katja coloured red and shook her head. "I can't..."

"Why not?"

"I'm just a simple flatlander," Katja blurted out. "You...you..."

The girl looked at Liselotte with such frank admiration that it made Liselotte feel uncomfortable.

"You're like Hille, Miss. When you were in the sea just now." Katja said. "So beautiful, and you know all these things...so much...even surgery!"

Fierce pride invigorated Liselotte. The full realisation of what she had done on that small islet by the Eendragt.

If I can treat a gunshot wound, I can also take over from Peter until he's better.

"How old are you, Katja?"

"Thirteen, I think, Miss."

"We're only a few years apart!" Liselotte smiled. "Just call me by my name. I think we shall become good friends.

Katja smiled shyly. "But..."

"No 'buts'," Liselotte decreed. "You see the differences between us, Katja. I see the similarities. We're both adrift, with uncertain futures."

Bleak futures. Which are not ours to control. Or could they be? How?

"My future isn't uncertain," Katja said proudly. "I'm going to be a handmaid in Rotterdam!"

Liselotte laughed, then looked at the distant towers. Their number was diminishing in the mist, their tolling bells dying down again.

"So, who rings the bells? The ones that don't exist."

"Folk say that on some nights you can hear the panicked shouts of men, screams of women, and wailing of children. And that those doomed folk ring the bells in alarm, summoning help that will never come."

Liselotte felt a chill crawl along her spine.

"Others say that you can hear the merfolk sing. That it is they who ring the bells to lure unknowing folk to watery graves."

Liselotte could well believe it, overlooking what had once been a battlefield between human and merfolk. The warning was clear; it was better not to underestimate the power of the merfolk.

Power.

On an impulse, holding the barbed merfolk spearhead at a safe distance so as to not accidentally cut herself on the wicked barbs, Liselotte threw off the blanket and drew her haversack to her. She pulled out Eyang, and then drew the keris from its sheath, which she left on the bag.

Eyang. Mermaid. Queen of the South Sea.

Liselotte rose to her feet and walked down the beach toward the receding water line, her mermaid keris in one hand, the merfolk spearhead in the other.

Hille, daughter of the king and queen of the Zeeuwse merfolk.

"Miss? Liselotte?" Katja got to her feet and followed Liselotte down the beach, though at a wary distance.

"Don't worry, Katja. I know what I'm doing."

She didn't really. It was intuition. If merfolk had the power to curse...they also had the power to bless. Landfolk deemed that it was Liselotte's duty to meekly accept she was someone else's legal property. Bartoen had reasoned Hille was his rightful property, a view that hadn't been shared by the merfolk.

When Liselotte reached the edge of the sea, Katja urged her to stop.

"Miss! You mustn't. Better to stay away from the water when the bells of the drowned land have just tolled. They could begin again."

Liselotte ignored her and walked into the sea until the waves lapped at her ankles. The bells had fallen silent so all she could hear was the occasional rumble of cannons at Bergen-op-Zoom, the gentle surf, the whispering wind, and seabirds crying out forlornly. It didn't take much imagination for those cries to assume the nature of a merfolk dirge. If those mysterious creatures existed still, they would be found here, at the edge of the Drowned Land of Reymerswal.

Liselotte raised Eyang high. Although there was no sun that she could see, the wavy blade of the keris shimmered nonetheless, its spiralling patterns seemingly alive.

Like a mermaid's tail.

She thrust the spearhead up, the smooth bone – polished by sea and sand – gleamed.

Liselotte crossed steel and bone.

The breeze didn't feel so cold now, but Liselotte's skin tingled and she felt goose bumps on her arms and legs.

"Hille of the merfolk," Liselotte called out, her voice loud and clear. "I beseech you to listen to me."

"Oh, dear Mary, Mother of God..." Katja uttered.

"My life!" Liselotte shouted over the water, then dropped into a whisper. "Hille, please help me live my life. My own life, as I choose it. Then, at the end, it'll be yours."

Without giving herself time to think about it, Liselotte clamped the spearhead between her knees – to free her left hand – and pressed Eyang's blade against her palm. The steel was razor-sharp and broke the skin easily. Liselotte completed the cut before she even felt the pain. Gritting her teeth, she formed her left hand into a fist and squeezed it.

She watched in fascination as a steady trickle of blood dripped down from her fist into the sea, where the bright red drops quickly diluted with the water to form vague stains that were pulled backward, before disappearing, consumed by the sea.

When the trickle of blood ceased, Liselotte dipped her left hand into the water. The sting of the salt water was such that she couldn't help but cry out in pain.

"Miss Liselotte!" Katja shouted in alarm.

Liselotte took hold of the spearhead again, clutching it tight despite the pain, and turned around, grimacing. "I'm alright. It just hurt a little."

Katja stared at her with wide eyes. "That wasn't Christian."

"It was something I needed to do," Liselotte said with conviction.

She walked back to her companion. Katja looked aghast.

"There's no harm done, Katja," Liselotte assured her. "Don't seafarers still honour Neptune? Some things are older...much older...like your *oma's* wisdom."

"Neptune?" The girl looked confused.

"Never mind. Just don't tell anyone," Liselotte concluded, sliding Eyang back into the sheath. "Not even Jasper."

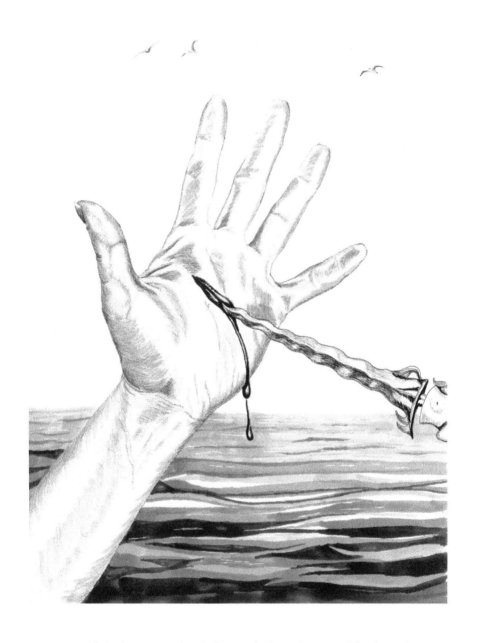

Liselotte completed the cut before she even felt the pain.

She recalled and repeated what Peter had said. "They're burning folk at the stake for less all over Europe."

"I won't!" Katja promised, her doubts replaced by a fierce loyalty that made Liselotte smile as she carefully tucked Eyang and the merfolk spearhead into the haversack.

"Good on you," Liselotte said cheerfully. "Thank you, Katja. And now, I suppose, we'd better get back to the others."

To tell them what I've decided to do, my earlier plan. Peter yearns for his ship. And a woman I think, in Flushing. He's in love. Christine? Dewi? Love is a powerful medicine. We have to get him to Flushing.

The two made their way back up into the dunes. After their voices died away in the distance, the only sounds that remained were the occasional booms from batteries around Bergen-op-Zoom, the cries of seabirds, the eternal rush of the sea, and something faint that sounded like an otherworldly song.

22. Last Stand at Lodiek Gap

LODIEK GAP ~ COUNTY OF ZEELAND ~ 1622.

Andries was crouched by Peter's side when the girls returned from their outing. Liselotte strode into the room and deposited her haversack and a blanket on the table.

"We'll stay here for the night," she said. "Hope the snares supplement our provisions and get a proper night's sleep. But then we must get off this island. Jasper, can we build a raft?"

"A raft?" Jasper asked incredulously. "To sail to Flushing?"

"Nay, to South Beveland. I saw it from the beach. It doesn't look that far. There must be other transport to Flushing from there."

"I suppose that's possible," Jasper mused. "We might reach Yerseke, if we time it on the outgoing tide."

"It's good to make plans," Peter said, in a weak voice.

"Peter!" Liselotte ran to her patient and crouched down by him.

"The fever broke," Andries told her. "About half-an-hour ago. He came to, just before you returned."

Peter looked pale and gaunt, tired beyond measure, but there was clarity in his eyes and his voice strengthened. "I consider myself fortunate to have run into you, cousins. The two of you can manage quite well without me, it seems."

He looked around. "We have acquired landbound lodgings. Where on earth are we?"

"In the city of Reymerswal." Andries answered.

Peter gave a small nod of recognition. "Very clever."

Andries felt his chest expand, but then breathed out deeply. "It was Jasper's doing. He sailed us here, even when the yawl was sinking. And Liselotte extracted the musket ball like a professional surgeon."

Peter looked at Liselotte. "If only you were—"

"A boy." She finished for him, with defiance. "*Ja*, then I could have been useful on your ship."

Andries was shocked by her insolence, but Peter accepted it with a little grin.

"My ship," Peter said slowly, and let out a deep wistful sigh. "Jasper?"

"Aye-aye, Skipper." Jasper stepped closer.

"The yawl is lost?"

"Regretfully so, Skipper. We intended to round Tholen but got caught in thick fog. The tide carried us over the Oosterskelde and into the Drowned Lands Sea. We struck a half-submerged oak. At the bow, Skipper, the wood was going soft. It wasn't pleasant."

"Like a hot knife through butter," Peter acknowledged. "The breach above or below the waterline?"

"Bit of both, Skipper. I rigged the jib round the bow, but the old girl was filling fast."

Peter regarded Jasper with amusement in his eyes. "What would you say to—"

"Peter," Andries interrupted hastily. "Jasper would like to muster as ship's boy."

Jasper nodded so mightily that his face became a blur.

"I see," Peter said, clearly pleased. He looked at Andries. "And how would you feel about that? Having this exuberant Fleming at close quarters for a year and more."

Andries's chest swelled again. It seemed as if Peter was giving him the final decision. The way he'd acknowledged Liselotte's input back in Oysterhout.

"I would enjoy his company, Cousin," he said truthfully. He grinned at Jasper's grateful look.

"That's good, Andries. That's very good." Peter looked at Jasper. "Consider yourself on my muster roll as cabin boy. Vouched for by Midshipman Haelen. The pay is double for this voyage. I'll get you kitted out in Flushing at my expense."

Jasper's mouth dropped open. Then he cheered loudly and spontaneously turned and hugged Katja, before jumping into the air, arms raised high. "I'm going to the East Indies!"

"Jasper," Liselotte said sternly. "Your captain needs some peace and quiet."

"Sorry, Skipper, my apologies."

Peter nodded. "But a word of warning. To all of you. Sailing to South Beveland may not be like rounding the Cape of Good Hope, but it won't do to underestimate the sheer power of *Zeeuwse* tides. They can rip a flimsy craft to pieces. There are submerged trees, farms, and villages between Reymerswal and Yerseke."

"Which can also rip a raft to pieces," Liselotte concluded glumly. "It was a bad idea."

"It was a good idea as a last resort. I suggest we post lookouts to spot passing boats. Tie my sash to something long to hail them, let them know we're *Oranjevaarders*."

233

"I was out earlier and didn't see any sails," Liselotte said. "Not on the Oosterskelde, nor over the Drowned Lands."

"The fighting at Bergen-op-Zoom?" Andries guessed.

"Enough to frighten the Devil out of anyone." Peter grimaced and adjusted his position a little. "Jasper, how long can a fisherman stay away from his catching grounds?"

"Not long at all, Skipper, tis fish or bust for most of us."

"So that's where you learned your ropes."

"In Heys, Skipper, near Bruges."

"I've sailed past. Do you know what they fish here?"

"Ouwe Gerrit, Katja's *opa*, came for sprats and mussels over the Drowned Lands Sea."

"The fishermen will come. Soon." Peter's eyelids seemed to grow heavy.

"You need to rest now, Peter." Liselotte said with a matron's sternness that was not to be denied.

Peter nodded weakly. "That would be good. Stay here tonight. Rest. Start looking for boats at dawn."

A round past the snares brought in a single meagre hare, an old tough one that had fought the noose tooth and nail.

"Not much meat on this one," Andries told Liselotte when he brought the mangled creature back to the guardhouse.

She was pleased, nonetheless. "It'll do for a broth."

She sent Jasper to the nearby bank of the Oosterskelde to fill the pail with seawater.

Andries accompanied him, to scout for a good place to watch the sea-arm from the next day. They settled for one of the more intact watchtowers that offered a wide view of the Oosterskelde, the desolated city, and most of the Drowned Lands Sea.

"Your sister, *Mynheer*, has asked Katja to be her handmaid," Jasper gossiped. "In Rotterdam!"

"Well, that's good, I suppose," Andries said, recognising that Jasper and Katja came part and parcel.

When they returned, the cauldron was on the fire, steam rising from the broth within it.

Liselotte took the pail and set it down next to the Amsterdam soap and her improvised and bloodied surgeon's apron.

"What are you going to do?" Andries asked.

"I've no spare shifts left," Liselotte explained. "And we're out of the strips I cut yesterday. We'll try to get this one as clean as possible and then make new bandages for Peter."

"Father always told us that filthy bandages needed to be burnt and not used again."

"You're right. I'm out of other options though, and the apron is less of a risk than the used bandages."

Andries nodded his understanding. "Don't start just yet."

He walked to the wheelbarrow to dig around in his duffel bag. He had been hoping to change his current worn and torn dirty shirt for a clean one, but having recently considered life without Peter's wardship, Andries knew where his priorities had to lie.

He walked back to Liselotte. "Here, I've got two spare shirts. Use these instead."

Her grateful smile was warming and almost worth losing two shirts for.

When the broth was ready, Peter was roused so that Liselotte and Katja could feed him. They then removed the bandages to inspect and treat the wound.

They ate next. Sitting around the table, the merry fire casting light and warmth on them, was almost homely, but they spoke little and then only softly, because Peter had fallen asleep again and needed his rest.

It didn't take long after the meal to divide the rest of the evening and night into watches and take turns to grab what much-needed sleep they could.

It still felt woefully short to Andries when dawn broke, but he did feel refreshed simply because he wasn't in danger of falling over from sheer exhaustion anymore.

He anticipated a long boring day when he embarked into the dawn with Jasper, who had brought one of the half-poles with Peter's orange sash tied to it to hail friendly craft.

They arrived at the watchtower on the eroded city wall.

The Oosterskelde was clear of mist, the cloud cover light and keeping pace with a brisk wind. The morning sun was consoling the city's woes with its first tentative rays that banished some of the eeriness.

Andries could barely believe their luck when, mere minutes into their watch, a longboat appeared from the east. Its mainsail caught generous wind to propel it forward past Reymerswal Island.

Jasper seized hold of Andries and pulled him down below the parapet. He hissed. "Those are Spaniards!"

"Dons? Are you sure?"

They rose slightly, peering over the parapet to look apprehensively at the many helmeted occupants of the longboat.

"*Ja*, absolutely certain. Those are some of the Count of Salazar's men. About thirty of them. But odd that it's just one boat, the Spaniards usually prefer larger numbers when they venture on the water."

Andries and Jasper looked at one another, then scurried over to the other side of the viewing platform atop the tower.

There were four more longboats. One was exploring the Drowned Lands Sea immediately to the south of the city. Three had pulled into the sombre lagoon at the market square. The lead boat was already spilling soldiers over its bow.

The boys exchanged a horrified look, and then – as one – raced down the tower's steps and hastened to the guardhouse.

"Fire out," Andries said hoarsely when they surprised Liselotte, Peter, and Katja with their sudden entry. "The Dons are coming."

"Spaniards?" Peter frowned.

"Salazar's men," Jasper said. "They're landing at the market square. At least eighty or ninety of them."

"We need to leave now," Andries added.

They scrambled about, dousing the fire, gathering things, packing up.

"Help me get up," Peter asked of Jasper.

"The wheelbarrow," Liselotte said. "The wheel squeaks."

"Won't be no good out in the dunes anyway," Jasper added. "The wheel will sink in the sand."

"Dunes?" Andries asked. "Shouldn't we hide in the city?"

"I doubt they've come specifically for us, there's no reason for them to know we exist." Peter said. "Scouting the area, more likely. Especially undefended places like Reymerswal. The dunes are less likely to interest them than the state of the walls and towers. I'll walk, use my musket as walking stick."

"Peter, that's not a good idea." Liselotte shook her head.

"There are no other options," he insisted. "Jasper, could you carry my duffel bag? And my powder and shot?"

Andries patted his pistol and axe before slinging his musket over his shoulder, next to his duffel bag. Liselotte hoisted her backpack on her back, hooked her quiver and Eyang to her belt, and drew the crossbow from her haversack. Katja had gathered the loose blankets, the cauldron, pail, and lantern. Jasper picked up Peter's bags and took hold of the pennant pole that he had propped up by the door. They were ready to leave and made their way to the arched gateway and the dunes beyond.

The deep soft sands of the dunes hadn't particularly bothered Andries when he'd gone round to set and inspect snares. Now that he was in a rush and loaded down by bags and weapons, he realised the extent of the hindrance formed by the unsteady footing.

Peter seemed determined not to slow them down, but the strain showed on his pale face as he leant on the musket and forced himself to keep up.

Andries reckoned they moved agonisingly slow, considering those eighty-some Spanish soldiers at the market square. Had they spread out to cast a wide net over the city? Or were they moving about more cautiously?

The answer came behind them, just as they were about to round a particularly tall dune that would have shielded them from sight.

"¡Oye! ¡OYE!"

Andries cast a backward glance to see three soldiers stand in the gateway. One of them waved urgently. "¡Regresar!"

"Scheit!³³" Jasper exclaimed.

"Aye, indeed," Peter panted. "Look lively now, keep moving."

They rounded the tall dune. The Spaniards disappeared from their view, but Andries could hear them exchange rapid bursts of speech, before shouting louder to draw the attention of their comrades.

"We have to hope that they'll dismiss us as shy local fisher folk," Peter said. "Not worthy of their time."

Andries thought that was hopelessly optimistic, but it seemed to encourage the others to redouble their efforts. They hastened along the narrow tracks that led through the grassy dunes.

When the path broadened between the crests of the last two dunes, they came to a halt, to regain their breath and stare with wide-eyed disbelief at the end of the island, even though they had known that it would come to this.

A broad bank of sand gradually bent south, tapering off as it reached its culmination by the restless water where the Oosterskelde and the Drowned Lands Sea met. The very end of the isle was marked by an old shipwreck, its ribs rising from the sand like ancient bones, some tattered strakes still clinging on to the bow.

---

³³ Shit

Some hundred yards farther out was another island – nothing more than a broad strip of dunes – but to get there with the tide high would require swimming, and there was nowhere to hide there anyway. South Beveland was visible but vague in the distance.

"Lodiek Gap," Katja said, pointing at the water between them and the other island. Strong eddies suggested there were various currents at play.

"Make for the wreck," Peter said. "Some cover is better than none."

Behind them they could hear orders issued and men shouting to and fro.

"They'll form a line across the dunes," Peter said. "To make sure we haven't tucked away behind the shrubs in a hollow. That will slow them down some, but we're in big trouble now."

The first Spaniards appeared on the path between the last two dunes just as Andries and the rest reached the wreck. The Spaniards pointed and hollered for reinforcements.

Ducking between the exposed ribs, Andries joined the others who had gathered in the scant shelter offered by the wreck's bow. Jasper dropped Peter's bags on the sand and clambered halfway up the stem to lodge the pennant pole so that the orange sash danced in the wind over their heads. He climbed back down, looking pleased with his act of defiance.

"Jasper," Peter asked. "Can you use a musket?"

"Aye-aye, Skipper." Jasper said confidently. "I was a soldier."

"A drummer boy," Andries couldn't help from commenting.

Jasper replied, "Everyone's helpful little brother who fetched things for them. Plenty were happy enough to let me handle their muskets. They liked teaching me. It's boring most of the time, being in the army."

"Take my musket," Peter said. "I certainly can't use it with just the one arm."

The doglock looked ridiculously large in the boy's hands, but he held it with the same confidence that had marked his tiller work on the yawl.

"You'll find powder and shot in my haversack, Soldier." Peter drew his pistol and found lodging against the hull's upcurved stem, as well as a convenient gap in the strakes to shoot through.

The Spaniards at the edge of the dune had grown in number, a score of them forming a broad line of halberdiers and musketeers. Another – far larger – group was nearing in the distance, spread out unevenly along the edge of the Drowned Lands Sea, but they seemed in no hurry.

The mathematics of it are clear, Andries thought as his courage sank rapidly. Even if all four of them hit their target, there would be sixteen Spaniards left to close the gap before the hull's defenders could reload.

"Jasper on the left flank," Peter said. "Andries on the right. Liselotte and Katja on me."

Andries regarded Katja. He drew his pistol from his baldric. "You think you can pull a trigger, Katja?"

Katja nodded solemnly and took the pistol from Andries tentatively.

"Thank you," Liselotte told Andries. "I'll help her prime it."

Andries took his place at the right, patting his axe for luck before attending to his musket.

"There's no point in surrendering," Peter said darkly.

Andries glowered at the Spaniards. The twins and Peter had come so far, only for it to end here. Apart from despair, it also filled Andries with anger at the unfairness of it.

The first group of Spaniards, deciding not to wait for the others, began to walk forward. Their line tightening as they hollered confident challenges at those concealed within the wreck.

"Hold your fire," Peter ordered. "Let them come closer first."

Andries targeted the biggest Spaniard he could see, the one he'd least welcome when the hull's defenders were inevitably overwhelmed. He was terrified, but Jasper remained calm and Andries couldn't let a mere cabin boy outshine him. Nor the girls, for that matter, who looked drawn and grim, but were focused on the foe.

Liselotte was mumbling names like a prayer. "Eyang. Hille."

The Spaniards sped up their advance, forming a tight wall of steel.

"Hold your fire," Peter repeated.

"Look!" Katja exclaimed.

Andries's eyes widened.

A ship was sailing down the Oosterskelde, out of sight of the main group of more distant Spaniards on the Drowned Lands Sea beach. The vessel's square sail appeared behind the smaller group of enemies lined across the last spit of Reymerswal isle. Those Spaniards were oblivious to the ship, all their eyes seemingly aimed at the wreck where their quarry had gone to ground.

The ship was close to twenty meters long, Andries guessed. It had a single square mainsail running parallel to its hull, two jib sails, and a rounded bow, as well as tear-shaped leeboards amidships. The poop deck was situated over a cabin with richly decorated gilded frames around latticed windows. Over a dozen crew were moving about on deck, some tending a large carronade on a swivel by the bow.

Most important of all, the stern sported a long flagpole from which flew a humongous prince's flag, the nine horizontal orange, white, and blue bands a beautiful sight to behold. The Republic's tricolour, red-white-and-blue, flew from the top of the mast, beneath a long orange pennant that danced a festive greeting at Peter's sash.

"The navy is here!" Andries said, barely able to believe it.

"A *statenjacht,*" Peter said. "God be praised."

"Bah." Jasper contributed. "Sea Beggars come to spoil our fight."

"Do they know we're here?" Liselotte asked.

"I don't know," Peter answered. "But they've seen the Spaniards. They're ready for them. Let's give them a hand, wait for my command to fire."

Andries focused on the Spanish soldiers, who were now close enough to read their facial expressions. They looked confident, nonchalant even as if this chore barely merited their full attention.

The *statenjacht* loomed behind them.

One of the Spaniards at the far end of the line, adjacent to the Oosterskelde, caught an inkling of something, and threw a casual look over his shoulder – to freeze on the spot.

He opened his mouth, but whatever came out was overpowered first by Peter's voice – "*VUUR!*" – and then by the immediate and almost simultaneous firing of two doglocks and two pistols.

Andries's ears were stunned. He hadn't heard the characteristic twang of Liselotte's crossbow through the roar of gunfire but saw the familiar blur of a bolt stirring gunpowder smoke as it streaked toward the foe.

There were cries of pain and anger somewhere through the powder smoke that quickly enveloped the wreck's bow.

"Reload," Peter said. He himself drew his sword. "Lively now."

Some shots rang out on the Spanish side, but no musket balls came hurling at the wreck.

They must be shooting at the statenjacht.

Andries reloaded frantically, expecting to see dark menacing shapes step through the dissipating cloud of powder smoke any moment.

Instead, there was a thunderous eruption from the *statenjacht*. Drawing abeam with the line of Spaniards, the Dutch crew fired the carronade.

Andries watched through the clearing smoke with disbelief. The line – already gapped by three soldiers who had fallen to the volley from the wreck – seemed to quiver for a moment, before spraying blood and disintegrating into agonised screams. Some cut short. A brief gory rain of red droplets pattered onto the sand around the stricken formation.

"Case shot!" Jasper shouted.

"*Oranje boven*[34]," Peter murmured.

Less than half the Spaniards remained standing, and they were reeling.

Musketeers on the *statenjacht* fired a volley, reducing the Spanish number further. Other crew lowered the mainsail.

The ship's bow slid along the beach, bringing the *statenjacht* to a halt. The musketeers on board started reloading.

"Huzzah!" The other crew hurled themselves off the bow onto the beach, brandishing pistols, axes, boathooks, and short swords. "*Voor Zeeland en Oranje*[35]!"

"Hold your fire," Peter commanded. "They're going in."

They were all youths, many with wisps of fuzz on their cheeks in poor imitation of beards. None wore helmets, most just simple knitted fishermen's caps, and some a few partial pieces of armour. Their breeches and jackets were brightly coloured. All of them were barefoot in the manner of sailors. One had skin as dark as ebony and strange short curly black hair.

Their apparent leader, who couldn't have been that much older than Andries, with a roughly hewn open face and stout frame, was simply dressed, dark breeches and a white, unlaced shirt. Untamed strands of long dark-brown hair surrounded his clean-shaven face. He opened his mouth wide and hollered, "*Zeeland en Oranje*! Kill the Spanish *klootzakken*!"

His crew ferociously roared their agreement.

---

[34] Literally 'Orange Above', referencing the orange pennant position over the tricolour, and the preference for the House of Nassau over the Habsburger kings of Spain. In modern parlay it translates into 'Go Orange!' or 'Orange Rules!'

[35] For Zeeland and Orange.

The leader sped toward the first survivor and made short work of him with his crude, heavy blade. His crew streamed around him to deal with the rest.

The other Spaniards, still well out of musket range, had paused but were now forming organised groups. Their number had grown. They easily outnumbered the Dutchmen on the beach.

"Peter," Andries said. "Those others will be heading this way."

"Get your gear," Peter commanded. "All of you. To the ship. Quick."

Jasper scrambled up the bow to reclaim the pennant pole, and then led the way to the *statenjacht*, waving the makeshift orange banner.

The *statenjacht's* crew saw the distant Spanish formations come into motion in a slow and measured advance. The young man in charge of the navy crew organised a skirmish line. They faced the enemy to cover the young leader and three of his sailors, who strode toward the small group that had emerged from the wreck.

The leader's face looked puzzled as he glanced at one of the motionless bodies on the sand. Stopping, he placed a foot on the man's chest, seized hold of the crossbow bolt that protruded from it, and yanked it out to regard it curiously. "*Sakkerloot!* [36]"

"I'm going to…" Peter stumbled. Andries and Katja were by his side almost immediately to steady him.

Liselotte turned and examined Peter. "He's passed out, lower him onto the ground."

They had barely done that when a loud voice boomed, "Well, well! What have we here then?"

Andries, on his knees next to Peter, watched Liselotte rise and turn to face the *statenjacht's* skipper. Her gown was in tatters. She'd lost her cap and her red hair was wildly spiked, all aflame in the sun. She had the crossbow in one hand. Her other hand rested on the hilt of the keris Peter had gifted her. The filled quiver was suspended from her waist belt.

The young skipper's mouth dropped open, but he quickly recovered.

"A veritable Goddess of War," he declared earnestly. "Jeanne d'Arc, I presume?"

"I, erm…" Liselotte seemed at a loss for words.

---

[36] From the French '*sacrelotte*', a corruption of '*Sacre nom de Dieu*' (in the holy name of God).

The boy bowed, swinging his arms about in a clumsy imitation of the courtly manners of yore – without taking his eyes off Liselotte. "Michael Adriaansz, at your service and enraptured by your dazzling appearance to be sure."

"Wholly captivated." One of his crew remarked.

"Spellbound," the second one added.

"Etcetera. Amen," the third one – with the ebony skin – concluded.

Michael Adriaansz gave them an angry stare. "You're ruining a fine introduction. And Jan, no need to get religious on us, utterly divine as…" He looked back at Liselotte. "This fierce and blindingly beautiful angel of war may be."

"Hallelujah," Jan added.

Andries was ready to huff and puff over the insolent manners of these youths but he couldn't really fault them for their mistake. Peter's party looked as ragged as refugees. He scrambled up, to establish proper social distinctions by introducing himself as VOC Commodore Haelen's second-in-command, but didn't get a chance to speak.

"Skipper!" One of the youths in the skirmish line shouted. "Incoming!"

The Spanish soldiers, having presumably tallied the numbers and found courage in the disparity, were speeding up their advance.

"Edge back! Steady!" Michael hollered. He lowered his voice and added conversationally, "We'll finish introductions later. I do beg your pardon, but there is a minor inconvenience headed our way."

"More than sixty of them," one of his youths added.

"We have a wounded man with us." Liselotte pointed.

"Understood," Michael answered, after a quick glance at Peter. "Geleyn, Cornelis, bring him on board. Jan, on me. The rest of you, follow us."

They trotted after Michael and Jan until they were amidships the *statenjacht,* where the two youths, with help from crew on the weather deck, helped the children scramble over the gunwales. Baggage and weapons were passed up next.

Michael and Jan stayed on the beach. The skirmish line was ordered to increase their rate of retreat. Geleyn and Cornelis passed Peter to outstretched hands on the *statenjacht* and climbed aboard. Liselotte and Katja knelt by Peter's prone body after he was laid out on deck.

"Tis done, Skipper!" Geleyn shouted, taking hold of a musket. "All guests embarked."

"Michael Adriaansz, at your service and enraptured by your dazzling appearance to be sure."

"Back!" Michael shouted at the skirmish line. "Back! Look lively now! Let's get floating!"

They turned as one and sprinted to the *statenjacht*. Passing their weapons over the gunwales to the crew on board, they put their shoulders to the hull and started heaving. Michael and Jan joined them, the skipper hollering encouragement in a torrent of insults.

"Call yourselves *Oranjevaarders*? Heave, you bunch of sissies!"

On board, Geleyn, Cornelis, and three others stepped up to the gunwales and lifted muskets to provide cover.

"Heave! Useless puny shrimps! Heave!"

"Jasper," Andries called out.

The Flemish boy understood. They raised their loaded muskets simultaneously to add to the *statenjacht's* firepower.

"Heave! Your little sisters could do a better job than this!"

The Spaniards, seeing their intended prey on the verge of escape, howled their anger and broke ranks to run to the beach at a furious pace.

"Heave!" Michael roared. "One more time, lads."

"They're coming closer!"

"She's shifting!"

"Heave!" Michael bellowed. "Deck hands, *Klaar!* There she goes. Deck hands, *Richt!* Beach hands DUCK! Deck! *VUUR!*"

The *Zeeuwen* on the beach crouched low. The musketeers on deck of the *statenjacht* fired a volley at the closest onrushing Spaniards. Andries felt the butt of his doglock punch his shoulder, and powder smoke sting his eyes. Smoke rolled along the gunwale and cries of pain rang out on the beach.

"On board! Get on board!" Michael ordered. The youths clambered up the gunwales, the musketeers extending helping hands. The *statenjacht* began to drift on the tide.

"Pelle!" Michael shouted to the stern. "Get ready!"

Michael organised the crew on the weather deck. The musketeers were to reload – Andries and Jasper following suit. Some youths were ordered to mind the jibs, which had been billowing about aimlessly.

The rest seized the halyard and hauled up the mainsail. It and the jibs caught the wind and the *statenjacht* gained speed fast.

Michael – eyes on the sails – ordered adjustments of the main and jib sheets, and then tasked some of his crew to secure them on belaying pins. The rest rushed for their weapons and then joined the musketeers at the larboard gunwale, to look back at the beach.

The first red-faced Spaniards had reached the bank of the Oosterskelde, roaring furious curses as they watched the *statenjacht* slip out of their grasp. One officer, however, was organising a line of musketeers.

"Any of you useless mongrels reloaded already?" Michael asked.

"*Ja*, Skipper!" Jasper held up his doglock.

The officer on the beach commanded his musketeers, "¡*Preparados*!37"

---

37 Prepare, as in ready your guns.

Michael took Jasper's musket – inspecting it briefly. He aimed at the beach and shot the Spanish officer, who crumpled to the ground. "WELCOME TO ZEELAND, *KLOOTZAK!*"

The Spanish musketeers scattered back in anticipation of more gunfire from the *statenjacht*.

"*Platbroecken!*" Jasper shouted at them triumphantly and thumbed his nose at them.

His insult was met by Dutch cheers, and then echoed. "*Platbroecken! Platbroecken!*"

Michael turned around to face his guests, focusing his attention on Liselotte again. "Welcome aboard *De Wilde Ruyter*[38]."

He added, with a wink, "Mercifully free of *Platbroecken.*"

Andries made to speak. It was wholly inappropriate of Michael to refer to the content of his breeches in this manner. He hesitated though, because he already admired this young swashbuckler a great deal and Liselotte, curiously enough, didn't seem to mind, regarding the young skipper with thoughtful bemusement.

"Skipper," Jasper spoke urgently. "There were three longboats that disembarked the soldiers on the beach. But there's a fourth longboat yonder, over the Drowned Lands Sea, and a fifth somewhere ahead of us on the Oosterskelde. Full of soldiers both."

Michael nodded. He turned to Jan, Geleyn, and Cornelis. "All wounded, divine war goddesses, and children to the main cabin, if you please."

Andries started to protest, "I'm not a..."

Jasper pulled his sleeve hard. "A skipper's word is law at sea."

Michael was already off. "Right, you lazy pox-ridden bastards. Battle stations!"

Resigned, Andries let himself be ushered toward the stern and then down the stairs that led to the main cabin of *De Wilde Ruyter*.

---

[38] *The Wild Raider/Rider*. In a seafaring context, *ruyter* (derived from an old word for raider) could be used to indicate the unruliness of a pirate or privateer and/or a mounted 'rider', symbolising speed.

22. De Wilde Ruyter

ON THE OOSTERSKELDE RIVER ~ COUNTY OF ZEELAND ~1622

The main cabin was large, occupying at least a quarter of *De Wilde Ruyter's* length. It was luxurious, with polished walnut cabinets and rich green leather padding on extended benches along both sides of the cabin. A long oak table stood between the benches, on the far end of which lay charts and writing implements. A collection of pewter jugs and goblets crowned the middle.

Liselotte wondered if the imposing snobbery reflected the character of *De Wilde Ruyter's* surprisingly young and remarkably cocksure skipper. His simple outfit didn't match this pomposity, but it certainly suited his audacity.

She was still somewhat stunned by the straightforward way in which this Michael had expressed interest in her, especially with his eyes. They hadn't conveyed forcefulness or command, just...

Invitation.

There was a long narrow mirror by one of the cabinets, surrounded by a gold-leafed frame. Catching sight of herself, Liselotte understood.

She looked a lot more dishevelled now than she had at the farm near Steynbergen, when Bettie's mother had assumed Liselotte was of an equivalent lower class.

I look like a beggar. Definitely the social equal of a forward scoundrel. It makes him carefree of etiquette.

Not knowing what to make of it, Liselotte opted to grumble. "Who does he think he is? Sending me below-decks?"

"If you don't know Michael Adriaansz," Jan spoke up behind her, with a pronounced *Zeeuwse* accent. "Then you're not from around here, are you, *meissie*?"

He was ushering Jasper and Katja in, followed by Andries and the two sailors carrying Peter.

They all stepped aside to allow the two sailors and their burden to pass.

"He speaks Dutch!" Katja said wide-eyed, unable to keep her eyes off Jan's black skin.

"Well, of course I do," Jan said, expressing surprise. "Why wouldn't I?"

Jasper stepped in front of Katja protectively. "Please forgive her, *Mynheer*. It's just that she's never seen an African savage before."

Geleyn and Cornelis laughed.

Jan sighed deeply and rolled his eyes. "I'm from Flushing."

"Nowadays, Jan," Geleyn corrected him. "You're from Flushing nowadays. Right Cornelis, let's put him down."

"Before that," Cornelis told the children, as he helped lower Peter on the nearest bench. "Our Jan was Viceroy of Gorée, so really we oughta be calling him Yer Majesty and whatnot."

"That's right," Geleyn confirmed. "King Jan."

Jan shook his head. "The title is actually 'Dammeel of Kajoor', and I was only a potential one."

"*Ja*, Yer Royal Majesty," Cornelis acknowledged.

Liselotte's attention was drawn to Peter, fearing to see fresh blood seeping through his bandages, but fortunately the wound seemed to have held well.

Jan addressed Andries. "Is that a gunshot wound?"

"*Ja*," Andries said.

Jan nodded. He turned to Cornelis and Geleyn. "Michael will have need for you on deck. Don't tell him they called me a savage."

"Aww," Cornelis said. "You know how he rewards such talk, Jan. I was looking forward to a keelhauling, I was."

Katja turned pale and looked to Jasper for reassurance, but his usual confidence was diminished.

"Don't you worry now," Geleyn told Jasper. "I'll request leniency for you, on account of you being Flemish."

"Everyone knows they're dull-witted," Cornelis assured Jasper. "It'll just be a flogging for you, lucky little devil that you are."

"Fifty lashes at most if the skipper is in a merciful mood," Geleyn promised.

"Which," Cornelis spoke soothingly. "Is worse than it sounds. Even the strongest boatswain starts getting a bit tired after thirty lashes or so."

"That's right," Geleyn said. "The last dozen are as soft as being stroked by a wench at the Malle Babbe on a Saturday night."

"Enough of that," Jan commanded. "Begone."

The two left, chuckling.

"Jasper!" Katja cried out.

"Don't worry," the boy tried to assure her, even though he did look a little shaken. "This is how sailors talk."

Jan barked a short laugh.

Liselotte went to Peter to examine his bandages more thoroughly.

Jan addressed Andries. "I'm very sorry about your master. But if it's a gunshot wound there's not much we can do. We've no barber or surgeon on board and carry urgent dispatches from Bergen-op-Zoom to the *Zeeuwse* Admiralty at Flushing. We're under orders and can't afford to lose time sailing in and out of a port to drop you off."

"He'll be alright," Liselotte said. "The wound was inflicted two days ago and has been treated. He needs rest. We were hoping to get to Flushing."

She slipped off her heavy pack and set it on the ground. "Katja, could you make him comfortable?"

Katja nodded and set to work with the blankets.

Jasper sat down and began to reload his musket. Andries deposited his duffel bag on the floor.

Liselotte regarded Jan. "So, who is this Michael then? And this crew of beardlings? Is the navy that short of grown men?"

Jan grinned broadly. "Michael was the first to volunteer, *meissie*, when Lieutenant-Admiral de Zoete asked who would be willing to risk a peek at Spinola's gun emplacements. This *statenjacht* is on temporary loan from the admiral for the purpose."

"An admiral!" Andries exclaimed, admiring the cabin.

Jan continued. "The admiral knows Michael's worth, and Michael knows what he's doing. He first went to sea aged eleven, four years ago and plenty of deeds to his name already."

"So, he's fifteen!" Andries sounded his disbelief.

"Aye, and a rising star in the fleet," Jan confirmed. "And some of us 'beardlings' have been with him since the start. We like to stick together. Now if you'll excuse me, there are some Dons that need to be taught a lesson. Stay put, you'll all be safe down here."

He made his way up the stairs.

Not long after they could hear cheers on *De Wilde Ruyter's* deck.

Andries and Jasper rushed to the starboard windows to peek outside.

"We've got the longboat in our sights," Jasper announced. "Looks like they were heading back, but they've come about again and are running from us now. If we can rake their stern, another round of case shot will do the trick."

Having witnessed the carnage on the beach, Liselotte could well imagine what case shot would do to tightly packed men in a longboat.

Orders were shouted above. Feet thumped on the deck, shortly after which *De Wilde Ruyter* changed course, the deck gently tilting down to starboard.

"Look!" Andries called in alarm, pointing through the larboard windows at a second longboat that had appeared behind *De Wilde Ruyter.* It was filled with armed soldiers.

"The Drowned Lands Sea lot," Jasper said. "They must have heard the gunfire on the beach."

Whereas *De Wilde Ruyter* was on an oblique course to a position behind the front longboat's stern, the new arrival was sailing in a straight line and making swift progress.

Shouts of alarm sounded above their heads, and then more thumping of feet on the deck.

"Skipper Adriaansz has to divide his crew now," Jasper told Andries. "There's not that many of them. I counted seventeen."

"They told us to stay here," Andries said.

"If the Spaniards board…" Jasper cast a worried glance at Katja.

"We won't let them," Liselotte declared.

She wasn't about to be banished to a cabin because some cheeky beardless boy had said so, no matter how much admirals trusted him.

Liselotte stood up and patted Eyang and her crossbow. "Katja, stay with Peter. Andries, Jasper, let's go."

The predicament they were in became even clearer when they emerged on the weather deck. Michael and half his crew were concentrated around *De Wilde Ruyter's* bow, exchanging musket shots with the longboat ahead of them or fussing over the carronade. The rest of the crew, commanded by Jan, had gathered on the stern, but only three of them had muskets.

The Spaniards behind *De Wilde Ruyter* were gaining fast.

"They're overbearing us!" Jasper said, pointing at the *statenjacht's* mainsail that seemed to falter somewhat. The longboat at their stern lay lower in the water and had a smaller sail but seemed to be blocking some of the wind.

A commanding voice on the chasing longboat hollered, "¡*Preparados*!" just as Michael's voice sounded from the bow, "*Klaar*!"

"They're going to fire at us," Jan shouted. "Get down, get down!"

The youths he commanded ducked below the gunwales. Liselotte motioned for Andries and Jasper to shelter behind the height differential between weather and poop deck.

"¡*Apunten!*[39]"

"*Richt!*"

Jan spotted Liselotte and her reinforcements. "I told you to stay below."

Michael's voice thundered "*VUUR!*"

The carronade on the bow spat deafening death at the front longboat, followed by agonised screams of pain.

"¡*FUEGO!*[40]"

The Spanish musket shots from the rear longboat sounded puny compared to the carronade, but the musket balls whistling over the poop deck were frightening nonetheless. Michael commanded his musketeers to pick off the remaining Spaniards in the raked longboat and more musket shots sounded at the bow.

"Now!" Jan ordered at the stern.

"Now!" Liselotte echoed instantly.

Jan's youths rose, the musketeers readying their guns, the others drawing pistols. Liselotte led the boys up the poop deck to extend the Dutch firing line.

Jan didn't protest. "*Klaar!*"

The longboat had come closer still. When Liselotte poked her crossbow over the gunwale, she could read a few bloodthirsty expressions, but most Spaniards were still focused on reloading their muskets. None had anywhere to run to. One of the watching men spotted her and leered, before licking his chops in exaggerated fashion.

"*Richt!*"

Liselotte, Andries, and Jasper aimed their weapons in unison with the beardlings. Liselotte targeted the leering man.

"*Vuur!*"

The volley briefly enveloped the stern in gun smoke. Shouts of panic and pain sounded on the longboat.

"Down!" Jan shouted. "Reload."

Liselotte ducked down and hauled back her steel string. The boys were scrambling to reload the doglocks.

The Spaniards held their fire. Grappling hooks clawed at the aft gunwales, accompanied by a frenzied collective roar from the longboat.

One of the beardling musketeers began to rise but was pulled back by a companion who was quicker-witted and realised that anyone poking their head up would be targeted by waiting Spanish musketry.

---

[39] Aim

[40] Fire

"Back to the weather deck," Jan shouted. "Stay low! Back! Back!"

They yielded the high ground of the poop deck in exchange for the cover offered by the drop to the weather deck. Michael and four beardlings from the bow joined them. Liselotte could feel her heart pounding in her chest.

A few desultory shots sounded from the bow. On the weather deck, those with loaded muskets and pistols – or readied crossbow – were told to crouch down, low down, out of sight of most of the poop deck. Michael took the rest back closer to the mast.

The first Spaniards to clamber over the stern howled in triumph when there was no immediate opposition to be seen other than a handful of *Zeeuwen* amidships.

More of their comrades spilled onto the poop deck. Liselotte could hear their boots and harsh voices as she crouched low, barely daring to breathe.

"Now!" Michael roared and sprinted forward, followed by the others in front of the mast. "Up! Up!"

The Dutch firing line rose as one to be greeted by Spanish calls of alarm.

Jan rattled, "*Klaar-Richt-VUUR!*"

Liselotte thought her eardrums would burst when she loosed her bolt amidst the gunfire. She immediately began drawing back her string.

"*Oranje en Zeeland!*" Michael thundered.

He and his beardlings propelled themselves onto the poop deck and jumped through the gun smoke, to fall upon the hurt and befuddled boarders. The musketeers followed.

Jasper and Andries wanted to join, but Liselotte told them to stay put.

Ferocious hand-to-hand fighting broke out on the poop deck, but the *Zeeuwen* clearly had the upper hand and it didn't last long. Roars of anger, clashing blades, and agonised shrieks filled the air.

The first Spaniard fled, clambering back to the longboat along the rope of a grappling hook. Only a few managed to follow the first, the rest cut down on *De Wilde Ruyter's* poop deck, now slippery with blood.

"They've had enough! They're clearing off," Jan shouted.

The beardlings cheered. "*Oranje boven!*"

Andries and Jasper joined in enthusiastically. "Huzzah!"

Liselotte was relieved it was over. Noise, confusion, fear, and pain seemed a more accurate association with fighting than the glory folk spoke of.

"They're running!" Michael said, wiping his bloodied sword on a fallen Spaniard's coat. He grinned when he spotted a crossbow bolt sticking from the man's throat.

He walked over to the front edge of the poop deck, eying Liselotte's reinforcements below. "Jan! I thought I asked you to keep this rabble in the cabin?"

"Aye-aye, Skipper, that you did and that they were told," Jan replied. "But that *meissie* is as stubborn as an ass. However, they were helpful and fought well."

Another shot sounded at the bow, followed by a cry of pain.

Michael jumped down onto the weather deck and beheld Liselotte with sparkling curiosity.

"Does the ass who defies my orders have a name? Who the devil are you, *meissie*? Other than a mutineer?"

Liselotte hesitated for a moment.

She was, of course, properly affronted by his assumption of familiarity, but…was also relishing the thrill of it.

It would be seemly to inform him that she was the daughter of a respected surgeon and Lady Saskia of the house of Krooswyck. To judge by his mannerisms, he was certainly no gentleman. Liselotte had every right to demand to be treated with the respect due to her station, but…there was a delectable sensation. She was tingling within in a way she had never experienced before.

Considering her present state of uncertainty and poverty, as well as the sea breeze tugging at her salt-crusted hair and the taste of brine on her lips, she felt more on a par with her piratical grandfather. She chose to prolong these curious senses Michael invoked, lest they depart too quickly at the behest of social conventions.

"I'm an orphan," she answered truthfully, adding proudly, "Granddaughter of a *Hollandse*[41] Sea Beggar and a Sussex smuggler. My name is Liselotte."

"Liselotte." Michael tasted the name with approval. "A Sea Beggar, eh? That does explain a thing or two."

He glanced at her crossbow and Eyang. "You're quite a wild one. I keep finding Dons you killed in battle."

---

[41] From the County of Holland.

He looked at Liselotte intently again. The invitation was back in his eyes.

He might as well be licking his lips. No shame at all!

"Michael!" Cornelis strode over from the bow. "There's none left standing on the front longboat."

As if to collaborate his claim, the longboat drifted back alongside *De Wilde Ruyter*, her mainsail floundering and deck piled with dead and wounded men.

"Good work!" Michael didn't take his eyes off Liselotte. She returned his frank gaze, not about to surrender a staring contest to this beardless leader of beardlings.

"But Michael," Cornelis said gravely. "Geleyn has been hurt. Shot."

Liselotte and Michael turned as one to see Geleyn staggering from the bow, supported by two other youths, his face rigid with pain, a growing bloodstain on his right thigh.

"Geleyn!" Michael called out.

"Spot of bother, Skipper," Geleyn managed a weak and apologetic grimace.

A shadow crossed Michael's face. "Geleyn, we have to make to Flushing. The admiral needs our report on time."

"I know, Skipper," Geleyn said. "Just make it quick, if you can."

"As if the Devil himself were on our heels," Michael promised. He addressed the other two youths and Cornelis. "Get him to the cabin. Make him comfortable. Jan!"

Jan came over as Geleyn was supported to the stairs.

"Set course to the Zuytvliet," Michael ordered. "Make full sail."

Jan strode about bellowing orders and beardlings dashed about to hoist the topsail. Liselotte noted that they had left the small duned islands of Reymerswal behind. Tholen still ran abeam to starboard – several church towers visible over a formidable sea dyke – with South Beveland coming closer on larboard. She could see a small fishing port there, modest roofs rising around a harbour, but their course would take them past it.

She went down the stairs to the cabin, passing the two youths who had carried Geleyn down and were on their way back to the weather deck.

Geleyn had been laid out on the table. Cornelis was inspecting the wounded leg.

Katja sat by Peter, who was still unconscious. The girl looked pale.

"I heard the fighting," she said, glancing at the cabin's ceiling.

"Jasper is alright, so is Andries," Liselotte replied. "Peter?"

A relieved Katja answered with a quick nod of assurance.

That forced march from the drowned city was too much for him. The fever hasn't come back though. Katja would have said if it had.

Liselotte put her crossbow down on the bench; clear of Peter's feet.

"Is it bad, Cor?" Geleyn asked his shipmate.

Cornelis nodded grimly. "Tis bad. The ball is still in your leg."

Not again.

"God's gonads!" Geleyn cursed. "I don't want to lose me leg, Cor. Don't let 'em cut it off."

Katja threw Liselotte a questioning look. Liselotte nodded, and the younger girl began to undo the straps of Liselotte's pack.

Jasper dashed down the stairs to deposit the two doglocks in the cabin. "We've been put to work by King Jan," he announced cheerfully, winked at Katja, and sped back up.

Katja rapidly retrieved items from the pack and organised what they would need, leaving Liselotte free to step up to the table.

"Have you got a galley on board?" she asked Cornelis.

"Huh? Why?"

"I need a fire."

"*Ja,* we have a galley." Michael's voice boomed through the cabin as he joined them. "But the fire was doused before we attacked at Reymerswal. Standard precaution. So, what's going on here?"

"Got a bloody musket ball stuck in me leg, Skipper," Geleyn said. "I told it to go away, but it won't listen."

Michael's face darkened. "We've set all sails, Geleyn. We'll fly to Flushing, I promise."

"Don't let 'em cut me leg off." Geleyn pleaded. "Please, Skipper. Better off dead than rotting away in hospital."

"Which is why I need fire," Liselotte told Michael. "I'll need to boil water and heat a concoction, before I extract the shot."

Michael was flabbergasted. "*Sakkerloot!* You'll do *what* now?"

"Save his life."

Their attention was temporarily drawn to the lattice windows. Dead and wounded Spaniards came tumbling past. They had been stripped to their underclothes on the poop deck and then tossed overboard to splash into the Oosterskelde.

Liselotte turned to Cornelis. "Take off Geleyn's breeches, but cut them open slow and easy around the wound first."

Cornelis let out a low whistle. "You've made an impression on the *meissie*, Geleyn. First time this request has been made without you paying for it."

"Shut up," Geleyn told him. He shook his head at Liselotte, managing a sweet smile. "Don't get me wrong, *meissie*, I'd love to. You're adorable, truly, but I'm a bit busy right now. Later, in Flushing."

Liselotte looked at them with disbelief. She recalled Henk. The Sheriff's men. Those mounted soldiers at the crossroads in Prinsenland. Andries in Father's library back in Oysterhout. Andries ogling Katja's exposed chest.

Are all of them seriously this obsessed?

She glanced at Michael, who seemed engrossed by the medical supplies and tools Katja was organising.

Is he?

She quickly looked away. He'd been honest enough about his interest, so she knew it was on his mind. She also knew who he was thinking of.

Irritated by the blush that spread on her cheeks, Liselotte spoke to Geleyn. "Fine by me. Your breeches, by the way, are dirty. And shreds of that filth will have burrowed their way deep into the wound along with that musket ball. Katja?"

"*Ja*, Mi—Liselotte?"

"Remind me what happens when wound rot sets in?"

"It eats the flesh. Leaving it behind dead."

"A gruesome sight," Liselotte added. "You'll watch it spread, Geleyn. Bit by bit, you'll watch yourself die. Worse than that, smell yourself die."

Katja, who had guessed Liselotte's game, revealed a streak of flatlander bawdiness. "He won't be able to honour his promise to you by the time we reach Flushing, Liselotte. The rot will be reaching his privates about then."

She giggled. "Oozing decay."

"That's cruel, *meissie*," Cornelis said disapprovingly.

"Michael!" Geleyn lamented, cupping his crotch. "Make them go away. Throw them overboard."

Michael finished studying the display of makeshift bandages, cauldron and crucible, pots and bottles, as well as unrolled mats that displayed gleaming steel instruments.

He gave Liselotte a curious look, then turned to Geleyn and Cornelis.

"You two will do what the *meissie* says," he ordered.

"Begging your pardon?" Cornelis asked.

"Skipper," Geleyn protested. "She's just a girl. And a Hollander by the sound of it! I need me a proper *Zeeuwse* navy surgeon."

Liselotte shook her head and poured the correct measurements of various ingredients into the crucible. Unbidden, Katja broke off a piece of Amsterdam soap and deposited it in the cauldron.

"Nay," Michael disagreed. "Not *just* a girl. She's a proper Sea Beggar. She's killed two Spaniards today. In battle."

"Three," Liselotte said. "I targeted one on the longboat. And I never miss."

"She killed a Dutch deserter too," Katja said, satisfaction in her voice.

"You hear that?" Michael asked Geleyn. "You be nice to the *meissie* now, if you know what's good for you. Liselotte?"

She looked up and instinctively caught the *duit* that tumbled through the air. She looked at it, and then at Michael, an unspoken question on her face.

"*De Wilde Ruyter* needs a ship's surgeon," Michael said. "You're hired. Welcome to the navy."

"For a single *duit*?" Katja asked. "Have you been hit by a windmill?"

Michael shrugged apologetically. "It's the family fortune I'm offering. I have no more."

"You *have* been hit by—"

Liselotte shushed Katja. The temporary commission pleased her a great deal. The *duit* didn't matter.

Michael looked at Geleyn. "You'll be treated by a proper *Zeeuwse* navy surgeon now, as per your request." He walked over to the paperwork at the far end of the table, dipped a quill in ink, and wrote something in one of the leatherbound notebooks.

Liselotte marvelled at being mustered. *I've joined the navy. Father will be turning in his freshly dug grave. Your daughter is an Oranjevaarder now. Oh, and my skipper fancies me. Turn, Father. Turn.*

One of the beardlings came rushing down the stairs, keeping his head low because of his height, crowned by a mop of pale blond hair.

"Begging your pardon, Skipper," he announced. "We've sighted sails."

"Thank you, Pelle. Tell Jan I'll be right up, oh and Pelle, tell Kokkie to light the fire in the galley."

"Aye-aye, Skipper." Pelle pounded back up the stairs.

"She's just a girl. And a Hollander by the sound of it! I need me a proper Zeeuwse navy surgeon."

Michael looked at Liselotte, all business-like this time. Her skipper now. "Anything else you need?"

"Someone to take Katja to the galley and help her carry some things. She knows what needs to be done. And a couple of men to hold Geleyn down."

"Do what now?" Geleyn asked anxiously, but he was ignored.

"He'll struggle," Liselotte added.

"I will? Skipper! Have mercy."

"And," Liselotte continued. "When I send word, to keep the ship as steady as possible for a stretch."

Michael nodded. "Cornelis will stay, and I'll send some hands down for the rest."

"Skipper, tis unseemly," Geleyn protested. "It bain't Christian."

"Do you want to keep your leg, or not?" Liselotte asked, impatience giving an edge to her tone.

"You heard the ship's surgeon," Michael said curtly. "You'll do exactly what she says, the both of you. Savvy Cornelis? Her orders are mine. Ignoring them will be counted as mutiny." He paused. "I never thought I'd say this to you Geleyn, but get those damned breeches off."

He turned to leave, then stopped and looked at Liselotte. "You're a *lieffie*. Violent and lethal, but a *lieffie* nonetheless. But I hope you know what you're doing."

"Aye-aye, Skipper," Liselotte answered, adding a confident, "I do."

23. On Passing Wolfersdiek

ON THE ZUYTVLIET SEA-ARM ~ COUNTY OF ZEELAND ~ 1622

Liselotte emerged on the weather deck, eager for a breath of fresh air. The wind had picked up. She looked in awe at the large spread of the square mainsail and the topsail overhead – sensing the sheer power up there as the elements were harnessed to do Michael's bidding.

Not entirely to his liking though, as the wind had turned. Sailing to the Zuytvliet hadn't been a matter of simply drawing a straight line there as on a sea chart. They'd had to tack again and again and were now not going to reach Flushing before nightfall.

Having spent an eternity in the cabin focused on Geleyn's wound, Liselotte had lost track of where they were. She noted the mellow evening sun. She knew she was surrounded by groaning timber, tight snaps of taut rigging, a creaking mast, and occasional slap as the bow hit a wave dead-on, followed by a light tremble that shuddered through the ship.

It...no, She, has come alive. A giant living being made of wood and canvas, speaking in sighs, creaks, and groans.

Liselotte took her cue from the crew, none of whom seemed remotely bothered by the apparent animation of *De Wilde Ruyter*.

She made her way to the bow, where she felt she'd not be in the way, as most of the crew were on the weather deck, ready for the next tack. Andries and Jasper were mingled with them, looking content enough. Michael, Jan and Pelle were on the poop deck, engaged in an earnest discussion that Michael broke off occasionally to give an instruction to the helmsman, or bellow an order over the weather deck.

Liselotte got to the blunt bow. The shores of nearby *Zeeuwse* isles were clearly defined by stout lines of sea dykes, behind which rose the occasional rooftop, or a huddle of them clustered around a church tower – even the outline of a city that they had passed to larboard.

Elsewhere, at greater distance, other islands were vague shadows at best, revealing no further secret other than their location. The sea, coloured by hues of green, was topped by white foamy heads and sometimes overshadowed by small clouds that were chased by the brisk wind.

The cannons at Bergen-op-Zoom still fired, but their sound was just a faint grumble now.

Liselotte's thoughts went back to the operation. It had required intensive effort to rid Geleyn's wound of the strands of wool from his cheap breeches. The wool had clung to the torn flesh, even fused with it, and that had required a scalpel's cut. The musket ball had gone in deep, but once she had located it with the probe, she managed to retrieve it in one go with the crane's bill.

Katja had anticipated Liselotte's every need, proving herself invaluable once more.

Geleyn himself had noticed little, because Liselotte had applied laudanum.

Michael had come down again, explaining that the distant sails had been Dutch merchants. He had stayed long enough to help restrain Geleyn during the extraction, fascinated by Liselotte's procedures, ejecting the occasional "*Sakkerloot!*"

Another successful surgery.

Liselotte heard footsteps on the deck behind her and turned, pleased to see it was Michael. She had been hoping to speak to him somewhere more private than the busy cabin, and here they were partially concealed by the jib sails. She didn't know what she wanted to say, but was certain there was much to talk about.

"We're making steady progress, in spite of the damned wind," Michael said, pointing larboard. "We've passed Goes on South Beveland. The smaller island between South Beveland and us is Wolfersdiek. That large mass ahead, that's Walcheren, where I hail from. Tholen is now far to our stern. Over there..." he indicated the land to starboard, "are the first reclaimed polders of the Drowned Land of North Beveland."

"More drowned lands," Liselotte said, shivering at the memory of the ghosts of Reymerswal.

"*Ja.* This is Zeeland after all. On North Beveland we lost Kortkene, Campen, Dyxhoecke, Edekinge, Out-Kats, Vliete, Wele, and more...all gone. The St Felix Flood took them. Same flood that took out Reymerswal ninety-some years ago. Just about all of Zeeland was swallowed up, only a few isolated polders held out against the great storm on Malign Saturday.[42] Imagine it if you can, an entire county gone, just like that." He snapped his fingers. "One hundred thousand *Zeeuwen* drowned."

---

[42] 'Malign Saturday' is what the *Zeeuwen* named 5 November 1530.

"Reymerswal was taken by the merfolk," Liselotte said. "King Nollekin and Queen Drimmeline wanted to save their daughter Hille."

Michael shook his head. "That's a fairy tale for children. Reymerswal fell because Lord Lodiek was a *bescheiter*.[43]"

Liselotte was somewhat peeved by his casual dismissal of something that was real to her, but her curiosity won over. "A swindler? How so?"

Michael placed his arms on the top of the gunwale, leaning down as he gazed out over the Zuytvliet. Liselotte did likewise, using the opportunity to move a bit closer to him.

Michael answered Liselotte's question, "It was Lord Lodiek's task to levy a dyke tax on all the freemen in Reymerswal. That money was earmarked for the water defences. That's what folk paid it for, their own safety. But Lord Lodiek used inferior – much cheaper – materials to fill up dyke sections that needed repairs. He charged the full amount and pocketed the difference. That carried on for over ten years. When the St Felix Flood struck the weakened dykes were quickly breached, the common folk condemned to death by drowning because of a corrupt ruler."

It made perfect sense in the manner that Michael described it, but Liselotte was reluctant to wholly accept it, having allied herself with the merfolk after all. She stroked Eyang's handle for reassurance.

I heard the bells toll. The others did too. That wasn't our imagination. I swore a blood oath.

Had the merfolk not sent *De Wilde Ruyter* to Liselotte's aid on Reymerswal? As well as this outrageously self-confident commoner, who spoke at times with surprising insight and knowledge far beyond his years. Whose rough voice made the word *'lieffie'* sound like raw poetry. Whose face – ruggedly hewn out of granite – was made striking by the energy he exuded.

His eyes have changed.

They had spoken with blatant honesty earlier in the day. Michael had made it light-hearted by his mockery of courtly manners and exaggerated compliments, but his eyes had conveyed desire.

He had wanted to take Liselotte as far as the stars could take them both, *should she so choose*.

The liberating sense that her own mind on this matter was of consequence to him, had been somewhat diminished by his apparent

---

[43] Literally, a 'beshitter'. Figuratively it indicated a deceptive, untrustworthy cheater. 17th century Dutch.

bold assumption that his sinful appetite was reciprocated. That was something to be scornful of, but...

It is mutual.

That insight made her heart skip a beat and her breath stall. It was a daunting aspiration, which her mind vehemently condemned as dangerous. This was the wolf from one of the cautionary tales in a book that she *had* been allowed to read. Encouraged to read even, respectable girls needed to be forewarned so that the wolf didn't swallow them whole.

Her heart spoke otherwise. Liselotte's physical response to his interest was unlikely to be one a respectable young lady ought to have. It was thrilling, daring, stimulating, and terrifying all at once.

She suspected that if he so much as looked at her in that peculiar way again, her resistance to doing something sinful would dissolve like candlewax touched by flame.

Faster and more furious than the St Felix Flood.

Since Michael had seen the medical equipment, however, his eyes had been more guarded, warily avoiding prolonged contact. Caution mixed with the longing.

Liselotte wasn't sure if she was relieved or disappointed.

She realised that Michael had been waiting for a response while her mind had been adrift, and quickly said, "It must have been terrible. I was thinking about it in Reymerswal, looking out over the Drowned Lands."

Michael shrugged. "The water comes, the water goes. We dance by the sea and drown in our homes. Then pretend we're hardened to such loss and blame the Devil or the merfolk. The worst is when it's preventable, like in Reymerswal. It's always us common folk who pay for the greed of our so-called betters. I doubt that will ever change."

He said 'us' common folk.

But I'm not who he thought I was. And he's started to suspect that.

"Michael, I..."

The words died when she saw that his scorn for *bescheiters* was replaced by frank admiration. "*Meissie*. Geleyn is an old friend of mine. I'm in your debt. Deeply so."

"Is he one of the ones who've been with you since you were eleven?"

"*Ja*, as are Cornelis, Jan, and Pelle. So, my crew wasted no time in telling tall tales?"

"They think the world of you," Liselotte noted. She shivered. "And I think we are in your debt. If you hadn't shown up at Reymerswal..."

He shrugged. "Killing Spaniards is my job."

Liselotte smiled at the utter confidence with which he said that. It was the swaggering bravado displayed by most youths of his age, but his was credible somehow. Michael exuded a remarkable – and contagious – trust in his own abilities. Having seen him in action made her suspect much of it was warranted. She decided to match his confidence with a newfound discovery.

"Well, extracting musket balls from gun wounds is my job, Seigneur."

"I watched you do it. You're skilled at it, Liselotte. But none of the 'Seigneur' stuff, if you please. I'm no gentleman; my father is a lowly brewery porter. You, however...tell me, when did they start teaching surgery to orphans?"

"About the same time they started teaching porters' sons to captain warships."

Michael chuckled. "*De Wilde Ruyter* is hardly a warship. But who knows what the future will bring? Who are the others? The older lad has to be your brother, you look much alike."

"My brother's name is Andries. We met Katja and Jasper just after Katja's *opa* and *oma* were killed by Dutch mutineers near Steynbergen."

She shuddered. "The bastards had already massacred dozens of refugees in horrible ways. We couldn't leave the children behind."

"The Flemish boy is handy, but a Papist no doubt. Can he be trusted? Who's to say he isn't a spy?"

"He's not," Liselotte declared firmly, having learned more about Jasper from Katja. "He ran away from their army."

"A deserter," Michael frowned.

"He's just a boy from a fishing village, pressed into service against his will. He's with us now. And the wounded man is..."

"Commodore Peter Haelen," Michael said. "I know of him. All of Flushing does. The Crazy Captain, they call him. Which begs the question, what are you doing in his company, Liselotte? You speak like a Hollander, a long way from home."

"Peter isn't crazy," Liselotte said pointedly. "We're on our way to his ship in Flushing. Andries and Jasper are on his muster roll."

"*The Coffin*?" Michael shook his head warily. "They say that ship is cursed."

Liselotte was confused. Peter had said his ship hadn't been named yet.

The Coffin? What a horrible name.

"He hasn't helped matters, to be honest." Michael said. "I recognise that he's driven by a vision, but it pays to heed folk around you. Setting up that dockyard without acknowleding local shipbuilders...calling it by a heathen name...building a ship with an outlandish design..."

"Heathen name?"

"Jayakarta Dockyard."

"What is Jayakarta?"

"It was the name of a Javanese port. But the VOC razed it to the ground. They've rebuilt it as Batavia."

"I've heard of Batavia. Peter is an *Oostvaarder*, he's been there."

"The Batavia Dockyard would have been a more apt name, less likely to ruffle patriotic feathers in Flushing."

Liselotte shrugged, using the movement to edge closer to Michael. She was sure Peter would have had a good reason when he named his dockyard. Her cousin didn't seem to do anything without first giving it thought.

Michael smelled of the sea. She drifted a little bit closer still.

"What about Jan?" she asked. "Where's he from? Is he a—"

"Slave? He's from West Africa and used to be a slave. But he's free now and a trusted friend."

"It must be hard for him," Liselotte reflected. "When you're...different."

"I suppose you would know, being a Sea Beggar *and* ship's surgeon, even though you're a *meissie*."

For a change Liselotte wasn't in the least concerned about the injustice of being forbidden to do things she was good at. She was wholly preoccupied with her urge to kiss Michael.

Reputation. Father's voice hissed in her ear. *Honour. Virtue.*

I'm not very good at being a respectable young lady anyway. I could have died, how many times the last few days? Are we truly safe? Or will we run into bigger Spanish ships, ending it all in a blaze of cannon fire? Before I've even really lived?

She shivered as she recalled the gruesome scenes at the crossroads in the forest near Steynbergen. It could have so easily been Peter's party on that bloody ground. Tortured at leisure. Everything that was normal, and always there, could be gone in the blink of an eye, accompanied by the sound of screams and brutal laughter. Both Michael and she could be dead in an hour's time.

Unkissed.

The sun was sinking, casting reddish and orange hues over sea and islands. They seemed to be in a world of their own on the bow.

If not now, when?

With courage she didn't know she had, Liselotte laid a hand on Michael's arm and took an audacious step forward, close enough to feel the warmth of his body. Liselotte pressed closer, leaning in on him, and turned her face up. Inviting.

Like in the books.

He reached out a hand and stroked her cheek. Tempted.

Just like in the—

His hand fell away. He took a step backward, slowly, regretfully, but definitely backward, away from Liselotte.

…not like the books at all.

She looked at him questioningly, her courage sinking.

"Liselotte, *Lieffie*," he said. "Who are you really?"

"Orphan and granddaughter of a Sea Beggar and a smuggler," she said stubbornly. "Michael, if my father had known what I've been doing since he died…fighting men, killing men, healing them…he would have disowned me."

He's done that anyway, by not mentioning me in his will. Like I don't exist.

Paradoxically, she felt gratitude for that callous and no doubt intended oversight.

He set me free.

Liselotte continued, earnestly, "It doesn't matter, not to me. All that is left of me is the girl standing in front of you. That's all there is."

"Your father was a surgeon?" Michael guessed. When she nodded, he added, "And Commodore Haelen? You called him Peter."

Cat's piss.

"My cousin. My brother is midshipman."

"*Sakkerloot, meis…Mejuffrouw.*" He shook his head, edging backward to gain a respectful distance. "*Mejuffrouw*, this was unkind of you. I want…wanted to…we almost…My lads, I myself, we've behaved like ruffians, common scoundrels. Which we are, but still…"

His embarrassment was genuine. Which made it all the more painful for Liselotte.

"Michael, please, don't."

"Nay, *Mejuffrouw*." He shook his head, regret in his tone. "Such things cannot work. It'll end in tears and idle folks' gossip."

Something that somehow feels so right?

"How do we know, if we haven't tried?"

She was wholly preoccupied with her urge to kiss Michael.

"You think none have gone before? Such things don't work out well. Your reputation would be shattered beyond repair. I'm a nobody from the Flushing slums, I can't afford to make enemies of respectable families. Your cousin has powerful connections."

"Peter would never—"

"Maybe, but that would make him a rare exception. There are other Haelens?"

"In Rotterdam." Liselotte reluctantly added, "I'm to be sent there."

"Your virtue a valuable family asset then."

She glared at him. "Your manhood an idle boast then."

He shook his head. "That might work on the weak-minded, *Mejuffrouw*. I care not. You know how they'll think about it in

Rotterdam. That's the way of the world. Some things aren't yours to give."

Fine. I'm not going to beg.

"I need to go check on my patients, Skipper Adriaansz. Presuming I have your permission to do that, at least."

"*Ja*, of course. Lise…*Mejuffrouw*. I'm in your debt and deeply grateful for what you've done for Geleyn."

Ja, sure.

Liselotte left the bow and stepped onto the weather deck – angry, empty, and defeated.

Platbroeck.

Most of the crew were gathered around the main hatch, which Cornelis had occupied like a stage. He was telling a dramatic tale, to judge by his tone and extensive hand gestures.

"And then…after the little *meissie* had described in horrible detail how Geleyn's dick was going to rot off…'ooze decay' the little 'un said, the surgeon herself said, 'Do you want to keep your leg, or not?'"

"Cornelis," one of the beardlings warned him, nodding at Liselotte.

Cornelis paused in the middle of a complicated gesture. "The surgeon is behind me, isn't she?"

Liselotte tried to ignore them, to keep her eyes focused on the low door to the cabin stairs. She wasn't in the mood for their banter, not right at this minute after…

I threw myself in his arms. All caution cast to the wind. Like a common tavern wench.

The crew had become suspiciously quiet. Despite her intention not to, Liselotte cast a glance at them, to come to a surprised halt.

They were all looking at her. One by one, they took their caps off and lowered their heads in respect.

"Three cheers for the *De Wilde Ruyter's* surgeon, lads," Jan shouted. "Hip Hip…"

"HUZZAH!"

Michael appeared, taking place at the side of the group. There was a sad smile on his face.

"Hip Hip," Pelle shouted.

"HUZZAH!"

"HIP HIP," Cornelis roared.

"HUZZAH!"

The crew threw their hats in the air and cheered. Liselotte bit on her lip, turned, and fled down to the cabin so they wouldn't see the tear that spilled down her cheek.

24. A Festive Display

ON THE VLAECK ~ COUNTY OF ZEELAND ~ 1622

Andries awoke before dawn, yawning contentedly. The benches in *De Wilde Ruyter's* cabin offered far more comfort than any of the other places he'd managed to snatch some sleep in since they had left Oysterhout.

And that after an ample evening meal of a simple but warm stew – as much as he had wanted – with reasonably fresh bread, ale, and celebratory brandywine.

Andries kept his eyes closed. He hoped to retain his warm sense of well-being as long as possible, but he couldn't prevent his mind from focusing on his surroundings and the others in the cabin. Geleyn was snoring. Peter drawing regular breaths. Jasper and Katja were sound asleep at the back of the cabin. Liselotte however, appeared to be awake. He could hear her sighing – tossing and turning.

She'd been making things complicated again. The crew on the weather deck hadn't been oblivious to her encounter with Adriaansz on the bow. They'd responded with knowing grins and much eye rolling. With so many topside, Liselotte hadn't technically been improperly alone with the ship's young captain. Yet, all had sensed that those two seemed to be in a world of their own.

Andries hadn't been pleased. First that scandal with the Oysterhout farm boy, and now skirting the edge of propriety in view of sailors. Even a landlubber like himself knew sailors gossiped more than old women at the market. Liselotte ought to know that she had her brother's reputation to think of, and Peter's.

It was inconsiderate of her, but then the crew had huzzahed her. That had filled Andries with pride at the respect that she commanded from that rowdy lot.

She'd turned shy and fled to the cabin, strangely quiet and subdued when Andries and Jasper had joined the rest of their party there. Jan and Pelle had come down for supper, but Michael had stayed away, choosing to eat on deck with his crew instead. That had been disappointing, as Andries looked up to him as a hero to emulate.

Andries was debating whether to diminish his own elation by inviting his sister to talk about whatever was making her unhappy, when Peter spoke softly.

"Can't sleep, Liselotte?"

"Peter!" Liselotte replied in a hushed tone. "When did you come to?"

"About half-an-hour ago, at a guess. I've been listening to the waves chat to the hull. It's good to be back at sea again."

"Are you thirsty, shall I get you some water?"

"Aye, that would be a fine thing."

Andries heard Liselotte get up to pour water from a pewter jug.

"Thank you, Liselotte. I take it we managed to get away from that Reymerswal beach then."

"*Ja*, we're moored on the Zuytvliet, at the end of Wolfersdiek. They said it was too risky to sail on to Flushing in the dark. I think they said we'd be off to a...head? At dawn."

"The Armuyden Hooft I suspect. On Walcheren's shore. It's sensible to be cautious. There are shallows in the waters of the Vlaeck, not to mention deceptive currents."

"There was another fight soon after Reymerswal. There were two longboats filled with Spanish soldiers on the Oosterskelde. We defeated them. Andries and Jasper fought really well."

Andries smiled, unseen in the darkness of the cabin.

Ja, I did.

"Good lads. Did any of the Spaniards find themselves at the wrong end of a crossbow?"

"Of course. One on the beach, one on the longboat, and one of the boarders on *De Wilde Ruyter*."

"*Opa* and *Oma* would have been proud of you. So am I, but I'm not so sure if the Rotterdam Haelens will view it that way? You might...exceed their expectations regarding proper behaviour. I don't think respectable young ladies are meant to swan about shooting mutineers and Spanish soldiers."

"I won't mention it to them."

"The other man in the cabin? The snoring one?"

"Geleyn. One of the crew, he got hurt in the second fight."

"What kind of hurt?"

"Musket ball, in his thigh. I extracted it."

"You really are something else, Liselotte. I reckoned your pack was too heavy, but I thought—"

"That I'd surrender and give up."

"That you would learn the lesson and lighten the load. Maybe lose a gown or two."

"Gown or two?" Liselotte laughed. "The only gown I own is the one I'm wearing."

"I see. My apologies. We'll make sure you're presentable before we get to Rotterdam. Can't have you reunited with the family looking like a Sea Beggar."

"They'll see me as I am. Is that so bad? Peter, do you think your father would be offended if I asked to stay with Aunt Mathilda and Uncle Karel?"

"Is that what you'd like to do? They're kind people, that much I remember."

"Very kind. Andries and I used to stay there a lot, back in Rotterdam. When our cousins still lived."

"It won't be my decision but if that's what you want, I shall certainly recommend it."

"Thank you, Peter."

"We're on *De Wilde Ruyter*, was it? Admiral de Zoete's *statenjacht*. Who's skipper?"

Liselotte hesitated for a moment, before she said, "Michael Adriaansz. They were scouting Bergen-op-Zoom."

"Adriaansz! The *Duvelsjong*[44] of Flushing."

"*Duvelsjong*?"

"That boy has more mischief in his little finger than seven shiploads of sailors on shore leave. He's always been destined for great things, or the gallows. Mind you, the first is more likely these days. He's a boatswain's mate in the fleet, and clearly de Zoete trusts him enough to let him command the admiral's own *statenjacht*. But the lad still frequents Flushing's taverns to cause mayhem when he can. The boy has quite a reputation."

"So I've noticed."

"How so, Liselotte? Has he misbehaved to you?"

Liselotte made a sound that seemed a combination of a sob and a laugh. "Oh, he's been more than honourable, Peter. Like a gentleman, in fact. You need not worry on that count."

Oh, that's a relief, Andries thought.

"Are you sure?"

"*Ja*, Peter. Nothing untoward has happened." She let out a deep and wistful sigh.

---

[44] Devil's child, used to indicate an unruly child.

"Well, that's good to hear. I haven't got a clue, Liselotte, how to ward a young woman such as yourself. I'm afraid I've let you run wild."

"Run wild? There wasn't much of a choice, as I recall."

"True. This last week, it must have been quite an experience for you."

Liselotte seemed to be mulling that over, before she answered. "What comes to mind are the horrors of the crossroads, the blood and pain, the tiredness from walking endlessly, sleeping on the hard ground, being cold, wet, scared, and hungry a lot of the time. But…"

"But?"

"I've never felt so free."

Free? What rubbish. We've been in danger for much of it.

"Aye, you've definitely been running around wild. It might be a challenge, getting used to the constraint of the civilised world again."

"I'll do my best."

"I think you'll manage, there seems to be little that comes your way that you aren't capable of dealing with."

Peter was slowing down, pausing longer between words.

"We're talking too much Peter, you need rest."

"*Ja.* I shall rest now."

Andries was relieved. Most of it had been a dull conversation with nothing to indicate a reason for Liselotte's subdued spirit. He dismissed his earlier concern; it was probably just one of those spells of strange emotional silliness girls were prone to.

Maybe he could surrender to some more sleep. He had certainly earned it. He recalled scenes from the previous day. The sheer terror and fear he'd felt had already faded, leaving him with recollections of stepping up to the gunwale with *De Wilde Ruyter's* crew to fire a volley at the onrushing Spaniards on the beach. Shoulder to shoulder with Jasper. Then again, at the longboat's boarders on the poop deck. Gunfire, smoke and screams below the proud spread of the prince's flag.

I'm truly an Oranjevaarder now. I fought and killed Spanish soldiers. For the Republic. In the name of the Prince of Orange.

Although it was less glorious, Andries was equally proud that he had been true to his promise to learn about sailing.

At first, when Liselotte had introduced herself to Adriaansz on the weather deck after the fight, Andries had been peeved with her omission of their social standing.

He had complained to Jasper about it. "She's letting them talk to her like they do to their wenches. It's not proper."

Jasper had looked about him, before answering in a low conspiratorial tone. "*Mynheer* Andries, this is a very tight-knit crew. We've got some acceptance because we did well in the fighting. But a unit like this, I've seen it afore, *Mynheer*. You must earn their respect. They won't give it if we insist that you're properly addressed as midshipman, as you should be, of course. But this lot won't be impressed. I think your sister has done you a favour. And I'm sure *Mejuffrouw* Liselotte can fend off unwanted attentions. They're a little bit scared of her."

Andries had mulled this over. He didn't agree with everything Jasper had said, as respect from lower classes for their betters should be a given. On the other hand, this crew, even though they were boys his own age or just a little older, far exceeded him in confidence. The way they swaggered about like old tars was intimidating. Commanding them one day would be easier when Andries was properly dressed, with an officer's sword at his side.

"You'd best call me Andries then, for a while," he grumbled.

Jasper had grinned. "*Ja*, Andries."

When Jan had presumed to start ordering the boys about, Andries had been reluctant at first, but soon started enjoying his apprenticeship. They'd been kept plenty busy, stripping the fallen Spaniards of weapons and armour, scrubbing the poop deck clear of blood, hauling at ropes during the tacking, and helping Kokkie prepare the stew.

Through it all, Jasper had patiently provided explanations about the tasks they were assigned, tasks carried out by other crew, as well as naming parts of the ship, rigging, and sails. He had done so in low murmurs, so as not to make clear to all just how little Andries knew.

By the time Liselotte was huzzahed, Andries had earned himself little nods of acknowledgement by the crew, as well as a few hearty slaps on his back that had filled him with pride.

It had been a perfect day, Andries concluded, before he sank into a slumber.

He dreamt about Truusje, back in Zevenbergen. This time there was no animosity, just her breasts, his hands caressing her body. He woke in a state of arousal. Half-submerged in his dream still, Andries brought a hand down—

He shot up, snatching one hand away with the other, guiltily remembering where he was.

The only other people in the cabin were Peter and Geleyn, both fretting lightly in their sleep.

Andries could tell that *De Wilde Ruyter* was under sail, the hull slicing through the sea. The curtains had been drawn shut, but gaps revealed daylight outside.

Andries made his way up the stairs. The hatch to the weather deck was open and voices drifted down.

"A sight for sore eyes, I tell you!"

"Will you look at that? Will you just look at that?"

"*Oranje boven!*"

"Spinola will shit himself!"

"Three cheers for Admiral de Zoete!"

Andries rushed the rest of the stairs two steps at a time, to burst onto the weather deck and make his way to the gunwale to stare.

The sun warmed a blue sky. They had left Wolfersdiek and South Beveland behind, coursing steadily towards the Walcheren shoreline, which stretched out on starboard as far as Andries could see.

They weren't the only ones out on the water. Sailing from the south, resplendent in the morning sunshine, was the most impressive spectacle that Andries had ever seen. Ships, large and small, almost a hundred of them.

All were festooned with flags that broke the monotony of the pale forest of sails. The red-white-and-blue flag of the Republic dominated, but there were also multi-banded prince's flags, Republic state flags with a crowned red lion on a gold field, and the *Zeeuwse* flag displaying a red lion on a field of blue and white wavy lines. Long narrow orange pennants completed the festive display, streaming playfully in the wind.

The most imposing vessels were a score of warships, three-masted and multi-decked, with two rows of cannon ports running from bow to stern, about twenty ports in total.

With another twenty on the other side. That's eight hundred cannons on the big ships alone!

"A fine sight, isn't it?" Michael Adriaansz joined Andries. "I guess Admiral de Zoete decided not to waste time waiting for us to return. This will make a big difference at Bergen-op-Zoom, some of the Don gun emplacements are very vulnerable."

"Good," Andries replied. "And a fine sight indeed. I've never seen anything like it."

He saw Liselotte and Katja from the corner of his eye, making their way back to the cabin.

"And this is just the *Zeeuwse* fleet. With all due respect to Prince Maurits's army, it'll be sea power that will win this war."

"You think we can win?"

"Of course we can! And we will." Michael studied Andries. "Your sister told me that you're a midshipman on Commodore Haelen's ship."

"*Ja*, I am."

"And yet, *Mynheer*, Jan had you on your knees scrubbing *De Wilde Ruyter's* deck yesterday. You could have told us you were an officer? You outrank all of us."

"Officer-in-training. I've never set foot aboard a ship until a few days ago," Andries confessed. "I'm still to learn. I didn't think it a good idea to pull rank. Your crew is very good."

Michael nodded. "You made a wise decision, *Mynheer*. My lot wouldn't have taken well to being ordered about by someone who's little acquainted with the sea."

He indicated the fleet. "We've got a surplus of arrogant officers whose sense of entitlement far exceeds their abilities. De Zoete is clever enough to keep me and the lads away from them. I'd say you took a promising step in becoming one of the good officers, *Mynheer*. And God knows, the Republic is going to need men like you."

Andries thought he would burst with pride. "Thank you, Skipper!"

A solitary boom sounded over the water. Andries looked toward the source of the noise, to see smoke drifting from a single cannon muzzle on one of the warships.

"That will be Admiral de Zoete's summons," Michael said. "If you'll excuse me, I've work to do. Oh, and please look after your sister, she's quite remarkable. I've never met anyone like her before."

He walked off, shouting orders.

Andries deducted that the fleet wasn't intending to stop altogether. Sails were shortened to reduce speed, giving *De Wilde Ruyter* the opportunity to come about and take up a position abeam the admiral's flagship. A longboat was launched to fetch Michael and Pelle, rowed by a score of stout *Oranjevaarders*. Michael took an armful of rolled up scrolls, presumably information on the Spanish siegeworks. Jan was left in command of the *statenjacht*.

After Michael had been rowed back from the flagship – he'd been aboard for less than half-an-hour –, he briefly spoke to Jan, and then summoned Andries and Jasper to join him in the cabin. Liselotte and Katja had been tending their patients; both Peter and Geleyn were awake.

"Commodore Haelen," Michael said respectfully to Peter. "It's good to see you in the land of the living."

"Thank you, Skipper Adriaansz. All thanks to the remarkable skills of my cousin."

*Sailing from the south, resplendent in the morning sunshine, was
the most impressive spectacle that Andries had ever seen*

"She ain't half bad," Geleyn admitted.

"And I must thank you as well, Skipper," Peter continued. "For coming to our assistance at Reymerswal. We were in a bit of a tight spot."

Michael nodded. "My orders allowed me to engage if absolutely necessary, Commodore. Seeing a handful of patriots flying the prince's colour, under siege by more Dons than ought to set foot on *Zeeuwse* soil, was necessity enough. We couldn't possibly let a bunch of Hollanders and a Fleming get all the credit for defending Zeeland from invasion."

"I'm from Brabant," Katja protested. "I shot a pistol."

"My apologies, *meissie*," Michael said, grinning at the girl. "I certainly can't have brave Brabanders defending *Zeeuwse* turf while standing by unemployed."

Katja grinned back at him. "Exactly."

Peter said, "You have our gratitude, Skipper. I take it that you've spoken to Admiral de Zoete?"

"*Ja*, I have, Commodore. I'm afraid we won't be able to take you to Flushing. The fleet sails to Bergen-op-Zoom and we have orders to join it. Spinola's earthworks surround the city but none are aimed at the Oosterskelde. We caught the Dons with their pants down, begging your pardon Commodore. We need to strike fast, and we need to strike hard."

"I understand," Peter said.

Liselotte, who had remained in the background, throwing the occasional uncertain glance at Michael, shook her head, mouthing a 'nay'.

Andries reckoned he understood her reaction all too well. He had hoped their next stop would be Flushing, reached comfortably in *De Wilde Ruyter's* admiral's cabin. No further adventures, he'd had more than enough.

He asked, "but how will we get to Flushing?"

"We've hailed one of the fishing boats that have come to gape at the fleet." Michael told him. "And will arrange a passage for you to Armuyden." He looked at Peter. "Commodore, I trust you're familiar enough with Walcheren to find your way to Flushing from there?"

"Aye, indeed. And once again, you have our thanks."

"How about me?" Geleyn complained. "I need my surgeon!"

"*Your* surgeon, is she now?" Michael responded. "The yawl is waiting to take you to the flagship, Geleyn. There's a sick berth waiting for you, and you'll have de Zoete's own physician at your disposal, compliments of the admiral. And Pelle for company, he'll be there to help Admiral Zoete interpret the maps we drew."

"I think I'll go with *Mejuffrouw*," Geleyn insisted. "I'm sure it's bad luck to change doctors in the midst of this most dangerous of, erm, medicinal phases and such."

"I'm sure it doesn't, Geleyn," Liselotte said, with a little smile. "But the compliment is appreciated."

"If you must hang from the yardarm for desertion, Geleyn," Michael said cordially. "You should have informed me yesterday. That would have saved our surgeon a great deal of trouble."

"Suppose so," Geleyn muttered. "The admiral's own physician, eh? How about his personal cook? Will he be at my disposal?"

"In your wildest dreams," was Michael's answer.

Things moved quickly after that. A fishing yawl had drawn alongside by the time Peter's party emerged on the deck of *De Wilde Ruyter*, packed and well. Peter was on his feet, using the pennant pole as support, a blanket around his shoulders. The crew shouted quick farewells. Andries saw Jan press two cleaned crossbow bolts and a folded piece of paper into Liselotte's hands. There was no time for longer goodbyes. Sails were being lengthened across the fleet. The sound of commands and pounding feet on decks filled the air.

Michael's young sailors passed down baggage and weapons to the fishermen aboard the yawl. They then helped Peter and the children climb down to the yawl along the rope nettings that had been cast over the gunwales for this purpose.

Statenjacht and fishing yawl separated. The first sailed off to war. The second set course for Armuyden.

Peter's Story
Hendrik van der Dekken

SEVEN YEARS EARLIER

CAPE OF GOOD HOPE, SOUTHERN AFRICA, 1615

The fierce storm appeared out of nowhere. It swept toward the convoy with unnatural speed. Wind and rain whipped the broad swells of the South Atlantic into ferocious waves. Dark clouds rapidly claimed the sky, dimming daylight.

The convoy had been spread out in a long line of nine East India merchantmen and one large yacht, all flying the VOC colours. The ships scattered in the face of the onrushing tempest.

Those at the rear, with the flat-topped Table Mountain abeam, came about to seek shelter in Table Bay. The majority tacked until they had rounded the Cape of Good Hope – the Storm Cape – and then made good use of the wind at their back to reach the relative safety offered by False Bay.

One of the ships, however, didn't deviate from her route to Cape Agulhas, the southernmost point of the African continent where the South Atlantic met the Indian Ocean. It was the merchantman *De Blokzeyl*.

De Blokzeyl's young First Steersman, recently promoted after a fever had taken his predecessor, hurried to the helm.

The tall stern figure of *De Blokzeyl's* biblically-bearded skipper was a familiar sight on the quarterdeck, for he rarely seemed to rest. Captain Hendrik van der Dekken was a man of few words but a superb sailor who ran a tight ship. There were few places on board of *De Blokzeyl* where the First Steersman couldn't sense the captain's relentless authority. It seemed at times that skipper and ship had merged into a single entity.

"Well met, Haelen," the captain greeted the First Steersman. "A fine day for sailing, nay?"

"Captain, the other ships are headed for False Bay," Peter Haelen said, pointing at the rest of the nearby convoy.

"Your observational skills are astounding," van der Dekken replied.

"Skipper, shouldn't we...?"

"Damn your eyes, Haelen. I'll have no outlandish profanity here, not aboard my ship."

"Aye-aye, Skipper. But the rest..."

"AMATEURS! COWARDS! DAMN THEIR EYES!" van der Dekken roared, before dropping his fury and assuming calm reassurance. "If it would settle your nerves, Haelen, you may tell the boatswain to take in the top sails and reef the mainsails."

"Aye-aye, Skipper." Peter Haelen retreated from van der Dekken, as the captain relieved the helmsman, taking place at the helm with keen confidence.

Walter Zundert, the boatswain, grumbled and shook his weathered head. "It don't bode well to underestimate these cape storms, *Mynheer* Haelen." Nonetheless, he bellowed orders and sailors ran to obey him, a great many ascending the shrouds to raise or reef sails.

The ship's *Koopman*[45] appeared on the weather deck, impeccably dressed as usual, his demeanour calm and confident as he took in the labouring crew and rapidly approaching storm.

"How goes it, Peter?"

"I'm not sure, Marnix. It appears Captain van der Dekken doesn't want to be slowed down by the storm."

Marnix Velthuys chuckled. "The man is obsessed with speed."

Peter nodded. It was true. He had lost count of the number of times van der Dekken had grumbled about the perceived sluggishness of the rest of the fleet. *De Blokzeyl* had frequently been called to heel by the yacht, when van der Dekken had once more coaxed the maximum speed to be had from the ship, only to have to take in sail and wait for the rest to catch up.

It was an open secret that van der Dekken was likely to leave the fleet behind once they had passed Cape Agulhas. Safety in numbers was an unassailable VOC commandment for the Atlantic Ocean. There was no such stipulation for the Indian Ocean, and many skippers viewed the dash from the Cape of Good Hope to Batavia along the Roaring Forties trade winds as a race, encouraged by bonuses awarded to the skippers who reach Java fastest.

De Blokzeyl's crew shared their captain's ambitions. They knew Hendrik van der Dekken wasn't interested in the bonuses, he just

---

[45] Commis. The VOC merchant on board of company ships whose authority exceeded the skipper on company matters.

wanted to beat the others and be counted a *Bestevaer*[46] among sailors. On previous occasions, the captain had divided the bonuses between the crew, with equal shares for all.

Nonetheless, the captain was a traditionalist. He had shown no interest in ship design innovations suggested by Peter, growling responses such as "Damn your eyes, Haelen, I'll not tolerate such heresy on *De Blokzeyl.*"

"And what do you reckon?" Marnix asked Peter. "About taming a tempest?"

Peter hesitated. He'd established a good relationship with Marnix from the moment they had left the Tessel roadstead. Despite being very different in nature, the men had woven their initial mutual appreciation into something resembling a friendship during their frequent encounters in the great cabin, where the ship's officers worked, relaxed, and took their meals.

"Your hesitation, Peter," Marnix observed. "Is answer enough. You don't want to be disloyal to your captain."

"There is a risk to it," Peter admitted. "But if anyone can pull it off, it'll be our skipper."

His was a sentiment shared by most of the crew. There was a fair share of grumbling as the men were set to work in the increasingly atrocious weather, but most of that was good-natured. Pride in showing the other crews a lesson in seamanship was the prevailing mood when *De Blokzeyl* was first clutched by the storm; the men blasted by the wind and whipped by the rain.

A man's conviction, however, can be subject to erosion. Admiration for the dramatic spectacle of nature's fury diminished as *De Blokzeyl* rode out hour after hour of the ocean's rage. Excitement at the challenge of it was dulled by the sheer endlessness of the raging maelstrom of towering waves, howling winds, sheets of rain, and incessant briny spray. Swaggering confidence changed to grim determination to see it through. Pride in *De Blokzeyl's* performance was replaced by an increasing awareness of the ship's vulnerability in the face of the ocean's unmitigated violence.

The first casualties were counted. A man swept overboard. A scream as someone plummeted down from a spar, cut short when he impacted the deck with an audible crack of skull and bones. A steady

---

[46] An honorary title for leading seamen that could only be conferred by seamen. It referred to a combination of 'Best Father', this applicable to the paternal role of a good skipper, and 'Best Sailor'. It was never bestowed lightly.

stream of lesser injuries kept the surgeon and his assistants busy. When men weren't needed, they sheltered below deck, but they were frequently summoned topside to perform one task or another.

For the first few hours of the storm, Hendrik van der Dekken bellowed commands at the boatswain, unperturbed by the storm's seemingly infinite energy.

Somehow, though, the skipper became detached from the rest of the crew, reducing his existence to a private battle between himself and the storm.

He stood at the helm, back straight, head held high, and most voluble as he raged at the elements. "Know this, ye winds, that I shall not yield. Damn your eyes! Rage if you want. Howl what you want, but I shall not yield."

It was Walter Zundert who somehow translated the captain's ravings into the orders that were required to keep *De Blokzeyl* from floundering in the tumultuous seascape of hungry waves and seething winds.

Word of the captain's behaviour began to spread. Dread took root. A sense of impending doom became prevalent.

At last the captain ceased his blusterous defiance of the storm, clutching the helm in silence instead, exuding his unshakable faith in *De Blokzeyl*. The mere sight of him sufficed to convince the hands on deck to carry out their tasks with quick efficiency. They saved their mutters until they had descended back into the focsle.

Those murmurs of discontent, fuelled by fear, swelled into resentment.

The first Peter knew of this, was when the constable came to the great cabin to share his opinion that Peter, as the highest-ranking ship's officer after the captain, had best visit the focsle to diffuse the situation.

Peter exchanged a glance with Marnix. If the constable felt that the men were beyond his control, things were bad indeed.

"I'll come with you," Marnix said.

As they made their way to the focsle, Peter cast a glance at Hendrik van der Dekken at the helm. He half feared that the captain would demand an explanation as to what Peter was up to. In van der Dekken's present state of mind, any suggestion that the crew doubted their captain's capacity might trigger a reaction that would only make things worse.

Van der Dekken, however, seemed oblivious to the First Steersman and *Koopman*. He remained silent and forbidding at the helm, rearing straight as a ramrod in his refusal to cower for the storm.

Although forewarned, Peter wasn't prepared for the enmity he encountered in the focsle. Both he and Marnix were popular with the men, but that seemed to matter little now. The men had gathered in a broad circle, leaning in on a centre formed by three sailors who seemed to have been chosen to speak for the collective.

Looking around, Peter read outright hostility on the faces of the usual malcontents. The majority, as of yet, seemed ready to give the First Steersman the benefit of the doubt, but they were wary and mistrustful. Still, many expressions also conveyed embarrassment, but it was mixed by stubborn insistence that they were in the right to be concerned.

Peter invited the sailors in the centre to give voice to the crew's grievances. They left him with little doubt that the collective opinion was that the captain's mind had keeled over, that *De Blokzeyl* was skippered by a madman, and that the survival of ship and her entire crew now depended on relieving Hendrik van der Dekken of command.

In short: Mutiny.

Privately, Peter shared the fear that the captain's mind had come undone.

The spokesmen posed an impossible ultimatum. Peter was invited to take the lead, thereby lending some legitimacy to the enterprise of deposing a captain, or express his opposition – defying the deeply unhappy crew.

"Whatever you decide," Marnix spoke in a low voice. "You will have my support."

Peter examined the core group. Jan-Pier, Tjores, and Korneel were prime first-raters. Like all underpaid sailors on a dangerous voyage, they had causes to grumble, but in the months that Peter had known them they had never engaged in airing their grievances. They returned his gaze frankly. Peter sensed that they were greatly reluctant in their role, but resolute in their conviction that all was lost if nothing was done.

If van der Dekken and his officers had lost their grip on men like these, there wouldn't be many on board who would lift a finger to prevent an outright mutiny.

"I will go talk to the skipper myself," Peter decided.

There were shouts, once again emphasising the crew's desire that van der Dekken was removed from command immediately.

Peter raised his hands to bid for silence. "If such a thing is done by force," he spoke loudly. "The VOC will brand every man jack of you a mutineer. I do *not* want to see a single one of you hung from the yardarm. That's my motivation."

"You could take the ship and run," Marnix added. "But you'd never be able to return to the Republic. Never see your sweethearts, wives, children, parents, brothers and sisters again."

"You dare threaten us?" One of the regular malcontents demanded furiously.

Korneel rose to speak with considerable volume. "Nay, Olle. That's not what I heard. *Mynheer* Haelen and *Koopman* Velthuys spelled out consequences, which are true enough, let's not fool ourselves."

Tjores nodded. "Let's give the First Steersman a chance to do it his way."

"Give him a chance," Pier-Jan concurred.

The opinions of those three settled it for most of the crew.

"Well played," Marnix told Peter as they emerged on the weather deck.

"Was it?" Peter asked. "I just don't know."

"*De Blokzeyl* is still a VOC vessel, isn't it? What do you think van der Dekken will say? Can he be reasoned with?"

"Damn your eyes." Peter sighed. "That's what he'll say. And then tell us to be on our way."

He approached the helm with great trepidation. At least the storm seemed to be lessening in intensity, but other than that Peter had little to be happy about and a great deal to fear.

Van der Dekken waited motionlessly for his First Steersman to join him at the helm, his eyes fixed on what passed for a horizon beyond the bow. With visibility still hampered by the storm, it wasn't until Peter and Marnix were within an arm's length of their captain that they realised they would not, after all, be required to try and counter insanity with reason.

The captain was stone cold dead. His muscles had gone rigid, keeping him upright, his hands gripping the helm in a lifeless vice.

"The captain is dead," Marnix said. "Long live the captain."

Peter barely registered those words, unable at that moment to fully comprehend that he was now captain of *De Blokzeyl*. Instead, a chill grasped his heart and a shiver traversed his spine as he wondered for just how long *De Blokzeyl* had sailed under the command of a dead man.

Marnix had similar thoughts. "Better not tell the men. Quick, help me prize him loose."

They struggled with the dead man's stiff fingers in the continued gloom of the storm. The sky thundered in triumph. Lightning bolts pierced the restless ocean.

Unexpectedly, Walter Zundert rushed to their rescue, adding his strength to the effort. "The men mustn't see Skipper van der Dekken like this, Cap'n," he grumbled to Peter.

His intervention was timely. The men had become restless in their impatience. The first of them, Jan-Pier, Tjores, and Korneel, strode across the weather deck to investigate, others appearing behind them. The sailors saw the boatswain at the helm, and the First Steersman and *Koopman* bent over the prone body of the captain.

Not the best impression to make. But better this than the sight of van der Dekken clinging on to De Blokzeyl with stubborn determination even in death.

Peter, Marnix, and the boatswain exchanged quick looks of understanding between them.

Peter said, "Thank you, Walter."

Marnix nodded his agreement. "Thank you, Boatswain Zundert."

"Pleasure, Cap'n," Walter Zundert answered. "*Heer*[47] Velthuys."

Jan-Pier, Tjores, and Korneel decided to forego a request for an explanation. They had all the facts they needed. Nodding briefly at Peter, they turned to face the rest of the gathering crew.

"Let's hear it, lads," Jan-Pier bellowed. "For Skipper Haelen."

Tjores, Korneel, and Walter echoed him: "Skipper Haelen!"

The crew cheered. One or two were unwise enough to throw their hats in the air, and these were promptly devoured by the wind, carried out of sight in no time.

"Congratulations, my friend," Marnix said in a low voice so only Peter could hear him.

"Bethanks to your support."

Marnix waved that away gallantly. "Get us out of this storm, Skipper, and then let's go make some serious money."

"Aye, let's do that."

---

[47] Lord. This was a common title used to acknowledge both aristocrats and the wealthiest burghers.

Part Three
Isle of Walcheren

See you, beneath yon cloud so dark,
Fast gliding along, a gloomy bark?
Her sails are full, though the wind is still,
And there blows not a breath her sails to fill!

(From 'Written on Passing Dead-Man's Island' by Thomas Moore, 1804)

25. At the Silly Sally

ARMUYDEN ~ COUNTY OF ZEELAND ~ 1622

Liselotte sat next to Katja on the fishing yawl's middle thwart, staring at *De Wilde Ruyter* as the *Zeeuwse* fleet sailed off to the Zuytvliet.

She hadn't been sure what might have been salvaged from the previous evening's disaster. She'd left in anger.

Not a good thing.

During her nearly sleepless night, Liselotte had struck upon the hope that a renewed day would provide an opportunity to talk with Michael again. Make peace.

She'd kept her distance when he'd come down to the cabin after he had visited the admiral's flagship, unsure how to carry herself. Then, before she'd even fully realised it, she'd been climbing down to take place in the fishing yawl.

Michael had shown himself briefly at the gunwale of the poop deck, to wave a farewell at the yawl. They'd already been too far away to read his face.

Was he relieved? Sad? Regretful? Disappointed? Indifferent?

It was a poor goodbye. Liselotte was unlikely to see him again. He was sailing off to war, where death's hungry maws awaited many. If he returned, she would have long been deposited in Rotterdam, in the company of strangers and bound by a myriad of rules.

Maybe it's better this way. I'd just make a fool of myself again.

Katja shifted closer, taking one of Liselotte's hands in her own. "Miss, what's wrong?"

"Nothing, Katja." Liselotte answered automatically.

"That's not true."

Katja glanced at the other members of their party, by the yawl's bow. The boys were telling Peter about the fights of the previous day, eagerly competing to spill heroic details and basking in Peter's compliments.

Leaning closer, Katja whispered. "Liselotte, you said we would be friends. Friends share their troubles, don't they?"

Liselotte bit on her lip, squeezing Katja's hand. "I'll tell you later then, *my friend*. When we're alone."

"It's *him*, isn't it?" Katja asked. "That Flushing rascal."

"Michael…"

"Well, whatever he's said or done, I reckon he's definitely been hit by a windmill."

Liselotte smiled but shook her head.

He was the sensible one. I was rash and impulsive.

Inwardly, she fumed. *Sensible after stunning me with that promise in his eyes first.*

She also remembered his clear regret. He had wanted to.

Liselotte sighed. In the romances, they would have run away and sailed into the sunset. Or, she reminded herself, met a less happy end like Tristan and Isolde.

He's gone now. Nothing to be done about that. Stop dwelling on it.

They were nearing their destination, so she tried to focus on Armuyden instead. Busy wharves fronted the city with multiple jetties extending out into the water. Modern ramparts, broken by gates, rose above the expansive wharves. A gigantic church rose tall over the red-tiled rooftops behind the formidable defences. It had a steep roof and a slender tower from which rose an immense steeple that doubled the height of the building. There was some raised terrain at the far end of the city, bearing several tall windmills, but nothing to compete with the sheer dominance of the church.

Armuyden made an imposing but pleasantly carefree impression in the sunshine – untouched by war.

They docked at one of the quays, by a short stone dock with steps leading up to the wharf. The fishermen refused payment, pleased to have contributed to the Republic's cause. They helped their passengers disembark and then made to depart quickly. They wanted to salvage the day's fishing, which they hadn't got around to yet. "Twere worth it for the mighty sight of our *Zeeuwse* fleet, and we have a few hours yet afore the weather turns foul."

Liselotte scanned the horizon on hearing those last words, but couldn't see anything to indicate a weather change.

On the wharf, Liselotte could see that Peter was swaying on his feet. He had been much weakened by his ordeal and efforts.

"Peter," Liselotte said. "We need to find you a bed."

He nodded, too weary to contest. "Into the city. First inn we see."

Even that was too far for him. By the time they walked through the nearest gate he had to be supported by Andries and Jasper.

The part of Armuyden they walked into was a poor neighbourhood. The houses were lined up neatly, but their frontages were narrow. Craftsmen worked in front of their shops, their tools and wares taking up much of the available space on the streets. They jested, gossiped, or haggled over prices with passing shoppers.

There was an inn at the nearest corner, strategically placed as to be immediately visible to anyone walking through the gate.

They stopped outside the door to read the sign that hung from a wrought iron bracket. It depicted a round-breasted, golden-haired wench holding up a foaming tankard below the words 'Silly Sally'.

Andries stared at the sign with a curious mix of apprehension and guilt on his face, which Liselotte thought odd.

"I'm not sure…" Peter said. "If this is suitable."

It was clearly eminently unsuitable, but Liselotte could see no other inns along the various narrow streets in their immediate vicinity. Peter was at the end of his tether. She didn't want him to pass out again and risk renewed fever. The Silly Sally would have to do.

She knocked loudly on the door.

When there was no response, Liselotte repeated her action.

A shrill voice complained. "Hold yer horses, we's all resting in here after a busy night."

"Good folk," Liselotte spoke in a loud voice. "We seek lodgings."

The door opened and a formidable woman appeared. She had small squinting eyes and a prominent nose with a sharp downward hook. Her hair wasn't covered but hung loose in unkempt tangles. A corset pushed up considerable breasts that threatened to spill out of her low-cut blouse. She clenched a pipe in her broad and somewhat crooked mouth and was clutching a pewter tankard.

"Not quite like the picture," Jasper whispered to Katja.

Liselotte tried not to grin at the comment. "Good morning, *Mevrouw*."

The woman took one look at the small group and shook her head. "Nay, nay, and nay. And that spells 'nay'. Them Dons are ruining me business, sending folk running to Zeeland and begging for charity. Well, I won't have it, do ye hear? I'm no charitable institution, I'm an honest businesswoman trying to make a living, that's what I am."

"We're not refugees, *Mevrouw*," Peter said. "Merely travellers who ran into some bad luck."

"Bain't none of my worry," The woman replied. "I run a respectable establishment, no room for beggars."

She started to close the door.

"Oh dear, Commodore Haelen," Jasper called out. "What shall we do now?"

"Commodore?" The door froze mid-swing.

289

"Take my money elsewhere, Jasper." Peter shook his purse to make it chink.

The door opened wide. The woman reassessed the motley group doubtfully. "I don't believe a word of this Commodore stuff. Will ye just look at yerselves? Greet Kals weren't born yesterday. But them coins sound real."

"We can pay our way, *Mevrouw* Kals," Peter confirmed.

"Yer wounded. Been up to no good, I has no doubt, and then show up here, armed to the teeth and with a purse full of coins? I'll not be giving the city watch a reason to come poking about me reputable establishment."

"We've been fighting the Dons," Andries said. "We're *Oranjevaarders*."

"Please, *Mevrouw* Kals," Liselotte said. "This is Commodore Haelen of the VOC and owner of the Jayakarta Dockyard in Flushing. We were on our way there when General Spinola invaded. We got caught up in the fighting."

"VOC?" The woman's eyes lit up. "Well, why didn't ye say so, Monseigneur? I can offer you the finest of lodgings. Come in, come in, do come in."

She ushered the group inside.

The taproom looked surprisingly clean and presentable, even if the furnishings were basic and the room smelled of stale ale and tobacco smoke. There were no other people inside.

Peter indicated a broad bench in a corner by a wide hearth, bereft of a fire as of yet. Andries supported him there and Peter sank down with a sigh.

Liselotte placed her hand on his forehead. He wasn't running a temperature.

"Better now," Peter assured her. "Not being on my feet helps. Sit, everyone."

They deposited baggage and weaponry in a corner and took place around the small table.

Greet Kals waddled over and started polishing the table with a filthy rag. "Would his Noble Lordship be wanting a flask of wine? There be no finer wine in Armuyden. Pon me honour, yer Nobleness! None of that Spanish muck either, proper Frenchie stuff. Perhaps a fine lamb shank to go with the wine? His Lordship must be famished. We serve a fine cheese omelette as well, none makes 'em better."

Upon seeing four faces light up, Peter said. "Cheese omelettes all around. With two loaves of your freshest bread, a jug of milk and a jug of watered-down ale."

"Anything his Nobleness wants. Greet Kals serves all polite words can buy and silver coins might desire." She made off to a stack of barrels in the far corner, hollering, "Marlies! Ye be needed in the kitchen. Get yer lazy arse outta bed you useless wretch. MARLIES!"

Peter sighed and apologized to Liselotte. "I'm sorry to have brought you to a place like this. Hopefully our stay won't be overly long."

"We go to Flushing, right?" Andries asked.

"Nay. Not immediately. Middelburg isn't far from here, four or five miles at most. My friend Marnix is at the VOC Chamber there, as are my funds."

"Peter," Liselotte said. "You really shouldn't be travelling. You need bed rest. I mean it."

"I agree," Peter said reluctantly. He was lost in thought for a moment, and then looked at Andries. "My midshipman will have to walk to Middelburg after our breakfast. Take Jasper with you and report to the VOC Chamber. The offices are in Biggekercke House. You'll find it between Breestraat and Rotterdam Quay. You can't miss it; the building is huge."

"*Ja*, I will, Skipper," Andries said. "But...what am I to say to the VOC?"

Peter answered, "That you are Peter Haelen's midshipman. I will give you a letter. I'm sure *Mevrouw* Kals can spare a piece of parchment and a graphite pencil."

"*Ja*, I could do that, Monseigneur." Greet Kals approached the table, carrying glazed earthenware jugs and mugs on a tray. "But seeing that graphite pencils don't grow on trees, I'll add the use of it to yer bill, of course."

"Of course." Peter said drily.

The innkeeper set the tray on the table.

A door flew open behind her. A dozen young women burst into the taproom in a cacophony of chatter and laughter. Their only attire consisted of the towels they were wrapped in. Their eyes grew wide when they saw the guests. They stopped in their tracks and giggled at Andries, Jasper, and Katja who were staring at them open-mouthed.

Greet Kals shrilled at them. "Can't ye see tis the finest of quality what frequents the Silly Sally? A Monseigneur from the very VOC itself, as befitting this fine establishment. Go on, get yerselves to the washroom, don't disrupt his Lordship no more."

Still giggling, the towel-clad gaggle fled to the other side of the taproom, disappearing through a door there.

"I does offer me apologies, yer Nobleship," Greet Kals told Peter. "My girls bain't the sharpest knives in the drawer." She looked at the boys with shrewd eyes. "Pretty though, bain't they?"

Andries and Jasper turned bright red. Greet Kals cackled at their discomfort, then said, "I'll fetch yer parchment and pencil, then see how Marlies is getting on with yer Lordship's meal."

Jasper peered at the door the gaggle of girls had disappeared through. "Normally you'd have to drag me in kicking and screaming, but I wouldn't mind having a bath right now – Ouch!" He looked at Katja in astonishment. "What'd you pinch me for?"

"Serves you right," Liselotte told him. "I saw a water pump outside, Jasper. You're welcome to go stick your head underneath if you need to cool off."

Jasper stared at the tabletop, abashed. "*Ja, Mejuffrouw.*"

Peter frowned. "This really is a most unsuitable—"

"We're not moving you about Armuyden anymore," Liselotte said in a firm tone that forbade dissent. "The sooner you're in a bed the better, Peter. You've been asking too much of yourself. I'd rather that fever doesn't come back."

"*Ja*…Doctor."

When Greet Kals brought the requested parchment and pencil, Liselotte spoke to her about getting a room for Peter. "We'll have need for it today, I'm not sure if we'll be here tonight. The boys are off to the VOC in Middelburg to get help."

Peter was writing on the paper with an unsteady hand.

"That be fine," Greet Hals replied to Liselotte. "But I'm charging ye for the full night."

Peter folded the parchment twice and addressed it.

Heer Marnix Velthuys
VOC Middelburg
Biggekercke House

He handed the letter to Andries and returned the pencil to the innkeeper.

"My girls bain't the sharpest knives in the drawer." She looked at the boys with shrewd eyes. "Pretty though, bain't they?"

Greet Kals led the way up the stairs – huffing and puffing –, followed by the boys supporting Peter, with Liselotte and Katja making up the rear.

The room was simple but clean. It contained a large bed, a chair, and a washstand. A boxed bed was built into the far wall, and a small hearth centred the opposite wall. A latticed window offered a view of a narrow street and the gate by the seafront.

Greet Kals boasted, "Nothing but the finest rooms in the Silly Sally, even if I say so meself. I'll have the fire lit, and water brought up for the washing basin."

"Bethanks, *Mevrouw* Kals," Liselotte said.

They helped Peter to bed. He was exhausted and drifted off immediately.

Liselotte sent Andries and Jasper back downstairs to fetch their belongings. Once that was done, Katja and the boys went back to the taproom to intercept the cheese omelettes.

Katja returned a short while later, with a mug of milk and a platter loaded with bread and steaming omelette.

"Thank you, Katja," Liselotte said, taking the platter and mug, her tummy rumbling.

"How is the Seigneur doing?" Katja inquired.

"Asleep now. It's all been too much for him. He shouldn't exert himself any time soon."

"He's stubborn," Katja said, approval in her voice for a trait highly prized by the Dutch.

"*Ja*, he is. But go down, Katja, before the boys eat everything."

The time came for Andries and Jasper to depart, armed with the doglocks, snaphance, axe, and Peter's letter. Jasper also insisted on bringing the orange pennant.

"Tis well known in Flanders that *Zeeuwen* haven't got common sense. So, I best spell out how dearly I love the Prince of Mandarin." He waved the pennant enthusiastically.

"Orange," Andries corrected him.

"That's the one. His Royal Citron."

Liselotte and Katja came out of the Silly Sally to wave them off. Katja was unhappy that Jasper was leaving and the boy took her aside to speak soothing words.

Liselotte smiled at Andries and adjusted his torn collar. "You be careful out there. Look after our Jasper now."

"Middelburg is less than a two-hour walk. We should be back before nightfall."

Liselotte looked up. A wall of clouds was drifting in over the horizon behind the windmills at the edge of the city, still a great distance away, but already spoiling the previously unblemished sky.

"Outwalk that storm. Try to stay dry. Here," she said, pressing one of Father's silver guilders into Andries's hand. "For emergencies."

"Bethanks," Andries took the proffered guilder and tucked it into his empty purse. "Jasper, let's go."

"Aye-aye, *Mynheer*."

As the boys started to walk away, Katja came to stand by Liselotte, silent tears rolling down her cheeks.

"Oh, *lieffie*." Liselotte folded an arm around Katja's trembling shoulders.

Poor girl, but it'll be worse next time they part.

She told Katja, "We have each other, remember?"

Katja nodded bravely and wiped her cheeks with her sleeve, sniffing.

Jasper turned to wave cheerfully, but his face fell when he saw Katja's expression.

"One moment, *Mynheer*, please." He told Andries and ran back to the girls.

"We'll be back before you know it, *meissie*," he told Katja. "Don't be silly now."

To Katja's surprise, and possibly his own, he leant forward and delivered a peck on her cheek, causing them both to blush furiously.

Quickly retreating, Jasper re-joined Andries and the two strode away, watched by the girls. Katja held a hand against her cheek, a wondrous look in her eyes.

"You know, Liselotte. I may have changed my mind about kissing. It's quite wonderful."

Liselotte smiled. "Well, at least someone got kissed."

"Oh!" Katja exclaimed. "Is that what the Flushing scoundrel wanted? How dare he? I told you he was hit by—"

"We both wanted to," Liselotte explained. "But we decided not to."

"Oh." Katja was unsure how to react to that, and Liselotte didn't want to explore the topic further, out here on the busy street corner.

"Let's go check on Peter," she suggested, and ushered Katja back into the Silly Sally.

Peter had come to again, leaning against the pillows in thoughtful silence. Someone had lit a fire in the hearth and filled the washing basin.

"I'll need to look at the wound, Peter," Liselotte told her cousin.

They undid, and burned, the old bandages. The wound was still red and irritated, but not festering anymore. Small amounts of pus seeped out, which was a good sign. Peter winced every now and then and uttered a groan when the tent was extracted, but Liselotte was pleased that he underwent the process without needing laudanum.

"No tent this time," she decided as they cleaned the wound. "That will help drain the wound and then hopefully the flesh will knit together. Peter, I'm serious about bed rest. If you do too much you will make it worse again."

Peter nodded, already drifting off. The girls bandaged him with the last of Andries's donated spare shirts, then cleared and cleaned up.

That done, Liselotte was at a loss. There was nothing to do other than wait, but she didn't want to be inactive. That would only invite contemplation and she wasn't sure if she wanted to dwell on things all that much. Better to leave it behind her.

"Katja, could you stay by Peter? I'm going to see if *Mevrouw* Kals is willing to part with an old bed sheet or two, so we can make new bandages."

"She'll not part with anything for free," Katja predicted.

"That's fine," Liselotte said. Peter needed clean bandages, and now that the wound was draining they would have to be changed regularly.

Katja was right. *Mevrouw* Kals was happy to add the price of two old bed sheets to the bill, along with the warning that any bloodstains on Peter's bedding would see a punitive addition of fees.

Clutching her prizes, Liselotte made her way back up the stairs. On the landing she encountered one of the girls she'd seen giggling in the taproom earlier. The girl was about eighteen, with striking raven-black hair, and voluptuous curves barely concealed by her flimsy shift.

The girl stared at Liselotte curiously. "If your master is such a fancy Lordship, *meissie*, then why does he make you wear rags?"

"We've had some mishaps," Liselotte answered. "We had to run from Spanish soldiers."

The girl came closer. "I'm Fleur."

"Liselotte."

"If your master is cruel, *meissie*," Fleur spoke very softly. "The two of you could stay at the Silly Sally. The other girl, well, she's a bit young yet but Marlies could use a scullery maid. You however..." She eyed Liselotte from top to toe with approval. "Could get started straight away."

"He isn't cruel," Liselotte said quickly, both aghast and amused at being offered employment at the inn.

"Good!" Fleur replied. She brightened. "Come, we'll see if we can get you something better to wear."

"I've no—"

"I didn't think so, it doesn't matter."

Fleur took Liselotte by the hand and led her up a set of rickety stairs to the loft. A dormitory took up the entire space, filled with narrow beds between chests, shelves, and lines of drying laundry. There was much cheerful banter as Fleur's companions busied themselves with their attire or frolicked in various stages of undress between drying bed sheets and clothes.

They all flocked around when they saw Liselotte. Fleur introduced her. "This poor *meissie* has only just managed to stay out of the clutches of the bloody *Spekjannuh*[48]."

The girls growled patriotic anger.

"So, it's up to us to do our bit in the war against tyranny, and help poor Liselotte out, dress her up in something respectable."

"*Oranje boven!*" There was a flurry as the girls rushed around digging items out of chests.

Liselotte protested. "But I can't accept—"

"Don't worry, *lieffie*," Fleur assured her. "We're as patriotic as respectable folk, none can take that away. A lot of the girls have favourites on that fleet that sailed past this morning. And this stuff..." She pointed at the finds the other girls were depositing on the nearest bed. "Is from our old lives. None of us will ever wear them no more."

Fleur began to go through the donations, occasionally sizing Liselotte up as she made her selections. "Right Liselotte, get those rags off."

Liselotte hesitated, an invitation for the girls to throw themselves at the task with merry laughter. They made quick work of it. In no time Liselotte was left wearing nothing but her battered stockings. She

---

[48] A rude nickname for Spanish troops. Referencing the state of affairs before the truce, when the losing, unpaid, and unsupplied Spanish soldiers would devour anything edible they managed to lay their hands on.

covered her breasts with one arm and reached out with her free hand to conceal her privates.

Fleur laughed. "Shy, are you?" She tossed a clean shift to Liselotte. "Here, for your modesty."

Liselotte quickly pulled the shift over her head. That left her far more comfortable with the rest of her fitting as they dressed her in a long skirt, shirt, jacket, apron, and simple cap. A mirror was brought over so Liselotte could inspect the result of their efforts. The clothes fit well enough, but hadn't been made to measure, falling down shapelessly. The material was cheap, but clean. It was the garb of a common farm girl, or labourer's daughter, and Liselotte was tremendously pleased with her flatlander wear.

Liselotte and Fleur made their way back down the stairs, with the bed sheets and Liselotte's old gown.

Katja's mouth dropped open when she saw Liselotte reappear.

"You're next." Fleur beamed at her.

Liselotte said. "This is Fleur, go upstairs with her. Don't be afraid, they mean well."

When Katja had departed, Liselotte recalled the piece of paper Jan had given her upon leaving *De Wilde Ruyter*. She retrieved it from her haversack and sat down on the chair to turn it over in her hands.

To Whom it May Concern was scrawled boldly on one side.

Liselotte sighed, that indicated it was unlikely to contain a personal message.

She unfolded the paper. It attested to the commission of Liselotte Haelen of Rotterdam as ship's surgeon aboard the *Zeeuwse* Admiralty's *Statenjacht De Wilde Ruyter*. Although it was dated, the letter omitted to specify the duration of Liselotte's commission.

It was signed:

On Behalf of Lieutenant-Admiral Willem de Zoete, Lord of Haultain, in Service of the Zeeuwse Admiralty and the Republic of the Seven United Provinces; Michael Adriaanszoon of Flushing, Temporary Skipper of the Statenjacht De Wilde Ruyter & Faithful Servant of the Stadtholder of Zeeland, Captain-General Prince Maurits of Nassau.

Liselotte grinned. She had hoped for a last personal word from Michael, but this was far better. A reminder that, like Adrian Haelen before her, Liselotte had served her country and a Prince of Orange, no matter how briefly. Perhaps it also signalled that she was remembered as ship's surgeon and not the improper wench at the bow.

Katja returned in a clean outfit, clutching a borrowed hairbrush. She set to work tackling Liselotte's hair, which put up a stubborn resistance to being ordered.

Katja demanded to know what had happened on *De Wilde Ruyter*.

Liselotte gave her a short version, admitting there had been a moment of a near kiss before reality set in.

"I'm a family asset," Liselotte said resignedly.

"Of course you are. Liselotte, I think those girls upstairs are… well…"

"Ladies of loose morals." Liselotte winced as Katja showed little mercy when she untangled a knot in Liselotte's hair.

Whores.

How often had the vicar back in Oysterhout thundered his outrage at the sinful state of such women? Devil-sent and inherently wicked, was what Liselotte had been taught. None of it fitted with what she'd experienced up in the loft. Apart from the setting, the girls were much like Liselotte's friends in Oysterhout in the manner they had conducted themselves, albeit a bit more underdressed.

"They are very nice," Katja said, with surprise in her tone.

"They are indeed."

When the time came for Liselotte to brush Katja's hair, the girl asked, "Can you do braids?"

It filled the time. Liselotte had just finished braiding Katja's brushed hair when their attention was drawn to the window. The daylight spilling in was undergoing a rapid change, darkening fast.

They went over to the window to stare outside. The distant wall of clouds Liselotte had seen earlier was advancing at a furious pace, whipped up by a vicious wind and consuming the sky over Armuyden. Down on the street, the craftsmen were busily carrying their tools, supplies, and products into their workshops. Passers-by walked with hurried tread, casting anxious upward looks.

The sky began to rumble ominously as the air took on a strange yellow glow.

"Storm," Katja whispered.

When the rain came, it cascaded down in an instant downpour. Farther on, deeper in the storm, the dark clouds flashed with brilliance, followed seconds later by the sound of ferocious thunder that seemed to rumble on forever.

The last people disappeared from the streets. The window's shutters trembled in the wind. Liselotte opened the window and struggled with the wind for control of the shutters. Bolts of lightning shot down from the sky, rapidly followed by the crack of thunder and the tremendous rolling boom that followed nearby impact.

Liselotte managed to draw the shutters and bolt them. She shut the windows and then stood mesmerised by the noise, as the full force of the heavens was unleashed upon Armuyden.

She shuddered, struck by recent encounters with flooded parts of Zeeland. Her mind's eye recalled images it had summoned by the Drowned Lands Sea. Water rushing over streets, unstoppable, snapping stout oak doors and gates like matchsticks to overwhelm those who had thought they were safe. Reymerswal must have once seemed as secure as Armuyden appeared to be behind its formidable defences.

We dance by the sea and drown in our homes.

The sea.

If it was this bad in the shelter of a city, what was it like out there, in the open? It must be horrendous.

"Oh!" Liselotte exclaimed, when the next bolt of lightning struck the raised terrain behind the city, the thunder drowned out by the near-immediate explosion of the impact. The glass of the latticed windows rattled, the floorboards shuddered, the sheer violence of the boom was deafening.

Katja tugged at Liselotte's sleeve, her face pale. "Liselotte, we must get away from the window."

Liselotte nodded and let Katja lead her to the boxed bed, where they sat down on the edge of the bed, huddled close together.

Katja patted Liselotte's hand reassuringly. "I'm sure Jasper and *Mynheer* Andries will have reached Middelburg in time to find shelter."

Liselotte drew a guilty breath. She hadn't even considered that yet, her worries had concerned someone else.

Out at sea.

26. Biggekercke House

MIDDELBURG ~ COUNTY OF ZEELAND ~ 1622

Andries and Jasper made good progress. The road between Armuyden and Middelburg was broad and in a good state, busy with traffic. It wasn't long before they could see the towers of Zeeland's primary city rising over the green flatlands – against the backdrop of the broad storm front developing in the west.

As they neared, approaching along the perfectly straight and busy Canal of Welzinge, the sheer size of the city began to overwhelm them. By the time they came close enough to make out a multitude of masts and rigging, rising amidst the rooftops behind formidable ramparts and redoubts, it had already become perfectly clear that this was a place of great wealth and power.

"It makes Rotterdam look small," Andries said in wonder.

"We'd better hurry," Jasper suggested. "That foul weather is making full speed right at us."

They passed through the modern Veersepoort, to discover that the end of Welzinge Canal formed a huge harbour right in the middle of the city. Towering wood cranes lined the stone quays in service of a great many moored merchant ships, large and small. It seemed that there were thousands of people around, passing by at leisure or busily engaged in tasks and errands.

Even as the boys gawped, a change of pace rippled through the collective whole, a sudden hurry to get things done and dusted.

The storm was hunting across the flatlands, furious in its approach to Middelburg, casting a towering shadow over all.

Fortunately, the Rotterdam Quay wasn't far ahead of the boys, and soon Biggekercke House rose prominently in sight over the lower rooftops to their right.

The streets were nearly deserted, just a last handful of folk hastening to shelter. The air became ominously yellow, full of tense pressure.

The boys – their hair whipped by the wind – gaped up at Biggekercke House as they made for the broad and stately front door. The building was endlessly long and rose five whole floors up. The façade of brick and ornamental stonework was shaped in imitation of Romano-Greek architectural prowess.

301

It grew dark as night. Andries had never felt so small before, at the foot of the monolithic building and at the mercy of nature's full fury.

Flashes lit up street, rooftops, and sky, followed by thunderous roars so loud that the boys could barely hear the doorknocker that Andries was rapping urgently.

The broad door opened. They made to go in, but found their way barred by two grim doormen. The men were dressed in the modest and sombre attire of clerks, but their tattoos, earrings, a missing hand for the one and a missing eye for the other, and most specifically their weatherworn faces, suggested they had served the VOC in another guise for many hard years.

"No beggars," the one-handed man barked upon seeing the boys.

"Fuck off, right now." His one-eyed partner suggested, patting the end of a wooden truncheon against the palm of his hand.

Andries took a deep breath. He spoke slow and loud. "I am Midshipman Haelen, in service of Commodore Peter Haelen. I bear an urgent message."

He produced the letter and held it up.

"You don't look like a midshipman to me," One-Eye growled.

"We've been fighting Salazar's tercios," Jasper told him. "And killed plenty, only yesterday on the Oosterskelde."

One-Eye's single eye widened. "The little shrimp-dick speaks."

"Pronck, Kagers. Enough of this," a voice behind them spoke. "You'll mind your manners; you aren't in the focsle with your shipmates."

The two doormen parted, to reveal an elegantly dressed man of Peter's age, with long dark hair that fell down in oiled curls, a thin, waxed mustachio, and neatly pointed goatee beard. His broad domed hat was awash with ostrich feathers, and a finely decorated sword hung at his side.

The two doormen parted, to reveal an elegantly dressed man of Peter's age,

"*Ja*, Monseigneur," the man with one arm transformed from ferocious to humble in the flash of an eye.

"Begging yer pardon, *Heer* Velthuys," One-Eye said.

"Well, let them in, let them in. And shut the door behind them, for goodness's sake."

The boys stepped into a high-ceilinged and long, broad hallway. A great many polished walnut doors and paintings in gilded frames lined it. A few people traversed the hallway, harried clerks carrying documents, or wealthy merchants conversing.

"*Heer* Velthuys?" Andries asked, as One-Eye shut the door. "*Heer* Marnix Velthuys?"

"That would be me." The gentleman regarded him curiously. "Who are you?"

"Midshipman Haelen, Monseigneur. In the service of Commodore Haelen. I have—"

"You are Peter's cousin!"

"*Ja*, Monsigneur, I have a letter from him, for you." Andries handed the folded parchment over.

Velthuys studied the front, and then unfolded the short letter to swiftly read it. A warm smile formed on his face when he folded the paper again. "Midshipman Haelen, it is a pleasure to meet you." He shook Andries's hand enthusiastically. "Your cousin is a very good friend of mine. Who's your young friend?"

"Skipper Haelen's cabin boy, Seigneur." Jasper answered proudly.

"Excellent," Velthuys said. "The more the merrier. Come, come. To my office. You have much to tell me, and we can't travel to Armuyden in this weather any time soon."

He looked at One-Eye. "Spronck, send word to the kitchen if you please. My guests will require a hearty meal."

"Aye-aye, *Heer* Velthuys."

Andries and Jasper exchanged a delighted glance.

They followed Marnix Velthuys deeper into Biggekercke House, their mission accomplished.

27. Mortified

ARMUYDEN ~ COUNTY OF ZEELAND ~ 1622

The tempest raged on. It appeared to abate a few times, only to renew its fury as wind, rain, and lightning hammered Armuyden with fierce anger.

Peter slept through it all.

When someone knocked on the door, Liselotte opened it to see Greet Kals fill the doorway.

The innkeeper cast a curious glance at Peter, before addressing Liselotte. "I don't expect none will come from Middelburg today, *meissie*. They'd be mad to venture out in this storm."

"*Ja, Mevrouw* Kals." The thought had already occurred to Liselotte. "We'll spend the night here."

"It might be wise to arrange yer supper afore it gets busy downstairs."

"Busy? But…" Liselotte glanced at the shuttered window.

Greet Kals chuckled. "I said none'll come from Middelburg. Plenty in Armuyden who'll need distraction. Speaking of which, twould be better if ye and the other *meissie* stayed away from the taproom this evening. It'd just be confusing to the punters, and we don't want no trouble now, do we? For yer sake as much as mine."

"*Ja, Mevrouw* Kals," Liselotte agreed, understanding the warning.

They negotiated a supper. Roast chicken, beans, and bread for the girls, chicken broth for Peter, and a few flasks of watered-down ale.

Peter was woken when the food came, to be spoon-fed the broth and undergo another change of bandages and wound treatment. He remained groggy throughout. Liselotte applied a little laudanum to make sure he'd sleep well, and then helped Katja clear up.

Their own supper had grown cold by the time they sat down on the floor to eat, but it tasted wonderful all the same.

The storm was finally dying down, the lightning and thunder moving farther away and the rain lessening in intensity. The taproom, on the other hand, became livelier by the minute. At first, it was mostly the continuous hum of conversation, but as the evening progressed this was frequently overpowered by outbreaks of raucous merriment, friendly shouts, and the higher tones of Fleur and her girls as they laughed and joked with the customers.

There was singing as well. Occasionally a great many would join in with a chorus, to fill the Silly Sally with an inebriated disharmony of song.

And Lo! Betwixt her creamy thighs
He discovered paradise, yo-ho!

Liselotte cast a worried look at Katja whenever such tunes became audible, but the girl grinned and even hummed along to a few of the ditties.

"I should hope we'll be able to sleep, with all this racket," Liselotte said.

Katja yawned. "I think I'll sleep very well. In a proper bed too." She indicated the box bed. "I just had a cot at home. I've never slept in a proper bed before, it's so soft!"

They blew out the candles before dressing down to their shifts and crawling into the box bed. It was a bit snug, but Liselotte found comfort in Katja's close presence.

Her friend was soon asleep, leaving Liselotte to stare into the darkness, somewhat anxious. She'd kept herself deliberately busy all day, but now there was nothing to keep contemplation at bay.

She hoped fervently that *De Wilde Ruyter* had withstood the storm and assured herself that Andries and Jasper must have found shelter with the VOC in Middelburg.

The tumultuous merrymaking in the taproom continued unabated.

Liselotte wondered if this had been the type of place frequented by Father, but couldn't imagine his dour presence amidst so much inappropriate mirth.

Peter had said that Michael had a reputation for causing mayhem in Flushing taverns. It was far easier for Liselotte to imagine Michael and his crew lustily joining in with the bawdy ditties in a place like this, a girl like Fleur on his lap.

Occasionally a great many would join in with a chorus, to fill the Silly Sally with an inebriated disharmony of song.

Hadn't Geleyn mentioned something of the kind? She recalled his voice.

"...as soft as being stroked by a wench at the Malle Babbe on a Saturday night."

Liselotte told herself to focus on more appropriate things, but the carousers downstairs weren't making it any easier, now all joined in a jubilant song about the adventures of a lusty young smith.

A door opened in the room next to theirs, and Liselotte could hear people stumble around.

A man's voice joined in with the chorus of the ditty that resounded from the taproom.

> With a jingle-bang, jingle-bang, jingle-bang, jingle,
> With a jingle-bang, jingle-bang, jingle, hi ho!

His contribution was met by the sound of giggling.

Liselotte tried to ignore them, trying to think of Rotterdam instead, but the walls were too flimsy to tune out the neighbours altogether.

She was relieved when their talk and laughter softened to murmurs that were drowned out by the continued intrusion of the taproom's collective merrymaking.

Just as she was beginning to doze off, Liselotte registered new sounds from the next room.

Her first instinct was that someone had been hurt. The man groaned every now and then, the woman was more consistent in uttering soft whimpers.

When the whimpers intensified into a sequence of impassioned yelps, Liselotte was mortified to realise what she was listening to. The heat of a blush spread on her face and she quickly covered her ears, struck by guilt at her sense of intrusion.

Curiosity and fascination, however, led her to uncover her ears again. The pace next door had quickened, the man adding groans of pleasure to the woman's now high-pitched gasps, the bed they were on creaking madly.

Liselotte stared wide-eyed into the darkness, unable to focus on anything else but the act next door. Her heart thumped. The pace of her breath increased. Her imagination rushed – uninvited – to provide images to match the sounds of passion. The expressions on unknown faces as the groans turned to husky grunts, and the gasps to repetitive squeals of intense delight.

Liselotte's body began to respond to the feverish activity of her mind's eye, becoming sensitive enough that the mere pressure of the blankets and Katja's warmth became a thrilling caress. Her nipples were roused, and her loins warmed. Only her young friend's proximity kept her from giving in to the powerful yearning to touch herself.

She gradually became aware that other rooms on the Silly Sally's first floor had become similar scenes of carnal vigour. Headboards thumped the rhythm to a chorus of bestial groans, fervent moans, and arias of '*ja ja ja*', – occasionally reaching a crescendo of intensity in a couple's conjoined rise to climax.

When Katja murmured something in her sleep, and then shifted to turn on her side, Liselotte could refrain no longer, so insistent was the ache. Under the pretext of scratching her thigh, she quickly cupped herself. A few applications of pressure were enough to release a surge of pent-up heat. A moan escaped from her lips as she shuddered with small convulsions.

Purged of the torment, Liselotte was left drifting in a languorous state of bliss, able at last to shut out the worst of the continued orchestra of obscenity around her. The warmth around her loins, on her chest and cheeks, slowly faded.

"Some things are not yours to give," Michael had said. How, she wondered as her eyelids grew heavy, could these sensations be possessed by anyone else, as if on a household itinerary in a will? How could they be anything else but her own?

29. Marnix to the Rescue

ARMUYDEN ~ COUNTY OF ZEELAND ~ 1622

Liselotte opened the shutters and window to air the room. The sky was overcast but dry. A gentle breeze conveyed the briny smell of the sea. Gulls screeched and squawked in their multitudes over the quays and harbour.

The world outside seemed refreshed, as if cleansed by the storm. It was a sense Liselotte shared; it was as if she walked with a lighter tread this morning.

Other than snorers in some of the other rooms, the Silly Sally was silent. Exhausted perhaps from the fervent passions of the night, the echoes of which lingered in a pervading mood of languid contentment.

Peter woke, looking rested. Liselotte and Katja tended his wound. It looked to be mending still. The girls had saved some of Peter's broth and half a loaf of bread. The fire in the hearth had died during the night, so they couldn't warm the broth up, but Peter didn't complain. All that done, the girls stilled their own hunger with the bread.

"I'm sure *Mevrouw* Kals would be amenable to frying up some bacon and eggs," Peter suggested.

"I suspect she isn't an early riser," Liselotte said. "It was quite lively in the Silly Sally last night."

"Oh, dear."

Katja said, "We slept like roses though, didn't we, Miss?"

"Ahem, *ja*, we did."

The clatter of hoofbeats and rumble of wheels on street cobbles drifted in through the window. A coachman could be heard urging his team to a halt.

"The bed was really soft," Katja enthused. "Do they have soft beds like this in Rotterdam?"

"You're headed for Rotterdam as well then?" Peter asked her. He looked at Liselotte with twinkling eyes. "What a fortunate coincidence."

Liselotte stepped closer to Katja and folded an arm around the girl's shoulders. "Katja has agreed to be my handmaiden and companion."

"*Ja*, I have," Katja confirmed happily.

Peter chuckled. "I suspected some such arrangement would be made."

"Well, Cousin. A certain someone is planning to take her best friend to the other side of the world."

"Aye, indeed. I'm pleased for you both."

There was commotion downstairs. Someone was knocking insistently on the door, while an irate Greet Kals shrilled her displeasure at the time of day as she moved through the taproom.

"A peek, if you would, Liselotte," Peter said. "It might be word from Middelburg."

Liselotte nodded and made her way to the landing where she could eavesdrop.

"Monseigneur!" Greet Kals exclaimed as a visitor entered the Silly Sally. "An honour to welcome you back again. Even though it be a tad earlier than usual, mayhap?"

A smooth, suave voice answered her. "My dear *Mevrouw* Kals, how lovely it is to see you once more. However, I'm here on other business today. I have been given to understand that one of your guests is my friend, Commodore Peter Haelen?"

"*Ja*, the commodore is here, *Heer* Velthuys, in my finest room, befitting a gentleman of his status. Nothing but the best for the VOC, eh?"

Liselotte went back to the room. She told Peter, "I think it's your VOC friend, *Heer* Velthuys."

"Marnix," Peter smiled. "I was hoping he would come."

"Is Jasper with him?" Katja asked eagerly.

"I don't think so."

The girls cleared the breakfast clutter. Then looked at the door expectantly, as did Peter.

Velthuys entered with all the drama of an actor strutting onto a stage, in an exquisite outfit and with a pompous whirl of the ostrich feathers on his hat.

He glanced dismissively at Peter. "Oh, it's you again."

Peter grinned at him.

Turning to Liselotte, Velthuys was all smiles. Twirling the pointed end of his mustachio with approval, he spoke, "You can be no other than *Mejuffrouw* Liselotte Haelen. The resemblance is remarkable, you look just like—"

"My brother, Monseigneur," Liselotte filled in, forgetting to mind her manners. Her response was an automatic one to a statement she'd grown very tired of hearing. Specifically the surprise always invested in it, as if it was a staggering discovery that twins were similar. "Begging your pardon, Monseigneur."

Velthuys waved her apology for interrupting him away with easy elegance, but there was a flash of disapproval on his face when he took in Liselotte's attire. "Now you mention it, you and young Master Andries do look alike. That wasn't who I was thinking of though, but I digress." He brightened and beamed. "It is a pleasure and honour to meet you, Mademoiselle. I've heard much about you already."

"From Jasper, Seigneur?" Katja asked. "He always talks too much."

Velthuys turned to study Katja.

"This is Katja," Liselotte told him. "My handmaid and companion."

"Jasper sends his greetings, young Miss Katja," Velthuys said. He looked at Liselotte. "As does your brother. They've remained in Middelburg at my request, hard at work right now I should think."

Velthuys turned to Peter. "I'm tremendously disappointed in you."

"I expected nothing less, Marnix."

"Getting shot at was very inconvenient of you. What were you thinking? You've made up for that blunder somewhat, by intending to return to Rotterdam's one of the city's missing treasures..." He indicated Liselotte. "Only to then let all of Rotterdam down by accommodating such a rare and precious jewel here, in Armuyden's infamous Silly Sally."

Peter began to protest, "It was—"

"Nay, nay." Velthuys lifted a hand. "There can be no excusing such an unforgivable disgrace." He tut-tutted, before smiling at Liselotte. "I'm pleased to assure you, Mademoiselle, that my arrival heralds the end of your ordeal."

Somewhat overwhelmed by Velthuys's easy charm, Liselotte answered, "How so, *Heer* Velthuys?"

"I have a spacious coach ready, Mademoiselle. To carry us to Middelburg in comfort."

"A coach!" Katja was thrilled.

Velthuys turned to Peter. "My Middelburg lodgings are at your disposal, Peter. Considerably more appropriate than the Silly Sally, I dare say. The boys are already installed. Do you think you can manage the coach ride?"

"I think so." Peter threw a glance at Liselotte, who nodded her agreement. The night's rest had benefited Peter and the journey shouldn't be long by coach.

Velthuys turned to Peter. "I'm tremendously disappointed in you."

"I expected nothing less, Marnix."

The coachman was a sturdy fellow who quickly dealt with the little baggage they had while Velthuys settled the bill with Greet Kals. After that, they helped Peter down the stairs and to the lacquered coach.

Velthuys stayed by the coach door, helping Peter inside. Katja drifted to the horses to admire their shiny coats as well as braided tails and manes. She engaged the coachman in a conversation that was beyond the comprehension of Liselotte.

Horse talk.

Liselotte was somewhat startled by an eruption of distant deep rumbling that filled the air with a low growl, nearly continuously renewed.

"The fleet," Peter said, leaning out of the rear coach window. "Not scattered by the storm and in action already. Sharp sailing."

Liselotte listened in awe. It sounded like a thousand cannons were blasting away at once, making enough noise to be heard all the way in Armuyden. What a spectacle it must be at Bergen-op-Zoom this morning. The crew of *De Wilde Ruyter* would no doubt be in the midst of the action; Michael keen to trade blows with the Spaniards.

"Come, come," Velthuys called out. "We mustn't keep Middelburg waiting."

When everyone had embarked the coach started moving, almost imperceptibly at first. Soon it rumbled over the cobbles of Armuyden and then out of the city into the green flatlands of Walcheren.

Peter sat on a corner of the rear bench, wrapped in blankets. Liselotte was by his side. Katja fidgeted restlessly at the other end, looking out of the window with happy wonder.

Velthuys sat opposite Peter, observing him with amusement. "Your midshipman and cabin boy have generously imparted the most remarkable stories, my friend. My apologies, I truly thought a quick jaunt into Brabant would be devoid of adventure."

"Worth every step of the way," Peter said. "Andries and Jasper have proved their mettle. They're both fine additions to the crew."

Liselotte swelled with pride, pleased to hear Andries spoken of in such positive terms. He had carried himself well in the various skirmishes during their escape from Reymerswal. He had even managed to be accepted by *De Wilde Ruyter's* crew somehow – she suspected Jasper had helped her brother with that. It gave her hope that Andries would be able to cope with the long journey to the East.

Peter turned his head to smile at Liselotte. "And the girls have surprised me at every turn."

"I dread to think, Mademoiselle," Velthuys said. "What terrors you must have endured. With such bravery too, if young Master Andries is to be believed. Rest assured that you no longer have to worry about such terrible things. My lodgings are humble, but you will not lack for anything there."

"Bethanks, Monseigneur."

Velthuys spoke to Peter, "Being terribly important as I am, I'm afraid that I must be most boring and head straight to Veere after dropping you off at Middelburg."

"Trouble?"

Velthuys rolled his eyes. "The usual. Envy of Middelburg's dominance of VOC Zeeland. Excitable chatter and squawking. I go to smooth some feathers and convince them it's in their own best interest to be reduced to a second-rank player, whilst at the same time coughing up their pledged dues."

"Politics," Peter said with dislike. "Still, a task that suits you, I should think."

"I'm suited for it, but it's numbingly dull stuff nonetheless, these local rivalries. The *Zeeuwse* cities bicker like children. In the meanwhile, my housekeeper, Hans Ernstra, is fully informed as to your situation and will make you comfortable and welcome. His wife has taken the boys into the city. They are to be fitted out for sea, but also social occasions, Peter, young Master Andries told me of your plans. There will be much interest in your return to Rotterdam, and that of your cousins. Three long-lost Haelens appearing all at once!"

"Nosy people," Peter said. "Not minding their own business."

"Rotterdam's finest," Velthuys confirmed. "I know you care not, but your cousins can make an impression that will stand them in good stead. It will require a few public performances of your own in their support. It's a dramatic stage that can be occupied for a few weeks at most, before interest wanes. *Carpe Diem*[49]."

"That is true and I owe them a great deal," Peter agreed. "Liselotte and Katja will need new outfits too."

"They'll be in good hands. *Mevrouw* Ernstra is aware that they are on their way. I've full trust in the Ernstras and told them not to spare any expenses. They're drawing from the Jayakarta account."

"That's fine," Peter said.

---

[49] Seize the day. Latin.

"Peter, you mustn't spend too much money on us," Liselotte objected. She touched Eyang's hilt, sure that no amount of finery could equal that most generous gift. Not to mention his guarantee of Father's debts.

"Don't worry about it," Peter said.

"My dear Mademoiselle," Velthuys enthused. "Thanks to your cousin we're both fabulously rich. Outrageously so. Obscenely even. Has he not told you that?"

Peter looked embarrassed. "There's a bit of money thanks to both of our efforts. I sailed fast. Marnix, as *Koopman*, bought and sold with skill. We shared two *Blokzeyl* voyages and worked well together."

"An understatement, if ever I heard one," Velthuys said with satisfaction. He looked at Liselotte. "Peter doesn't always understand how people work. He relies on me in these matters, which is very clever of him."

Peter nodded. "I never had much time for social niceties."

"A polite way of saying Peter can be a walking disaster at times, Mademoiselle. Oh, the tales I could tell you! Another time perhaps. As for outfits, Mademoiselle, this particular expenditure is an investment. People will be observing you from the moment you set foot in Rotterdam, so you must shine at your brightest. You can't possibly arrive dressed in these rags. The Haelen family stands to benefit from a positive impression of both your brother and yourself."

Liselotte looked down at her Silly Sally clothes, which she found pleasing because they were unpretentious.

All that's left of me.

Moreover a gift that represented heartfelt generosity from Fleur and her girls, no matter how low the monetary value and social status.

She wasn't pleased to hear them described as rags. Recalling what Michael had said, she asked sweetly, "To be a family asset, *Heer* Velthuys?"

Velthuys clapped his hands with delight. "Young Master Andries said you were clever. I'm pleased you understand, Mademoiselle. Precisely that. A precious family asset. Interest in your arrival may allow you to enhance your family's social elevation."

"Politics," Liselotte echoed Peter. She glanced sideways at her cousin, but he had settled into the corner and was drifting off. Katja's face was still pressed to the window, the girl wholly enthralled by riding in a coach.

Liselotte looked back at Velthuys. "Monseigneur, I've never considered marriage, I'm not sure—"

316

"My dear Mademoiselle," Velthuys exclaimed in mock horror. "That I find difficult to believe. I have four younger sisters and they spoke or thought of little else at your age, as should be. It must be these dreadfully inappropriate adventures Peter has dragged you into, but as I mentioned, you'll no longer be distracted from more worthy pursuits befitting a young lady."

Liselotte wanted to shrug her disinterest in these pursuits at him, but that would have been rude. "I think my primary concern, *Heer* Velthuys, is Peter. He still requires treatment."

"Which will be provided for," Velthuys said cheerfully, but his eyes scrutinised Liselotte's face carefully. "By Middelburg's finest physicians. They've been sent for in expectation of our arrival."

"Peter is *my* patient."

Velthuys glanced at Peter, who appeared asleep, then leaned in a little closer to Liselotte. "My dear Mademoiselle, I'm going to be brutally honest with you. It is, no doubt, a fine thing that you did out there, extracting that musket ball. Commendable in the absence of any other alternatives. However, it's wholly unseemly for a young lady to indulge in this profession. The *less* said about it, the better. If your primary concern is indeed Peter's welfare, you would be mindful of his reputation. And your brother's."

Liselotte stared at him in silence.

Velthuys threw her a radiant smile and settled back, all amiable once again. "Please understand, Mademoiselle, that Peter's welfare is dear to my heart. I've made a considerable investment in his project, the only investor he could find, I might add. I very much desire that he succeed. Sail to the East Indies and back in record time, prove to doubters that he is right about his ship's design, and raise outrageous profits in doing so."

"We have that in common then, Monseigneur." Liselotte acknowledged.

"Oh, we have something more in common," Velthuys assured her. "I was trying to tell you earlier, Mademoiselle, that you bear a striking resemblance to Saskia van der Krooswyck."

"You knew my mother, Monseigneur?"

"The Velthuys and van der Krooswyck families have long moved in the same social circles. Saskia and I were not of the same age as I trailed her by a decade, but I encountered her often enough in my childhood. When she was your age."

Liselotte was fascinated, despite her growing uneasiness about Velthuys. "What was she like?"

"She was kind to me, told me stories, and made me laugh with her jokes. Our elders considered her clever and dutiful. The unfortunate scandal caused some consternation."

"Scandal?"

Velthuys regarded her curiously. "Surely you know, Mademoiselle?"

"Nay, Monseigneur, what happened? Please tell me."

"What happened was Simon Haelen." Velthuys said it regretfully, but he was clearly relishing the gossip. "A young promising physician, to be sure, but the Haelen family pedigree is…well, there is none to speak of, at least not in polite circles. But Saskia and Simon were head over heels, forever seeking each other's company to the tune of wagging tongues. There was nothing that could keep them apart, it seemed. The van der Krooswycks tried, even offered Simon thousands of guilders to quietly take his leave. Do you know what answer your father gave them?"

Liselotte shook her head, barely believing that this was Father of whom Velthuys spoke.

"He turned all the offers down, and in between his rejections he quoted selections from Ovid's *Art of Love* at them. Poetry!" Velthuys laughed. "It was daring, I have to admit that much."

"Father wouldn't—"

"He would and he did. Very eloquently too. I heard it first-hand from several van der Krooswycks who attended that meeting with him. They were not amused. The family subsequently issued an ultimatum to Saskia, to choose between her inappropriate suitor and her family. It was either one or the other."

Liselotte looked at Velthuys open-mouthed, willing him to go on — though her own existence was a reasonably sure prediction of the outcome.

Velthuys continued, "Saskia made her choice. They slipped out of the St George's Gate one morning at dawn, walked to Delft, and were wed in the Saint Hippolytus Chapel by noon. His parents then sailed them back to Rotterdam in a borrowed fishing yawl."

"Oh!" Liselotte clasped her hands to her heart.

"The van der Krooswycks were forced to disown Saskia, Mademoiselle, and had to learn to live with the shame."

Shame?

Liselotte reminded herself that Velthuys had identified himself as a natural ally of the van der Krooswycks. "I'm sure, Monseigneur, that I can be forgiven for my gratitude that they wed, it being the reason I exist, shameful as that may be to some."

Velthuys chuckled. "As a matter of course, Mademoiselle. I've never held it against Peter, and I have much enjoyed talking to young Master Andries."

His face transformed, from amiable to calculating. He spoke slowly with sharp clarity. "But it will be remembered in Rotterdam, I assure you. Your arrival will rake up memories. The specifics might not be recalled, but people will remember there was a scandal. Some might even wonder if your likeness to Saskia is just outward, or also inward – someone likely to lose all self-control."

Liselotte stared at Velthuys; barely able to believe he had just fired such a broadside at her.

"*Heer* Velthuys, what do you think you are sugges—?"

"I refer, perhaps," he interrupted her. "To an improper dalliance with a common *Zeeuw*."

Liselotte stared at him, hard. "Monseigneur, I don't know what Andries told you—"

"Oh, you need not worry on that count, Mademoiselle. Your brother was most loyal to you. But it struck me as odd that he chose to reiterate several times just how *proper* your encounters with the young navy skipper had been. He clearly thought it important to mention with some frequency. Even that cabin boy was impudent enough to believe it was his business to support young Master Andries's claims on this topic."

Oh, Andries.

"Monseigneur." Liselotte looked Velthuys straight in the eye. "Nothing untoward happened."

"Perhaps it's just my imagination, Mademoiselle. I've met this Michael Adriaansz. He certainly has a magnetic quality; it's what makes him a natural born leader. As the boys told their stories, I thought to myself: Take two young people who encounter each other as they fight side by side for survival. Spirits on fire. Blood heated by battle. Hearts pounding. Sweating. On the intimate side of death, but then...they emerge victorious. All that excitement! Such an occasion may lead to an illusion of a common bond, a faux feeling of connection..."

His eyes pierced Liselotte's and she struggled to maintain an even gaze, in uncomfortable recognition of his evaluation.

Velthuys broke the intensity, tacking his personality again with ease. Relaxing back on the bench, he added teasingly, almost playfully, "Add a goblet of wine, a sunset over the sea..."

"Nothing untoward happened," Liselotte maintained, but she remembered her moment of surrender when she had pressed herself against Michael in invitation of a kiss.

"I'm happy to take your word for it, Mademoiselle." Velthuys smiled. "With my humble apologies if my words suggested otherwise."

Liselotte's head was spinning from his rapid changes of character, as well as his summary of what might have transpired on *De Wilde Ruyter*.

Michael was right to be cautious.

Velthuys continued. "However, I would request that you be mindful that such matters can damage Peter's enterprise, my anticipated profits, and your own prospects. It may not seem so, but my primary motivation is your own welfare. It's tied to Peter's enterprise, Peter himself, and our promising midshipman."

"I understand, Monseigneur," Liselotte acknowledged.

His face brightened with lively interest. "Learn to trust me, Mademoiselle, and I will help you make your entry in Rotterdam society in a fashion that will long be remembered. For all the *right* reasons. It would be an absolute delight to do so, and if I'm seen as your patron in these matters your star will rise high. Follow my advice and you might regain what Saskia threw away."

"I'm grateful, Monseigneur."

Liselotte looked out the window and pretended to be fascinated by the rising contours of Middelburg. She had admired the brotherly way Peter and his old friend had talked with each other, but based on her own conversation with the man, she didn't like Marnix Velthuys very much.

30. Died and Gone to Heaven

MIDDELBURG ~ COUNTY OF ZEELAND ~ 1622

They arrived in Middelburg before noon. The rest of the day passed by in surreal fashion.

Velthuys's 'humble' lodgings turned out to be a large three-storey house at the far end of Breestraat. Imposing stone ornamentation enhanced the brick façade and it had a multi-stepped gable resembling castle-like crenulations.

The housekeeper stood by the door to greet them when the coach rolled to a slow halt on the cobblestones.

Hans Ernstra was dressed in sombre attire of good make. He was middle-aged, with a balding crown and a stern face, with which he regarded Velthuys in the manner of a loyal hound awaiting his master's command.

He and Velthuys exchanged words as servants helped Peter inside the house and then transferred the baggage. Katja marvelled at the ostentatious wealth of the Breestraat while Liselotte thanked the coachman – much to his surprise and bemusement.

"I must be on my way," Velthuys said. "Veere awaits. I should be back in a few days at most."

He looked at Liselotte. "Mademoiselle, it was a pleasure meeting you. I already look forward to our next encounter."

"Your return is much anticipated, Monseigneur," Liselotte answered dutifully, hiding her relief at his prompt departure.

Velthuys lowered his head briefly in graceful acknowledgement, gave Katja a curt nod, and then left.

Ernstra invited the girls into the house, naming half-a-dozen servants lined up in the hallway. A maid led the girls up the staircase to the first-floor landing. The house exuded wealth with its furnishings and decorations.

"Is this a palace?" Katja whispered to Liselotte.

It felt palatial enough. They were brought to a spacious room, with two broad beds to either side of a hearth with a marble mantlepiece. Both beds had a washstand at their feet, as well as large closets. Paintings of ships out at sea hung on the walls. The floorboards that were visible were polished to a shine, the rest covered by a thick woven rug.

The small pile of their meagre belongings on the middle of the rug emphasized their change of fortune.

"Luncheon will be served in the dining room in thirty minutes," the maid announced. "There is clean water in the washing basins, should you desire to freshen up."

With that she closed the door and departed. With no clean spare clothing to speak of, all the girls could do was scrub their hands and faces, and then straighten their skirts, aprons, and coats as best they could, before venturing back into the house in search of the promised food.

"How do we behave?" Katja inquired softly.

"I don't know," Liselotte answered.

It wasn't immediately clear where the dining room was, so the girls wandered about the ground floor, peeking into rooms if the door was open and admiring the overwhelming luxury of all they saw. Liselotte had known such wealth existed but had never been this close to it.

One open door, at the very end of the central hallway, revealed a bedroom. Peter reclined on the bed within, and two elderly men in respectable garb fussed about at his bedside. Peter's chest was covered in small, lozenge-shaped creatures.

Leeches!

"They're bleeding him," Liselotte hissed.

She supposed it was to be expected. A lot of physicians applied leeches instantly, before making a diagnosis. "But he's in no state to lose blood."

Katja pulled at her sleeve, whispering urgently. "Miss Liselotte, you heard what *Heer* Velthuys said."

"You were listening?"

"Of course I was. I bain't stupid. Well, a little, I didn't understand all of it. But I know *Heer* Velthuys is too important to pick a fight with. And *Mynheer* Haelen is tough."

Liselotte sighed. "You're right, Katja. What would I do without you?"

Katja shrugged shyly, but she was pleased with the compliment.

The front door opened, and the hallway filled with the excited chatter of boys – voices that sounded familiar.

Andries.

"Jasper!"

Liselotte and Katja hurried to the front door but froze when they saw the apparent strangers who strode toward them.

Or were they strangers?

Liselotte shook her head in confusion. "Andries?"

§ § § § § §

"Well?" Andries asked his sister. "What do you think?"

He twirled around to give her a good look at his new outfit. Finely embroidered matched dark-blue breeches and doublet, black leather boots, a short red cape that reached halfway down his back, and a magnificent domed felt hat replete with ostrich feathers.

Then, being a gentleman now, Andries graciously indicated Jasper, whose breeches and doublet were of a simpler and less ostentatious make, albeit in the same colour blue. Jasper too wore a domed felt hat, with a smaller brim and a neat clutch of pheasant feathers pinned to it.

"Jasper!" Katja exclaimed. "Look at you!"

Jasper beamed. "All proper now."

"Well?" Andries asked Liselotte again, wanting her to be as proud of him as he himself was. He frowned. "Why are you dressed like a flatlander?"

Liselotte smoothed the front of her skirt, "These were a gift. There wasn't much left of my gown. You look very nice, Andries. And all cleaned up!"

"They have a huge brass bathtub," Jasper said. "You should see it, Katja. Big as a boat."

Mevrouw Ernstra had entered the house behind the boys. She was *Mynheer* Ernstra's age and similarly dressed in sombre tones of quality. She directed several servants who followed her – carrying packages – to a side room, and then stepped up next to Andries, with a carefully maintained expressionless face.

"Oh," Andries said. "*Mevrouw* Ernstra, let me introduce you. Liselotte Haelen, my sister, and Katja, handmaid to Liselotte."

"A pleasure to meet you, *Mejuffrouw* Liselotte, Katja." *Mevrouw* Ernstra said. "Master Andries, your luncheon should be ready in the dining room. Could you show the young lady and her maid the way? Please do not wait for us. I must speak with *Mynheer* Ernstra first, there are still things to be arranged, and..." She nodded at Liselotte, with a strange twist of the lips that might have been a forced smile. "We have a busy afternoon ahead of us."

The gleaming black lacquered table in the dining room was loaded with platters. The temptations offered by cold meat cuts, cheeses, bread rolls, and fruit beckoned. They had been left a free run; there was no one else present.

They eagerly loaded large pewter plates with as much as they could fit on them, but then hesitated – anxiously studying the polished lacquer of the table and chairs, as well as the bright colours of the embroidered seat covers.

"Are such chairs really made to sit on?" Katja asked.

"*Ja*," Liselotte said, "But let's go sit there."

She indicated the fire that crackled merrily in the hearth at the end of the room. Descending around it, they sat down on the ground to enjoy the luxury of the fire's warm glow and abundance of food on their plates.

The boys had much to tell, in between bites. About their journey to Middelburg and initial reception at Biggekercke House, but especially their good fortune since. They'd lunched as guests of the VOC, after which Velthuys had taken them to his lodgings on Breestraat. The first tailors had been summoned for measurements almost immediately – grumbling as they came through the rain but unwilling to risk displeasure. Dinner had been lavish, and the evening filled with more fittings. This morning, they had been out in Middelburg, visiting this shop and that.

"I'm getting a sword," Andries said proudly.

§ § § § § §

Liselotte nodded. She was pleased for him.

Katja was fascinated and wanted to know all about the shops. The boys were eager to provide more detail. Liselotte did her best to follow the enthusiastic descriptions, but her mind was elsewhere.

Velthuys had offered to act as her guide to Rotterdam society. Liselotte had never in her life spent even a single second thinking about Rotterdam society. Its existence had loomed up sudden and unexpected, like a predatory tree trunk in the shallows of a drowned land.

Liselotte accepted with regret that Rotterdam wouldn't be how she had experienced it as a child. Returning at her age, as a *precious family asset*, was likely to be daunting, filled with potential pitfalls that Liselotte was barely aware of.

More fighting to be done. Just on a different type of battlefield this time, one she dreaded as much, if not more, than the bloody Reymerswal beach by Lodiek Gap.

Turning Velthuys's offer down would be rude, considering that Peter and Marnix Velthuys were good friends. Foolish too. Liselotte had no idea now what to expect of Rotterdam, and more importantly what would be expected of her.

She grinned doubtfully. Michael had spoken of Peter's 'powerful connections', and Liselotte had no doubt that Marnix Velthuys was ranked high in that group. Even a *Zeeuwse* boatswain's mate had shown a better understanding of how this society business worked than she did. This was going to be a difficult challenge.

It felt like capitulation of sorts, to fall into line. To exchange dagger and scalpel for a delicate fan and dainty handkerchief. Peter had warned her it would be necessary, in their pre-dawn conversation in *De Wilde Ruyter's* cabin, but he couldn't guide her in this. He hadn't been back for more than fifteen years and admitted he didn't understand or care for society.

Good for him. Not a luxury I have though.

Most of all, Liselotte's mind wondered at the revelations about Saskia van der Krooswyck.

Had Father really been a lovestruck young man who had armed himself with poetry? Liselotte simply couldn't imagine it. He had never spoken about Mother much, other than to frequently assure Liselotte that if Mother had lived she would have been most disappointed in her daughter.

Saskia van der Krooswyck had always been a faceless and unknown presence, though Velthuys had suggested that Liselotte could catch a glimpse of Mother by looking into a mirror.

Velthuys had clearly raised Mother's past scandal as a cautionary tale, to issue a warning, but Liselotte couldn't help but be deeply impressed.

Young Saskia had defied her family and forsaken her wealth and status, to stroll to Delft and *do as she damn well pleased*. Liselotte was immensely proud of that defiance.

Her attention drifted back to the conversation by the fire in the dining room of the house on Breestraat.

The boys revealed what they knew about the afternoon's planned itinerary for the girls. It was disappointing to hear that they wouldn't get a chance to walk around Middelburg to see the city. All the tailors and required merchants had been summoned to Breestraat, in a tightly arranged schedule.

Mynheer and *Mevrouw* Ernstra entered the dining room, to note with some surprise that the table was empty of occupants, who were gathered around the hearth instead.

Mevrouw Ernstra herded Liselotte and Katja into a large corner room at the back of the house. It had a floor of blue and white tiles laid out in a chequered pattern. An unbelievably huge copper bathtub dwarfed various cabinets and washstands. It had curved stems, like bow and stern, on either end. Steam drifted from the water in the tub, as well as a rich flowery perfume.

The windows – set in the two outer walls – were open but concealed from sight by long white curtains that caught the breeze to fill up like sails.

Mevrouw Ernstra nodded at the maid present in a corner, then told Katja, "Watch and learn."

With that, she left.

Liselotte looked at the maid, uncertain as to why she was there.

"I'm to help you disrobe, *Mejuffrouw*," the maid said, eyeing Liselotte's attire curiously. "And help you wash."

"Oh, don't worry," Liselotte told her. "My handmaid will attend me."

"As you wish. Am I dismissed, *Mejuffrouw*?"

"Erm, *ja*, and bethanks."

The maid left and shut the door behind her.

"Am I really supposed to undress you now?" Katja asked.

"Nay, of course not." Liselotte rolled her eyes with exaggerated exasperation. "I can undress myself, I'm not helpless."

Katja grinned. "So, what am I to do then?"

"Take your clothes off."

"*Wablief*?"

"What we're going to do, *Lieffie*, is have a bath. That tub is big enough to fit us both and even then, there'd be room for more. I don't know about you, but I've never had anything other than lukewarm water in a tin tub. Have you seen that steam?"

"*Opa* took our tin tub from its hook on Saturday afternoons," Katja chatted as they undressed. "And then we took turns to bathe."

They entered the tub. The water was soapy and perfumed by rose petals, as well as exceedingly hot, almost excruciatingly so. What's more, there was a lot of it, reaching Liselotte's shoulders as she sat down.

"I've just died and gone to Heaven," Katja spoke with absolute certainty, after lowering herself down at the other end of the tub.

Liselotte agreed. She had never experienced anything like it. She closed her eyes as she relished the near complete envelopment by the scalding water, breathing in the scent of roses.

Opening her eyes again, Liselotte laughed when she took in Katja's enraptured expression.

"Hey, *meissie*," she called out, and splashed a handful of water at Katja, who felt obliged to retaliate. They were splashing away when—

"I think it's here, *Mynheer.*" The door was swung wide open, and Jasper burst into the room, his face turned backward to the hall. When he looked front-and-centre, he froze. "Wrong room." His eyes widened. "I think I just died and done gone to Heaven!"

He made a rapid retreat, shutting the door just in time to prevent getting hit by two bath sponges that were hurled at his head, along with giggles and cheerful curses that would make a sailor blush.

Liselotte suffered through the afternoon's fittings in silent misery. One tailor after the other came by. They had female assistants to wield the tape measures, while the artisans discussed materials and styles with *Mevrouw* Ernstra.

Liselotte was pleased that Katja was happy with the prospect of three outfits befitting a handmaid and companion but was concerned by the increasing number of orders made for her.

What do I need ten gowns for?

Mevrouw Ernstra provided explanations, describing how different occasions required different outfits, but Liselotte soon lost track of what was suited for what.

The rapid realisation of the complexity of this kind of life was dizzying. Father had stuck to boasting about the superiority of their class, demanding meek obedience, and living simply – on the cheap. They rarely had guests. Liselotte's experiences clearly weren't going to suffice to keep her afloat in this strange new world.

Her interest was roused when a jeweller came and laid out a row of short and slim daggers, with delicate handles of pedigreed silver and elaborately decorated sheaths.

Liselotte drew one of the daggers out of the sheath. To her surprise, the narrow blade was blunt.

"The Monseigneur told me," *Mevrouw* Ernstra said to Liselotte, "that you hail from aristocratic stock, *Mejuffrouw.*"

"I don't think that part of the family would agree, *Mevrouw,*" Liselotte confessed.

"So, I've heard, *Mejuffrouw.* But nonetheless, you have the right to wear a ceremonial dagger."

"I can wear a dagger?" Liselotte asked, perking up.

"*Ja, Milady,*" the jeweller confirmed. "And these here are fine accessories for public functions."

"They're very beautiful," Liselotte complimented him. She looked at *Mevrouw* Ernstra and patted the hilt of her keris. "I shall wear Eyang then."

"My dear." *Mevrouw* Ernstra shook her head. "That heathen knife is not appropriate."

Liselotte couldn't resist contesting that claim. "Maybe, but you can't stab anyone with these others. I've stabbed a man with Eyang. The blade went in really easy."

Mevrouw Ernstra gasped for breath and had to sit down to recover, a maid sent to fetch a glass of water.

Feeling guilty, Liselotte agreed to one of the ceremonial daggers, stylistically decorated to resemble a dolphin.

Eavesdropping in the hallway later, Liselotte heard *Mevrouw* Ernstra complain to her husband. "Those Haelens are little savages, Hans. Eating on the floor like peasants. The girl had her maid in the bath with her! Both indecent and that boy running in and out! And that poor jeweller was scared to death when the girl started talking about stabbing people with that vicious knife she insists on carrying."

Mynheer Ernstra had commiserated. "You know what they say about Brabant and Brabanders. We should have foreseen this."

Liselotte had grinned at first, until she realised that the Ernstras were likely to make report to Marnix Velthuys. He had expressed his desire for Liselotte to behave appropriately.

I didn't even know I was causing trouble.

The sense that things were watched, discussed, and then judged was stifling.

Liselotte was curious as to some of the gowns, having seen samples of materials that were unbelievably smooth and soft, but simultaneously viewed them as items of bribery.

Here's a piece of fabric to ooh and ah over, don't you worry your pretty head about anything else.

Like a child. A spoiled child.

Peter asked to see Liselotte before supper. He was sitting up in bed, with a trace of his old energy.

"I think I just died and done gone to Heaven!"

A young clerk, not yet twenty, was seated at a nearby table, quill scratching on parchments. Long dark curls framed his narrow, studious face. His brown eyes were brimming with keen sharpness that hinted at intelligence. Liselotte saw a pile of familiar papers from Father's strongbox laid out on the table.

"This is Rolf Romeyn, temporarily attached to the Zeeland VOC Chamber," Peter introduced the clerk. "Rolf, this is my cousin, Liselotte Haelen."

"A pleasure, *Mejuffrouw*."

"Likewise, *Mynheer*."

"I'll speak to Andries separately," Peter told Liselotte. "*Mynheer* Romeyn has drawn up a contract for your brother's employment as per the agreed conditions, with specifications for sums advanced in order to resolve an unfortunate issue, and the future recuperation of the advance."

Liselotte nodded her understanding that Peter was talking about Father's debts.

"Anyhow," Peter continued. "Young Rolf is very clever. Even if I myself wouldn't return, your brother will be cleared of any obligations after his first tour. He will be free of debt. Which brings us to you, Liselotte."

"Me?"

"I trust that Katja has asked you for decent wages?"

Liselotte squirmed a little. Katja hadn't mentioned it at all. Liselotte herself had given the necessity of it thought but had let her mind wander off into a fantasy in which she would set up a physician's shop in Rotterdam to earn an income. It was less attainable than the desire to fly to the moon and back, so hardly helpful.

"You're not to worry," Peter said. "I'll pay Katja's wages for a period of two years. We can review her contract when the boys and I return from the Indies."

Liselotte was overwhelmed. "Peter! That's so generous of you."

Peter shook his head. "I'm aware that we owe Katja a yawl. I don't think we would have got very far without it."

Liselotte shivered; her mind drawn back to the bloody crossroads near Steynbergen. "Nay, we wouldn't have."

"There's a selfish reason too," Peter confessed. "If she's safe with you, it'll give Jasper peace of mind and that will be worth a great deal to me."

Peter shifted, slowly and with a grimace, to reach for a small purse. He passed it to Liselotte.

"There's ten *stuivers* in there. Tell Jasper and Katja to go to a church or chapel in the morning. There are plenty in Middelburg. A *stuiver* or two should get prayers said for her *opa* and *oma*."

"That's very thoughtful of you. I think they will both appreciate that. As I understand it, Katja's *opa* and *oma* had pretty much adopted Jasper as their future grandson-in-law."

"And who can blame them?" Peter asked. "As to the other eight *stuivers*, present them to Katja as muster-bonus. Tell them both to take the day off after they've had the prayers said. There is plenty to explore in Middelburg. Let's give them a happy memory."

Liselotte smiled. She was sure that Katja and Jasper would be delighted with the freedom of a large bustling city for a day.

She spotted a great many bottles and pots on a table in a dark corner. Wandering over, she said, "Is there such a thing as a muster-bonus for handmaids?"

Rolf chuckled.

Liselotte studied the labels of the containers; it was clearly a cache left by the visiting physicians. Most of the contents met with her recognition and approval.

"There is for sailors. And Katja has sailed with us. Part of the crew." Peter shrugged awkwardly. "I'm fond of the symbolism of things."

"Part of the crew," Liselotte confirmed, empowered by the words.

Even if just for a short while. Part of De Wilde Ruyter's crew as well. As ship's surgeon.

"Peter, I know I'm not supposed to stick my nose in, but what did the doctors say? I'd like to know."

"You've earned the right to know as far as I am concerned. They hope to have a diagnosis tomorrow morning."

"A diagnosis? Peter, it's clear. You got a hole in your shoulder that needs to heal."

He sighed. "They have determined that I have a melancholy personality and that my black bile has become unbalanced. They now need to consult the stars and draw up a horoscope."

Cat's piss! These physicians are positively medieval.

Liselotte kept her face neutral, not wanting to alarm Peter unnecessarily, but she resolved to try and keep a close eye on what these old-fashioned relics from the past decided upon as treatment.

This is the seventeenth century! Modern times. The wound is knitting. It needs to be kept clean. It's that simple now. He's on the mend. Katja and I did that.

Pleased with the progress of his recovery, Liselotte took her leave, clutching the little purse of *stuivers*.

§ § § § § §

Supper started with a skirmish when one of the attending servants made clear that Jasper and Katja were expected to eat in the kitchen, "with the other servants."

Andries was embarrassed but reluctantly accepted that this was the normal way of doing things.

His sister, however, protested with enough vigour to cause one of the servants to depart to fetch reinforcements.

"Miss," Katja said. "It doesn't matter, we can eat in the kitchen. Can't we, Jasper?"

"That's not a problem, *Mejuffrouw*."

"Liselotte..." Andries said.

"I want to eat together," Liselotte insisted. "As a special celebration, and as a memory for all of us when you two are at sea."

Andries understood but was wary of contesting the matter with the Ernstras, both of whom entered the dining room enveloped in an air of righteousness.

They expected a confrontation.

Andries didn't like the unfairness of that. *What are they up to?*

"We made an exception for the luncheon," *Mevrouw* Ernstra said. "Out of consideration."

"From the kindness of our hearts," *Mynheer* Ernstra added in a dour tone, as if his trust had suffered a mortal blow.

"You need to understand," *Mevrouw* Ernstra lectured. "That civilised behaviour is an expectation here in Zeeland. You're not in Brabant anymore."

"I do understand," Liselotte said. "I'm doing my best. We're all trying. But just this night then—"

"Oh, the impertinence!" *Mevrouw* Ernstra exclaimed with dramatic exasperation. "Hans, do something."

Mynheer Ernstra complied with her request by giving Andries a meaningful look.

It was clear for all to read.

Keep your sister under control.

"Oh!" Katja exclaimed. She cast a worried look at Liselotte, as did Andries. His sister was staring at *Mynheer* Ernstra as if debating whether to stick him with her keris or shoot him with her crossbow.

Andries grinned foolishly. Events on the Eendragt and Oosterskelde had made clear who was in charge. Still, he was wary of offending the Ernstras in that they were extensions of Marnix Velthuys, a man who had been most generous with his time, resources, and praise.

Looking at Jasper and Katja, however, – especially Jasper – had become impossible without an immediate succession of recent memories passing by Andries's mind's eye.

When Andries had spoken to Peter earlier in the day, to review the contracts that Andries had promptly signed, Peter had spoken of 'his crew' on the yawl. Andries recalled other words Peter had uttered back on the yawl.

It is a strength of unity that will carry a crew through the heart of the worst storm.

It was a notion that Andries was beginning to understand. He had seen it on *De Wilde Ruyter*. He himself felt stronger because of Jasper's support. This was one of the things to learn.

"*Mynheer* Ernstra, *Mevrouw* Ernstra," Andries spoke up. "You are right to insist on proper behaviour. And have been most kind in your consideration, as you said."

They acknowledged his words with short nods.

"But I too would ask for one last extension of your goodwill. We shared a bad time out there, many things happened. Soon, Jasper and I are to sail to the East, for the benefit of Monseigneur Velthuys, and we won't see Liselotte and Katja for a long time, many years even. Please, can we have this one last evening? Tomorrow we will do as you wish. *Including* my sister."

He cast a sideways glance at Liselotte. Surely, she would understand the game.

"*Ja*, we will all do as you wish," Liselotte agreed, contrite and meek. "I will do as my brother asks."

Andries bit on his lips to prevent himself from laughing at her performance.

Mynheer and *Mevrouw* Ernstra accepted the twinned request and promise with as much non-verbal disapproval as they could muster. Then curtly announced they would not be eating in 'mixed' company and withdrew.

"Thank you," Liselotte said to Andries. She took his hand in her own and squeezed it gently, then swiftly kissed him on the cheek. Andries was pleased he had impressed her.

Servants brought in flasks and steaming platters and then left the children to it. There was a wide selection of roast meat, vegetables, fruit, and bread. They piled their plates full and sat by the hearth again, comparing it to the meagre comforts of the guardhouse in Reymerswal.

After they had eaten, Jasper discovered that one of the smaller flasks contained brandywine. They mellowed by the warmth of the fire to enjoy a rare moment of peace and companionship. The flames in the hearth invited song and they obliged in harmony. The poignant tones of the tragic demise of an *Oranjevaarder* filled the room.

> *There was a proud ship that sailed on the lowland sea*
> *It sailed by the name The Golden Vanity*
> *And we feared she would be taken*
> *By a Spanish galilee*
> *As we sailed upon the lowland, lowland, low*
> *As we sailed upon the lowland sea.*

31. The Hysterical Lunatic

MIDDELBURG ~ COUNTY OF ZEELAND ~ 1622

They were served a light breakfast of some bread and cheese in their rooms early the next morning. A steady stream of packages reached the house soon after, mostly for Andries, though there was a sturdy sailor's outfit for Jasper which he couldn't stop parading in with the swagger of an old tar.

There was one early set for the girls. Liselotte fell head over heels for the made-to-measure green gown with fitted bodice and a closed round skirt. It was accented with brown velvet bands and had wide virago sleeves. The whole was completed by a white ruffled collar – and Liselotte couldn't believe how elegantly it suited her.

Mevrouw Ernstra nodded approvingly as Liselotte admired herself in a standing mirror but tut-tutted when Liselotte attached Eyang to the gown's narrow leather belt, next to a small flat purse made from the same material as the gown.

Katja had a matching outfit, of the same colour and material, but of a simpler design and with a modest flat lace collar. She was delighted, proclaimed that she had never owned such fine clothes before, and then rushed away to show off to Jasper.

The two youngsters left soon after. The mission to have Katja's grandparents named in prayer to honour their passing lent them gravitas, but there was an underlying energy as well. The two were thrilled with their new outfits and the anticipation of exploring a big city with *stuivers* to spend.

Liselotte accompanied them outside and reminded Jasper to refrain from outbursts of Flemish pride. "Don't let them know you're a Catholic."

Jasper had nodded as gravely as he could but was clearly bursting with impatience to be off.

Liselotte waved at them from the porch, and then walked back into the house that felt emptier in the absence of the two youngest members of Peter's crew.

Andries was in the parlour, trying yet another outfit on. Liselotte noted that the door to Peter's bedroom was slightly ajar, so walked quietly through the hall to glean if anything useful could be learned.

The physicians were back, speaking to *Mynheer* Ernstra.

"We have studied the iatromathematics of the matter," one of the physicians said.

The other one, who sounded sterner, added, "Specifically the placement of Mercury, the wound's location being one in Gemini's sphere."

"Fortunately," the first physician spoke, "the alignment of the planets bodes well for the treatment of Commodore Haelen."

Liselotte shook her head.

Hocus Pocus.

"I was given to understand," *Mynheer* Ernstra said. "That it was mostly a matter of keeping the wound clean and under observation."

"If only it were that simple," the stern physician said reprovingly. "Then the likes of us wouldn't have to spend decades mastering our profession."

The other one added, "things have already been made far more complicated through that initial treatment by an inept layman. These matters should really be left up to experts in the art of diagnostics."

Liselotte balled her fists.

"*Ja*, Monseigneurs," Ernstra answered. "But as I understand there was no choice in the matter at the time."

"Nevertheless," the stern physician said. "It has brought an imbalance to his humours. There is bad blood within."

Great, they're going to bleed him again. Just what he doesn't need!

"*MEJUFFROUW* HAELEN!" *Mevrouw* Ernstra appeared in the hallway, face and voice full of disapproval.

Mynheer Ernstra stepped out of the bedroom, staring at Liselotte with reproach.

"We've been warned about this," he told Liselotte resolutely. "And the Monseigneur has left explicit instructions that you are *not* to be involved in Commodore Haelen's treatment."

Mevrouw Ernstra, who had approached Liselotte, added, "It simply isn't seemly. Folk would be quick to talk about the shame of such an outrage."

"God forbid," *Mynheer* Ernstra added.

"Do recall your promise before supper last night. Come to the parlour, *Mejuffrouw* Liselotte." *Mevrouw* Ernstra said. "Another gown has arrived for you to try on."

"Enough new clothes to keep you fully occupied," *Mynheer* Ernstra said soothingly, as if to signal the end of the matter. "The generosity of the Monseigneur knows no limits."

"*Ja*," *Mevrouw* Ernstra added. "*Mynheer* Velthuys has offered you nothing but hospitality and fine gifts. A modest young lady should be grateful."

Liselotte stood her ground, unwilling to admit defeat, not with Peter's health at stake.

"Please, *Mynheer* and *Mevrouw* Ernstra, those men don't know what they are doing. They haven't a clue. Please believe me, for Peter's sake."

"You would claim to know better than two of your elders? Highly learned and esteemed experts in their field?" *Mynheer* Ernstra shook his head. "The sheer impudence of it." He looked at his wife. "Take her to the parlour."

Mevrouw Ernstra reached out to take hold of Liselotte's arm. Liselotte evaded her easily, but began a retreat to the parlour, as ordered. The alternative of being dragged there like a wayward child didn't appeal to her.

I'm not a child.

Ernstra paced through one of the doors, disappearing deeper into the house. His wife ushered Liselotte to the front of the house. She opened the parlour door and beckoned for Liselotte to step through.

Peter screamed.

It was an agonised scream of raw pain that seemed to tear through Liselotte's very soul. "What the Devil!"

"Your language, *Mejuf*—wait, come back. Don't go there."

Liselotte was halfway to the bedroom door when another drawn-out scream from Peter filled the air.

Andries ran into the hallway, in an ungainly fashion because he was somewhat hampered by the sword attached to the belt of the seafarer's outfit he wore. "Liselotte, what's going on?"

"I don't know," Liselotte answered without breaking her stride. She burst through the bedroom door to the sound of yet another scream, Andries hot on her heels.

The two physicians had restrained Peter to the bed with several stout leather straps. One stood by the bedside, a bloodied scalpel in his hand. The other was just approaching the bed, bearing a small cauldron that contained a rancid smelling substance. Peter's wound had been cut wide open. Blood welled from it, mixed with glistening oil. Peter had passed out after his last scream.

"What have you done?" Andries cried out.

"They've cut the wound open," Liselotte said, dazed by the stupidity of it. "It was healing!"

337

"How dare you intrude on us?" The man with the scalpel – the stern one – asked. "This is preposterous."

Liselotte asked. "What's in that cauldron? What are you using it for?"

"Now look here," the man said. He lifted the scalpel and shook it at Liselotte in admonition, in the manner of a schoolmaster.

There was a scrape, a swift blur, and then the physician was presented by the sight of his short scalpel blade crossed with the tip of a gleaming seafarer's sword.

"I am Midshipman Haelen," Andries told the physician. "You will stop threatening the Commodore's cousin at once. Lower that scalpel. Good. Now tell us what you are doing to my captain."

"There's no need for this." The physician retreated a few nervous steps.

Liselotte glanced at her brother.

Andries has his moments.

Andries slid his sword back into its scabbard. His latest outfit wasn't like the other fancier ones. This one was the same type of good quality practical seafarer's gear that Peter wore. Liselotte reckoned it suited Andries better than the ostentatious ones that left him looking rather pretentious.

"What's going on in here?" *Mynheer* Ernstra filled the doorway. *Mevrouw* Ernstra appeared behind him, peeking over his shoulder.

"I'll tell, it's not a secret!" the other physician said, putting down the steaming cauldron on a small table by the bedside. "A tried and tested remedy. Certainly not worth this undue and disgraceful fuss. We've opened the wound and poured in boiling oil to cleanse it. Next, we'll apply the mixture in the cauldron. It contains paraffin wax to help mould it to the wound's shape, mixed with mercury, lamb fat, toasted cheese, and fresh hog dung."

"Fresh hog dung?" Andries asked full of disbelief.

"Like HELL you are," Liselotte barked. "You're not putting *scheit* into Peter's wound."

"*Mejuffrouw* Haelen!" *Mevrouw* Ernstra protested. "Your language! Your manners!"

"Don't you understand?" Liselotte despaired. "These *platbroecken* will kill Peter. You don't insert faeces into a wound, you just don't."

"The girl is in hysterics, *Mynheer* Ernstra," was the stern physician's diagnosis. "It's the only explanation for this ludicrous behaviour."

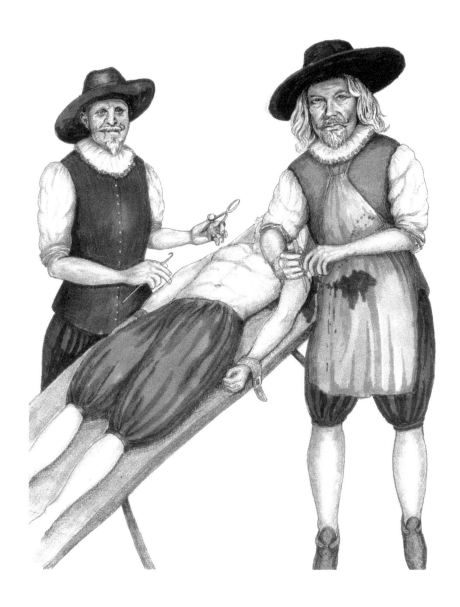

"They've cut the wound open," Liselotte said, dazed by the stupidity of it. "It was healing!"

"Clearly on the edge of lunacy," his colleague agreed. He looked at Ernstra. "There is treatment for female hysteria. But she needs to be restrained, her clothing loosened to let her breathe. She should be bled immediately. Fortunately, we brought enough leeches."

"Fumigated as well, I should say," the stern one said. "I'll take it upon myself to—"

"BY GOD'S GONADS!" Liselotte screamed at them in fury.

Ernstra's eyes bulged. "Enough of this blasphemy." He seized hold of Liselotte's arms and pulled her out of the bedroom.

Andries made to come to her assistance, but found himself restricted by *Mevrouw* Ernstra, who grabbed him by the back of his doublet's collar and steered Andries into the hallway.

"Get your hands off me!" Liselotte struggled as Ernstra dragged her in the direction of the front door, but Ernstra was strong and lent determination by his anger.

"You ungrateful, wretched wench." He snapped at her. He nodded at one of the maids who had appeared. She opened the front door.

"The Monseigneur will hear of this!" *Mevrouw* Ernstra added.

Without slowing down, Ernstra shoved Liselotte forward, out of the house and on to the porch steps.

Liselotte stumbled, recovered, and turned. She expected Andries to be exiled with her, but *Mevrouw* Ernstra was directing him into the parlour.

"Andries!"

"Liselotte!"

"*Mejuffrouw*," Ernstra spoke solemnly. "You can stay out here on the porch until you are ready to apologize most profusely for your shameful behaviour."

"They're going to kill Peter with that stuff," Liselotte pleaded.

Ernstra shut the door. She could hear his muffled voice through the door, as he told *Mevrouw* Ernstra, "She has nowhere to go in Middelburg. She'll sit on the porch, be stared at, and feel miserable. When she gets hungry, she'll knock and offer her apologies."

Anger crossed Liselotte's face.

Klootzak.

32. The Boatswains

MIDDELBURG ~ COUNTY OF ZEELAND ~1622

Liselotte paced the cobbles in front of the house on Breestraat. Everything had gone horribly wrong in very short order. Velthuys would be furious, but Liselotte was past caring. Those idiots inside were going to murder Peter.

She touched the hilt of Eyang for reassurance and was struck by a thought.

Take Peter to Flushing.

That had been her plan back at Reymerswal.

Liselotte looked around at the Breestraat. She didn't think it looked welcoming or friendly. It was as if Middelburg itself was infused with hostility.

Flushing it is then.

Somehow.

Liselotte grasped Eyang's hilt tightly.

First things first.

She needed to get back into the house and talk to Andries.

"Excuse me," a deep male voice said.

Liselotte barely registered it, preoccupied with eyeing the ground floor windows.

Might there be something open around the back? Those bathroom windows?

"Excuse me, *Mejuffrouw*." The voice was insistent. "Begging your pardon. Tis about that keris…"

Liselotte turned to see two sailors. They were keeping a respectful distance but even so the two men appeared as giants, both standing six-foot tall and broad with muscles. Their bared forearms were resplendent with ink. Both had elaborate mermaid tattoos to admire, with tails that rippled when their arms flexed.

"Excuse me, Mejuffrouw." The voice was insistent. "Begging
your pardon. Tis about that keris…"

One was an old salt, with long white hair tied at the nape of his neck, a silver-streaked grey bushy beard, and a weather-beaten face that spoke of a wealth of experience. Despite his age, his bearing was straight and his presence powerful. The other sailor was Peter's age, with trimmed beard and brown hair cropped short. He carried himself with quiet confidence.

The younger one was leading a horse that pulled a cart, with a flat bed on which rested some neatly folded sails.

"My apologies," Liselotte said. "I wasn't paying attention."

The old salt pointed at Eyang. "That keris, *Mejuffrouw*. There's only one like it."

"Begging you pardon, but how did you get it?" the other sailor asked.

They know Peter!

"The keris was a gift, from Commodore Peter Haelen. I'm his cousin, Liselotte Haelen."

The two men exchanged a puzzled glance.

"You're his cousin, *Mejuffrouw*?" the younger sailor spoke. "I thought Skipper Haelen's cousin was a lad, about your age."

"My brother, Andries." Liselotte glanced at the house. "Who are you?"

"Walter Zundert," the older man said. "Former boatswain to Commodore Haelen on *De Blokzeyl*."

"Korneel Jansz," the younger man introduced himself. "Current boatswain to Skipper Haelen. I came to Middelburg today to pick up some stud sails and old Zundert here, who's come looking for work. We heard the captain was here, is he in the house? Is it true that he's been wounded?"

Liselotte glanced at their mermaid tattoos again and released her grip on Eyang's hilt. "Peter is in the house, but it isn't good. He was shot by a sentry at Tholen. It was night, they thought we were Spanish. The wound was treated out there and he was on the mend, but now they've got Middelburg physicians in charge." She paused. "Very old-fashioned. Those *platbroeck* doctors are literally killing him right now."

"Killing?" Zundert was dubious. "This is Seigneur Velthuy's place, isn't it? He wouldn't allow the skipper to be harmed. Surely—"

"*Heer* Velthuys isn't here. Those quacksalvers are stuffing pig *scheit* into the wound. Pig *scheit* and toasted cheese."

"Toasted cheese." Jansz shook his head in wonder. "But *Mejuffrouw*, physicians work with strange methods all the time, far beyond the understanding of mere mortals such as us."

"The hog dung will make that wound fester," Liselotte insisted. "And rot. My father was a physician, he taught Andries…and myself. I've done operations. As ship's surgeon even."

"Ship's surgeon?" Zundert shook his wizened head. "*Mejuffrouw*, you take us for fools, there's no such—"

Jansz fell in by laughing. "*Meissies* don't—"

"HELL'S BELLS!" Liselotte exclaimed. She retrieved Michael's letter that she had carefully tucked away in the small purse at her belt. "Here, read it yourself."

Zundert took the letter and began to read it, very slowly, his lips moving as he did so.

Liselotte turned her attention back to the house. For a moment she had hoped the sailors might help her, but that seemed unlikely now.

"It's true," Zundert told his companion with wonder in his voice. "Appointed by Adriaansz."

"The *Duvelsjong* himself!" Jansz exclaimed. "*Mejuffrouw*, you come highly recommended then."

"I treated one of his sailors," Liselotte said. "And Peter."

"Liselotte!" Andries came rushing out of the narrow alley by the side of the house, in his seafarer's kit, the sword scabbard slapping against his leg.

"Andries!"

"Officer on deck," Zundert said in a low voice.

The boatswains straightened their backs.

"Andries, this is Boatswain Zundert and Boatswain Jansz." Liselotte said. "Masters, this is my brother Midshipman Haelen, in service of Peter."

"Seigneur!" the two boatswains exclaimed as one.

Andries nodded at the boatswains, but then faced Liselotte. "Peter has become unresponsive. They tried antimonial wine, but that didn't work."

Liselotte's face clouded over. Antimonial wine was a toxic brew that was meant to provoke vomiting as a means of shocking a patient back into consciousness.

"They were talking about fumigation next, and otherwise trepanning."

"Trepanning!" Liselotte was horrified.

"Begging your pardon," Jansz said. "I know what fumigation is, but trepanning?"

"They'll cut a hole in his skull," Andries said.

"Supposedly to release evil spirits," Liselotte added. "It's barbaric. I told you they were killing Peter."

"Is that true, Seigneur?" Zundert asked Andries.

He didn't hesitate to answer. "My sister was well taught in these matters, by the best. If she says so, then it's true, Boatswain. This will harm my cousin."

Jansz shook his head. "Can't let that happen."

"I agree." Zundert looked at Andries. "What would you have us do, Seigneur?"

§ § § § § §

"Me? Have you do?" Andries looked from one to the other.

"They're part of Peter's crew," Liselotte reminded him.

Andries understood.

"Just say the word, Seigneur," Jansz growled.

Andries suppressed the rush of panic that had numbed him at Steynbergen and Tholen. Liselotte was fighting for Peter's life again. Jasper and Adriaansz had been right about filling certain roles at the wrong time. Now was the right time though, this time he would help Liselotte straight away.

Wasn't that why he had snuck out of the parlour and found a servant's entrance at the side of the house? It was a pity he wasn't wearing one of his more flamboyant outfits, but this one would have to do.

He drew his sword.

"There's a small door in the alley. I jammed it open. Follow me."

He could barely believe that the two enormous men obediently fell into step behind him, followed by Liselotte – who was grinning fiercely.

They made it to the hallway unseen, emerging in the middle of it. Mevrouw Ernstra was by the front door, her back toward them, speaking to the VOC clerk on the porch.

"Nay, *Mynheer* Romeyn, I'm afraid Commodore Haelen is indisposed today."

Andries motioned for the others to follow him to the bedroom door. He opened it and strode in.

Mynheer Ernstra was in the middle of the room, his back to the door, observing the bed. Peter lay prone, the leather straps now undone, a bandage bound sloppily about his shoulder to contain the vile mess the physicians had smeared in and on the wound.

Ernstra turned around. "We were not to be distu…"

His eyes widened.

The physicians looked up, perturbed. One had lit a long pipe with wide bowl; the other was fussing over a set of fumigation bellows.

The sterner man with the pipe said. "Really, *Mynheer* Ernstra, we can't be expected to work if we're continually interrupted like this."

The other one, with the bellows, shook his head. "This is not a sight for children. We need to pull the patient's under-clothing down. It's imperative that we blow tobacco smoke up his rectum immediately."

"You can go blow it up your own arse," Liselotte snapped at him.

They both looked shocked.

Andries brandished the sword menacingly and ordered, "Step away from the Commodore. Now."

Ernstra looked at him with contempt. "Who do you think you are? You have no right!"

The housekeeper's wife wailed a plaintive "Hans!" from the doorway, even as Rolf Romeyn stepped past her, taking in the scene and trying to make sense of it all.

"Seigneur Haelen!" Zundert barked. "Permission to speak?"

"Erm, *ja* Boatswain," Andries said.

Zundert looked at Ernstra, his face apologetic. He spoke in a soothing regretful tone, "I'm very sorry *Mynheer*, but Midshipman Haelen is obliged to follow his orders. He's just doing his duty. A little enthusiastically maybe, but that is ever the way of the young."

"Orders? Duty?" Ernstra asked with disbelief. "Whose orders?"

"Why, Lieutenant-Admiral Willem de Zoete, Seigneur. And the *Zeeuwse* admiralty."

Ernstra frowned. "I wasn't aware that de Zoete had issued orders to this…midshipman."

"The Admiral has summoned all *Oranjevaarders* to his banner, *Mynheer*. A general mobilisation of all ships in Zeeland."

Ernstra shook his head. "This is a VOC matter. The VOC is exempt from the general mobilisation, as you should know…?"

"I'm Boatswain Zundert, *Mynheer*. You are correct about the VOC being an exception. But my Skipper Haelen here, he don't sail for the VOC no more. He does captain a ship, and as such, he is to report to the admiralty, Seigneur."

"This is ludicrous," the stern physician announced. "This man is in no state to travel anywhere. The admiral may say what he likes, but in affairs of health a physician's word outweighs his."

"True, Seigneur," Zundert generously conceded. "But as a civilian caught up in navy business, Seigneur, your words are outranked by a navy surgeon's. Wouldn't you agree?"

The old sailor glanced at Andries, tapping the letter Liselotte had shown her brother the previous evening against his arm. Andries nodded his understanding and tried not to grin.

"Well, *ja*," the physician said. "But there are no navy surgeons here."

His colleague argued, "Fumigation is urgent. We cannot wait for the fleet to return."

Relishing the moment, Andries announced. "In the name of Admiral de Zoete, I would call upon *De Wilde Ruyter's* ship's surgeon to make a pronouncement on this matter."

The ship's surgeon of the admiral's very own *statenjacht* flashed one of her wolfish grins and stepped forward, eager to be of assistance. "Gentlemen, as navy surgeon I deem Commodore Haelen fit to travel at once."

The stern physician spluttered. His colleague began to cough, then choke on his coughs.

"Try blowing some smoke up your arse," Liselotte advised him sweetly.

Ernstra shook his head firmly. "This is ridiculous, Boatswain." He looked at Andries and said through clenched teeth. "Master Andries, this is just a farce. I must ask you to—"

"Here," Zundert thrust the letter at him. "Read it for yourself."

Ernstra did, with growing disbelief. "*Mynheer* Romeyn? As senior VOC employee present…"

Rolf came closer and took the proffered letter, reading it intently.

"Who is this temporary skipper?" Ernstra asked him. "What's his rank?"

"Doesn't matter, *Mynheer* Ernstra," Rolf answered him. "In this matter Adriaansz speaks with Admiral de Zoete's authority, as does Midshipman Haelen. Under current conditions, it would seem that Commodore Haelen is under admiralty orders."

The stern physician reddened in anger. "A girl can't be a surgeon. She's a hysterical lunatic!"

Liselotte took the letter from Rolf and waved it at the physician. "Skipper Adriaansz says I can. Admiral de Zoete says I can. Now get out of my way." For good measure she added, "In the name of Count Maurits, Prince of Orange."

Liselotte squeezed past him to attend to Peter. "*Mevrouw* Ernstra, if you please, I need two cauldrons of boiled water."

Mevrouw Ernstra looked at her husband, who nodded wearily.

"Very well, *Mejuffrouw*."

"Doctors," Ernstra said with reluctance. "I will see you out."

The physicians protested, until both Zundert and Jansz took a step forward to help convince them that it was a good time to depart.

Those left in the room could hear their outraged protests and Ernstra's apologies all the way to the front door.

Rolf motioned Andries and Zundert to him. "Well played, but you're lucky they weren't too familiar with the matter."

"Familiar?" Andries asked.

Zundert grinned. "I may have exaggerated things a mite, Seigneur."

Rolf explained to Andries, "For *Mynheer* Haelen to actually fall under the admiralty's authority, he needs to be afloat on a ship with the Republic's flag raised at the mast. Not in a sickbed in Middelburg."

"It worked though, eh?" Zundert said, clearly pleased with himself.

Rolf nodded. "It was well conceived."

"But you knew it wasn't entirely valid?" Andries asked Rolf.

Rolf cast a glance at Peter who was being tended by Liselotte. "*Mynheer* Haelen was fine yesterday. Before those..." He shook his head.

Looking back at Andries and Zundert, Rolf said, "Listen, I'm just a low-ranking VOC employee. It won't be long before Ernstra gets in touch with Biggekercke House to verify what's what. You need to get the commodore out of here as soon as possible. Preferably now. I'll talk to *Heer* Velthuys when he gets back. He trusts me."

"And take Peter where?" Andries asked.

"Why, Seigneur," Zundert said. "To his ship, of course. Time to hoist the colours."

"Flushing!"

"Flushing," Rolf confirmed. "Go make it legal, Midshipman, get the captain on his quarterdeck."

33. Queen of the South Sea

ZUYT WATERINGE ~ COUNTY OF ZEELAND ~1622

Katja and Jasper came strolling down the Breestraat just as Zundert and Jansz installed Peter – unconscious still – on the folded sails on the cart's bed. The children carried various packages and bags. Neither of them seemed surprised that the Haelens had outstayed their welcome, nor perturbed that they were all promptly moving on to Flushing.

"We came back to drop some things off." Katja indicated their haul. "But still have things in the house as well."

Andries pointed at the bundles on the cart. He and Jansz had hastily gathered all their belongings from the bedrooms and bundled them in bed sheets.

Liselotte knew that Andries regretted that they didn't have the time, or space on the small cart, to collect his new outfits from the parlour. Her brother seemed resigned to the loss, at least pleased that he was wearing his seafaring kit.

Liselotte wore her green gown, Katja was wearing the complimentary companion's version, and – like Andries – Jasper looked quite the part in his new sailor's gear.

Liselotte got on the cart, to rest Peter's head on her lap after she had covered him with one of their blankets. The others walked when they departed, Jansz leading the horse.

Liselotte was barely aware of the city as they moved through Middelburg's streets and squares. Her attention was focused on Peter. She had cleaned the wound as best she could back at Breestraat and had appropriated some of the physicians' lye to pour into the wound before bandaging Peter up. As soon as they reached the Jayakarta Dockyard in Flushing though, she would have to open the wound up again to ensure it was entirely clear of the foul elixir poured in by the quacksalvers. Jansz had told her it was about five miles to Flushing.

We should be there in a few hours.

Nonetheless, Liselotte was worried about Peter's mind. He seemed to have gone into a shock of sorts and his forehead was glowing hot again. Treating the wound was riskier if Peter was too weakened, but it had to be done.

They left the city behind and entered the green flatlands of Zuyt Wateringe.

Katja and Jasper had taken an immediate liking to Zundert and Jansz. Now that there was no city noise to contend with, they proceeded to share their Middelburg adventures as if the two boatswains were old friends. Most of their tales involved the discovery of various foodstuffs. These were duly produced to be shared around. Saffron biscuits, spiced biscuits, sugar-coated almonds, marzipan, gingerbread, and preserved fruit – there seemed to be no end to the delights offered by Middelburg.

Andries dropped back to offer Liselotte some of the delicacies that were doing the rounds.

"How's Peter doing?" he asked.

"Not too well," Liselotte said, taking a spiced biscuit and some marzipan. "He's still unresponsive, which isn't surprising considering the efforts of those two fools."

"We did the right thing," Andries said, though he added, "*Mynheer* Velthuys won't be pleased with us. It's a shame, I liked him."

"He might not be as displeased as you think, Andries. I heard Ernstra speak to the physicians. Velthuys wanted those *platbroecken* to keep the wound clean and monitor Peter. Not embark on medical misadventures. Velthuys and Peter are good friends I think, and Velthuys told me that he very much wanted Peter to succeed on his...your...next trip to the East."

"You think so?" Andries didn't seem convinced but cheered up a little.

Liselotte was of that opinion, though she reckoned that Velthuys was far more likely to forgive Andries than accept Liselotte's behaviour. He'd made his expectations clear. She had certainly not met them. She grinned, recalling that she'd cursed like a sailor. The Ernstras would probably report that word for word.

So much for Rotterdam society.

As they progressed, Peter remained unconscious, though he did speak every now and then. "At the helm! Rising tall in death. Don't tell the men. Mustn't tell the men."

Zundert turned to throw a concerned look at Peter.

Liselotte soothed her cousin. "Hush Peter, hush now. It'll be alright."

"Nay, nay, nay, we must stop them. Dewi! Christine!"

Liselotte stared at the distant towers of Flushing. She was certain there was a woman that Peter was in love with, either this Dewi or Christine. She dearly hoped that they would find this woman in Flushing and that her presence would soothe Peter's soul.

They were approaching the city when Zundert took over the horse's lead rope from Jansz. Like the other inhabited cities Liselotte had seen in Zeeland, Flushing was defended by a modern system of ramparts and bastions. They took a road leading left instead of heading to the nearest gate, moving past the ramparts and toward a pair of windmills rising on the city's eastern edge.

Jansz fell back to cast a glance at Peter.

"How is the skipper doing, *Mejuffrouw*?"

"He's feverish again, Boatswain. A cause for concern."

Peter jerked around for a moment, moaning, "*Tebing Yang Menjerit.*"

Liselotte recalled that he had uttered those words in the guardhouse at Reymerswal. She also noted Jansz's response to the words, as a brief shadow flitted over his face.

"Boatswain Jansz. Do you know what those words mean?"

He hesitated.

"Master Jansz," Liselotte pleaded. "The more I know the better. He's said those words before, as well as…" She frowned as she tried to recollect. "…*Lauwtan Tulan*?"

"*Lautan Tulang*," Jansz said, dread in his voice. "It means 'The Ocean of Bones'. They are painful memories, *Mejuffrouw.*"

"Why, what happened?"

"It was in the East Indies, *Mejuffrouw*. On our last voyage. We'd been sent to, ahem, 'pacify' the Wandan Islands. For the nutmeg."

"Pacify?"

"It was a bloodbath, *Mejuffrouw*. Most of the *Blokzeyl* lads were horrified by what happened. Not many Wandanese survived."

"I see," Liselotte said. She recalled the recognition she had seen in Peter's eyes at the bloody crossroads near Steynbergen, when it seemed he had stared thousands of miles away.

Was his mind entangled in vivid memories of such cruelty now?

They were turning around a broad corner. Liselotte could see that the area between the windmills and the city ramparts was a hive of activity. There were many – mainly low – buildings, as well as rising masts and rigging that suggested the presence of a harbour. Beyond that, a grey glimpse of the sea.

"The skipper took it especially hard, *Mejuffrouw*. He had, ahem…well…it's…" Jansz looked embarrassed. "Not quite appropriate."

"You must tell me though. I need to know. It may help me treat my cousin."

"He had a native sweetheart, *Mejuffrouw*. Not a doxy, like many of the lads. But a proper local lady, a chieftain's daughter. He was…"

"In love?"

"Well, *ja*. Smitten. And she loved him too, I think. The skipper was absolutely devastated when she…when…"

"She died?"

Jansz nodded. "He blamed himself. Her name was Dewi, *Mejuffrouw*."

"Dewi."

It explained the heart-breaking poignancy Liselotte had discerned whenever Peter had mentioned that name. But it didn't match the longing she'd heard in his voice when he had told her that he wanted to be with…someone. That optimistic hope hadn't been for someone who had died, but for someone alive and within reach.

Liselotte hoped to find an answer in Flushing. If it wasn't Dewi…

It must be Christine. Who is she?

They entered the busy area between windmills and harbour, a collection of cottages, taverns, open-air roperies, storage yards for timber, and dockyards – filled with the noise of hammers and saws. Nobody paid them much attention as they progressed, most folk having tasks to attend to.

"Master Jansz," Liselotte said. "Does the name 'Christine' ring a bell?"

He narrowed his eyes, reluctant to answer. "It be ill luck, *Mejuffrouw*."

"I must know. Surely it'll be bad luck for many if Peter doesn't pull through?"

"True," Jansz admitted, shrugging. "And the core crew know anyway. It's to do with Dewi, *Mejuffrouw*. The skipper wanted to call his ship *De Dewi*, but *Heer* Velthuys insisted on a proper Christian name. So the skipper, with his sense of humour…just a minute."

Christian. Christine.

"To the right here, Master Zundert," Jansz called out.

Zundert led horse and cart through an opening between two workshops. They emerged on a large rectangular yard, fronted by a small house, various workshops, sheds, and, at the far end, a slipway that led down to water. There were men about, but none were working, puffing at their clay pipes or engaged in games of dice instead.

In the middle of the space, on rollers and supported by beams, stretched a long black hull, partially masted. The ship was deserted and made a gloomy lifeless impression.

Zundert brought the cart to a halt. Liselotte jumped off and walked along the length of the ship. Jansz followed her.

He said, "The skipper intends to name her—"

"*The Christine*," Liselotte whispered, looking at the ship in awe. She had seen big ships in Rotterdam when she had been a child, but never up close. The sheer size astonished her.

She stopped in her tracks when she reached the bow and saw the figurehead. It was a brown-skinned mermaid, elegant, bare-breasted, with a crown made of seaweed.

Liselotte's hand automatically reached for her keris.

Eyang. Queen of the South Sea.

Absorbed by the mermaid, Liselotte was at first unaware of the commotion around the harbour. Folk pointed, shouted, beckoned, and then drifted to the edge of the quays or slipways. It wasn't until the craftsmen in the Jayakarta Dockyard – as well as the new arrivals – made their way to the water that Liselotte took her eyes off the figurehead, looking past the mermaid at…

He certainly knew how to make a dramatic entry. *De Wilde Ruyter* sailed into the harbour festooned with flags. Balanced precariously on the bowsprit, Michael Adriaansz clutched a jib stay with one hand and waved a massive flagpole with the other. The huge multi-banded prince's flag attached to it streamed regally in the wind.

"VICTORY!" Michael roared at his gathering audience. "VICTORY!"

The cry was taken up by his beardlings.

"VICTORY FOR ZEELAND AND ORANGE! HUZZAH!"

Liselotte watched, open-mouthed, as the *Duvelsjong* returned home to Flushing in style.

She stopped in her tracks when she reached the bow and saw the figurehead. It was a brown-skinned mermaid, elegant, bare-breasted, with a crown made of seaweed.

34. Hell Hath no Fury

FLUSHING ~ COUNTY OF ZEELAND ~ 1622

The news filtered through to Jayakarta Dockyard in bits and pieces.

Admiral de Zoete's fleet hadn't been scattered by the storm, having found safe anchorage on the Eendragt for the night. At dawn the fleet had set out for Bergen-op-Zoom and appeared there wholly unexpected. No Spanish guns had been pointed seaward yet. The bombardment had been one-sided; as had the subsequent destruction of Spanish soldiers, siege guns, camps, and supplies. It was a blow well struck at Spanish strength and morale, hampering their siege.

The admiral had acknowledged the contribution of Adriaansz's thorough reconnaissance by electing *De Wilde Ruyter* to bear the good tidings to Flushing. It was a high honour for such a junior rank, but clever politics because Micheal and his crew were Flushing natives.

Church bells tolled in joy over the rooftops of the city. The progression of Adriaansz and his officers through the streets to the city hall was marked by the sound of cheering. Zeeland had taught Spinola a painful lesson and Zeeland was ecstatic.

Liselotte heard much of this later, as Peter's wound needed her attention first. The small house at the dockyard had an office downstairs and a bedroom upstairs. Peter was brought to the bed, their luggage carried up, and then Liselotte shooed everyone but Katja out. The girls tore up one of the Breestraat bed sheets to fashion makeshift surgical aprons and washed their hands with the now rapidly diminishing supply of Amsterdam soap.

Using laudanum to spare Peter the worst shock, Liselotte and Katja embarked on a thorough cleansing of his wound, using a dilator to expand their reach.

Katja offered to bandage Peter up after, and Liselotte descended the stairs in search of water to wash her hands with.

The office was milling with men.

"I asked them to wait for you," Andries told her.

A meeting.

"Thank you."

Jasper hovered close to Andries. Zundert and Jansz were there, as well as two men Liselotte didn't know. A broad-shouldered stout man was introduced as Jan-Leyns Visscher, a master carpenter from Domburg. The other man was in his early twenties, exceedingly tall, with long straw-coloured hair and an easy smile. He was introduced as First Steersman Hidde Tjippema.

"I'm also known as 'that darned Frisian'," he said cordially.

"If you'll excuse me," Liselotte showed them her bloodied hands. "I'll wash my hands and be with you in a moment."

"There's a pump around the corner of the house," Visscher advised.

Andries and Jasper followed Liselotte outside, inquired after Peter, and then told Liselotte of the news surrounding *De Wilde Ruyter's* triumphant return.

Liselotte mulled it over as she washed her hands.

Surrounded by well-wishers, Michael would be basking in his well-earned achievements. For a brief – thrilling – instant, Liselotte envisaged his face lighting up with joy upon seeing her, ignoring all and sundry to sweep her into his arms.

Don't be stupid. He's made it clear enough. As has Velthuys.

That left awkwardness and possibly the interest of gossipers.

You have Peter to think of now. And be glad you have. Those quacksalvers nearly killed him.

Trailed by Andries and Jasper, Liselotte made her way back to the office.

Tjippema and Visscher had already been told about the circumstances of the hasty departure from Middelburg.

It turned out there was a problem in meeting the requirements spelled out by Rolf. The ship was ready to launch, the ship's carpenters and riggers waiting for just that to happen to complete the masts. There weren't enough crew though.

"We're at least a dozen short for a launch," Tjippema said. "I'm pleased with the addition of midshipman and cabin boy, but we need strong grown men for this."

"I had been hoping that the coxswain and constable might have returned," Jansz explained to Liselotte. "Jan-Pier, Tjores, and some of the crew have been sent on a recruiting mission to the Republic's major ports, but there's no sign of them yet. That leaves us with seven sailors."

"Eight," Zundert said. "I'm sure the captain will offer me work."

"No doubt about that, Walter," Tjippema confirmed. "Welcome back."

The office was milling with men.

"My apologies," Visscher said. "But I know *Heer* Velthuys as a very reasonable gentleman to deal with. This sudden rush to launch instantly is based on the assumption that he will challenge Commodore Haelen's departure from Middelburg, isn't it? Maybe we worry about nothing."

"Tis better to be safe," Tjippema said. "It could be said that our midshipman, two boatswains, and cabin boy, not to forget *De Wilde Ruyter's* ship's surgeon…" He nodded at Liselotte. "Have kidnapped *Heer* Velthuys's houseguest. So we need to protect our crew."

"He can see sense clear enough," Zundert said. "But he's a proud man, our Marnix Velthuys is. I suggest that Korneel, myself, and any reliable man from the rest of the crew do a round of Flushing."

"We've tried that before," Jansz said. "They've got it into their heads that the ship is cursed. And you know what thick skulls us *Zeeuwen* have."

"He says confidently to a Frisian, famed for our obstinacy," Tjippema noted dryly. "It's true that there's reluctance, but folk will be celebrating and in good spirits after the *Duveljong's* news. I can think of no other option, I will draw some funds from the ship's chest for your tavern visits. Tell them we only need their services for half a day."

§ § § § § §

Time crawled to a halt after Zundert and Jansz departed with four sailors in tow. Liselotte went back upstairs to mind Peter. Andries and Jasper wandered around the office, looking at drawings, diagrams, and calculations that were scattered about.

After a while Andries went upstairs to inquire as to Peter's health. He was worried to see Peter in a feverish state. His cousin mumbled and muttered restlessly.

Liselotte told Andries that Peter had been in love with a chieftain's daughter in the East Indies.

"That's the Dewi he's been calling out for. I'm not sure, but I think he watched her die. The other stuff is to do with a dead captain sailing a ship and keeping that information from the crew."

Andries shivered. "Worrying."

Liselotte nodded. "Andries, can you do me a favour? We're nearly out of Amsterdam soap, do you think you could find some in Flushing? Do you still have that guilder I gave you for emergencies?"

"Yes, I do. I'll take Jasper and go straight away."

"Bethanks."

Pleased to be useful, Andries went downstairs to tell Jasper that they were going on a mission in Flushing.

The boys had no problem securing a chunk of Amsterdam soap from a grocer's shop, but Andries was in no immediate hurry to return to Jayakarta Dockyard. Liselotte had implied she still had some soap left. There was little for the boys to do at the dockyard and a whole city to explore.

The harbour adjacent to Peter's dockyard was but one of many. Broad canals divided the city proper behind its ramparts, and there were all sorts of ships berthed wherever they looked, accompanied by a myriad of activities. Andries led them aimlessly along the quays, drinking in the sights of Flushing, and pleased when his appearance drew envious or admiring glances. He wished he had one of his more imposing outfits, but at least he and Jasper looked like *Oranjevaarders* in their seafaring gear.

"*Mynheer*, what precisely are we doing?" Jasper asked.

"We're promenading, Jasper."

"What's that?"

"Ambling around with no specific purpose, to see and be seen."

"Begging your pardon, *Mynheer*, but that just sounds like a daft way to waste time."

Andries laughed. "You've got Katja's eye, Jasper, so have less need to promenade. But have you seen how many girls have looked our way?"

"Ah, so!"

"Well, well, if it bain't our mutineers!" A voice called out behind them, slurring slightly.

Andries and Jasper turned to see Cornelis and Pelle of *De Wilde Ruyter* swaying on their feet, their arms around each other's shoulders for support, their faces stupidly happy.

"We saw *De Wilde Ruyter* sail in," Jasper told them.

"All of Flushing did!" Pelle laughed.

"Heroes! Returned from war." Cornelis said. "Now showered with praise and...and..."

"Brandywine," Pelle completed.

"Brandywine!" Cornelis was struck by a thought. "Join us for a drink? The lads will be pleased to see you and it's your victory too. You helped us fight the *Spekjannuh*."

"*Ja*, do," Pelle encouraged. "We'll buy you a drink."

"We have to get back to the dockyard," Jasper told Andries.

"*Ja*, you're right Jasper, we should," Andries agreed. "But we won't stay long. Just for one drink. We've earned it!"

Cornelis and Pelle led the way.

Jasper followed, muttering, "I suppose one drink won't matter."

Andries ignored the cabin boy's reluctance, happy to toast to victory with fellow fighting men, like a proper *Oranjevaarder* should. And this time, he looked the part.

§ § § § § §

Liselotte's worries mounted.

Peter's condition was worsening, his feverish mind increasingly in a delirious state as he struggled with the memories from his past that haunted him so. Liselotte applied more laudanum and prepared a concoction to fight the fever.

Zundert and Jansz returned in the late afternoon. There was a hurriedly assembled meeting in the office, but they had no success to report.

"We must launch," Liselotte insisted. "I believe it will be good for Peter to be on his own ship, out on the water."

To her surprise none contested this, instead nodding their assent.

It was agreed that they'd try again that night, as Flushing's taverns had become the focal point of the victory celebrations, with ale and brandywine flowing in abundance. It might be possible that the false courage of inebriation would erode superstitions.

At first, Liselotte was so occupied with Peter that she wasn't concerned that Andries and Jasper were late in returning. Amsterdam soap shouldn't be hard to obtain, so she assumed the boys were taking in the sights of Flushing.

When they hadn't returned by suppertime, Liselotte started to worry and Katja started to fret. They wandered outside, hoping to see the boys return.

"Not like Jasper to skip a meal," Katja said. "I could go look for them. I'm not afraid."

Liselotte looked at her friend, struck by the memory of the conversation with Peter at the old barn near Zevenbergen, before Andries had departed on his errand. Except, this time Liselotte was playing Peter's role. Without realising it she echoed his words, "I don't doubt it, but that may be a problem in itself."

"*Wablief?*"

Liselotte looked down at herself. Everything seemed much the same, barring the splendour of her new gown. Yet, she felt distanced from the person who'd been perched on those beams at the barn, little expecting what lay ahead. It hadn't been long ago at all, but at the same time seemed a lifetime away.

"Listen, *lieffie*," Liselotte told Katja. "You're not going into a strange city on your own. The streets will be full of drunk men."

Katja shuddered, then nodded.

And we can't the both of us go. One of us has to stay with Peter.

Liselotte looked at the rooftops over the nearby rampart. The sky was a low mass of dark clouds. Twilight had come early. The merrymaking within the ramparts – drunken balderdash – could be heard all the way at the dockyard.

The memories of the old barn reminded her that Andries had nearly been killed when on a shopping errand in Zevenbergen. She tried to reach out to him with her mind. Sometimes she could get a sense of her brother, but there was nothing now.

§ § § § § §

Andries was intoxicated and happily content. The strong ale served in the Malle Babbe was delectable and the companionship of *De Wilde Ruyter's* crew intoxicating.

Although they formed a distinctly exclusive group in the taproom, the crew had made abundantly clear that they counted Andries and Jasper as their own, welcoming the boys with open arms. Elated by the sense of belonging and brotherly comradeship, Andries had downed tankard after tankard, and reached into his purse to buy a round or two – maybe three. He couldn't recall ever being happier.

This is the seafarer's life!

The owner of the Malle Babbe, pleased that the presence of Flushing's heroes had drawn so many to his establishment this evening, announced a 'round of the hayloft' for the *Oranjevaarders*. "One on the house! The girls will reward your *Zeeuwse* courage!"

The proposal was met by loud approval from the main beneficiaries, and cheers from the many onlookers in praise of the tavern keeper's patriotic generosity. "*Oranje boven!*"

Only Jasper looked uncomfortable.

"*Mynheer,*" he said to Andries. "Ish late, sjouldn't we get back? The girlsh will worry."

"Thatsh right!" Cornelis jested. "With all reshpect, Jashper-lad, but thish ish mensh work."

He cupped his crotch and jerked his hips to and fro.

There was no way Andries was going to leave now. He told Jasper, "You go on ahead. Let 'em know we're fine. Tell Lishelotte I'll be back latersh."

Jasper departed – unsteadily – and Andries followed Adriaansz and his crew through a maze of passages and stairways. They emerged in a broad loft that smelled of fresh hay, stale ale, and sweat. Low partitions running along the length of the sides of the loft created semi-private cubicles, the booths filled with beds of hay covered by blankets.

Grouped in the middle were a flock of scantily dressed young women, all cheering the arrival of Flushing's heroes.

§ § § § § §

"The mutton stew is getting cold, *Mejuffrouw*." Tjippema joined the girls in the yard. "But I suspect you have something else on your mind. Are you worried about Midshipman Haelen?"

"And Jasper," Liselotte acknowledged. "I'm going to go look for them."

"Not on your own, you aren't," Tjippema replied calmly.

"It isn't safe, Miss," Katja said. "You said so yourself."

Liselotte bristled and patted Eyang. "I've got my keris."

"Peace, *Mejuffrouw*," Tjippema said. "I'll explain myself. I never thought the skipper would part with that keris. He clearly holds you in high esteem, as do Walter and Korneel, so I'll mind your thoughts. If you are concerned about your twin, then I am concerned too. Added to which, the midshipman and cabin boy are crew. My responsibility."

Liselotte was pleased with his words. It was nice to be treated in this measured fashion after being viewed like an ignorant child in Middelburg. It was also a relief that she didn't have to tackle this latest problem on her own. She hadn't been looking forward to venturing into Flushing by herself. "Bethanks, *Mynheer* Tjippema."

"Let's think about this. Do Master Andries and Jasper know anybody in Flushing?"

"Not that I know of..."

"Miss! Liselotte!" Katja rattled. "*De Wilde Ruyter's* crew."

Liselotte slapped her forehead. "Of course!"

"The *Duvelsjong*?" Tjippema asked.

Liselotte explained, "We sailed with Adriaansz and his crew. Fought the Spaniards side by side."

Tjippema nodded. "They're likely holed up in the Malle Babbe then."

"If Jasper is someplace called the Malle Babbe," Katja declared firmly. "Then I'm going to kill him."

"Speaking of the Devil…" Liselotte's voiced trailed off as she watched Jasper stagger into the dockyard, unsteady on his feet.

Is he wounded?

The two girls and First Steersman ran toward Jasper. Seeing them, the boy's face lit up with a silly grin. Then he lost his balance and collapsed onto the ground.

Liselotte and Katja rushed to his side and turned him over gently, Liselotte automatically scanning for any tell-tale blood that might indicate a wound.

Jasper chuckled happily and reached into his doublet to withdraw a rectangular package that he offered to Liselotte. "Got your Amsjersjham shoap, sho we did."

His breath stank of ale.

"*Sotte Snotoor*![50]" Katja cried angrily.

"You've been drinking," Liselotte stated. "Where is Andries?"

"Andriesh ish wif Adrianshzn," Jasper explained. "In the Malle Babbe."

Thunder crossed Katja's face.

"Very well," Liselotte scrambled up. "Katja, I need you to look after Peter for me. Take Jasper upstairs, it looks like you have a second patient to take care of as well."

Katja helped Jasper up and ushered him toward the pump by the corner of the house.

Jasper said, "I can ekshplain—"

Katja didn't give him the chance, unleashing her opinion in a torrent of scorn. The two reached the pump where the girl emptied a pail of cold water over Jasper's head. When he protested, she upended another full pail.

"I suppose disciplinary measures won't be necessary," Tjippema remarked. "I somehow think your friend is a worse *Kenau*[51] than the cat o' nine tails."

---

[50] Used here as 'daft infant'. 17th century Dutch.

"She's a regular little *Kenau*, and I'm very proud of her," Liselotte answered.

"I'm freeshing!" Jasper cried plaintively as Katja scolded him into the small house.

Liselotte laid her hand flat over Eyang's sheath. *"Mynheer* Tjippema do you know how Peter came by Eyang? The keris?"

"It was gifted to him by a young woman called Dewi," Tjippema said. "A native of Wandan. I'll go fetch Zundert and Jansz. We'll need their help in this."

Liselotte drew Eyang, once again captivated by the swirling metals on the irregular blade.

Dewi's gift to Peter.

She looked at the figurehead of the ship, the oriental mermaid.

Peter wanted to call his ship *De Dewi.*

It's all connected. Christine is really Dewi. Peter's ship. The ship is a homage, the two have become one in his mind. The ship is a labour of love in more than one way.

This confirmed what her intuition had been telling her. Peter needed to be united with this love of his.

She recalled their conversation in *De Wilde Ruyter's* cabin, how he said he had been listening to the waves chat to the hull. She herself had marvelled when the *statenjacht* had appeared to become a living being under full sail.

She needed Peter's ship to take on that sense of soul. Peter's creation was lifeless on the dry. The ship had to be launched. If that didn't get Peter back, nothing would. His mind was beyond her ability to heal. Liselotte was very taken by her cousin, but there were dark depths to him that she couldn't fathom.

Determined, she slid Eyang's blade back into the sheath.

Tjippema returned with Zundert and Jansz and explained the situation to them, concluding with orders. "Send the men who were going with you on that second recruitment drive out on their own. I'll need Zundert to accompany *Mejuffrouw* Haelen and myself. You, Jansz, need to take charge here. The both of you, not a word about the Malle Babbe to the others."

---

[51] Kenau Simonsdochter's legacy. 'Kenau' is used in Dutch to refer to a particularly obstinate, self-willed, and dominant woman. I'm not sure when this started, but using it seemed apt.

The boatswains acknowledged the orders. Liselotte departed Jayakarta Dockyard in the company of Tjippema and Zundert, in search of Andries at the Malle Babbe.

§ § § § § §

The two groups in the loft spent some time exchanging jests and sharing laughter. The *Oranjevaarders* made loud boasts about their virility, the women issued flirtatious invitations and promises of heavenly delights. After about ten minutes of this, two of the wenches stepped out of the group of young women, seized Adriaansz, and dragged him into one of the cubicles. He pretended to struggle and hollered for help, but was answered by the cheers and jeers of his crew.

Other girls clearly had favourites among the crew and singled these out. The remaining crewmembers made their own selections.

Andries was left on his own, facing two dark-haired wenches. The older one tried to entice him with lewd invitations. Her brazenness was an uncomfortable reminder of Truusje at the Sail & Anchor, so Andries stretched out a hand to the younger one, who was looking at him with shy apprehension.

"Aww, Sailor," the older one said. "Little Lientje is new here and not much used to real men like you. She barely knows what she's supposed to do."

Andries recalled Truusje's bold audacity and his own humiliating performance. The memory made Lientje all the more desirable.

"Nay, I want this one," he insisted, seconded by his growing arousal.

"Well, you're not having her," the older one said. Her tone was final, but she smiled and then laughed as she pulled Andries into an empty cubicle.

She fell on the blankets, pulling him down with her.

"You can play the hard man with me," she promised him. "Oh so hard."

She had Andries's face pressed firmly between her breasts, making it difficult for him to speak - or disagree. He nodded his agreement.

§ § § § § §

The Malle Babbe was teeming with merrymakers, most of them thoroughly inebriated, all of them rough types. Liselotte looked out of place in her green gown and received curious looks. Any comments her presence might have elicited – or more forward approaches – were discouraged by the two sailors who flanked her, looking large, alert, and protective.

Spotting Cornelis at the stacked barrels in a corner ordering a tankard of something, Liselotte made her way to him. He recognised her with astonishment.

"You shjouldn't be here," he slurred.

"Where is Andries? My brother, where is he?"

"Drunk ash a shailor," Cornelis said proudly. "With resht of crew."

"And you let him?" Liselotte fumed.

Cornelis looked at her in puzzlement. "Let him?"

"He doesn't have any money for drink. How much did you give him?"

Cornelis shook his head, immediately regretting the movement. "Andriesh had plenty coinsh in hish pursh. He bought roundsh for ush all."

"I see." Steel anger filled Liselotte. "Where is he?"

"Upshtairsh, in the loft." Cornelis pointed at an open door through which Liselotte could see a set of stairs.

"*Mejuffrouw*," Tjippema said. "That is no place for a young lady. One of us will go."

Liselotte ignored him and marched toward the door, followed by Tjippema and Zundert.

He used my inheritance. To get drunk in a tavern. I'm going to kill him.

The tavern had a confusing layout, but she found a second set of stairs and pounded up.

"*Mejuffrouw*," Zundert called out. "You really don't want to see…"

Liselotte stormed into the loft.

§ § § § § §

The loft was alive with the sounds of copulation. The dark-haired girl was torturing Andries. After she had expertly relieved him of his breeches, she had placed herself on his hips, slipping her sleeveless shift over her shoulders to bare the glory of her breasts. The flimsy shift fell over their waists, concealing the sight of that which Andries was acutely aware of nonetheless.

She had pressed his erection against his belly and was slowly rubbing it with hot soft wetness.

Andries moaned at the sensation of it. "I want in," he said hoarsely.

366

She laughed. "I'm sure you do. But you've got to ask nicely."

Someone called his name.

Thrusting against the girl's motion, Andries begged, "Please."

§ § § § § §

Liselotte's first impression was that she had walked upon a battlefield. Her blood chilled when she saw horizontal bodies everywhere. Then she registered this was a different type of carnage, accompanied by the amorous chorus she'd heard at the Silly Sally.

She stalked along a line of stalls, peering into the booths.

Pelle was in one of them, with a willowy blonde wrapped around him. He looked at her with glazed eyes, raised a hand, and uttered a cheerful, "It's the doc, hello Doc."

Whereas the activities at the Silly Sally – heard but unseen – had provoked a response from Liselotte, she found the Malle Babbe's loft unappealing. Her eyes wandered over bare flesh and genitals with clinical disinterest.

She found Andries, on his back, a bare breasted dark-haired girl their age astride him.

"Andries!" Liselotte fumed.

His head was back, eyes closed, mouth open and he groaned. "Please. Please."

"ANDRIES!"

§ § § § § §

Registering the owner of the voice that was calling out his name, Andries opened his eyes with utter disbelief.

It can't be.

It was.

"You *KLOOTZAK*!" Liselotte spat at him.

35. *Klootzak*

FLUSHING ~ COUNTY OF ZEELAND ~ 1622

"*Godverdomme*[52], Liselotte!" Andries cursed.

The girl on his lap scrambled up, looked at Liselotte apprehensively, and swiftly scurried away, deeper into the loft. Andries reddened and grabbed his shirt to cover his lap.

"Get dressed."

"No, you can't make me." He objected defiantly.

"BOATSWAIN," Liselotte hollered.

"*Mejuffrouw*?" Zundert stepped to her side.

"Take the midshipman back to the Jayakarta Dockyard, if you please."

"Aye-aye," Zundert acknowledged. He looked at Andries without sympathy. "You heard, *Mynheer*. Either you get your breeches on, or I'll roll you into a blanket."

"You have no right," Andries told Liselotte. "I can do what I want in my own time."

"If you want to turn into Father, fine." Liselotte hissed. "But not with my money. I trusted you."

Andries looked down, ashamed but not yet defeated. "I'm not getting dressed."

"Very well," Zundert said. Without further ado, he seized hold of Andries and proceeded to roll the boy into a blanket, after which he simply lifted the bundle over his shoulder.

"Let me go!" Andries shouted. "Zundert! I order you to let me go! Liselotte has no right!"

Tjippema stepped forward. "You want to calm down this instant, Midshipman. You are under orders and you'll find that a ship's surgeon outranks you."

---

[52] God Damn it.

"Godverdomme, Liselotte!"

"Look at the bright side, *Mynheer* Andries," Zundert declared cheerfully. "You and I can have a long chat all the way back to the dockyard, about clever ways for *snotneuzen*[53] to interact with second officers, versus insanely stupid ways."

He walked toward the door. Andries – constricted by the blanket – hung over the boatswain's shoulder in defeat, helpless fury on his face.

Tjippema collected the boy's clothes and followed, glancing at Liselotte, who nodded and made to go with him.

She stopped in her tracks when she heard a familiar voice boom, "*Sakkerloot*! That was quite a show, *Mejuffrouw*."

Liselotte turned to look at Michael. He was sitting up in a stall opposite to the one just vacated by Andries, torso bared and flanked by two naked girls.

One of them sat up straight, looking at Liselotte curiously. Liselotte looked at her pert breasts, glistening with traces of semen, and for a moment hated the wench with all her heart.

Focusing on Michael again, she said, "You're a *klootzak* too."

With that, she followed Tjippema out of the loft.

"*Mejuffrouw*! Liselotte! Wait!"

Michael followed Liselotte onto the landing. She kept her back to him, making for the stairs that Tjippema was already descending.

"*Sakkerloot*! Surgeon, I command you to stop and bloody well talk to me. That's your skipper's order."

Liselotte stopped, duty bound, and turned around, only to immediately cover her eyes. "Michael! You're naked."

"Am I? Oh, *ja*," he agreed. "But honestly, folk don't come to the Malle Babbe for the fashion. You shouldn't be here."

Liselotte spread her fingers wider to peek. He had made no effort to cover himself. This time she couldn't maintain a physician's professional disinterest. As if aware of her covert gaze, the thing twitched.

"Michael, it's moving. Cover yourself up, make it go away."

"Don't go anywhere," he said, turned, and walked back into the loft.

Liselotte stared at his buttocks.

"*Mejuffrouw*," Tjippema said. "I'm no expert, but I don't reckon this is appropriate."

"I've been ordered to stay and talk by my skipper," Liselotte said lamely.

---

[53] Literally 'snotty nose'. Used to indicate someone still wet behind the ears.

"Even so."

"I'm sure I'll survive the shock, *Mynheer* Tjippema."

Michael reappeared with a blanket draped around his waist. "Listen Liselotte, I understand you were concerned about your brother, but you can't just march in here like that. You could have waited for him to come back tomorrow and scolded him then. Not in front of his mates."

"That was my money he was spending tonight. Without asking."

"Oh."

"*Ja*, 'oh'. And he's been commanded by *Mynheer* Romeyn of the VOC to be at the dockyard and help Peter out. Not go gallivanting about Flushing."

"Regardless, I'm not your brother's keeper. He chose to join us, and I welcomed him and the Fleming because we fought side by side. That's no reason to call me a *klootzak*, is it now?"

Liselotte placed her hands on her waist and glared at him. "Why ever not when you behave like one?"

"Behave?" He looked puzzled. "Oh, do you mean Tries and Eva?"

"Did it mean absolutely nothing to you? Back on *De Wilde Ruyter*?"

"Liselotte, I …you and I, we aren't—"

"Clearly not when I find you in the arms of two whores so soon after. Was I just an easy catch? A tasty side dish?"

Michael shook his head, hurt. "That's not fair on Tries and Eva. They're very nice girls. From the slums. I grew up with them."

Liselotte took a deep breath, thinking of Fleur and the girls in the Silly Sally. "Nay, that was wrong of me. I apologize for that. But you, you're still a *klootzak*."

"Maybe I am, but will you at least listen to me? For one, we're only here for a few days. Then it's back to Bergen-op-Zoom for us. To fight a war, Liselotte, in which it's not difficult to get shot to bits. We're just trying to make the best of it while we can. So was your brother. Do you think becoming an *Oostvaarder* isn't fraught with danger?" He shrugged. "Men have needs."

"And we don't? Do you think you're the only ones? I would have…never mind."

He looked genuinely shocked. "*Mejuffrouw*…"

"Don't you '*Mejuffrouw*' me right now, Michael. Don't you dare."

"Sorry, Liselotte." He looked at her earnestly. "A second explanation might be that I was desperately trying to forget someone whom I just can't stop thinking about."

"*Ja,* sure." Liselotte wanted to believe him but didn't allow herself to. He had the same easy charm Velthuys had, and she had seen there just how many other faces that masked. There was nothing to be salvaged here. She'd landed herself into another fine mess. She half turned to go.

"Liselotte, don't go like this," he pleaded. "I understand that you're upset. I really, genuinely, didn't intend to cause you grief. Can I at least make it up to you? Tell me what you want, I'll do anything."

What if you are what I want?

Liselotte became suddenly aware of the weight of Eyang resting on her flank. There was something else she needed and wanted far more than this scoundrel.

She faced Michael again. "Anything?"

He became cautious but couldn't back down. "If it's within my power," he promised. "Anything."

36. A Perfect Moment

FLUSHING ~ COUNTY OF ZEELAND ~ 1622

Peter's condition worsened during the night. His wound was healing well under the circumstances, but his mind was engaged in a struggle with his dark past. He mumbled of wading through blood. He agonised over something he named the Screaming Cliffs. He spoke feverishly of folk so malnourished they stumbled around like the living dead, the life in their eyes already extinguished. During a more peaceful moment he smiled with longing as he recalled swimming with a mermaid in an azure sea. More native words spilled from his lips, making no sense at all to Liselotte. *"Guna-guna!"*

Liselotte went down to the office to find Jansz, still awake. "What does *'guna-guna'* mean, do you know?

He turned pale. "Black magic, *Mejuffrouw*. From the East Indies. They also call it the Silent Force. Is the skipper—"

"I don't know, Boatswain. I just don't know."

"For what it's worth, *Mejuffrouw*. I think you're right about getting the skipper afloat on his ship. I've sailed with him for six years. He's a different man under sail."

"Thank you." Liselotte went back upstairs.

She took Eyang, sheath and all, and tried folding Peter's hand around the hilt.

Might the connection with Dewi...

He pushed it away, back at Liselotte. Sounding lucid for a moment, without coming to, he said solemnly, "She has chosen you."

Chosen me for what? To bring Peter back to us?

Dawn found her cousin's small crew assembled outside the house, sipping warm goat's milk and yawning at the morning. Visscher had assembled his group of Domburg carpenters nearby.

Liselotte and Katja joined the crew; both dressed in the complementary green outfits. Andries avoided Liselotte's eyes, looking away with guilt and anger on his face.

"Mejuffrouw," Tjippema said. "Are you sure—"

"Ja, *Mynheer* Tjippema. I'm sure."

"Look!" Jasper cried, pointing at the entrance of the yard.

Michael had kept his promise and had come to Jayakarta Dockyard, looking suitably contrite and repentant. His fifteen able-bodied crew followed.

Jan nodded respectfully at Liselotte. Pelle tried to smile but turned red. Cornelis cheerfully yelled, "Good morning, all!"

Some of the others who followed them cast apprehensive glances at the dark shape of Peter's brainchild. Most were still befuddled and sleepy.

De Wilde Ruyter's crew mingled with Peter's crew, and then all of them, even Andries, looked at Liselotte.

"Bethanks to all of you for being here today." She smiled. "Let's get Peter's ship launched."

The quays started filling up as word spread. When those at Jayakarta Dockyard were ready, it seemed that half the city had streamed out of homes and businesses to gather around the harbour.

The murmur of conversation formed a continuous hum that rose in volume as the crew formed a large circle on the weather deck.

Liselotte walked to the centre of the circle, with Katja and Jasper flanking her. Katja carried a silver standing cup, Jasper a bottle of the finest Schiedam gin. They had been instructed by Boatswain Zundert what to do.

The crowd around the harbour hushed when Jasper poured gin up to the brim of the silver cup. Katja solemnly presented the cup to Liselotte, who touched Eyang's hilt for luck.

She took a small sip from the cup, after which she poured the remaining gin over the deck, loudly calling out, "I christen this ship *The Christine*. And wish fair winds for all who sail on her."

The supporting beams propping up the hull were hammered away by the carpenters, who then scurried to a safer distance. A great many thick hemp cables that ran from ship to stakes in the ground turned taut as they took the weight of *The Christine*. The crowd buzzed.

The two boatswains and Michael hollered orders. The crew hauled at ropes all around the ship, their muscled arms straining. Liselotte and Katja grabbed the end of one rope to offer what help they could. Tjippema had added his strength to another rope, as did the boatswains and Michael.

The Christine jolted into movement.

Cornelis set in a bawdy capstan ditty concerning the misadventures of a dozen sailors on shore leave and a vicar's daughter. The men joined in enthusiastically.

The Christine began to rumble along the slipway. Seagulls swirled overhead, issuing plaintive screams.

"On my signal, lads!" Korneel thundered. "NOW! Loose! Loose!"

Ropes were released, nothing now withholding *The Christine*. The ship lurched forward, gathered speed, and then hit the water in a violent explosion of spray. The bow plunged deep, but then rose with equal force, after which the ship glided gracefully across the water, before she slowed to a halt on an even keel.

"She floats," one of Michael's crew uttered in amazement, surprise that was echoed by the crowd around the harbour.

"She sure does," Michael shouted. "Three cheers for *The Christine*!"

The crew roared a first "Huzzah!"

Seeing and hearing Flushing's heroes lauding the strange ship encouraged the first of the spectators to join in with the second "Huzzah!"

Nearly all present combined their voices for a thunderous third "HUZZAH!" that was heard all over Flushing.

Katja tugged at Liselotte's sleeve and pointed at Jayakarta Dockyard. Liselotte looked to see a familiar coach come to a halt. Marnix Velthuys emerged from it, staring at *The Christine*. Rolf Romeyn also stepped out of the coach.

"Go check on Peter please, Katja," Liselotte said.

Katja made her way to the stern, to enter the skipper's cabin where they had brought Peter before the launch.

Velthuys was pacing along the bottom of the slipway as the carpenters prepared a small jolly boat.

Tjippema approached Liselotte. "We're ready, just awaiting your orders, *Mejuffrouw* Haelen."

Staring at the jolly boat as it launched, both Velthuys and Rolf on board, Liselotte said, "Belay that a little longer, *Mynheer* Tjippema."

She motioned Andries to her. He came, looking sullen like a beat dog.

"Velthuys is on his way," Liselotte told him. "Do you want to give the order?"

"Why me? If you're trying to make up for what you did—"

"I'd rather eat hog dung. But you're going to sail with these men. If I were you, I'd give them something other than the sight of you rolled into a blanket as a memory. Also, whatever else, you are an *Oranjevaarder* and grandson of a Sea Beggar."

Andries nodded. "Just don't expect me to say 'bethanks'."

"I'm not. Just do it…" Liselotte checked the progress of the jolly boat. "Right about now."

Andries straightened, looked around, and then bellowed, "Hoist the colours!"

"Aye-aye, Midshipman! Hoist the colours!"

Liselotte made for the quarterdeck, brimming with accomplishment as she watched orange pennants and tricolours unfurl atop the masts. At her request, a multi-banded prince's flag rose up the flagpole at the stern. It was the flag Adrian Haelen had fought under.

All the flags and pennants were streaming in the wind by the time Velthuys and Rolf ascended the weather deck to cheers of *"Oranje boven!"*

Velthuys stood on *The Christine's* weather deck, looking up at Liselotte who was looking down at him defiantly. Glancing around at the crew who formed an expectant audience, Velthuys made to go aft.

"As you desired, *Heer* Velthuys," Liselotte spoke loud enough for all those topside to hear. "*The Christine* has been launched, her skipper is alive and well on board, her crew eager to be Java bound."

Velthuys stopped. For an instant, Liselotte could see admiration on his face, followed by a scowl, and then a wide smile as he turned to take in the crew. "It was well done lads! A splendid effort! You will be rewarded with the riches of the East."

The men cheered. Velthuys turned with a swirl of the ostrich feathers on his hat and stalked to the stairs up the quarterdeck. The crew drifted away to various tasks that needed to be done to anchor *The Christine* closer to the Jayakarta Dockyard.

Liselotte half-turned to face Velthuys. Tjippema and Andries joined her.

"You play a wild game," Velthuys said to Liselotte in a low voice. "A risky one."

"The stakes were high," Liselotte countered. "Those physicians were killing Peter."

"This is true, Monseigneur," Andries added. "My father would have been furious at the treatment. Peter nearly died."

"Nonetheless," Velthuys declared. "There are other ways of making your objections known. The poor Ernstras are still in shock."

"We tried. They wouldn't listen. Peter is alive." Liselotte said. "That's what matters, *Heer* Velthuys, is it not? Peter is alive."

Velthuys glanced at the forecastle, from which Michael was observing the quarterdeck. "Did he really make you a ship's surgeon?"

"*Mejuffrouw* Liselotte is on *De Wilde Ruyter's* muster roll as ship's surgeon, *Heer Koopman*," Tjippema said. "I read the attestation signed by Skipper Adriaansz on behalf of Admiral de Zoete."

Velthuys nodded. "Thank you, First Steersman." He looked at Liselotte. "One would hope for the *ship's surgeon* that her patient fares well."

Liselotte was uncertain if there was an underlying threat in his acceptance that Peter was her patient. She wasn't given time to contemplate it, as the skipper's cabin door opened.

Leaning on Katja, pale and gaunt, Peter stepped out on the quarterdeck, exclaiming, "*Wah! Gila*[54]!"

Liselotte's heart rejoiced.

Her cousin walked forward slowly, taking in the sight and sensation of *The Christine* afloat with wonder. Turning to his cousins, First Steersman, and friend, he said. "I seem to have missed a bit."

---

[54] Interjections of positive surprise, Indonesian.

"Wah! Gila!"

"Skipper!" Zundert couldn't hold back any longer and stepped forward, flanked by a beaming Jansz.

"Walter!" Both Peter and Velthuys cried out.

Activities on the weather deck and forecastle ceased as men drifted aft to look at Peter.

"Tis good to see you both, Skipper, *Heer* Velthuys," Zundert said. "I heard you were recruiting, don't know if you can use an old salt like me?"

"I've got a boatswain already," Peter said regretfully.

"And a good one, Skipper," Zundert confirmed. "That's all right, I'll settle for—"

"We need a Second Steersman," Tjippema suggested.

"Aye, indeed." Peter confirmed. "And none better, Walter. Will you accept a position as Second Steersman?"

Zundert's eyes grew wide. "Bethanks, Skipper."

Jansz faced the men on the weather deck. "A cheer for Commodore Haelen and Second Steersman Zundert, lads! Hip hip..."

All those on deck roared, throwing their hats in the air.

Peter looked at them in wonder. "Did Jan-Pier and Tjores return? So many of them now."

"*De Wilde Ruyter's* crew helped launch," Liselotte explained.

"Flushing lads! How did you manage to convince them?"

Liselotte hesitated, glancing at Andries. It was probably best to leave the Malle Babbe's hayloft unmentioned altogether. She could see he agreed on this, at least.

"Andries thoughtfully provided leverage," Liselotte said.

Peter smiled at Andries. "Then you succeeded where the rest of us failed. Well done, Midshipman."

Andries managed an embarrassed smile in response.

Michael's voice boomed from the weather deck. "Permission to ascend the quarterdeck, Commodore?"

"Please do, Skipper Adriaansz," Peter replied.

Liselotte was relieved to see that the interactions so far hadn't weakened her cousin. Instead, he seemed to be growing stronger by the minute, taking deep breaths of the briny air, eyes shining as they kept on wandering along the length of *The Christine*.

Michael climbed the steps and came closer.

"Commodore, *Heer* Velthuys," he greeted them respectfully. "*Mynheer* Tjippema, *Mynheer* Zundert, Surgeon Haelen, Midshipman."

Liselotte smiled at him. He'd kept his promise and helped achieve what had seemed impossible.

"Adriaansz!" Peter said. "This is the second time that I find myself deep in your debt, *Mynheer*. Surely that deserves a reward, have you one in mind?"

Velthuys took a purse from his belt, shaking it to make the coins inside chink. "This should be ample, Peter."

Michael cast a glance at Liselotte, and then shook his head. He walked to the helm and looked at Peter. "May I, Commodore?"

"Please do." Peter nodded at the helmsman who stepped aside.

Michael took hold of the helm, closed his eyes, and breathed in deeply. When he opened his eyes again, he smiled approvingly. "She's a good ship, Commodore."

"Aye, indeed."

Michael surrendered the helm back to the helmsman. "There is a reward I should like to claim, Commodore."

"Well, name it man!"

"I would like your permission to promenade *Mejuffrouw* Liselotte, Commodore."

Liselotte looked at him in astonishment. He'd redeemed himself, that much was true, but it wasn't as if she was likely to forget the Malle Babbe's loft any time soon.

Velthuys's eyes narrowed. He caught Liselotte's eye and shook his head subtly.

Peter looked at Michael curiously. "You save the day twice and all you want as reward is to take Liselotte for a walk?"

Michael looked at Liselotte. "I should like that very much. With a chaperone in attendance, of course." He nodded at the purse Velthuys was still holding out. "And the money would be nice for my lads."

Peter looked between Michael and Liselotte. "This is not for me to decide. Liselotte, what say you?"

Liselotte looked at Michael.

Still a *klootzak*, but...

"I would like that, Peter."

"Very well. Katja my dear, would you care to accompany your mistress?"

"*Ja*, Seigneur!"

"Good, now, the rest of you, there's work to be done!"

"Back before dark, Adriaansz," Velthuys growled at Michael as he surrendered the purse. He turned to Liselotte, a smile on his face but his eyes cold. "So, you take after your mother?"

"*Ja*, I do," Liselotte replied without shame. She added proudly, "I am Saskia van der Krooswyck's daughter."

Michael fished a coin out of the purse, before tossing the bag to Jan on the weather deck. "Divide it equally between yourselves."

He then looked over the railing to inform the men crewing the jolly boat that they were coming down.

Once ashore, Michael led Liselotte and Katja through the streets of Flushing, stopping by a bakery. He produced the coin and pointed at various treats that were duly packed in paper. The baker refused Michael's money and doubled the original order, packing it neatly in a wicker basket and adding a small flask of ale. "*Oranje boven*, Michael," he said.

They went on their way.

"I like this hero business," Michael told Liselotte. "Could get used to it."

"*Ja*, I noticed you like it."

He shrugged and handed the basket to Katja. "Here, brave Brabander, you're in charge of the provisions. And you'll have to taste it all to make sure it bain't poisoned."

Katja was swift to take the basket but looked at him suspiciously. "Are you trying to bribe me?"

"*Ja*, I am. Is it not enough? We can go back for some more."

"Nay," Katja shook her head, eagerly perusing the contents of the basket. "This'll do just fine."

They passed over a large public square dominated by the Grote Kerk, Flushing's main church. Its tower was crowned by a sequence of domes.

Michael pointed at it. "The Jacobstoren. Surrounded by scaffolding six years ago. I got into a world of trouble when Geleyn dared me to climb it all the way to the top. By the time I got down, half the city had come to watch."

Liselotte laughed, before turning to more serious matters. "So, you're headed for Bergen-op-Zoom again?"

"Ja. I'll lose *De Wilde Ruyter*, but that was just temporary, we knew that." He sighed. "They've plenty of cannons in the city, but not enough gunners. We'll be assigned to the garrison, along with many other sailors from the fleet."

"The garrison! Oh, but if the city falls…"

"It won't, I have a cunning plan to prevent that from happening."

"How so?"

"We win, Liselotte." He said happily. "It was the *Zeeuwen* who relieved the siege of Leyden, it'll be the *Zeeuwen* who'll take Spinola down a notch at Bergen-op-Zoom."

Fired at by Spanish siege guns.

"Well, you're braver than I am."

"I doubt that. But I'd fight the damned Dons anywhere, be it on land or sea. They could even stick me on a horse if they wanted to, and I'd do my best not to fall off."

"Ha, Michael the '*Ruyter*'[55]."

"I like the sound of that, actually. But my talents would be wasted on horseback."

They reached a gate surrounded by angular earthworks. Through it, Liselotte could see a road flanked by flatlands to the right, and low dunes on the seaside to the left.

"Michael, where are you taking us? Outside the city?"

"Away from curious eyes," he answered, and indicated Katja. "Don't worry, we're chaperoned. I'm not about to cross swords with a Brabander."

Liselotte glanced at Katja, who was fully occupied sampling the treats in the basket.

"A chaperone who was easily bribed," she said. "But it's not as if a Hollander requires help to fend off a *Zeeuw*."

Once out of the shelter of the city, the wind had free play with them. It was blustery out in the dunes, the low grass dancing wildly to the tune of passing gusts.

"This isn't really the weather for a walk," Liselotte noted.

Michael looked surprised. "Isn't it? It's a beautiful *Zeeuwse* breeze, a fine day for sailing."

He lifted his arms so that his sleeves billowed in the wind. "Come!" He shouted and started running down the path, whooping loudly. "Look at me! I'm a sailboat!"

Liselotte exchanged a glance with Katja, who tapped a finger against her temple and mouthed, *hit by a windmill*.

Liselotte laughed but followed Michael. She ran through the sand, holding out her arms to let the wind tug at her wide green virago sleeves.

Michael ran back, sprinted around her in a wide circle, and then fell in by her side, a broad grin on his face.

Liselotte couldn't help but laugh for the sheer careless freedom of it.

---

[55] Playing on the '*Ruyter*' also being a word for horse rider.

They ran out of the dunes onto a broad beach. Steel waves pounded the sand and dark clouds drifted by. The wind plucked and tugged at clothes.

Liselotte came to a halt in front of the thunderous surf, to catch her breath. Without warning, Michael lifted her up and dashed into the sea up to his knees, carrying her in his arms.

"Let go of me!" Liselotte shouted.

"Uh? Alright then." He loosened his grip.

"Nay!" She clutched on to him. "Don't you dare drop me in the water."

"Make up your mind!" He laughed, and spun around wildly, before carrying her back to the beach.

Katja had taken seat in the hollow of a dune, out of the wind, and applauded them.

"Well," Michael said with satisfaction as he set Liselotte down. "We've danced by the sea, Liselotte. A fine *Zeeuwse* custom."

"You scoundrel," Liselotte replied, although she was far from upset.

They joined Katja and dropped onto the sand. Having become quite the expert with regard to the content of the basket, Katja solemnly handed out treats on which they nibbled.

The wind picked up and changed direction ever so slightly, negating some of the shelter offered by the hollow. As they huddled close together to stay warm – Liselotte in the middle – she reflected that it was rather nice weather for a walk.

"I'm so full," Katja complained, and then curled up on the sand, placing her arms on Liselotte's lap and resting her head on them.

"So, here we are," Michael said. "It's nice to do something fun together. Without people shooting at us."

"*Ja*," Liselotte agreed. "You were right, back on *De Wilde Ruyter*, you know."

She told him about Velthuys's warning, and how she had used Michael's letter to save Peter.

"*Sakkerloot*," he said. "Well played."

Liselotte looked down at Katja, stroking the girl's head. Her friend's eyes were closed and she was breathing regularly, as if sleeping. Even asleep though, Liselotte reflected in a bawdy instant, Katja was ensuring propriety guarding Liselotte's lap as she was.

She leaned against Michael, enjoying the solid comfort of his presence and the rare sense of feeling secure. "Anyhow, it wouldn't have worked. As a Hollander I could never be seen at the side of a mere *Zeeuw,* even if he is Michael de *'Ruyter'* himself."

"Likewise," he agreed with a chuckle. "Flushing would have exiled me if I were to be with a *Hollandse Kenau.*" He paused, "there's something I'll regret for the rest of my life though."

"What's that?" Liselotte asked. She turned her face to his, swimming in his eyes, her blood rushing with the roar of the surf.

"Unless..." he brought his face closer to hers. "A memory for us both..."

"You impudent *Zeeuw,*" she answered before responding and pressing her lips against his.

For a blessed moment, the rest of the world ceased to exist. It was both endless and ended far too soon.

"That was so *mooi!*[56]" Katja's eyes sparkled as they walked back to the dockyard. "So mighty *mooi,* Liselotte."

"What was?" Liselotte asked, thinking back of the grim waves pounding the beach, the mighty rumble forming a continuous, liquid heartbeat of the sea.

"You and him."

"Katja! I thought you were asleep. You peeked!"

"Of course I did! So, so mighty *mooi.*" Katja sighed. "Like the bedtime stories *Oma* used to tell."

"*Ja,* like a story," Liselotte had to agree. Not just the first, but also the second, and especially the third and fourth much longer kisses had all contributed to what had been a perfect moment.

Just like in the books.

---

[56] Beautiful

Peter's Story
The Flying Hollander

A WEEK LATER

FLUSHING ROADSTEAD ~ COUNTY OF ZEELAND ~ 1622

The tide had started to recede. The wind was favourable. *The Christine* sailed out of Flushing at a pristine speed, the crew preparing to hoist more sails once they were clear of the shore.

Peter Haelen, former VOC Commodore and now skipper of his own ship, stood on the poop deck, surveying all with happy approval. He had dreamt of this moment often but had never fully anticipated the sheer exhilaration and explosion of pride that would accompany the momentous occasion of *The Christine* embarking on her maiden voyage.

In such fine company too. Pier-Jan and Tjores had returned with a score of recruits, old comrades all. The two were on the weather deck, where Korneel was explaining something to Andries and Jasper. Steersmen Tjippema and Zundert stood near the helm on the quarterdeck, pointing up at *The Christine's* completed topmasts and rigging. Katja leaned on the railing, a smile on her face. Marnix and the young VOC clerk, Rolf Romeyn, were looking out at Flushing. Marnix had requested passage to Rotterdam and Peter had acquiesced gladly.

Peter shared the poop deck with Liselotte. She looked pale and somewhat absent – missing her *Duvelsjong* no doubt. *De Wilde Ruyter* had departed a few days before. Yet, Peter had learned to respect his cousin's determination, and even now her apparent vulnerability was accompanied by newfound confidence.

She had given her brother credit for the launch, but when Katja had come to the captain's cabin where Peter had been coming to, the girl had told Peter that Liselotte had been behind it. Both Tjippema and Zundert had commented that Liselotte had been, albeit briefly, *The Christine's* first skipper. Peter also suspected that Liselotte had been the driving force behind the escape from Tholen and Middelburg.

It was only right that she was on board for *The Christine's* maiden voyage. She had earned it.

Peter took a deep breath before hollering his orders. All remaining sails were hoisted and a series of stud sails set.

The Flushing seafront was teeming with onlookers, all sensing this was a special departure. They weren't disappointed. When the full set of *The Christine*'s sails, jibs, and studs caught the wind, the ship accelerated fast. To the surprise and wonder of those on shore, it continued to speed up, cleaving through the waves at a tempo none could recall ever seeing before.

Thus, *The Christine* was given her third name in Flushing, ere departing Zeeland on course for the North Sea and an uncertain but seemingly less bleak future.

"Look at that Hollander go!" People told each other excitedly. "Look at her fly! A flying Hollander to be sure."

The name spread from mouth to mouth while folk watched in astonishment as the ship swiftly left Flushing in her wake. "There she goes, *The Flying Hollander*."

END OF BOOK 1
The Flying Dutchman
BLEAK FUTURE

The story of Liselotte, Andries & Peter Haelen
will continue in

Book 2
The Flying Dutchman
MALIGN SHADOWS

& Book 3
The Flying Dutchman
INFERNAL FATE

A Hearty Bethanks

With many thanks for input that has improved this tale:

Fellow authors Jaq D Hawkins & Guy Donovan who went above and beyond the call of duty to help streamline this story.

For brainstorming & feedback: Famke Kalkman, Jovannah Bär, Tristan Mostert, Rob Visser, Joyce Keyzer, Lou Yardley, Nick Cranch, Dan Shelton, Peter Dekker, Nany Trivita Kusuma, Jan Willem Oudwater & Franka Oudwater-Smit.

Tom and Nimue Brown for the fantastic cover image depicting Liselotte and Peter Haelen on the poop deck of *The Christine*.

Julie Gorringe for her amazing illustrations. We agreed that she would choose the subject/character/scene she wanted to draw, and Julie never ceased to amaze me.

Defragged History for inspirational YouTube docs regarding the VOC and the Eighty Years War. This eased travelling back to the seventeenth century and helped frame the Eighty Years War in *Bleak Future*. Also, Yvette Boertje for narrating the Drowned Land of Reimerswaal.

The Zeeuwse band BLØF for their songs 'Dansen aan Zee' ('Dancing by the Sea') and 'Aan de Kust' ('On the Coast'), which helped me think of Zeeland. And as ever, singer-songwriter Boudewijn de Groot.

Authors Johan Fabricius, Tonke Dragt, & Thea Beckman for an enchanting childhood.

Last-but-not-least: Piet Visser.

Some Notes

This is a *historical fantasy*, a fantastic alibi for any historical inaccuracies. Nonetheless, my aim was to root a subtle element of fantasy in a firm foundation of reality. Some readers enjoy a bit more insight into various processes behind a story and might find the following interesting. If you don't, there's nothing lost by skipping this last part. I hope you enjoyed the story as much as I have and many thanks for reading it.

Piet Visser & Philipp Körber – Unearthing a 1901 newspaper snippet announcing Gebroeders Kluitman's publication of Piet Visser's *De Vliegende Hollander,* I was intrigued by a brief sentence that revealed the Alkmaar publisher had actually asked Piet Visser to do a thorough rewrite of an earlier story, namely German author Philipp Körber's *Der Fliegende Holländer*, first published in 1849. *The Flying Dutchman* was wildly popular at this time, namely due to Richard Wagner's 1843 opera *Der Fliegende Holländer*. Kluitman had Körber's book translated to Dutch in 1870, with a second edition appearing in 1885. I managed to get my hands on a copy of the 1885 edition. To my bemusement the book starts with the memorable opening sentence '*It was a dark and stormy morning*'.

The first chapter covers an event that is absent in Piet Visser's rewrite, however, a Pieter van Halen and Andries van Halen appear, albeit with different characteristics than in Piet Visser's story.

Gebroeders Kluitman, now Uitgeverij Kluitman Alkmaar B.V. – Piet Visser's regular publisher still exists. I am much indebted to Elles van Roosmalen and Piero Stanco for answering my 'extraordinary' questions, and also giving me their blessing to retell Piet Visser's story, this its third incarnation and this time in English.

Peter Haelen versus Pieter van Halen – Piet Visser used the name Pieter van Halen. Van Halen is a familiar name thanks to the most bodacious and excellent band that goes by this name. To stress that the band has nothing to do with Piet Visser's protagonist I used the older spelling variety, making it Haelen and dropping the 'van'. I considered this necessary because I was continually distracted by the need to play 'Jump' at top volume whenever I typed 'van Halen' (true story). The Dutch 'Pieter' is pronounced as the English 'Peter', so it seemed simpler just to use the English spelling. Although I've rounded Peter Haelen out a bit, his character remains very loyal to Piet Visser's protagonist, and as such partially to Körber's earlier representation of the *Flying Dutchman's* captain.

Liselotte Haelen versus Lotje van Halen – Absent in Körber's work, Liselotte appears very briefly as 'Lotje' in Piet Visser's story, and has a total of about two lines, very much relegated to a young damsel in distress. She is not described, nor provided with an age, though at a guess she's younger than Andries. Whereas I have faithfully followed Piet Visser with regard to Peter, I would claim ownership of Liselotte's character but she doesn't like being owned and would likely shoot me with her crossbow if I tried to make that claim.

The following line in *Bleak Future*: *"I'll go to my room,"* Liselotte spoke *in the submissive obedient tone she had used in Father's presence. "And wait to be rescued by gallant heroes."*

...is a little joke, referring to Piet Visser's main bit of dialogue for his 'Lotje' in *De Vliegende Hollander*, namely: *"Oh Father,"* the girl said, *"Let's count ourselves lucky that we've such a brave and courageous hero protecting us."*

In Piet Visser's version of the fight with the bandits Lotje gets to scream in fear and needs to be rescued by Peter and Andries. She also uses smelling salts to help revive her father who's in shock after the fight, an action by Lotje that sparked Liselotte's gift for healing. Lotje survives and then abruptly disappears from the story.

Andries Haelen versus Andries van Halen – Andries would likely be horrified by what the Vissers have done to him. Körber's original Andries van Halen was a six-foot-tall, muscular, handsome, blond sex-bomb who never failed to draw the eye of any who pass him by. A walking six-pack, in other words, with a charming and funny personality to boot.

Körber's Andries doesn't play a major part in the story. He's the second son of a reverend, and duly recruited by his cousin Peter. He accompanies Peter to the East, and we are told rather than shown that Peter loved him like a son. Upon return, however, Andries had become depressed by the long sea voyage and longs to return to his family and study to become a clergyman like his father. This causes Peter a measure of disappointment that Piet Visser would much enhance in his version.

Andries is one of the few named characters in Piet Visser's story. He's presented as a nice lad who develops a father-son relation with Peter, but then...stuff happens that represents an unexpected U-turn of his character (this will appear in *Infernal Fate*). I've tried to insert a less pleasant side to Andries much earlier, also because I feel the parodoxical 'anti-mirror image' between the twins has been an interesting way of exploring their similarities and differences.

Marnix Velthuys – Although unnamed in both Körber's and Piet Visser's stories, he plays a very important part as Peter's friend who watches over Peter's interests there where the young shipbuilding genius simply doesn't have the savvy or social skills to do so. The basic common history of the two friends described in *Bleak Future* is much as it was presented by Körber and then greatly expanded by Piet Visser. Much of 'Peter's Story Despair and Hope' is a loose rewrite / creative translation of scenes from Piet's *De Vliegende Hollander*. Chapters two and four (Peter's arrival and the fight with the bandits) also contain dialogue and scenes from Piet's work – this was entirely Piet's invention as Körber leaves Andries's recruitment uneventful and brief.

Michael (Michiel) Adriaansz – Piet Visser makes no mention of him, but did place Haelen's dockyard in Flushing at a time that Adriaansz was present in the port, and notorious for his rowdy troublemaking skills. He had first gone to sea as an eleven-year-old in 1618. Somewhere between 1618 and 1622, he had been captured by the Spanish and imprisoned in the city of Corunna in Galicia. Organising an escape, he and a number of comrades walked all the way back to the Republic. In September 1622, Adriaansz was involved with the siege of Bergen-op-Zoom as cannoneer. Although *The Christine* is fictional, I doubt someone like Adriaansz would have remained unaware or uninterested if such a ship had been built in Flushing, therefore I couldn't resist including him in the story.

Michael (Michiel) Adriaansz was later to add 'De Ruyter' to his name and he would gain everlasting fame as Admiral de Ruyter. There are various theories as to Adriaansz's choice for 'De Ruyter'. One is that he had an uncle with that name who he was fond of, another that this denotes the sea raider/rider connection as Adriaansz had operated as privateer in his early days at sea. Readers of *Bleak Future*, however, know that Michael was gifted the name by a *Hollandse Meissie* on a windswept beach in Zeeland.

Greet (Griet) Kals – Other than Lotje van Halen, Greet Kals is the only other female character in Piet Visser's story (there is no mention of her in Körber's work). Although stereotypical, her appearance is one of the gems in Piet's story and very much reminiscent of Madame de Thenardier from Victor Hugo's *Les Miserables*. In Piet's book she's the innkeeper of the Old Cauldron near Oysterhout. I moved her to the Silly Sally in Armuyden so that Liselotte could encounter Greet Kals in her natural environment (an inn), rather than a much briefer appearance on the doorstep of the Haelen house after the fight with the bandits. In *Bleak Future*, Peter briefly recounts his stay at the Old Cauldron – overhearing the bandit plot to rob his uncle's house. Piet Visser devotes much more time on Peter's stay and escape from the Old Cauldron, but that wasn't possible to include in a story told from the perspective of the twins.

Jasper of Heys – appears as Thomas in both Körber and Piet Visser's stories, one of the very few named characters. Körber portrays him as a loyal but otherwise unremarkable young sailor. Piet Visser has expanded on this. Peter and Andries encounter Thomas after they leave Oysterhout, an amiable, helpful, and funny little chap full of mischief, who had indeed deserted from the army (it's not specified whose army) by pretending to be dead. Peter musters him as ship's boy. Piet Visser devotes an entire chapter to various pranks and jokes by the boys, completely ignoring the fact that they're moving through a countryside that, historically, was swarming with Spinola's tercios.

Katja of Steynbergen – is partially my own invention, loosely based on the lovely Timmer girls from the Timmer farm near Ommen.

Saskia van der Krooswijck – Inspired by my maternal grandmother's mother, my great-grandmother *Oma* van Wagtendonk, who I met several times when I was very young. She was from an aristocratic family, fell in love with a dockyard worker and was disowned by her aristocratic family for the crime of marrying a commoner.

Adrian Haelen – Inspired by my maternal grandfather's own grandfather (both called Adrian), a common labourer but larger-than-life character in many ways. I knew his daughter, my great-grandmother *Oma* Swank. I am tempted to appropriate Piet Visser's novels on the sieges of Haarlem, Alkmaar, and Leiden during the Eighty Years War and attempt a rewrite with Adrian Haelen and/or Elizabeth of Rye as protagonist(s) in all books. That, however, is a project for the future. Should it ever happen, references to this couple in *Bleak Future* will have laid the groundwork. Should it never happen, Adrian was very useful in allowing a brief exploration of the opening decades of the Eighty Years War.

Skipper Hendrik van der Dekken – doesn't feature in Piet Visser's story. I opted for a more likely Dutch spelling of the name 'Hendrick Vanderdecken', introduced in English literature as captain of *The Flying Dutchman*. The first time it's used is in the short story 'Vanderdecken's Message Home' (by anonymous), published in Blackwood's Edinburgh Magazine in 1821. The name appears again in Frederich Marryat's book *The Phantom Ship,* published in 1839. John Boyle O'Reilly's poem, 'The Flying Dutchman', also names Vanderdecken as captain. As such, van der Dekken is a fictional character, rather than a historical one, although based on a historical Dutch skipper renowned for his obsession with speed and record-breaking voyages (the Frisian skipper Barend Fokke). The English stories place van der Dekken as a VOC captain in the latter half of the seventeenth century, but also place his home port in Terneuzen, the harbour of which at the time barely had enough space for a dinghy to turn around, let alone an East India merchantman. I have taken the liberty of placing him much earlier and adapting his story to fit Peter's. His character has been much influenced by John Boyle O'Reilly's depiction of the unfortunate and doomed skipper.

Jan-Leyns Visscher – I don't know if the Visscher carpentry firm in Domburg was active in shipbuilding. I do know that it had been established in Domburg for five generations by 1622.

Philip Vysscher (born 1450-1460)
Jans Philipszoon Vysscher (born 1485)
Philip Janszoon Vysscher (born 1520)
Leyn Philipsen Vysscher (born 1548)
Jan Leynszoon (Jan-Leyns) Vysscher (died 1642)

Both Piet Visser and myself are direct descendents of these Visscher master carpenters from Domburg and I rather liked the notion (no matter how unlikely) that our family built *The Flying Dutchman*. After all, someone had to.

King Jan – A historical character from West Africa, known by his Dutch name Jan Kompany or Jan Compagnie. He was acquainted with Michael de Ruyter when the two were young boys in Flushing, and it's been documented that the two met again along the West African coast when de Ruyter was an Admiral and Jan the Viceroy of Gorée. There is no known documented evidence as to the extent of their friendship, but many fictional accounts of de Ruyter's childhood make mention of Jan and include him in a Flushing gang of mischievous misfits led by Michael (also including Cornelis, Geleyn, and Pelle). I particularly liked the accounts that explained Michael and Jan became good friends because Michael showed zero tolerance when Jan was exposed to racism.

Jan-Pier, Tjores, & Korneel – appear as Kees, Klaas, Gerrit and a fourth unnamed sailor in Piet's story. I chose new names based on a popular Dutch shanty ('All Those that want to go Privateering') which features bearded sailors named Jan, Piet, Joris, & Corneel in modern versions, and Jan, Pier, Tjores, & Korneel in older versions.

De Blokzeyl – It's highly unlikely that Hollanders, from the dominant province in the Netherlands, would have called one of their merchantmen after a small fishing town in rural Overijssel (present day Blokzijl). In his story Piet Visser had the tendency not to name secondary characters or ships, leaving me free to do so. The choice of *Blokzeyl* is entirely inspired by my father, who grew up in this town, often took us to visit, and has retained a special connection with Blokzijl throughout his life even writing a book about it (*Blokzijl helpt Nepal*).

De Feniks, De Zierikzee, and De Assemburg – have all been named in honour of respectively Famke, Gerrit and Arjen. They know why I chose these names.

De Wilde Ruyter – is fictional, but a *statenjacht* was a common sight on the inland waters of the Dutch Republic. They were usually lightly armed with a cannon or two for signalling purposes. Apart from ferrying admirals and highly placed dignitaries about, they could also be used for reconnaisance, transporting troops or goods, supplying fortresses and towns, and relaying important communications.

Zevenbergen – I was able to reconstruct Zevenbergen as it would have been in 1622 because of good historical documentation. I felt the slower pace in Part One of *Bleak Future* allowed for a bit of sight-seeing so that the reader could get a brief taste of what life was like in one of the smaller Lowlands towns.

Steynbergen (Steenbergen) – The Spanish attack on Steynbergen was intended as a diversion, but without cannon and gunners in the town and duly intimidated by a symbolic bombardment with field guns, the town was quick to surrender.

Bergen-op-Zoom – Catholic inhabitants did open a gate for Spinola's tercios, but patriots managed to shut them again in the nick of time. The bombardment of the city in *Bleak Future* was unlikely to have started so soon. It took far longer to prepare trenches, redoubts, gun platforms etc. However, I was unable to resist the drama of guns thundering over the horizon to add to the tension. I do know that Spinola's siege positions along the Oosterskelde suffered from the attentions of the Dutch navy, but the fast response by the whole of the *Zeeuwse* fleet after a recon by Adriaansz is – as far as I know – an invention.

Reymerswal – Reimerswaal wasn't entirely deserted in 1622, nor was it as intact. I've presented it based on descriptions of the city's state at the end of the sixteenth century rather than the beginning of the seventeenth. Historically, a few fishermen's families still lived in the remnants of the drowned city in 1622. The last of them left in 1630. I am much indebted to Frans van Eekelen who recounted the story of the merfolk curse in 'The Curse of the Mermaids, Steenbergen, a city with a history'. In this version the merfolk visit Bergen-op-Zoom, Steenbergen (Steynbergen), and Reimerswaal to ask for water and bread. They are given both in Bergen-op-Zoom, only bread in Steenbergen since the folk there reckoned mermaids had enough water already, and nothing in Reimerswaal. I rewrote the original curse which was "Bergen-op-Zoom will continue to exist. Steenbergen will flounder. Reimerswaal will cease to exist" to give it a bit of extra flavour.

The other parts of the story told by Katja are a fusion of various Zeeland legends recounting the misfortune that befell those who caught and tried to imprison merfolk. There are parts of Zeeland where the locals will swear on their pretty bonnets that ghostly bells can be heard tolling over (or even in) the sea on some nights. The story told by Adriaansz with regard to van Lodiek's corrupt practices is historical. After a decade of saving money by using inferior materials to repair dykes, the weakened dykes were quick to succumb to the St Felix Flood.

There are no visible traces of the city today. The Oosterschelde Museum in Yerseke displays models of Lodiek Castle and archaeological finds from the drowned city.

The Merfolk Spearblade – Strange items can be found on beaches (or in fishing nets) around the North Sea, including tools and weapons. In Zeeland's past these were sometimes seen as evidence of a realm below the waves, the items presumed to have belonged to the merfolk. These days the assumption is that these items hail from Doggerland, the landmass that once connected France and the Low Countries to Britain but was swallowed by a series of devestating floods. I owe thanks to Hester Loeff who regularly tweets about Doggerland finds & the Zeeland coast.

Physicians & Quacksalvers – The sixteenth century was marked by an improved understanding of the human body but a reluctance to challenge the established principles of Galen's four humours. I've carried this on into the early seventeenth century. Some physicians were remarkably effective, others did indeed still consider drawing up a horoscope more effective than an actual physical examination of the patient. Doctors did some crazy shit, truly, too much to list here. Trepanning was real (and in a few circumstances very helpful), as was fumigation. Blowing tobacco smoke up a patient's rectum to revive them, especially after a drowning, continued into the eighteenth century. It's where the expression 'blowing smoke up your arse' originated. Paraffin wax, mercury, lamb fat, toasted cheese, and fresh hog dung were all substances inserted into open wounds to promote 'healing'. I don't know if they were ever combined, I do know there were 'experts' daft enough to have given that a try. Liselotte's understanding of medicine is based on what would be the cutting-edge innovative modern thinking at that time.

I am indebted to Mark Kehoe's articles in *The Pirate Surgeon's Journal* (www.piratesurgeon.com), which formed my primary source.

Other *Flying Dutchman* stories – I've based two Sussex Smugglepunk short stories on a misunderstood inventor and airship-builder called Peter van Haelen who becomes doomed to fly an airship for eternity.

Both stories involve frit crew who need clean underwear after encountering *The Skirring Dutchman*. You'll find the short story 'The Skirring Dutchman' in *Taught By Time: Myth goes Punk* by Writerpunk Press (Seattle, WA, USA), and the short story 'Learning the Ropes' in *Harvey Duckman Present Pirate Special 2020*, by Sixth Element Publishing (UK). The stories can be read as stand-alone, but are connected to each other. The Cider Brandy Scribblers Anthology *SCADDLES* contains the full 'The Flying Dutchman' poem that features at the beginning of Part One of *Bleak Future*. Parts of that are a creative translation of Jan Slauerhoff's *'De Vliegende Hollander'* and parts my own reworking of main themes in Slauerhoff's work. Felix Clement, of The Captain's Beard, has also put a version to music in 'The Dutchman'. Though unnamed, *De Blokzeyl* as well as *De Christine* (in her incarnation as *The Flying Dutchman*), appear very briefly in a short story I wrote called '*Rousing the Duvelsbeest*'.

Piet Visser – Little is known about the man, other than that he was a teacher and a prolific writer. The Digital Library of Dutch Literature states he lived from 1887 to 1929. Wikipedia mentions 1887 to 1927. Our family records indicate 1877 to 1930. I suspect 1877 is more likely, because 1887 means that he would have been thirteen years old when he wrote *De Vliegende Hollander*. He wrote around 21 books, mostly boy's adventure stuff. He was a second cousin of my great-grandfather (also called Piet Visser). Many thanks to my uncle Karel Werschkull for helping me out with the family tree.

Piet's daughter recalled a family anecdote that he started writing (*Heemskerck op Nova Zembla*, 1900) after reading a book on Nova Zembla and concluding that there was much room for improvement so he might as well try writing the story himself. Oddly enough, or perhaps not, that was precisely my reaction when I read his *Vliegende Hollander*. Possibly something that runs in the family? My reaction to his book was that it seemed terribly old-fashioned, but in his day Piet Visser was considered an innovative force who did much to modernise Dutch juvenile fiction.

Piet Visser & 'the Bontekoe Connection' – *Scheepsjongens van Bontekoe* (*Java Ho!*) by Johan Fabricius is an immensely popular children's book in the Netherlands, first published in 1924. By 2003 it had been reprinted 28 times, with hundreds of thousands of copies sold. I devoured this book as a child, it was my favourite and it's no exaggeration to say I must have read it about a hundred times.

Fabricius was inspired by Alexandre Dumas's short story 'Bontekoe' in *Les Drames de la Mer*.

Dumas was inspired by the journal that Skipper Willem IJsbrandtsz Bontekoe published in 1646, entitled:

Journael ofte Gedenkcwaerdige Beschrijvinge van de Oost-Indische Reyse van Willem Ysbrantsz Bontekoe van Hoorn, begrijpende veel wonderlijcke en gevaerlijcke saecken hem daer in wedervaren. 1618-1625.

(*Journal or memorable description of the East Indian voyage of Willem Bontekoe from Hoorn, including many remarkable and dangerous things that happened to him there. 1618-1625.*)

Bontekoe's *Journal* was a bestseller and has been reprinted more than seventy times since the first edition. There have also been many adaptations and translations.

As mentioned in the dedication, Philipp Körber was also inspired by Bontekoe's journal, somewhat obsessed with it even. Körber wrote his own take on the journal entitled *Wilhelm Isbrands, gennant Bontekoe, reisen in den indischen Meeren* (1850).

I was pleasantly surprised when I read some academic research on Dutch juvenile fiction and discovered that Johan Fabricius had another source of inspiration, namely: Piet Visser. Specifically in relation to Piet Visser's first book, *Heemskerck op Nova Zembla* (1900). There is even a scene in *Java Ho!* that seems to be copied almost word for word from Visser's Nova Zembla story. Since anything I'm going to write about *The Christine's* journey to the East Indies is bound to influenced by a book I've read a hundred times, I was pleased to discover the hand of Piet Visser in Fabricius's masterpiece.

Nils Visser & 'the Bontekoe Connection' – Figuring it would be remiss of me to abstain from family tradition, I added two Bontekoe items to Bleak Future. The first is mention of Bontekoe's ship *De Nieuw Hoorn* when Liselotte contemplates household VOC names. The second is one of Fabricius's characters. Readers of *Java, Ho!* will have hopefully recognised said character, who will continue to play a minor part in *MALIGN SHADOWS*. They may also encounter another old friend in the second book of the trilogy.

YouTube – I've made a number of YouTube videos and there's another one in the planning.

The Dutchman's Legacy features the aforementioned song ('The Dutchman') by Felix Clement and 376 years of illustrations, from Bontekoe's *Journal* in 1646 to Bleak Future in 2022.
https://www.youtube.com/watch?v=Zht7_R_GTRM

Flying Dutchman (Vliegende Hollander) features 'The Flying Dutchman' song by the Jolly Rogers and focuses on the cover art of all three books in the trilogy by Tom and Nimue Brown.

https://www.youtube.com/watch?v=X2Px-ZEGnxY

The Drowned Land of Reimerswaal is a splendid narration of two chapters from this book by Yvette Boertje of Defragged History.

https://www.youtube.com/watch?v=Q0in_X5sbVI

That's all for now, but more will follow as we track the Haelens to Rotterdam and then set our course for the East Indies.

Nils Visser
Brighton, 2022

Lightning Source UK Ltd.
Milton Keynes UK
UKHW010749190822
407536UK00004B/285